Ne Obliviscaris: Do Not Forget

Harriet. Caught between the steady and the charismatic. Wavering. Two very different men. She's trouble. Can't stay out of it. Still digging away. In serious danger of collapsing the fragile corners of her triangular existence into one big hole.

Can Mark really put his fear of marriage behind him? She's only looking for one answer. Unless of course 'that gorgeous hunk of a blonde' in charge of her school gets there first. *Him*? Unlikely. Different worlds. Too many questions.

A weft of answers weave their way through the story. In and out. Criss-crossing the threads of rivalry, jealousy, anger, passion and desire. Ride all Harriet's emotions as she takes you on the rest of her journey. Then ask. 'Was she ever in control of her dreams?'

Ne Obliviscaris: Do Not Forget is the sequel to Margaret's first novel *A Question of Answers*.

Author Biography

Margaret Henderson Smith, a psychology graduate, taught in a priority area school before establishing her own Private Pre-school and Care & Service Agency.

Whilst teaching she introduced a school magazine for which she wrote her own children's stories. This was judged the regional winner in a competition organised by the local press.

Her writing began some years ago, when as a member of the young mums' church group she broadcast her own 'thought for the day' on Radio Merseyside. Early retirement has enabled her to pick up the threads and arima published her first novel 'A Question of Answers' last year.

For more information please go to www.margarethendersonsmith.co.uk

With love and thanks to
John

Jane & Richard
Gail & John
Elizabeth & Derek
Pat & Howard
Gill & Malcolm
Peter
Janet & Alex
Jenny & David

for their continued interest and encouragement.
With special thanks to all the girls up there who read the first one and
wanted the answers.

And a message to those significant others still loved but gone before:
'I haven't gone wayward in your material absence. It's nothing to do with
me. These characters just take on a life of their own.
Don't they Pepper?'

I am particularly grateful to Ian and Sue Flindt of 'Flindt Photography' for
allowing reproduction of the image for the book cover from their Bedruthan
Steps collection. This remains the intellectual property of 'Flindt Photography'.

Ne Obliviscaris

Do Not Forget

Margaret Henderson Smith

Published 2009 by arima publishing

www.arimapublishing.com

ISBN 978 1 84549 406 3

© Margaret Henderson Smith 2009

Printed and bound in the United Kingdom

Typeset in Garamond 11/14

Swirl is an imprint of arima publishing.

arima publishing
ASK House, Northgate Avenue
Bury St Edmunds, Suffolk IP32 6BB
t: (+44) 01284 700321

www.arimapublishing.com

Chapter 1

'It's a question of answers,' thought Harriet, trying to extract some coherence from the bubbling excitement gathering in her mind. She clutched the brown envelope to the cat as she went to play the messages. 'Me, a dame?' The words rang in incredulity stirring the delirious bubbles to a frothy intensity before the nerves in her stomach pierced every last one of them bringing her sharply back to reality. The cat, tired of being squashed between her ribs and a brown paper envelope broke loose, leaving her free to press the button for the first message on the answer machine. She took another deep breath. One of them had to be from him. She needed some explanation for it all.

'Ooh 'arriet. 'ave you 'eard the news? They've just mentioned a Mr. Bridgewater, 'arriet. Somethin' to do with donations and cash for 'onours. 'e denied all knowledge but 'e's up for questionin' along with a few more of 'em from that parliament place. It's got to be 'im, 'asn't it 'arriet? I 'ope they don't come askin' me any questions, I 'aven't got a clue what's goin' on. Well we 'aven't 'ave we 'arriet? Them 'onours are not for the likes of us, are they 'arriet? Just for the likes of our friend Joris Sanderson I would say: those with influence, those in 'igh places. They're from another world those that get them. Oooh 'arriet, it's got to be 'im though. It's got to be that Tarquin Bridgewater. Well fancy that 'arriet, would you believe it? Ooh, what do you think 'arriet?'

Harriet didn't. She couldn't think beyond the disappointment of it not being *him*. She twisted his ring round and round on her finger. 'Tarquin Bridgewater! He can have all the honours he wants including mine.' She glanced at the cat. It wasn't listening.

' "I've arranged for us both to attend a very special ceremony…",' his words returned. 'On his own, he can go on his own. I'm not accepting that BOGOF. Hmm. Buy One, Get One Free. He can keep it!' She wondered who else he'd lined up. Belinda Oxfordshire came to mind. She turned to the cat. It became a blur as it sat on top of her handbag on the bottom stair. She could hardly see it through the tears. She turned and bent her head. Her finger pressed the salty wet button and she waited in hope for the second message.

'Hi Harriet, it's Mark. Be back on Friday, they've cut the trip a bit short. By the way Hat I've got something to ask you when I get home and I definitely want you to wear the blue one. Missed you Hat, hope you haven't backed the wrong horse!'

Harriet jumped in surprise. This was the first she'd heard from him in three months. She wiped the tears from her eyes and played the message again. He wasn't due home until the end of the month, there were almost four weeks to go. Long enough for her to think her way out of her dilemma. She hadn't wanted to go there, at all. She had no spare mental capacity to get her head round Mark coming home. Besides he'd gone off in the foulest of moods. He'd made no contact with her. It was supposed to be all over between them. The gap he'd momentarily left was soon filled with that clawing, aching need for Mr.

Sanderson. It swirled through her every fibre like some bonding compound settling in every cell of her body. He had become her consciousness, a filter through which her whole world was totally sublimated.

' "Save that one for me," ' he'd said. His words rang loud in the silence of her mind.

She blamed herself for the break-up of their tenuous relationship. She knew it was her own folly that had driven him into the arms of Belinda Oxfordshire. That deep pain of loss had nailed itself to her every thought, her every movement.

'There's no way I'm going back there.'

She took the ring off her finger, held it to the light and read the inscription again.

' " 'our perfect day' ne obliviscaris JS" .'

The cat followed her to the dining room as she went to find the dictionary:

' "ne obliviscaris (L.) do not forget". Latin. Pepper. Latin, of course.'

She knew he was a classics scholar. She knew his intellectual capacity was far and away above hers. This so, so intelligent man with his alarming breadth and depth of knowledge constantly feeding his wry sense of humour. His smile always flickering first in indecision before spreading across his strong, serious face, then finally breaking full to show the slight irregularity that so enhanced his otherwise even teeth. She let her disappointment slide as she recalled the toss of thick blonde hair and the curl, insistent, resting on his collar. She pictured him, six foot or more of unequivocal good looks. His strong, handsome features; his twinkling, laughing clear blue eyes; his generous wide smile, his strong broad shoulders.   Harriet had to stop right there. It was a perfect day. How could she ever forget that? She ran her fingers across her left breast. He'd touched it. He'd slipped her bra strap from her shoulder and gently lifted her into his hand as they lay in the flower-filled meadow. He'd softly kissed her before returning the buttons on her jumper to their buttonholes, save the last two. These he had left open for the buttercups lifted from the array of flowers he'd strewn on her skirt.

The cat leapt ahead racing to sit on her bag, just beating her to the hall. She nudged it off and sat on the bottom stair. She found her address book. She opened it at the last page where she'd kept them. She touched the shiny deep yellow petals before threading their stalks through the ring she still held in her hand.

' "This hand for the moment, just for the moment, Harriet." ' She could hear his words. She could feel herself surrendering to the weight of his body on hers. She was still in the field of flowers. The doorbell rang. Quickly she closed the book on the flowers and placed the ring back on her finger.

'It's *him*,' she thought. Her body wrenched in delight.

'Hi `arriet, it's only me and I'm fumin`.'

Harriet swallowed hard on the disappointment as she weighed up Tricia's drenched jeans. She hadn't realised the sharp shaft of sunlight that had lit the inner face of her ring only a few minutes ago had been followed by the most tremendous downpour.

'Get in Tricia. It's starting again. Looks like someone's cascaded a puddle at you. You're drenched!'

'Drenched 'arriet, that's an understatement. I 'ad to park 'alf way up the road because there was a dog, 'ad a face like a butcher's block, sittin' right by your gate and I wasn't gettin' out to 'ave that thing go for me, I can tell you! Anyway I was just walkin' along, very gingerly I might add, when this bloody big silver Mercedes screeched right past me. I've never seen a dog move so fast in all my life! Before I knew it that same flippin' car was back again drivin' on the wrong side of the road, almost on the pavement I would say.'

Harriet looked swiftly at Tricia, surreptitiously sliding the ring off her finger as she did so. She clasped her fingers hard against it, impressing it into the palm of her hand.

'A silver Mercedes? It wasn't *him* was it Tricia?'

'It bloody well was 'arriet. I saw 'is number plate when 'e got past and as sure as I'm standin' 'ere, she was sittin' alongside of 'im. I'd say they were 'avin' a very speedy gawp at your 'ouse 'arriet.'

Harriet could feel the pain cutting its way into her throat. She couldn't bear the thought of Tricia confirming her worst fears.

'I thought she'd changed 'er mind about buyin' it 'arriet? Unless of course they're plannin' on movin' in after their weddin'?'

She felt sick. 'No Tricia, it's all over between them. He told me this morning, I haven't had chance to tell you yet.'

'All over 'arriet? It didn't look that way to me. 'er 'ead was bobbin' around all over the place like a blonde straggly mop that wouldn't keep still. Was that a metathingy 'arriet? I think I might just be gettin' the 'ang of those things now. Anyway, where was I? It was so close to 'is I don't know 'ow 'e could see to drive! Bloody annoyed I am. 'e's not gettin' away with this. 'e's ruined my jeans not to mention my suede jacket.'

Harriet closed the front door and ushered Tricia into the lounge.

'Do sit down Tricia, I'll just put the kettle on.'

Harriet placed the kettle under the tap and let it fill and fill. She became transfixed by the running water as her mind raced away.

'You're not tryin' to get 'im back for soakin' me are you 'arriet? Anymore water down that plug 'ole and you'll end up drownin' the whole world, never mind 'im!'

Harriet jumped. Clinging on to her ring, she wrenched the tap shut.

'Anyway, enough of 'im 'arriet. Did you get my message then, the one about Tarquin Bridgewater? 'e's up for questionin' 'arriet, or at least a Mr. Bridgewater is. It's got to be 'im though, 'asn't it 'arriet? There's somethin' very fishy about 'im comin' into our shop wantin' to know if 'e's left 'im anythin' all the time. I wonder what it's all got to do with those 'onours 'arriet? We'll soon know once

Simon Barnes gets 'is 'ands on 'im. No doubt we'll catch 'im and our friend Joris Sanderson on telly with their top 'ats on, oh and 'er no doubt. What's the bettin' she 'asn't blackmailed 'im into resumin' their engagement with an 'onour thrown in for compensation. Mr. and Mrs. That's not good enough for the likes of 'er. No she's got to be a dame to 'ave a title, too. You see if I'm not right. Mr. and Mrs Joris Sanderson, sir and dame of the realm. Or would she be a lady? Oh I don't know 'ow it all works 'arriet. You can just see it though. Can't you 'arriet?'

Unfortunately Harriet could just see it. Tricia had just reinforced every doubt, every negative feeling she'd had since she'd come home from school. Instinctively she wanted to tell her everything. She couldn't bring herself to do it. She was not prepared to betray their friendship now gelled out of their mutual but dichotomous desire for Mr. Sanderson. Besides Harriet would then have to admit all. She'd never openly confessed her side of the feelings they both shared for him. How could she tell her she thought she was on the brink of marriage, only to be fobbed off with some ludicrous title. How could she tell her that?

'Ooh, thanks 'arriet.' Tricia followed Harriet into the lounge, clutching on to her mug of hot tea, a little unsteady as she tried to close the door behind her. They sat down on the sofa and for a moment they looked at one another in silence.

'It's no good 'arriet, I just can't get that man out of my mind. Goodness knows I've tried 'ard enough. My Bob keeps asking me what planet I've gone to. Good job 'e doesn't know 'arriet. Do you know 'arriet, I lie in bed lookin' at Bob. 'e's gone all porky round the middle and I think 'e 'asn't 'ardly bothered keepin' 'imself in good shape for me and then I think about Joris Sanderson. If ever there was a firmed up man it's 'im. Oh 'arriet 'e's doin' my 'ead in. I just feel like grabbin' 'im and threatenin' 'im with my body when 'e looks at me like that. As you know 'arriet I've 'ardly seen 'im for the last three months, goodness knows where 'e's been, but yesterday 'e was in the office all mornin'. I could 'ardly keep still, 'til I saw 'er through my one-way mirror, flouncin' in. She said in that snooty voice of 'ers "Just popped in to have a word with Joris. Is he through the back?" and I told 'er he left 'alf-an-hour ago, completely forgettin' 'is car was still outside. She gave me a filthy look 'arriet, marched straight through and I went 'ome before I saw either of them again. Goodness knows what was goin' on back there.'

Harriet caught her reflection in the porcelain mug. Distorted. She didn't like what she saw. She quickly placed it to her lips and swallowed long and hard before returning to Tricia.

She made a swift decision.

'Tricia, I want to tell you something but please, please don't tell anybody. Not even Bob.'

'Too right 'arriet, I 'ardly tell my Bob anythin' these days in case I give myself away, if you know what I mean? 'e really lost 'is temper when 'e thought I was pregnant. Remember when 'e went down and made minced meat of that

Simon Barnes? Well ever since then I'm very careful what I tell 'im. 'e's been very touchy since then. I don't go to that garage anymore, either. Not since 'e told me where 'e found out. Not with that one behind the till gettin' 'er wires crossed and tellin' 'im the wrong story. If she's goin' to watch the news on the telly that one, she wants to get 'er facts straight before she goes tryin' to break up marriages. I very nearly lost my Bob over all that I did!' She looked at Harriet. 'You did lose your Mark didn't you 'arriet? I know you've never exactly told me that, but you've 'ardly ever mentioned 'im since 'e went away.'

Harriet took a deep breath and looked down at the floor. 'I've just played a message from him Tricia. He's coming back on Friday.'

'Well, that is a relief 'arriet. I didn't like to see you all on your own for so long. 'e is comin' back 'ome, 'ere, isn't 'e 'arriet? You do mean 'e's comin' back to you, I 'ope?'

'Looks like it Tricia.'

'Well you don't seem too 'appy about it 'arriet. You'll soon get used to 'avin' 'im around again. I know, 'arriet. It's your 'ouse. I've never seen it look so tidy since 'e's been away. Well, 'arriet just don't put up with it. Do what I do 'arriet. Just 'ide anythin' small 'e leaves out and if it's big make sure you put it just where 'e can trip over it. It's very easy to convince them they left it there themselves once they've landed on their bums! 'e'll be like my Bob. 'e'll be so fed up of trippin' up and losin' things 'e'll soon get the message.'

Harriet laughed, then her face straightened. 'I've got a bit of a dilemma, Tricia. Promise not to say anything.'

'Of course I won't, I promise 'arriet.'

'Well you know I've been trying to make a few improvements at school…'

'Oh yes 'arriet. I know you've worked very 'ard down there. I thought you were still doin' it to take your mind off Mark bein' away. It does 'elp when you've got plenty to do.'

'True,' said Harriet, brushing the remark aside. 'The thing is, he's too pleased with what we've all done together, really.'

'What do you mean 'arriet, too pleased? 'ow can anyone be too pleased? Especially 'im. You've worked your socks off 'arriet and it'll be 'im that gets all the thanks.'

'No Tricia, that's just the problem. He wants to make sure I get all the credit. Just a tick.'

Harriet went into the hall. She pushed the cat off the brown envelope she'd left on the bottom stair.

'Here, take a look at this.'

Tricia took the letter out of the envelope and her mouth opened wide in disbelief as the contents became clear.

'Ooh 'arriet, 'e's not tryin' to give you one of those dodgy 'onours is 'e 'arriet? Ooh 'arriet I wouldn't touch it with a barge-pole if I was you. You don't want to be up for questionin` with Tarquin Bridgewater, do you? Ooh do be careful `arriet.'

'You're right Tricia, absolutely right. It's in the system though. I don't know if I can get out of it just like that.'

'Course you can `arriet. It says somethin` there about tellin` them if you're goin` to accept it or not. You just `ave to let them know `arriet.'

'But I might offend him Tricia. I've still got to work there. He couldn't have done it without the approval of the governors, or the director. They'll see it as turning down an honour for the school.'

'Ooh `arriet, I never thought of it like that. I wouldn't like to be in your shoes. `e's a busybody `arriet. Why couldn't `e just leave you alone. You've got your Mark comin` `ome. What's `e goin` to say?'

'I daren't go there Tricia. I just daren't mention it to him. He can't stand him.'

'My Bob, neither.'

'Anyway Tricia, I've got some long and hard thinking to do. I certainly don't want to become a local celebrity. Can't you just imagine Simon Barnes having a field day with that one?'

'Oooh yes `arriet, `e'd never leave you alone, I'm sure. Not to mention our friend sir Joris.'

'Exactly Tricia. I don't know what he was thinking of. Didn't he warn me to stay away from Internews TV?'

'`e certainly did `arriet. In fact I remember `is exact words. `e said "For heaven's sake Miss Glover don't go anywhere near Internews TV." Then `e said somethin` about you `avin` legal contractual obligations to fulfil `arriet and you weren't to cause `im any further embarrassment. Do you think `e's tryin` to drop you in it on purpose `arriet? You really `ave got to be careful. I certainly wouldn't trust `im after the way `e's broken my `eart `arriet.' She looked down at her soaked jeans. 'I'm tellin` you `arriet they're back together again. Why else would they be drivin` past your `ouse like mad things. Do be careful `arriet.'

Tricia became more strident as her concern mounted. She shrilled in unconscious unison with the ringing phone.

'Won't be a tick,' said Harriet.

'You are joking.' Tricia could hear her saying from the hall. 'No, I'm afraid not. We can't do viewings at the weekend.' She faltered. 'I'm expecting my husband home. That's the last thing he'll want.'

'You `aven't gone off to the South Pole and married `im in secret `ave you `arriet? Did I `ear you callin` `im your `usband? I said it would be your turn next `arriet when I threw that confetti all over you at the church gate. Remember when your Clarissa got married?'

Harriet paid scant attention to Tricia's meanderings. She was absolutely furious.

'You were right Tricia. It was them. A viewing anytime over the weekend for Ms Oxfordshire and Mr. Sanderson. Yes, they said they knew they'd previously changed their minds about buying it, but as the market seems to be heading for free-fall they fear these type of properties will become increasingly unavailable. They want to view it again and come back with a swift decision.'

'Bloody cheek 'arriet. No you couldn't 'ave married your Mark or you'd be wearing a ring 'arriet. Let's see that 'and again.'

Harriet held her left hand out to finally convince Tricia.

''ere, what's that you've been clutchin' in your other 'and arriet?'

'More tea Tricia? Pass your cup over.' Harriet, still furious and now flummoxed reached for the cup. She clasped her hand around the handle and immediately the ring dropped to the floor.

'Ooh 'arriet. Congratulations! You wanted to keep it a secret. Well don't you worry 'arriet, I won't tell anyone. That's two of your secrets I've got to keep today. No thanks 'arriet. It's very kind of you but I won't 'ave anymore tea just now. I'd better be goin' I'll 'ave Bob back 'ome soon. 'e'll be wantin' 'is tea, though 'e's porky enough I would say. I'll speak to you soon.'

With that Tricia was gone. Harriet closed the front door, stunned she'd gone off in such a hurry. She hadn't given her a chance to explain anything. She looked at the cat. It had resumed its position, squashing her bag sideways as its paws well over-stretched the full length of the zip.

'Now Tricia's thoroughly confused thanks to them. I'm sick of trying to tell them my correct title is the one that sits with my maiden name. We wouldn't have this ridiculous charade if Mark hadn't gone along with it.'

The cat yawned at her. 'No, it's not boring. It's typical of him. He thought it would be better to just let them think we're married. It was better for potential buyers. Marriage equates with stability. Oh he'd never admit that, but I know that's definitely where he was coming from. You can tell him if you like.'

The cat jumped down, brushed against Harriet's legs and sauntered to the kitchen.

It had been Harriet's misfortune to meet another Glover. 'Huh, a commitophobe's dream,' she thought. ' "Why bother getting married? We're a Hat and a pair of Glovers already." ' Harriet recalled his words as she followed the cat into the kitchen. Her eye caught the green light on the answer phone. 'Just what did he say exactly?'

She listened carefully as she played the message again. 'He's got something to ask me when he gets home. He wants me to wear the blue one.' She recalled Clarissa's wedding. Mark had loved that outfit. ' "Missed you Hat, hope you haven't backed the wrong horse!" '

'He wants me to wear the blue one, too!' She recalled Molly's wedding. Mr. Sanderson had told her he'd never seen her looking more beautiful as his eyes ran the full length of her blue bridesmaid's dress. She opened her right hand and replaced his ring onto her finger.

' "This hand for the moment, just for the moment Harriet." ' She could hear his words. She could see the twinkle in his eyes losing to the serious expression on his face. She went back to the bottom stair and lifted both hands to hold a head full of broken dreams. 'Already back with Belinda Oxfordshire?' Tricia had just presented all the evidence. 'No, I'll not wear the blue one for some dubious honour. I'll wear the blue one for Mark. There's no way I've backed the wrong horse!'

She took the ring off her finger and hid it at the back of the bottom drawer in her dressing table, somewhere between her pants and bras and socks.

Chapter 2

Harriet struggled to keep her spirits afloat as she drove to school the next morning. She stopped at the lights and looked across to Starboard Marine North West on the corner. She couldn't bear the thought of them both being in his office all yesterday afternoon. How could so many dreams come crashing down so soon? Her depression turned to anger.

'Well if that's the way *he* wants to play it, that's fine with me,' she declared to herself. The lights changed. She forced the gear lever into first and almost stalled as her feet lost the necessary coordination to move the car forward. She jumped at the excessively loud blast of the horn from the driver in the huge black people carrier behind. Up went her two fingers at him. She was shocked. Never in her whole life had she ever done anything like that before! She glimpsed his sharp thin nose struggling to maintain his spectacles as his own two fingers jerked them out of line in angry response, just catching his silvery grey hair. 'That's a prat to get away from,' she thought as she gathered speed through the traffic. She kept glancing in her mirror. Still behind. He seemed to be following her. Then she lost him.

With great relief Harriet drove through the school entrance. No sign of Mr. Sanderson's car, either. She spotted Mr. Brown, the school caretaker, poking away at the flower beds. He was smiling to himself. He kept looking into the big fat sack of spring bulbs at his feet which was fraying round the edges. Offering spikes of coarse hair to his sleeping beauties. She wasn't too fussy on Mr. Brown, not since he'd accused her of treading on his geraniums and got her into trouble with Mr. Sanderson. She decided to park as far away from him as possible.

'Not there, Miss, if you don't mind. Can't you see I've put the cones out? We're havin' those railin's painted tomorrow. That's if the wind dies down. We don't want everyone's car covered in dark green spots. Do we? Tomorrow.'

'That's not today, though, is it? Surely it won't do any harm. I've locked it now. Anyway there isn't a cone at this end.' Harriet gathered up her bags.

'There doesn't have to be Miss. If you count the railings as I did you'd see that distance at the end is exactly the same distance that's at the other end. And the other end hasn't got a cone because the gate's there and this end's got the wall.'

Harriet looked at her watch. 'I'm going to be late. I promise to move it at break.'

Mr. Brown leant his hoe against the wall, put his hands on his hips and shook his head as he watched Harriet walk away. Her hair had blown all over her face. Sitting in uncooperative strands so she could hardly see. That always made her bad-tempered. She pushed her bags hard against the old heavy door, forcing it to open. She heard it swing closed behind her as she scrambled along the corridor to her classroom. Mrs. Bustard was waiting for her.

'Oh there you are Miss. I just 'ad to thank you again for givin' me that lottery ticket back. Once our Danny's in 'ere I'll be on me way to the post office to get the money. You are a good'n Miss Glover. Just look what a difference you've made to this place. I can't keep our Danny away now. 'e just loves comin' 'ere. 'e's still a little bugger at 'ome though. I say why can't you be'ave yourself for me, never mind Miss Glover.' She looked sideways at Harriet and then her eyes landed on the floor. 'If you get what I'm tryin' to say?'

'Well they didn't all turn into angels overnight, Mrs. Bustard,' reassured Harriet, 'but at least they're trying.'

Mrs. Bustard wasn't listening. She flew to the window and started hammering on it, shouting to Danny. 'What do you think you're doin' round there? You were supposed to be takin' your coat off.'

Harriet hurried behind her to open it.

'Look, I've got you some onions, me dad likes onions. 'e won't leave us if we give 'im onions.'

She looked at Mrs. Bustard. Mrs. Bustard rubbed the corner of her eye. 'Get round 'ere this minute will yer and put them bloody things back.'

They watched Danny, his cupped hands overflowing with bulbs, struggling his way back to Mr. Brown's sack. Mr. Brown was nowhere to be seen. Danny returned with his pockets bulging.

'And you can just give *them* to Miss. Go and 'ang that coat up.'

The bell rang just as Harriet closed the door behind them. She popped the bulbs on to the corner of the lunch box trolley. It was time for the fray.

Harriet wasn't in the mood.

'Sara Atkins,'

'Yes Miss,'

'Danny Bustard,' she continued.

'You know I'm 'ere Miss 'cos you've just seen me an' I want me onions back.'

'Sabaru Camaboolla,'

'You've seen 'er an' all and I want me onions back.'

The titters started and before Harriet knew it the quiet corner was in uproar. The door swung open. Harriet turned. Her cheeks flushed bright red to the roots of her hair. The classroom suddenly silenced.

'Miss Glover, I'd like you to meet Mr. Whittle, area Chief Inspector of Schools.' Mr. Sanderson's voice was stern. He was decidedly unamused.

Harriet stood up. For one terrible, brief moment she watched Mr. Whittle brush the grey silvery hair from the left lens of his glasses as he pushed them up his narrow, sharp nose. He took her hand and offered a thin reluctant smile. Inside she breathed a sigh of relief. 'No, it couldn't possibly be that man,' she thought, 'he'd have followed me all the way here.'

'Is that car yours Miss er?'

'Glover,' Mr. Sanderson finished for him.

'The one over there, by that cone rolling around. That one on its own parked behind the railings next to the wall?' Mr. Whittle snapped his fingers into the air and then pointed out of the window.

Harriet's stomach knotted. She could see Mr. Brown carrying what looked like a roll of wire under his arm. She watched him running after the cone as it parked itself alongside the wall. She glanced at Mr. Sanderson. She decided to take a chance. 'No, sorry, not mine. I got a lift in today.'

Mr. Sanderson tilted his right eyebrow as he looked at her, then scratched his head.

Harriet tried to swallow. Her mouth went very dry. She coughed. The annoyance on Mr. Whittle's face spread to the space he was standing in.

'So this is where the honour is to be bestowed. Hmm, I see.' He turned to Mr. Sanderson. 'You know, I had a most disagreeable experience driving here. Apart from getting lost of course.'

Mr. Sanderson's face straightened. He took a deep breath. Harriet could just see his shoulders lifting before she turned away.

'Quiet now, Danny. Mr. Whittle is a very important visitor.'

The children were starting to get restless. Harriet was grateful. Danny seized the opportunity. He stood up and then pulled at Mr. Whittle's trouser leg. 'Miss 'as stolen me onions. Tell 'er to give 'em me back.'

'Er that will be all Miss Glover,' Mr. Sanderson suddenly declared to a very red faced Harriet. She watched him quickly steer Mr. Whittle towards the door and breathed a brief sigh of relief. She knew that wouldn't be the end of it.

She returned to her chair and called the children to order before continuing with the register. She could hardly conceive of her misfortune to have been face to face with the man she'd been so rude to. ' "Area Chief Inspector of Schools".' Mr. Sanderson's words rang around her head. All day.

The clang of the 3.30 bell surged down the corridor and hit the door full force just as Harriet opened it. The children spilled into the corridor and Harriet, not anxious for confrontation, returned to her desk to gather the mountain of books and papers that threatened to keep her company for the whole of the evening.

She was so grateful the visitation of the morning had not been repeated. She looked out of the window and saw her car sitting there in sheer disobedience, defying the rolling cone as it swung semi-circular in the wind between the last railing by the wall and the back end of her car. There was no one in sight. Harriet rushed to get out before anyone appeared. She swung her bag over her shoulder and with her chin propped up the colliding books and papers spilling from her ageing brown holdall. Two bags, hands full, she struggled along the corridor and just turned the corner to see Mr. Sanderson, Mr. Whittle and Mr. Brown huddled on the sunken old doormat, completely blocking the main entrance door.

'That's it,' she thought, 'that's all I flipping well need.'

She quickly turned back and decided on the fire-exit at the end of the short corridor the other side of her room. She only ever used it for fire drill. There were no windows down there and it smelt horribly of the store cupboard that backed onto the wall of her classroom. She threw her bags down. Precarious. In an instant the mountain of papers slid off the top of her holdall to rest piled high against the doors. She pressed the bar down, hard, as hard as she could. The wind whooshed under the doors as they shot open. The playground was instantly littered with blowing and swirling A4 sheets.

'Oh sod! Didn't I just need that?' Harriet was furious. She grabbed what she could from the doorway, gathered up her bags and hurried over to the car. She scrambled in, reversed and heard something crunch against the wall. 'Oh, sod that, I'm out of here.' She tried to ignore the dragging sound from the rear of the car as she drove forward. She was more intent on getting away without being seen. She turned the steering wheel down hard left to get her out of the gateway. She glanced into her rear mirror. Needed to make sure the coast was still clear. Mr. Sanderson, Mr. Whittle and Mr. Brown suddenly came into full view, stepping out from the main entrance door. She obeyed the compulsion to look again. The mirror framed the three of them pointing at her car while the sheets of white A4 paper pretended to be giant angular snowflakes in front of their noses.

She clattered her way to a halt at the traffic lights outside Starboard Marine North West. It was getting dark. The lights from the showroom lit up the three or four gangly boys chewing gum with skewed ties and shirt tails dangling below their blue school blazers. Suddenly they relinquished the desire to shoot their arms and legs out randomly at unsuspecting passers by. They gathered up these involuntary spasms to point in unison at the back end of Harriet's car. They let rip. They were swinging round the traffic lights in crippling mirth, shouting and pointing at Harriet whilst she waited for the lights to change. They turned green. She was getting used to this. Up went her two fingers at them just as Belinda Oxfordshire came out of the door. Harriet had seen that face turn puce before. She clanked away at great speed and didn't slow down until she was safely on the drive at 4 The Willows.

Chapter 3

Like a spring lamb, the cat leapt from nowhere to greet her as she struggled out of the car.

'Well at least *you're* pleased to see me,' she said as it tried to catch her swinging bag. It followed her to the gates. She closed them and hardly dared look behind for fear of seeing her half-trailing bumper.

'That's funny Pepper. What was it and where did it go?'

She got on her hands and knees and searched under the car in desperation. It was pitch black down there. She pushed herself further forward and flattened herself between the paving stones and the exhaust pipe. In the blackness she suddenly thought about Danny's 'onions'. 'Oh bother! I meant to get those,' she muttered to the cat. 'Now where is the sodding thing?'

'You won't find it under there Miss Glover. I'd come out if I were you. I'll show you just where it is.'

Harriet froze. She didn't want to come out. The thought crossed her mind to just stay there. Forever. She wriggled herself backwards and then twisted round coming eye to eye with Mr. Sanderson's highly polished black shoes. He placed his hand under her elbow to ease her struggle from the ground. Then he let go and stepped back a pace.

'You've just about managed to infuriate most of us today, Miss Glover. Come, take a look at this.'

He ushered Harriet forward as he reached to open the gate. He swept his hand at his silver Mercedes. 'Just look Miss Glover. Just look at that.'

Harriet couldn't see anything. She looked up at him, completely blank.

'Not there, Miss Glover. Back. Kerbside, back!'

Harriet moved along. Then she could see everything. The gutter was littered with splinters of orange plastic. There was a huge awkward angular piece trailing strings of wire jutting out from underneath the car right next to the inside edge of the tyre. Mr. Sanderson bent down. He tugged it as hard as he could but it wouldn't budge. 'Goodness knows where else it's gone. What damage it's done. Just what is it with you today, Miss Glover?'

Harriet could feel herself beginning to tremble.

'Well I'm very sorry Mr. Sanderson. How would I know where *that* came from? I still haven't found out what's been going on with the back end of my own car. Why do you think I was underneath it?'

Mr. Sanderson flicked his hand towards the wheel.

'That's why you were underneath it Miss Glover. In its former life it used to be a traffic cone. You know, those orange things. Usually all over motorways. Remarkably similar in appearance to dunces' hats?'

'That's politically incorrect of him to say that. I'll tell him. Not just now. No. Some other time.' The thought trembled its way to her consciousness. Then faded.

He looked straight at her and continued. 'That was Mr. Brown's cone as a matter of fact. That is before you managed to drag it out of school. The foolish man's obviously decided to wire it to the fence to make his point. Regardless, don't feel you are now so elevated Miss Glover that you can park wherever you so choose. Brown's got a job to do like the rest of us.'

Harriet covered her mouth with her hand. She was shaking from a mix of fury and disbelief. It was the slam of a car door from behind them both that pulled her back to reality. She could hear the engine ticking over. She saw Belinda Oxfordshire get out of *his* car. She walked straight past her as she beckoned Mr. Sanderson into the waiting taxi. He locked his car. 'See me first thing in the morning, Miss Glover.'

Harriet watched them drive away. She placed her hand on the bonnet of his silver Mercedes and looked through the window at the very seat that had taken her to their field of flowers. She felt her eyes fill full. The tears spilled over her lower lashes making her red cheeks wet and shiny. She could feel them glowing in the dark as she opened the front door to let herself, her bags and the cat in.

She went straight into the lounge and from the window caught the street lamp lighting the bonnet of his car as she closed the curtains on it. The phone rang. She let it ring and then went back into the hall to listen to the message.

'`ello `arriet, it's only me `arriet. I think I know why you aren't answerin` this `arriet. It's because you've got our friend there I would say. I just drove past the end of your road `arriet and I saw `is car there. `asn't `e gone `ome yet `arriet?'

Harriet lifted the receiver.

'Oh, hi Tricia. Sorry about that. You wouldn't believe it Tricia. He's not here. He's just got into a taxi with that vile woman.'

'What do you mean `arriet? `e's just got into a taxi with that vile woman? Well I know exactly which vile woman you're talkin` about but what were they doin` at yours and why `as `e left `is car at your `ouse `arriet?'

'Because he's just squashed a wired up traffic cone under his back wheel and he can't move it.'

'Where did it come from `arriet?'

'Wouldn't you know? Me!'

'What on earth were you doin` with a wired up traffic cone `arriet?'

'It's a wonder you didn't hear me clanking to a halt at the traffic lights outside your place, Tricia. I saw *her* come out. Were you still there?'

'I was `arriet. I didn't `ear you though. I was too busy tryin` to push `er out of the front door. She said Joris was pickin` `er up. She was standin` out there quite a while before I saw `er get into `is car, though. They must `ave been comin` to view your `ouse again `arriet. I thought you told the agent you didn't want them round?'

'I did Tricia. Yes, of course that's it. They were obviously trying it on themselves. Well, they both got more than they bargained for.'

'Anyway `arriet, what was makin` all this clankin` noise that I was supposed to `ear but didn't?'

'That flipping traffic cone Tricia. I must have got caught up with it coming out of school. It obviously dropped off in the gutter before I turned in and he drove straight into it.'

'Serves 'im bloody well right 'arriet. 'e drives far too fast for my likin`. 'e shouldn't be drivin` so close to the kerb either. That's 'ow 'e managed to drown me yesterday and 'e shouldn't be screechin` to a halt like that. Well 'e must 'ave done 'arriet to get 'imself all caught up in your traffic cone. I'll just go and explain all of that to your Mark.'

Harriet clutched at her stomach trying to control the lethal cocktail of shock and fear suddenly fuelling her nerves. 'Did you say Mark, Tricia?'

'Yes 'arriet. 'e's standin` outside by the taxi 'arriet waitin` for me to tell 'im "What the 'ell's been goin' on." 'is words, not mine. 'e told the guy to carry on to ours when 'e got to your road and saw our friend's car parked outside your 'ouse. 'e said somethin` about 'opin` you 'aven't backed the wrong 'orse 'arriet. I told 'im I didn't think you'd turned to gamblin` on the 'orses just yet, 'arriet, especially as you two 'ad both got married. "Well that's very romantic Mark. A secret weddin` on the ice," I said. Do you know 'arriet 'e didn't know what I was talkin` about? So you 'aven't got married then? What was that ring you dropped then 'arriet?'

'Oh nothing Tricia. Just something I found on the shed floor. Probably out of Mark's tool box. He had a load of old curtain rings in there. You know what he's like? Can't throw anything away.' She felt unnerved. Mark would wonder. She hoped Tricia hadn't blown it before he'd even got home.

'Oh there I go again 'arriet, gettin` the wrong end of the stick. I 'ope you don't mind me sayin` this 'arriet, but I'm quite relieved. It was a shock when you 'ad that ring. I think I just needed a little bit of time to get used to the idea. Anyway, good job I was in. I'd 'ardly managed to close the front door when the bell started ringin`.'

'Oh thanks Tricia. He wasn't due home until Friday. Nothing like letting me know. Send him back please Tricia. I'll talk to you soon.'

Harriet, stunned, replaced the receiver then raced upstairs to try to sort herself out before Mark arrived. She powdered over all the red blotches left on her face and quickly brushed her hair. She looked more closely at her eyes in the mirror. Didn't want Mark to see she'd been crying. She hadn't seen him for well over three months and neither of them had spoken. Not since shortly after the wedding. Not since her mother had stood up and announced to all of Clarissa and Henry's guests that she and Mark were to be married and that she and Mark were expecting a baby. Mark had stormed off to the South Pole. It was over between them. Oh she knew he had to come back, but once they'd sorted their affairs out, that would be the end.

And as far as Harriet was concerned that would have been most convenient had Mr. Sanderson's "very special ceremony sometime following the spring" been of the kind to join them as man and wife. 'Huh! Bloody fat chance,' she thought, remembering Tricia's response to the lack of opportunity she'd had to give him her all in Switzerland. 'Now this. It's as if the field of flowers never happened. It's as if Molly's wedding had never happened. His beautiful words and the ring. How could it all roll back so quickly as if none of it had ever happened? He told me he'd finished with Belinda Oxfordshire. Why would it suddenly be all back on?'

Harriet decided she would be very pleased to see Mark. Very pleased indeed. She felt annoyed that after all this time Tricia was the one he'd seen first. Some of the old insecurities started to surface. Tricia hadn't wanted to see the ring. She'd left in a hurry. She remembered how Tricia used to play up to him. How Mark never exactly discouraged it, though he'd never, ever have admitted it. Of course once Tricia had become gainfully employed by Mr. Sanderson at Starboard Marine North West, Mark didn't get a look in. By that time Harriet wasn't too bothered anyway. She was far too concerned with trying to keep Mr. Sanderson all for herself.

'Bloody fat chance,' she reiterated to herself. 'Definitely why she rushed off though when she thought the ring had meant marriage, not giving me a chance to explain.' Harriet pushed the thought to the back of her mind.

She felt strangely nervous. In twenty two years they had never been apart for so long.

"Do be nice to Dad when he gets back." Clare had advised on the phone. "Rachael and I don't want to end up products of a broken home. What's it all about anyway Mum? What does it matter if he won't marry you? Why should it bother Granny anyway? You've just got to break loose from Granny. It's her fault you split."

If only it had been as simple as that. Harriet had never confided in her girls about Mr. Sanderson. About the unrelenting pangs that constantly seared and ached their way deep into her body, deep into her mind. She had no will to resist this gorgeous deeply charismatic man. This man of intellectual stature, of strong, handsome features, of laughing, quizzical, serious, questioning, twinkling clear blue eyes. This man with his mop of blonde hair and always the curl resting on his collar.

The doorbell rang. Harriet's stomach churned and she tried to close the thoughts off as she went down the stairs to open it.

Chapter 4

'He's not in the wardrobe then?' said Mark as he closed the front door behind him. Harriet took a deep breath. She was furious with herself for dragging that traffic cone home. Of course *his* car was the last thing Mark needed to see.

'Look,' she said, 'I really am sorry about that. It's just been one of those days when absolutely everything's gone wrong.'

'Including me coming back early Harriet?' He put his suitcase down and looked straight at her from under fast puckering eyebrows.

'Where's the rest of your luggage?'

'It's on its way Harriet. Is that all you've got to say to me after all this time?'

'Well your opening shot was a bit below the belt. Why would *he* be in the wardrobe Mark? No room. It's still full of your old jumpers and shirts and ties and shoes and sailing gear and that magnifying glass; since I didn't know where else to put it. It's been on the window sill where you left it all the time you've been away. I only moved it a couple of days ago. I bet they're glad to see the back of you at base camp, or whatever you call it. I'd be surprised if anyone could find anything once you'd put your hands on it.'

Harriet looked up to see him grinning at her. 'Come here Hat.' He stepped forward and wrapped her in his arms.

'Daft bat Hat. Have you missed me?'

'Like you'd miss sitting on a thistle,' Harriet replied into his jacket. It felt good being in his arms again. It felt good hearing his voice in the house again. 'And what about me? Have you missed me?'

'Didn't you get my message then Hat?'

Harriet looked up at him and nodded her head. They smiled and suddenly his lips were pressing hard into hers. He stopped to let her fall back into his arms. He looked at her and then returned his mouth to hers. Now he was gentler, kissing her again and again before finally letting her go. The cat hadn't finished trying to tie them together at their ankles.

'Better move Hat, before she trips us up.'

They went into the lounge and sat down, looking at each other from opposite sofas.

'So what's that lard ball been up to Harriet? What's his car doing here, anyway?'

'I thought Tricia was going to explain,' said Harriet not wanting to go over it all again.

'Tricia was too busy punching at my middle, telling me how porky Bob's gone and how lean and fit I look.' He grinned at Harriet. 'Well if you're honest Hat you've got to agree. I've had a fair bit of humping and shifting whilst I've been down there.'

'Yes Mark. There's no need to show off about it. I've managed to lose quite a bit of weight myself, actually. Or hadn't you noticed?'

'I have noticed Harriet. I think I prefer you the way you were. You've not been losing it for that lard ball, I hope?'

'And you've not been losing it for Tricia, I hope?'

'Get real Harriet. Anyway, what's been going on? Looks like his back tyre's come to grief with a wired-up traffic cone. What's he doing round here anyway Harriet? That thing sitting out there's going to really get on my wick before too long.'

'Well they were both in it actually.'

'Both?'

'Oh he had Belinda Oxfordshire sitting alongside him, so I can only assume they wanted to see this again. The estate agent phoned to try to arrange another viewing for them this weekend, but I as good as told him to get lost.'

'Why Harriet? People are allowed to change their minds you know. Let's go while we still can. You obviously decided to keep the house on the market whilst I was away.'

'Well, I would, wouldn't I Mark? You blazed out of here telling me we were finished, don't forget? We'd have still needed to sell it to be able to tie off our affairs.'

'So they're still together then? After all she took at the wedding? I don't know how he survived that little lot. It looked for all the world like something you'd both cooked up between the pair of you. Well you ending up with his carrier bag. She thinks it's her nice new hat and you turn it upside down and press it flat to her head covering her in cat's mess. She must be pretty gone on him Harriet.'

Harriet could feel herself going bright red. She didn't wish to be reminded of all that right now.

'There's a lot to fill me in on Harriet if we're going to make a go of it, I mean a serious go of it this time.'

'How serious is serious Mark? What exactly are you trying to say?'

'Well I'm not going to say anything while that lard ball's car's sitting out there. How long are we supposed to put up with it?'

'Give him chance Mark. It can't be more than an hour ago they both went off in that taxi. Anyway I shouldn't think he'd be able to arrange anything until the morning.'

Suddenly there was a heavy clank of metal outside and the sound of men's voices shouting instructions at each other. Mark rushed to the window and pulled the curtains back far enough to see the silver Mercedes being carried away on the back of a yellow pick-up truck.

'It's gone. All back to lard ball. Good riddance.'

Harriet swallowed hard on the ache that came into her throat. She couldn't deal with that man any more. The hints, the suggestions, the promises, the ring and now the honour. How could he be back with Belinda Oxfordshire after all that? She watched Mark's changing expression. Relaxed now.

'Come here Hat. Oh I've missed you. I thought for sure I'd lost you to him. You did get my message didn't you Harriet? You've still got the blue one? You might have to take it in a bit though Hat. Will you marry me Hat? Say you'll marry me Hat.'

'Are you absolutely sure that's what you really want, Mark?'

'As long as you haven't slept with *him* while I've been away. Yes, that's what I really want.'

'Well, thanks a bunch Mark. Is that the best you can do for a proposal?'

'Come off it Harriet. Your mother announced to the whole room you were pregnant. Where did she get that one from?'

'I told you Mark, where does anyone get anything from? I don't know. She probably got me all confused with Susan. She had a little girl by the way.'

Harriet could feel the first heat of a returning blush. She beckoned the cat to her lap. 'Anyway I'm not pregnant. I never was pregnant and I certainly haven't slept with him.'

'Yet.' The word jumped silently, involuntarily, into her mind. She pushed the cat off her knee and went into the kitchen.

'OK Hat. Calm down. It's been a real wind-up coming home to that bloody car of his. What was I supposed to think seeing it parked outside?'

'Well, as you rightly say, he's obviously still with Belinda Oxfordshire so he's not going to be interested in me, is he? Let's just forget about him Mark.' She turned and caught his grin as he moved towards her.

'Still a Hat and a pair of Glovers, then?'

'Still a Hat and a pair of Glovers Mark. It's good to have you home.'

'It's good to be home Hat. Come here my little sex goddess. I've never forgotten that night on the rug.'

Harriet didn't answer. She'd done her utmost to forget that night on the rug. Trying to keep Mark from watching the ten o'clock news. Trying to stop Mark from seeing her tussle with Simon Barnes on the doorstep. Trying to stop Mark from finding out about the £3,000 'tip' she'd inadvertently left for Charles Ormerod the steward on the ship.

'It had better be a takeaway tonight Mark,' she suddenly said remembering how near she was to being recognised in the wine shop that night.

Chapter 5

Harriet drove to school the next morning not knowing what to expect. She stopped at the traffic lights outside Starboard Marine North West and recalled Belinda Oxfordshire's misfortune of the night before. Stepping out of the doorway only to catch the very rude sign she'd given to those gangly boys on the corner. With all the kerfuffle of the evening she'd quite forgotten about Mr. Whittle. She'd done the very same thing to him on the way in to school yesterday morning. He wasn't going to forget that one in a hurry. She looked at her watch.

'Eight o'clock. The earlier the better. Let's get it all over and done with Harriet,' she thought.

She drove in through the school gateway and into the car park littered with the A4 sheets from yesterday afternoon. She was grateful there was no sign of Mr. Brown. *That* she didn't need just at this moment. She parked well away from his precious railings, not that there were many cones left in place after the gales of last night. She struggled with her bags and for a moment felt most relieved there was also no sight of *his* silver Mercedes. Then she remembered, it wouldn't have been going anywhere after last night. She pushed her way through the door not knowing whether he was there or not. She felt her stomach knot and then release as a nasty nervous pang shot through suddenly making her feel very sick.

All was quiet.

'No, he's not in yet,' she thought as she turned into the corridor. Then she felt horribly sick again. She could hear voices coming from her classroom. Loud voices. One unmistakably cultured. One unmistakably *his*. Mr. Sanderson and Mr. Brown gabbling away. The door flung open.

'She's just arrived Mr. Brown,' Mr. Sanderson said, holding on to the door as he beckoned her into her room.

Harriet rushed forward and somehow managed to catch her foot in the wheel of the lunch trolley. Down she went with great force and sent it propelling at top speed in one straight line towards the French doors where Mr. Brown was standing looking out at the rubbish in the playground. A couple of stray lunch boxes clattered to the floor, but the one on the top tier saved itself for Mr. Brown and bounced on his head just as the trolley hit him full force on the shins. Harriet lay on the floor in a heap. Her bags had all but emptied. She was surrounded by paper, art work and exercise books. Her handbag had emptied of more personal effects.

'That ruddy woman,' blurted Mr. Brown as he placed his hand on the corner of the trolley to try to regain his balance. He pressed down far too hard and the trolley shot from under him flipping sideways to catch him on the back of his head as he rolled over on the floor. 'That ruddy woman. She's a health and safety menace. Get her out of this place. It's her or me. I'm taking this to the union. You see if I don't?' He struggled to his feet and nursing his head disappeared as fast as his legs would carry him. Mr. Sanderson marched after him.

Harriet picked herself up from the floor. Her bags had initially cushioned her from the worst of the impact until everything had flown out and left her sprawling. She gathered up her stuff, took her coat off and sat on her chair in a dazed, detached state. Then the full horror kicked in. She looked across the room to see her wall covered in graffiti. She looked around to see torn-up books all over the floor, the science corner trashed and worst of all, the hamster's cage was empty. She couldn't believe her eyes. 'Who could have done all this?'

'Well done Miss Glover.'

Harriet jumped.

'You've managed to send Brown home just when we need him most. From which entrance did you leave the building last night?'

Harriet suddenly remembered and went bright red. 'The fire-exit, Mr. Sanderson. I went out through there. I'm sure it was open.' She pointed to the wall behind her, the one that housed Mr. Brown's cupboard on the corridor side.

'Well after you managed to leave them that way, Miss Glover. You left the damned things open. Not to say you had absolutely no right to be using them in the first place. Brown did an early check on all the doors and he swears they were locked at the time.'

Harriet didn't know where to look. This gorgeous, gorgeous man was angry with her. Very angry. All they'd had together just felt like a dream. It was surreal, weird. She couldn't handle it any more.

'Come to my office Miss Glover. Just leave everything as it is. Now.'

Harriet followed him to his office. He closed the door behind them and ordered her to sit.

'Well that's Mr. Whittle and now Brown wanting to see the back of you and I must say one can hardly blame them, Miss Glover.'

Harriet looked at the floor and then up at him. His face was set with anger. She watched him pace the floor.

'I appear to have had this irrational thing for you Miss Glover. Totally against my better judgement, I might add. Your behaviour has been atrocious. I'm shocked at the way you've conducted yourself Miss Glover. I would never have expected it of you, but I now have it on two counts that you've been making Anglo-Saxon gestures at people, both of whom now consider my professional judgement to be compromised. You've amazed us all by your outstanding achievements here and yet you let yourself down in this manner. Mr. Whittle is now seriously questioning my judgement in recommending you for a damehood. You've now placed me in a very embarrassing situation. You've well and truly put me on the spot Miss Glover. These things don't happen as quickly as that without exerting some influence and I'm not prepared to make a fool of myself trying to undo the process in hand, not that I consider it to be one of my better decisions just at this moment.

As for Belinda Oxfordshire, I feel you more than made your point at the wedding, Miss Glover. However much you dislike her and in some respects I can sympathise with your view, but never, ever should it be a reason for downright rudeness. Of course what you fail to realise is I'm treading a careful line here. Her emotional state is affecting her business acumen. I've got to stick with it I'm afraid. We don't have any grounds whatsoever for dismissing her, although I suspect she is manoeuvring this house purchase thing to suit her own ends. As you are probably aware she's had a complete change of mind with regard to pulling out of the purchase of your house. She's attributing it to the downturn in the market for some reason best known to herself. I suspect it's more about cornering me. However, as the company surveyor we are obliged to respect her opinion. I can certainly see where Ted was coming from. Something of an easy way out. Unfortunately I don't have the luxury of being able to hand in *my* notice, as he did. Anyhow this is not your concern. I think I've explained all this to you before.'

'No, not all of it Mr. Sanderson. Hardly any of it. I thought you were back...' There was a sharp knock on the door.

'In.' Mr. Sanderson opened it before Amanda Woods had finished pressing the handle down.

'That will be all for the moment, Miss Glover. I suggest you take some basic equipment to the library until we can get your room cleared up.'

Harriet returned to her classroom, trembling. She gathered a few things together. Picked up her bags and went off to the library. Of all he'd just said the only words she could clearly remember related to Belinda Oxfordshire. 'He said he sympathised with my view, in some respects. He feels, quite rightly, that I dislike her. She's cornering him into viewing our house together. He said she was manoeuvring this house thing to suit her own ends. Oh Harriet. You've done it again. You've completely got the wrong end of the stick. You stupid girl.'

The silent scolds filled the cool library air as she dropped all her things on to the table by the blackboard. It would seem he wasn't back with Belinda Oxfordshire after all. For a split second the excitement and relief mounted then collapsed into a black hole of utter despair as her mind cleared. ' "I appear to have had this irrational thing for you Miss Glover. Totally against my better judgement, I might add." ' Her eyes filled with tears as she recalled his exact words. 'It's not just her who's out of his life, it's me as well.'

The door flung open. Mr. Sanderson marched straight over with her address book in his hand.

'You missed this one Miss Glover.' He passed it over.

One of the two buttercups she'd placed between the last page and the back cover had edged its way forward of the corner. For a moment they both looked at it.

'I'd advise you to skip assembly this morning Miss Glover. Concentrate on getting your class settled.'

Then he was gone. Harriet replaced the buttercup to its safer place next to the other one, closed the book and returned it to her handbag. Those were the very buttercups he'd strewn on her skirt. He'd placed in the buttonholes he'd left open on her jumper.

She swallowed hard on her tears. She had a full day ahead of her. She didn't know how she was going to make it.

With her bag on her shoulder she walked along the corridor to gather her class. Mrs. Bustard was waiting for her.

'Bert and me won't be goin' to that barn dance tomorrow night, on account of 'er.'

Harriet didn't know what she was talking about.

'Well, 'aven't you noticed 'ow our Bert deliberately gets 'imself out of order when 'e's dancin' so 'e can end up with 'er? 'e 'asn't been comin' 'ome very early lately, either. Our Dannybabes is startin' to get really upset at 'ardly ever seein' 'im any more. I'm sure it's 'er 'e's been seein'. Anyway I told 'im it 'ad been cancelled. I don't know where 'e's comin' from. 'e 'ardly ever gets one anymore. She'll soon find out if 'e tries it on with 'er.'

Harriet blushed. She already had red eyes, a red nose and now bright red cheeks. She didn't need this.

'Look Mrs. Bustard it's easy to let your imagination run away with you. Now you get yourself down to the post office and claim that money. Get planning your next holiday with Danny and Mr. Bustard. He won't give barn dancing a second thought if he's got something really special to look forward to.'

Mrs. Bustard caught Harriet's arm. 'Do you think so? You're a good'n you, Miss. I feel better already.'

Harriet lined the children up along the corridor wall and sent them in fours to go and get their work trays. Already the classroom was starting to be cleared. Mr. Sanderson hadn't wasted any time requisitioning the local authority's cleaning-up squad. She marched the children along the corridor and into the library. This was going to be a very makeshift day.

'Sara Atkins,'

'Yes Miss,'

'Danny Bustard,'

'Me mum said 'er mum's after me dad Miss. I'm not 'avin' me name by 'ers on the register anymore.'

Danny folded his arms and slumped on the carpet pouting his lips at Sara Atkins. 'I'm not bein' register monster any more eiver, not 'til 'er mum gives me my dad back. Tell 'er Miss. Go on tell 'er.'

'That's enough Danny,' demanded Harriet as Sara suddenly burst into tears. That's quite enough.'

Much to Harriet's relief Danny spent the rest of the day in a sulk. He never referred to it again. At three o'clock she marched all the children and their work trays back to the classroom. That was the best part of the day for Harriet. The 3.30 bell couldn't come fast enough. She just wanted out of the place. She just wanted to go home. It was not to be.

For some reason the corridor cleared quickly. Even Mrs. Bustard didn't linger. Harriet wondered if she'd regretted confiding in her that morning. She felt sad. She hoped Mrs. Bustard was over-reacting. She didn't like to see Danny and now Sara getting upset.

The door swung open jogging Harriet from her thoughts. She looked up.

'Oh, Mr. Sanderson, I wasn't expecting…' He didn't give her chance to finish.

'That woman was supposed to be here at 3.00. She's not answering her mobile, either. Mrs. Harrington said she left the office at 2.30 or thereabouts. Plenty of time to get herself here. Can I rely on anyone these days?'

'Are you talking about Belinda Oxfordshire, Mr. Sanderson?'

He nodded his head. 'She'd promised to give me a lift. I've left some urgent stuff at home and she was supposed to be collecting it at the same time. Damn! Anyway not your concern. I've had a call from the leader of Brown's union. Now that is your concern Miss Glover. He wants a meeting with us both to discuss what he feels is your deliberate attempt to disable Mr. Brown.'

Harriet could feel the colour draining from her cheeks. It required little prodding to recall knocking him off his ladder a few months ago. And now this.

She watched Mr. Sanderson. Impatient. Staring out of the window. Drumming his fingertips on the top of her table. Bored with the syncopation he banged his hand down to terminate it.

'Still no sign of that infuriating woman.'

'Look Mr. Sanderson. Can I give you a lift?'

'Me and how many traffic cones, Miss Glover? No sorry, that was unfair.' He looked at his watch. 'I'm about twenty minutes south west of here Miss Glover, Lower Tideside. You know it?'

Harriet nodded her head. She knew it very well. Mark and her had often ended up there taking a Sunday afternoon stroll along the cliff tops to watch the sun dance along the estuary tide before lighting up the hills on the other side. It was a beautiful and very expensive place to live. She hadn't realised *he* lived there. She felt weak at the thought.

He looked round the classroom. 'We'll need to reinstate the science corner. Nothing of value taken Miss Glover?'

'Just the hamster as far as I know. Unless they let it go. No one's found it yet anyway.'

'Quite, Miss Glover. I was thinking more of the IT equipment. I can do without the inconvenience of insurance claims.'

'If you would like a lift home Mr. Sanderson? It's no trouble at all.'

'Thank you Miss Glover. That would be a great help.'

Harriet gathered her things. Walked in silence with Mr. Sanderson to her car.

He opened his hand. Clicked his thumb impatiently against his index finger. 'Keys Miss Glover if you don't mind.'

She offered no resistance. Handed them over in a total daze. He unlocked the car, ushered her to the front passenger seat and then closed the door firmly shut. She just managed to pile all her stuff into the back before he sat next to her. Scooted the seat back. Leg length. He needed it. He pressed the clutch firmly down and ran rapidly through the gears before hitting the accelerator hard to rev the engine. He released the handbrake. Into first. They were away.

'I'm most obliged to you Miss Glover. This won't take long.'

He was soon out of town following the country roads into the lanes. She glimpsed the tips of the hills coming into view. As they climbed she could see the whole of the river dancing and sparkling in the sunlight. She looked across at him. Almost lost for breath. This was bringing back too many memories. 'This man. This absolutely gorgeous man. Why can't he just be mine?' She tried desperately hard to control her thoughts. She feared for where they might take her. What she might say. How far she would go.

'Nearly there Miss Glover. Just after that 'For Sale' sign.'

She followed his hand as he went from the steering wheel to the gear lever. His foot still struggling for space as he depressed the clutch.

He changed down. Her eyes were drawn to the sharp crease in his trousers. Running the full length of those solid, sturdy legs. She watched his hand return to the steering wheel. His jacket sleeve falling slightly back.

'Oh those gold cufflinks again, holding those immaculate white cuffs. Those strong beautiful hands.' Harriet could feel all sense of control draining away.

'Left here, down this lane and that's mine. You can just see it over there looking straight across the river.'

She looked across. They'd soon passed the nearest house, the one up for sale, just a little way back, before they'd turned into the lane. This one was different. It was huge with tall trees flanking the edges of the massive gardens. He drove straight in waving to the gardener busy tidying away his things. Harriet could see a fairly elderly stout lady, occasionally lifting the gravel to her toes as she walked towards them. Mr. Sanderson crunched the car to a halt.

'Everything alright Mrs. Harris? Have you got a lift home?'

Harriet's stomach knotted. 'I don't know where she lives,' she panicked to herself, having visions of getting lost. Never quite being able to get back to 4 The Willows.

'Oh yes thank you Mr. Sanderson.' She nodded towards the gardener. 'Mr. Swift's nearly finished. He said he'd be up for giving me a lift, thank you. Oh by the way, that lady friend of yours called round about an hour ago. The tall one with the blonde hair. I never could remember her name. Er, let me think now, Sandra, Linda, now which one was it?'

Harriet quietly started to seethe. 'How many flipping lady friends has he got?' She undid her seatbelt. Fidgeted in her seat.

'That would be Belinda Oxfordshire Mrs. Harris. Exactly what was her excuse?'

'Well she was panicking about something or other she should have had but didn't. Anyway I told her I was unable to help and suggested she tried to get you at school. Then she suddenly remembered that was where she was supposed to be going. To collect you. She said she'd completely forgotten and then went off in a real panic.'

Curious, she pushed her head into the car to get a closer look at Harriet.

'Hello I'm Mrs. Harris, Mr. Sanderson's housekeeper.'

She thrust her arm past Mr. Sanderson to offer Harriet her hand.

'Very pleased to meet you,' Harriet said. 'I'm Harriet. Just giving Mr. Sanderson a lift home. I offered. Couldn't have him hanging around waiting. Forever. I'm a teacher at the school. You've probably realised.'

'Well you did your best to give him a lift Harriet.' She tilted her head towards Mr. Sanderson. Her plump rosy cheeks waggling behind her. 'For sure *he's* not the one to be driven by anybody. I've seen him budge a taxi driver out from his seat before today.' Her face broke into a huge smile.

'Hmm, quite,' muttered Mr. Sanderson. 'Anyway Miss Glover needs to get home. Must press on Mrs. Harris.' He looked behind him. 'There's Mr. Swift. He's just backed his car out.'

'Oh right, thank you Mr. Sanderson. I saw you coming. The door's ajar. I'll see you in the morning then.'

Mr. Sanderson continued crunching the golden stone chippings as he drove down the drive to stop at the wide steps leading to his front door. Harriet took a deep breath. She could see the Georgian windows with their small oblong panes of glass shining yellow in the light that beamed from the old lamps hung either side of the door. Every now and then it broke. Splintered. Sparkling into the heavy, obscured glass circles set like patchwork in the old frame. This was some house. It was double fronted with huge oblong bays either side of the pillars supporting the entrance porch. She looked up to see them rise beyond the first floor to the roof where they terminated in dormer windows either side of the central stack of chimney pots.

Harriet could just see in. The front rooms were subtly lit. Mrs. Harris knew just how he liked it. For all her attempts to place him somewhere in her mind, she could never have imagined so grand a residence. She could just see him wining and dining. The rich. The famous. The elite. The Prime Minister. All his circle of very important friends. Here. In this house. The mass was draining from her body. She felt almost a shell. Trembling. Weak. Her stomach churning at the prospect of being part of all that. She knew she'd never fit in. Her thoughts terminated in a wave of hopeless resignation.

He got out of the car. Harriet was determined to stay put. She scrabbled on the floor for her handbag. Placed it on her knees. A draught of early evening air chilled her legs as he opened the door.

'Will you pop in for a moment Miss Glover whilst I gather this stuff together for Belinda Oxfordshire? I'd be most grateful if you could drop it into Mrs. Harrington or Starboard Marine North West on your way in tomorrow morning. Either would do.'

Harriet, clutching her bag stepped out. He closed the car door behind her. Led the way up the steps. He turned to look at her, pushing the front door open. She felt hot. The ground from under her strangely starting to sway.

'What a house. This man. That ring. Why did he ever give it to *me*? We lay in the field of flowers...'

She cringed. Her thoughts. Unrelenting.

'I want, I mean I wanted this man to actually undress me in the flowers. I wanted him to actually make love to me.'

Overwhelmed, she pulled the two sides of her coat together across her chest. Threw her bag over her shoulder. Followed him in. Stood in the centre of the square entrance hall by the beautiful old fireplace. Drawn to the huge, luxurious flokati rug meeting the hearth. Her eyes followed the winding staircases up to the galleried landing. One either side. The banisters angled back to disappear behind the huge chimney breast as they ran into one.

Harriet struggled. Tried to appear normal. She'd never seen such a clean, light, tastefully furnished house in all her life. White walls. White everywhere The stair carpet matching the soft furnishings. Carrying just a hint of ochre. She felt uncomfortable. As if it was almost wrong to stand on it. The woodblock floor. Gleamed its warmth all the way to the study on the right. He showed her in.

'Take a seat Miss Glover. I promise not to keep you a minute.'

She sat in the armchair behind the door. Looked around at the expensive cream furnishings. Paintings of the sea. Set against the white walls. All of them. Differing scenes of yachts, racing, running, tacking, heeling. Each one splashing colour into the exquisitely designed interior. The few glass ornaments in their maritime capacity tastefully extending the theme. Cautiously distributing any and every shade of aqua into the room but never deviating from that.

She thought about her own house. She thought about 4 The Willows. She cringed again. 'This man most definitely belongs to a different world. The world of the titled. Oh no. Not me. I don't want to go there. I can't go there. I don't want to be honoured at the Palace.' Again she thought about the ring and the field of flowers. She thought about the ship, the cat, leaving all that money behind. She thought about Simon Barnes, the Prime Minister and the grand opening of Starboard Marine North West. She thought about the wedding and her mother and banging that carrier bag down on Belinda Oxfordshire's head. She thought about yesterday and Mr. Whittle and Mr. Brown and dragging the traffic cone home. Then she thought about Mark. Felt bad. She knew he wouldn't exactly approve of where she was. She could feel herself going hot all over. She stood up just as Mr. Sanderson came through the doorway.

'Sorry to keep you Miss Glover.' He handed her three files keeping a large brown envelope back. He waved it at her. 'This one. She was supposed to be picking this up herself. It's highly confidential Miss Glover. That's why the envelope's unmarked. Can I trust you with it?'

He smiled as he passed it over. 'Are you sure you can manage all this Miss Glover? I won't be in tomorrow. As soon as they've delivered the car I'll be off to join the family gathering. A funeral unfortunately but these things have to be done.'

'Oh, I'm sorry to hear that Mr. Sanderson.'

'Thank you Harriet. It's a distant relative on my mother's side but she's always been close to the family.'

As she always did, Harriet recovered a little at the use of her Christian name. He stood back and in a moment's silence he watched her pull the two sides of her coat together. His eyes rested on her right hand.

'Maybe we should do these up Miss Glover. It's cold out there.'

Before she could speak Harriet could feel him sliding each button into its buttonhole until he'd finished the last one just below her waist. He lingered and then pressed his hand against it. Against her stomach. He lifted her right hand into his. 'No ring Miss Glover. I was asking too much of you?'

Harriet could feel herself blushing. 'We're from different worlds Mr. Sanderson.'

He shot her that serious, penetrating look. The look that collapsed her rationality. The look that undressed her mind, undressed her resolve. The look that left her mentally naked. For all the world she wanted him to just take her in his arms, to just lie her down there and then in front of the big old fireplace. She wanted him to undo all those buttons he'd just done up on her coat. She wanted him to slip it off her shoulders. To slip everything from her body. She wanted to lie bare on his beautiful deep pile rug. She just wanted this gorgeous, gorgeous man to make love to her.

His hand reached for the car keys in his pocket.

'That's not an issue Miss Glover. Your penchant for upsetting people, however, is a very different matter.'

He took a deep breath, raised his eyebrows and opened the entrance door ahead of her.

'You'll need these Miss Glover and thank you indeed for the lift home.'

Harriet took hold of the keys. He stepped out to open the car door for her.

'Careful how you go,' he said.

Harriet reversed. Caught his wave as he closed the front door. She crunched her way forward shifting the gravel into two tracks all the way to the gates. She halted to give way to the headlights of a dark blue car just turning in. As they dipped she looked straight in. She wished she hadn't. Oh how she wished she hadn't just seen Belinda Oxfordshire.

Chapter 6

'You're late tonight Hat,' said Mark as he met her at the front door. 'Nothing to do with lard ball I hope?' He put his arm around her, drew her close and kissed her on the cheek.

'It was actually. Belinda Oxfordshire reneged on giving him a lift home so I stepped in.'

'Why?'

'Because he was standing there pretty much expecting one. I could hardly do anything else.'

'He could have called a taxi.'

'He doesn't do taxis, Mark. He can't stand being driven. I don't suppose there's many taxi drivers out there too keen on being kicked out of their seats.'

'So you got kicked out of yours then?'

'Something like that.'

'The overbearing tyke. Why did you let him Harriet? That car's falling apart as it is. It won't stand much of his kind of driving.'

'You're absolutely right Mark,' agreed Harriet, furious at having left him with Belinda Oxfordshire. 'Next time he can just hang round until she turns up.'

Mark grinned. 'Mind you Hat if you hadn't annihilated his car with that traffic cone he wouldn't have needed a lift.'

'How did you know it was a traffic cone, Mark? It was practically powder.'

'I sat on the kerb making a three-dimensional puzzle out of the bits in the gutter.'

'You didn't Mark. What a cringe! Anyway how do you know it had anything to do with me?'

'I undid the rest of the wire left trailing from the back end of your car whilst you were washing the dishes last night.'

'You didn't say.'

'There are a lot of things I don't say Harriet.'

'Did anyone see you sitting out there?'

'Daft bat Hat. Just as if. How did you manage to collect a traffic cone, anyway?'

'It was the caretaker's fault, wiring it to the fence to try to keep it in place. You know how windy it was yesterday.'

'Enough said, Hat. That reminds me. I want to go down to the club to check the boat. I'm not sure it was such a good idea leaving it down there for the winter.'

'We didn't have much choice Mark. If you remember you were going away. There's no way I could bring that thing back on my own.'

'OK keep your hair on Hat. I'll take *your* car. See if that lard ball's done it any damage. Oh and I'll get something to eat at the club if that's alright. If I've got to start shifting boats to sort ours out I don't want to be down there all night.'

'That's fine Mark, we're late anyway. I'll have mine with the cat.'

Mark grinned, reached for his jacket, grabbed his keys and kissed her goodbye. Harriet was relieved to be on her own for a couple of hours. Needed to get her head round *him* and that beautiful old house. She waved him off as she brought her school bags in from the car. She hung up her coat and then picked up the envelope she'd left on the window sill. The brown formal envelope. The envelope containing the letter she'd try to push to the back of her mind. The one she'd not yet told Mark about. Her stomach dropped. She just hoped he hadn't seen it.

' "There are a lot of things I don't say Harriet." ' The words he'd just spoken came back. She hoped against hope he hadn't seen it and was keeping it to himself. She was furious at her own carelessness. For leaving it lying around like that. She took it upstairs and carefully hid it at the back of the same drawer underneath the ring, the pants and the socks.

The phone rang. Harriet jumped. Perched on the edge of the bed she pressed the receiver to her ear.

'Oh, hello Harriet. It's Mummy here. Just phoning to see if Mark's home yet. It was this week, wasn't it? Only I remember thinking it would give you both three weeks together before Christmas. Time for you both to settle down again. You are going to settle down this time, aren't you Harriet? I do hope you've stopped going round with that common girl. I know she was completely responsible for getting you into trouble with that television crew. I couldn't stand another dose of that Harriet. It's taken me all this time to convince my friends at the Women's Institute it was actually nothing to do with you at all. Rather it was all down to that awful chit of a girl. Harriet are you still there?'

'Yes Mummy and Mark's already home.'

'Oh thank goodness for that Harriet. I never liked the thought of you being in that house all by yourself. Anyway Harriet I'm phoning to tell you James and Geraldine have invited us all over on Christmas Day so you and Mark won't have to worry about anything.'

'Who's all, Mummy? We've got Rachael and Clare coming up with the lads.'

'Oh Geraldine knows all about that. What they've done Harriet is booked the Tideside Hotel for us all. There'll be Clarissa and Henry as well so there'll be twelve of us.'

'Very nice too,' returned Harriet. 'What about Paul and Susan?'

'Oh they're off to Susan's mother, I'm glad to say. Daddy and I can't stand the noise. Of course the baby's gorgeous Harriet. You haven't seen her for a while, have you? She's gone quite chubby. But can they get her to sleep during the day? She bawls the place down. Susan seems to spend most of her time driving her round in the car.'

Harriet suddenly felt irritated. 'Why should Susan find it so easy to get pregnant?' She tried to rationalise her thoughts. Tried to stop the jealousy from settling in her mind. 'Well I suppose I've never, really seriously committed to it.'

She thought about the way she'd hedged and flirted with the idea. Sinking into utter despair when the odd gamble hadn't paid off.

'Are you still there Harriet?'

'Sorry Mummy, go on.'

'Yes Harriet and then we'll all be going back to theirs for tea. I've already told her you'll be going. She left booking it all a bit late but they told her they'd just be able to manage twelve on the last two tables. Geraldine asked them to push them together. So much nicer for us all to be together, on the one table.'

'That's a relief Mummy. Save a lot of work. Now what do you and Daddy want for Christmas?'

'We'll have a think about it Harriet. I told Daddy we're not asking anyone what they want this year. Everyone's going to get a surprise. I do think that's what Christmas should all be about.'

'Sorry Mummy, must go. I think that was the door bell.'

'Oh that's alright Harriet. Our meal's just about ready.'

'Bye Mummy, speak to you soon.'

Harriet straightened her jumper as she weaved her way round the cat to the bottom stair. 'Well it's definitely not *him*,' she thought, rapidly justifying their energy supplier to herself. She'd had enough of these uninvited bombardments. She swung the door open.

'Thanks to you I've now had to chase over here to collect that little lot Joris gave you.'

Belinda Oxfordshire didn't look too pleased.

'I was on my way. I don't know why he couldn't have waited for me. I rather think you were just a little bit too quick offering him a lift.' She peered down her nose at Harriet.

Harriet could feel herself beginning to tremble. This was the first time she'd actually come face to face with her since flattening that carrier bag on to her head. She thought it better to try to be nice.

'Oh I'm sorry. It *was* you I passed on the drive then. Had I realised you could have had them there and then.'

'Quite!'

'Hang on.' Harriet hurried back into the hall. The dump at the bottom of the stairs consisted only of her handbag and school things. No sign of the files and brown envelope.

'In the car. I'll just get the keys.' Harriet shouted. She couldn't find them.

'I'm in a hurry, actually. What's the problem?' Harriet could hear her calling into the hall. Her voice was impatient.

'I'm really sorry, I seem to have mislaid the car keys. Won't you step in?'

'Most certainly not. Not without Joris. I'd have seen you in court if it hadn't been for Joris talking me out of it.'

Harriet paled. 'He would have explained it was a genuine mistake then, getting the carrier bags mixed up.'

'I really don't wish to go there at this particular moment. Let's not beat about the bush over this. Joris and I may have temporarily parted company largely due to finding an item of your very grey underwear in his pocket I might add.'

'How do you know it's mine?' trembled Harriet.

'Come off it. I'm a fair bit younger than you but I wasn't born yesterday.'

Harriet winced. Felt the pain of a carving knife going through her.

'Just lay off him will you? He's way out of your league. You've screwed up our engagement and I'm going to make jolly sure it's back on well before he collects his knighthood. Sometimes Joris can be just a little too charming for his own good. You're not the first to try to come between us and I don't suppose you'll be the last. I advise you to back off now whilst the going's good.'

Harriet's mouth fell open. She frantically started rubbing the side of her face. She was lost for words.

'If our engagement isn't reinstated well before the ceremony, then I sue. I'll sue you for everything you've got. I've taken legal advice. You don't stand a chance Harriet Glover.'

Harriet suddenly felt very sick. Creasingly sick.

'I'll use everything at my disposal to get him back, believe me. By the way, in light of what I've just said I think it would be wise to cooperate over this viewing we've requested. I want to survey it at the same time, so be prepared for out! Now, the things I've come to collect if you don't mind.'

'I think the car door might be open actually.' Harriet moved forward. Belinda Oxfordshire stepped back on to the drive.

The car wasn't there. For a moment Harriet thought it had been stolen. She looked at Mark's car and then suddenly remembered. He'd taken *hers*.

'I'm afraid I'll have to pass it all to Mrs. Harrington in the morning. Mark's taken the car.'

Belinda Oxfordshire swiftly turned. Marched out of the gate to her car. In a flash she'd turned it around and was out of sight. Harriet felt like she'd just had a jug of boiling hot water poured over her. Scalded. A disintegrating jelly. She closed the front door, flopped on to the sofa in the lounge then immediately stood up and went to the kitchen to pour herself a glass of wine. Her shaking hand could hardly unscrew the lid from the bottle. The cat brushed at her legs.

'Oh no Pepper, that does it. That definitely does it. I've said it so many times but that man's out of my life for good. Just let me get out of both of their lives.'

She wished Mark was home.

She fed the cat. It made her feel sick. At the best of times she hated the smell of cat food. She couldn't eat. She couldn't sit. She couldn't do anything save pace the floor to the window and back, hoping to see Mark drive in.

The phone rang again intensifying the cycle of fear clutching at Harriet's mind. She let it run.

'Only me Mum. Rachael here. Is Dad back yet?'

'He is,' cut in Harriet, relieved to hear her voice. 'He was a couple of days early as a matter of fact. It's good to have him home Rachael. Anyway how are things with you?'

'Excited. You know that heavy metal group Mum? Rapping Hammer and the Ironing Bards. Think they come from somewhere over the water. You should have heard of them. They're local lads Mum. They were doing a gig down here and we both got Rapping Hammer's autograph.'

'Rapping Hammer? I've never heard of him Rachael. Still I'm very pleased for you both.'

'They're very famous Mum. They buzz world wide.'

'Sorry Rachael, I still haven't heard of them.'

'You will. They're fab. Anyway that's not all. They're back up your way for Christmas. Doing a Boxing Day gig at the Arena Central. We're all going to see them. To celebrate.'

'To celebrate?' queried Harriet.

'Yes to celebrate Mum. Christmas is going to be a bit of a wow for us all. Another surprise to come.'

Harriet pretended her mother hadn't just mentioned it. Hadn't just mentioned Christmas dinner, out. She didn't want to spoil Rachael's moment. 'Well Rachael that sounds like something special for us all to look forward to.'

'Oh it most certainly is. Clare told me not to mention it until the very last minute but I had to tell you at least that much. We're all going to have such a lovely Christmas together. Must go Mum and don't tell Clare I said anything.'

'That's a promise,' agreed Harriet, 'we'll look forward to the surprise. Take care, we'll phone at the weekend.'

Harriet replaced the receiver. Then she remembered Geraldine knew all about them coming up for Christmas. 'Mummy must have forgotten it was going to be a surprise.'

Her thoughts returned to the brown envelope. To Belinda Oxfordshire. To *him*. Her stomach hurdled. She felt sick. 'Oh hurry up Mark. Where are you?'

The cat licked her lips, looked up and meowed.

'I need him Pepper, like I've never needed him before.'

Chapter 7

'Hi Hat, sorry I've been so long. Some pillock dumped his boat right across ours. I had to wait for Greg and Pete to give me a hand shifting it. His trailer tyres were both flat. So chocked I'd have clouted someone else's if I'd done it myself. Anyway, who ever it was has managed to prang ours alright. It looks like it's gone through. I'm damned annoyed. I'm going to email Bridgewater tonight and tell him it's about time he got that yard sorted out.'

Harriet looked blank.

'Are you OK Hat? You look awful?'

'Just worried about the stuff I forgot to get out of the car.'

'What stuff Hat?'

'The stuff Mr. Sanderson gave me to pass on to Belinda Oxfordshire. She's been round. She wasn't too pleased when I told her it was in the car and you'd taken it.'

'I didn't notice any stuff Hat. Where was it?'

'On the front seat. I only grabbed my bags from the back seat when I came in.'

'Better go and look,' volunteered Mark.

'Oh no, don't tell me that's gone missing now,' said Harriet following Mark to the car.

'These what you're talking about?' he passed her three files.

'There was a large brown envelope Mark. With the files. Is it not there? Have a look under the seat.'

'No 'fraid not Harriet. There's nothing else down there. Sure it wasn't in the hall on the window sill?' Harriet's stomach churned again.

'It was a large brown envelope Mark. Oh come out. Let me have a look.'

Harriet scrambled in and felt every possible surface, front and back. It simply wasn't there.

'Oh no Mark. What have you done with it?'

'Look Harriet I didn't even know the stuff was there.'

'Well did you lock the car when you got out or not?'

'I'm trying to remember.'

'Well just remember Mark. I don't know what was in that envelope. Think! Think!'

'No, that's it. I got caught by Graham Whiteside. He called me over to look at the boat. I just got straight out. It's been damaged Harriet. Damaged.'

'So you didn't lock it then?'

'Could well be.'

'That's it then Mark. Someone's pinched it. I'm in it now.'

'Am I fed up with that bloody school and that lard ball. If it was that important he'd no right expecting you to deliver it for him. Just deny all knowledge of it Harriet. Let him think he never gave it to you in the first place.'

Harriet just stared at the car seat.

'I'm more concerned about the boat. Wait until I get my hands on that cheeky sod.'

Mark slammed the car door, locked it and they both went inside. Harriet was used to having bad days. But this. This one had excelled itself. She flopped into Mark's arms before he'd barely turned round from closing the front door. She buried her head in his jumper to feel the warm shreds of damp wet wool clinging to her cheek.

'Steady on Hat. It can't be as bad as all that.'

She struggled to stop the tears but the point of inevitability was gone. She could feel him patting her back, trying to calm her down, as she sobbed away into his chest.

'Come on Hat. It can't be as bad as all that. Freezing in the South Pole with only a few bearded anoraks for company, now that's bad. But getting into this state over a brown envelope Harriet. What's the point? Lard ball should never have passed the responsibility over to you in the first place.'

'You're right,' snuffled Harriet. 'As always you're absolutely right.'

'Of course I am Harriet. So far this homecoming has been *dominated* by *him* and I'm getting a bit tired of it. The sooner we get that ring on your finger the better.'

'Do you really mean it Mark? Why should you suddenly want to commit after all these years? You've been away, granted, but now you're back. Why should it be any different?'

'I've had plenty of time to think Harriet whilst I've been chipping the ice off my fingernails. He's playing about with you Harriet. I've had enough of it. You're mine.'

'But you've always said that Mark.' Harriet sniffed and blew her nose on the tissue she'd pulled from her sleeve. 'You always said we're a Hat and a pair of Glovers. We don't need to be married for that. Why should things be different now?'

'The mind plays funny tricks when you're down there Hat. I left in a rage, I know. I didn't really know how it would go with you two. I didn't want to lose you Harriet. Not to him or to anyone else.'

Harriet snuggled closer. She delighted in the warmth, the security, the comfort, the familiar.

'I thought I'd lost you Harriet. I don't want you getting out of reach.'

'Out of reach? What does that mean, Mark?'

'The brown envelope on the window sill Harriet. It's not there now. What was in that?'

'Oh just an income tax thing.' Harriet could feel herself going red. She wasn't prepared to squander Mark's feelings. She wasn't prepared to risk this long awaited opportunity to marry him. 'I've put it away now. It was just a notice of coding.'

'I'm telling you this Harriet. We're getting married and I don't want any brown envelopes of any description in our lives. Understand?'

42

Harriet understood.
'Did you get something to eat at the club Mark?'
'No, I didn't with all that going on. I'm starving.'
'Let's go to the takeaway then. I haven't eaten either.'

* * *

Mark marched into the lounge. 'Well done Hat, all ready to light.' He put a match to the fire and protected the kindling flame with the fire guard.
'Wine shop as well Hat. We've got something to celebrate!'

Chapter 8

Harriet kissed Mark goodbye then gathered up the empty cartons and stained wrapping paper from the night before. They'd managed one and a half bottles of wine between them and tidying up wasn't on the agenda. She'd wanted to get that rug out of her mind. *His* flokati rug and all the desires that went with it. She wanted to return Mark to their rug, to that night when she'd done her utmost to keep him from watching the ten o'clock news. She wanted to forget *him*, Belinda Oxfordshire, the brown envelopes and all the nightmares of the last couple of days. She smiled, recalling how the fire had danced and crackled its heat on to the rug as Mark had slowly undressed her. How they'd made love with that heady passion neither had felt since their university days. She felt an overwhelming sense of warm satisfaction. He'd given her the honeymoon on the hearth rug he'd promised her when he got back. She knew it would be a difficult day in school today. She didn't want to see *him*. She didn't want *him* to disturb her thoughts. Her decisions. Her mind was made up.

She backed the car off the drive, glancing at the files she'd placed on the empty seat next to her. She looked at her watch and decided her best course was straight to Starboard Marine North West. She was too late to catch Tricia at home now.

She turned right at the traffic lights, went round the block and parked in the main car park at the front of the showroom.

'Oh there you are `arriet,' came Tricia's voice through the open window of the car. 'I was expectin` you. Only I've `ad Miss Snootypants on the phone going on about these things you're supposed to be bringin` for `er. She said there were three files and a brown envelope and I was to make sure everythin` was there or she wouldn't be takin` any of them.'

Harriet suddenly felt ill. That was Mark's solution blown out the window.

'I haven't got the brown envelope Tricia. Mark took the car to the club last night and left it open, didn't he?'

'Ooh `arriet did somebody take it then?'

'Well I can't think why else it wouldn't be there. I've searched the car high and low.'

'Ooh `arriet. It might `ave `ad another stash of `is money in. What did it say on the envelope?'

'It didn't Tricia. It was blank both sides.'

'Oooh come in `arriet. I've got plenty of brown envelopes in my drawer. Not stashed full of fivers I might add. I'll get one and we'll find somethin` to fill it with. Leaflets I would think. Like the rest of them. She's not goin` to know what was in `ers. Is she? Unless `e's been up to `is old tricks again `arriet. In which case she'll be very disappointed.'

'I'm not so sure Tricia. I don't really know what to do.'

'Look `arriet there's no way `e's goin` to tell `er over the phone what was in it, is there? Such people keep everythin` as secret as they can. Look at those things Tarquin Bridgewater keeps askin` me for. I `aven't seen any yet, never mind them bein` in brown envelopes. `e won't even tell me what I'm supposed to be lookin` for so it's `ardly goin` to matter what we put in `er envelope is it?'

Harriet was desperately trying to get her head round the skewed logic as she got out of the car. From the corner of her eye she saw a silver Mercedes heading towards the lights.

'Oh Tricia. In quick! It's him. Quick fill it up with something.'

They shot in and Tricia grabbed a couple of handfuls of promotional leaflets from the top of her desk. She fumbled in the drawer for a large brown envelope while Harriet kept a look out through the one-way mirror.

'There `arriet. Made it. Just in time if you can see what I can see.' She thrust the envelope against the files in Harriet's hand. 'There we go `arriet. She won't know any different and `e'll think it's `er that's pullin` a fast one. I'd say that was a good day's work `arriet and we `aven't `ardly been `ere five minutes. Ooh eh, `ere `e comes.'

The door swung open. Mr. Sanderson marched straight over.

'Right Miss Glover. Pleased to see you haven't mislaid them after all.'

He snapped his fingers at the pile now under Harriet's arm. She passed them over. He picked up the brown envelope, shook his head and then placed it between the top two files.

'All present and correct?'

Harriet and Tricia nodded their heads.

'Mrs. Harrington make sure Belinda Oxfordshire gets them will you? She'll be calling in sometime this morning.'

He looked at his watch.

'I'm late. Should have been on the road an hour ago.'

Harriet and Tricia watched him back out of the car park and away.

'Where's `e off to in such an `urry then `arriet? `e didn't even `ave the good manners to say good mornin`.'

'No you're right Tricia.'

'Too busy flappin` and fussin` about all this stuff, I would say. Now where would `e be goin`? Not to school `arriet. I shouldn't think you'll be seein` `im down there today.'

'Oh no. That's it Tricia. I've just remembered. He's off to a funeral today. Some relative or other.'

'That should take `is mind off that brown envelope then. At least she's not goin` with `im. I think I might just tell `er `e said somethin` about deliverin` leaflets to every `ouse in `every road from `ere to your school `arriet. Just a minute.'

Tricia recovered another large brown envelope from the drawer and proceeded to fill it from the stack on her desk. She pulled the first one out from between the two top files, ripped it open and merged both contents.

'There we go `arriet. That should keep `er on the trot for a while.'

'Isn't that a bit risky Tricia? She'll blow her stack and it might come back on us good style.'

'Now don't you worry `arriet. I'll just mention it in passin`. She'll be the one that puts two and two together to make five. She won't deliver them `arriet. Can you see `er doin` that. She will `ave a big row with `im over it though. With a bit of luck `e'll get so fed up `e'll give `er the push. I've `ad enough of `er takin` over this place `arriet. Quite enough.'

'Couldn't agree more. But he's going to know what we've been up to if you tell her that.'

'Of course `e's not `arriet. Trust me. `e's been bringin` boxes of these bloody things in all week. `e's got everyone you can think of `arriet lined up to deliver them. `e told me to start puttin` them in brown envelopes ready to give out. `ow do you know the envelope you lost wasn't full of them anyway, `arriet? `e'll think it's been `im that's got everythin` mixed up, not us.'

'Oh brilliant, thanks Tricia. I'm off the hook. Better go. Good luck with B.O.'

'She'll `ave plenty of that by the time I've finished with `er. I'll phone you later `arriet.'

Chapter 9

Harriet drove home, grateful for *his* absence. Grateful for the uneventful day. She wondered how Tricia had got on with that Belinda Oxfordshire. She wondered how she could square it with Mark, refusing to sell her their house. He wanted to get married. He wanted a fresh start. She couldn't cope with the thought of *them* being together in 4 The Willows. She knew she'd never settle down to marriage with Mark knowing that *he* was in their bedroom with *her*. The thoughts flooded her mind, flooded her body. She swallowed hard on the pangs of pain that physically caught her breath.

'That man. Oh that man. Did he look absolutely gorgeous this morning?' Her body responded to the question as the desire for him surged through her yet again. She thought of how she'd wanted to lie with him on that luxurious rug in front of the fireplace in that grand, distinguished hall. In that beautiful old house. Then she tried desperately hard to pull away from her thoughts. 'Entertaining the Prime Minister? That's not me. Get real and stay real Harriet.'

Suddenly the harsh, shrill ringing of the phone sent her thoughts crashing. She was grateful to this impromptu aid for returning her to reality.

'Oh `arriet I'm so glad you're there. I just can't wait to tell you about `er comin` in for those things this mornin` and even better than that `e came back again just before I was about to go home.'

Harriet caught a gasp of envy on her breath.

'Go on Tricia. Don't keep me in suspense.'

'Well `arriet, I was just finishin` renewin` my lipstick. Well you never know when `e's goin` to pop back do you? Not that I'm bothered about `im. Oh `arriet you know that's a fib don't you? I've never been able to get `im out of my mind all day. `e looked gorgeous this mornin`. Didn't you think so `arriet? You know that look `e `ad like `e `adn't long been out of bed? Did you notice `ow `is mop of blonde `air was all ruffled `arriet? Ooh `arriet I've got a confession to make. I've been in bed with `im today `arriet.'

Harriet's stomach turned over. She couldn't speak.

'Only jokin` `arriet. It's still fat bloody chance I can tell you. I thought I'd got `im out of my system `arriet. But there you go. It's like when I was tryin` to give up smokin`. It was bloody `ard goin` but I got there in the end `arriet.'

Suddenly it was Tricia's turn to go quiet.

'Are you OK Tricia?' asked Harriet.

'Oh sorry `arriet. It just crossed my mind. There's one big difference though about what I just told you. I wanted to give that up. I don't want to give `im up though `arriet. I can't stop thinkin` about `im. I just `ad to let my thoughts take me where they wanted to go `arriet.'

'Likewise,' Harriet said to herself. Then she sat on the thought. She felt momentarily sick recalling Belinda Oxfordshire's threats. Her mind struggling to surrender to the fact *he* was not to be her destiny. Fear caught hold. How was she going to unravel herself from that dubious honour?

'Are you still there `arriet? It seems like we're takin` it in turns to go quiet `arriet. Are you alright?'

'Oh yes thanks, sorry Tricia. What happened with Belinda Oxfordshire then?'

'Well `arriet she crashed through those doors, I thought they were goin` to come off their `inges, so I rearranged myself behind my desk, that's after I pulled tongues at `er through my one-way mirror first. Then she came stridin` over. I thought she was goin` to topple off those big `igh `eels I did. She placed both `er hands on the desk and said, "Well?" So I said "No I'm very sorry we don't `ave any wells `ere. I would try the garden centre if I were you. They do plenty of things to catch drips." So she said "Are you calling me a drip?" So I just gave `er one of my quizzical smiles `arriet and then watched `er face start to go purple. "Three files and a brown envelope if you please. They're here. Joris phoned me again to tell me they were in your safe keeping." "Oh did `e?" I said. "And did `e tell you what was in this one?" At that point `arriet I pushed the brown envelope right up to `er nose. "No actually. Joris is full of surprises. Just another one I suspect." Then I stretched right over my desk and stared at those knittin` needles she calls `eels. So I said "Well I wouldn't be advisin` you to wear those." Oh you should `ave seen `er face `arriet. She said "What do you mean?" So I said, grabbin` an `andful of fat brown envelopes from the shelf under my desk, "Well I don't know what's in yours but this lot's full of these." I picked up a pile of leaflets off my desk `arriet and shoved them under her nose as well. "Mr. Sanderson is `avin` a publicity drive. `e's openin` a coffee shop in `ere. After the sailin` lessons being so successful for the children in `is school I believe `e's workin` with Tarquin Bridgewater to try to get all the parents and the rest of Stetmead by the looks of it, interested in sailin` and `is coffee shop of course. Which I shall be runnin` for `im." '

Harriet pricked up her ears. This was the first she'd heard of it.

'What did she say then Tricia?'

'She said, "I happen to be aware of that. Anyway, Joris wouldn't for the life of him have me delivering leaflets. There'll be something rather more important than that for me in this.", in `er posh voice. So I said, "I wouldn't be so sure, `e said somethin` about all `ands to the pump. Come to think of it you can get *them* in the garden centre too." '

Harriet's state of tension was fast reducing. It usually did once Tricia got going. She started to laugh.

'Then she said, "What's this obsession you've got with the garden centre Mrs. Harrington? I've got no intention of going there." Then I said, "Oh you've just reminded me. `e mentioned somethin` about you goin` along there to see `ow they run their coffee shop. It wouldn't surprise me if `e didn't want you to call in while you're doing your delivery round. From what I remember I think `e was lookin` for someone to do all the roads between `ere, the garden centre and `is school. I might `ave it wrong, but I think `e was talkin` about you. Anyway you'll soon know if you find a load of these in that brown envelope." Ooh `arriet you should `ave seen the look on `er face. Then she said, "There had better not be," and then she flounced out `arriet.'

'Oh Tricia, you certainly took that one right to the edge,' said Harriet, not wishing for any more to worry about.

'Serves `er right `arriet. We'll deny all knowledge. `e's been flappin` about with this bloody lot all week. `e'll just think `e's got `imself all mixed up. Oh `arriet I meant to say. `e plans on givin` this lot out at the barn dance tomorrow night at your school. Guess who `as got that job `arriet? Me! Bloody cheek, especially as `e wants me to draw everyone's attention to the prize draw number on the bottom of the paper. I thought why can't `e ask `er? Then I thought maybe `e just wants the chance to see me `arriet. `e did `ave that look on `is face when `e said I might like to join in the fun.'

'Oh, I see,' replied Harriet, 'what's the prize then?'

'`e said somethin` about free sailin` lessons `arriet. So I said to `im, you'll never get anyone round `ere interested in sailin` anyway especially if they've got to pay, so `e said "Fair point, I'll look into that." Ooh `arriet `e was leanin` against all those ropes when `e said it. You know the ones that turn into sheets. I was meltin` `arriet. Just meltin`. Then I said " `ow about a brand new boat? And a few sailin` lessons personally taught by you. That would bring everybody on board." Ooh `arriet was that one of those meta-thingies? I'm gettin` really good at those now. Sorry `arriet I've just interrupted myself. Now where was I? Then `e patted me on the back and congratulated me on my brainwave. "Something like a Mirror or a Wanderer. I'll get on to those boat people in Essex. See what they can sort out." So I said "You could `ave a runners-up prize Mr. Sanderson say for about ten people? `ow about a day trip on your yacht from `ere to all the way round Anglesey and back? It's not really fair is it to only `ave one big prize and leave everybody else out." '

'What did he say to that then Tricia?'

'`e said "I think not Mrs. Harrington." Then he went. I `aven't given up on it though `arriet. You never know. We'll just make sure our numbers go into that `at.'

'He won't even give it a second thought Tricia. Believe you me.'

'We'll see about that. `e will if I `ave anythin` to do with it `arriet. On second thoughts I don't think I'd `ave the courage to ask `im again. Or would I?'

'I'll give you a lift then tomorrow night, shall I Tricia?'

'Ooh, thanks `arriet. That's very kind of you. I feel much better about goin` now.'

'So do I Tricia. I've had enough of that place. I'll pick you up tomorrow evening then at six o'clock.'

Harriet replaced the receiver to the brush of soft fur against her legs. 'Oh alright. If you're that hungry you'll jolly well eat the packet stuff.' She went to the kitchen with the cat meowing, running at her feet. She shook the dry pellets into the bowl. The cat sniffed at it and walked away. 'Look here, my stomach's not in any fit state to cope with that revolting jelly meat you call food.' She watched the cat sidle its way out of the cat flap. Then she felt very guilty. She took a deep breath and opened the tin at arm's length. She heaved at the smell and felt the cat's gaze from the window sill. She'd barely placed it on the floor when it shot back in. She heaved again just as she heard Mark opening the front door.

'Hi Hat. You're looking a bit green. You OK?'

'I'm just about to be sick. `scuse me.' Harriet rushed upstairs.

'It was only last night Hat,' shouted up Mark.

'What was only last night?' called back an irritated Harriet.

'Forgotten the rug already Hat?'

Harriet appeared, arm across her stomach.

'Cat food Mark. It does that to me. Remember?'

Harriet caught the scepticism in his face.

'No Mark. Don't go there. I really don't need it right now.'

'Are you sure you didn't have it away with lard ball, Harriet? Marriage isn't going to be easy for me you know. I'm not up for it if everyone and the cat thinks you've been with him.'

'Well thanks Mark. If I'd been with *him* I'd have stayed with *him*. Don't you think? Especially after the way you walked out of here.'

Harriet suddenly felt the need to change the subject. 'Anyway we're under a lot of pressure to sell and move out. Belinda Oxfordshire's well and truly set her sights on this.'

'No problem there. A fresh start wouldn't go amiss Harriet. What's with you? I thought we both wanted that?'

'No Mark not with them. Anybody else yes. But not with them. I wouldn't be able to stand the thought of them both living here. Here in our bedroom. No!'

'Him in our bedroom with her you mean, don't you? Anyway I thought they'd be buying it as a company investment.'

'Oh I don't know what they'd be buying it for, do I Mark? How do I know what *he's* up to. She probably sees it as a handy little pad, a base for seduction. If she can manage to pull it off, that is. She'll do her best.'

'If they're still together why does she need to bother?'

'That's the point Mark, they're not still together, but she's doing her level best to get him back. That's why the sudden interest in this again. Reading between the lines he doesn't want to know but he'll go along with it. He hasn't got any grounds to dump her.'

'He's been confiding all this to you then, has he?'

'No Mark, I just said "reading between the lines," didn't I? Anyway we're not selling to them!'

'You're not selling to *her* you mean Harriet? Have you not noticed we're sliding into a deep recession? If we get married I want a new start. I don't want to be living anywhere in the shadow of lard ball. I haven't noticed anything selling around here. Same old boards. Nothing's changed since I went away. It'll only get worse. There's no way we'll get another buyer if we let her go.'

Harriet suddenly went very quiet. Wrong subject. She didn't want to face up to this just now.

'Well do you want to get married or not Harriet?'

'Of course I do Mark.'

'Well stop being so stupid. If I can jump such a huge hurdle for you, it's not much to ask in return.'

Harriet swallowed hard. If only she could get *that man* out of her system.

'Had a good day, then?' she said.

'Not bad, not bad. We've managed to generate a fair bit of panic down there. It might bring them all to their senses. What *is* the point of going back year on year looking for trends on which to base predictions when it's obvious the bloody stuff's melting like billy-oh all around us. It's an ark we'll be needing Hat. Never mind looking for another house.' He moved forward to peck her on the cheek.

'Any messages from Bridgewater? I'm fuming about that boat.'

'Not as much as *he'll* be fuming about that brown envelope,' thought Harriet.

'No, Tricia rang, that's all,' she said. 'I'm giving her a lift to school tomorrow evening. He's asked her to go to the barn dance to give out a load of brown envelopes.'

'So what's he up to now Hat? Brown envelopes full of what?'

'Promotional leaflets. He's trying to get everyone interested in sailing and "Why not chat about it over a coffee?", sort of thing.'

'Where, at the sailing club? Bridgewater won't want it packed out with the whole of Stetmead.'

'No, not there. In the new coffee shop he's opening at Starboard Marine North West, of course.'

'So it was full of leaflets then. There you go Hat. What was all the panic about? Whoever pinched that one last night's in for a bitter disappointment.'

'I just hope you're right Mark.'

Chapter 10

Harriet and Mark woke up to noisy splinters of rain. Hitting the window. Pelting their way through the early Saturday morning.

'Sleep well Hat?' Mark stretched the words at her as he got out of bed to make the tea.

'I did thank you, and you?'

'Not bad, not bad. That boat's been on my mind though. I want to get an early start if that's alright with you. The sooner I can get down there the better.'

'It's raining Mark. You won't be able to do anything with it in the wet.'

'No, I'll get it into the shed. I've got a couple of guys coming down to sort it out.'

'Who?'

'Oh they're a couple of chaps who specialise in GRP repairs.'

'How did you get hold of them, then?'

'Well in the end I had to phone lard ball's place, didn't I?'

'Who did you speak to Mark? Tricia didn't mention it.'

'She probably didn't even know it was me. I was only on a second before she put me through to enquiries.'

'So who did you speak to then Mark?'

'I presume it was lard ball. I didn't exactly announce myself.'

Harriet felt her stomach wrench. He was being evasive.

'What did he say?'

'Give him his due he said I'd get a call back in ten minutes. And I did. Even lard ball has his uses.'

Mark thumped his way down the stairs. Harriet lay in bed stunned by the revelation. Her common sense told her it was nothing, absolutely nothing. Perfectly logical that Mark should use Starboard Marine North West. There wasn't anywhere else. She wondered why he hadn't made himself known to Tricia. Why she hadn't recognised his voice but the fleeting curiosity soon faded to the aching desire igniting her body only thinly veiled under her nightdress. 'Just a mention of *him*. I've got to learn to deal with this.' She made no effort. Her thoughts went spinning back to the field of flowers. Still not fully awake she slipped her nightdress off and pulled the duvet back to cover her bare body. She decided this would be the very last time he'd ever make love to her.

It was harder to thump *up* the stairs with a tea tray of mugs full to the brim. The individual thuds of Mark's imminent return reluctantly dispersed her daydreams and she quickly slid her nightdress back over her head.

'Tea up Hat. Gone back to sleep again?'

'Something like that,' she replied, wishing she hadn't just gone there. Floundering her way back to reality. She thought about the ring. ' " *'our perfect day' ne obliviscaris JS* ".' He only wanted me to wait for him. What am I doing marrying Mark?'

'Apparently, one of those guys was saying, lard ball's family tree takes him back to Danish royalty.'

'What made him tell you that Mark? It was only a call about getting the boat mended.'

'Well I had to ask him who he was referring to. The guy kept talking about "The king." '

Now she knew just why she was marrying Mark.

'Oh, I see,' replied Harriet nudging herself into his arms. He clasped her tightly. She knew something was coming.

'Out of here. Out of that dump you call school. Right out of *his* life. That's the way it's got to be Harriet.'

Suddenly a soft lump of fur landed on top of them.

'Down Pepper. Off! That's something else that's going to change Harriet. That cat can stay in the kitchen at night. It always used to.'

'Better the cat on the bed with me than anyone else, Mark. You were away a long time you know.'

'Too long Hat.' He rolled back the duvet just to look at her. Just to make his point. He stared in amazement. 'Wow Harriet you can see right through that between the folds. You are beautiful you know. Come here my little ice maiden. We've got plenty to make up for.'

'Ice maiden? And exactly what do you mean by that?'

'I drew picures of you in the snow Harriet. I carved you naked in the ice Harriet. Every curve, every inch. I laid you down Harriet. You'll never know how much I wanted you.'

'That's sweet Mark. And what happened to me? Did I just melt away?'

'Something like that Hat, something like that.' He whispered the words into her hair as she nuzzled into his neck. This was nice. This was secure, warm and comfortable. But she couldn't leave it there.

'When I melted away Mark. You didn't go and carve another one did you? Of Melissa? She was down there wasn't she? With Geoffrey?'

'Geoffrey couldn't go Harriet. He rolled off Scafell when they were on their walking holiday. A bit difficult hobbling over the ice with both your legs in plaster.'

'Well, thanks a bunch for telling me Mark. No wonder you couldn't bring yourself to phone me whilst you were away. You had her all to yourself, then?'

'She needed to talk Harriet. It gave her the breather she wanted. It's not exactly working out between her and Geoffrey.'

'Are you trying to make me feel better Mark. By any chance?'

'Just call a halt Harriet. I came back to you didn't I? I've asked you to marry me haven't I? I don't suppose for one moment your behaviour's been too exemplary whilst I've been away.'

'Just what are you admitting to Mark?'

'Exactly what you're admitting to Harriet. Nothing.'

Harriet could feel herself being overtaken by a very bad mood.

'And have you got to go down there again? With her? I bet she can't wait. Poor Geoffrey I bet he's having a bit of a struggle performing his nuptials with both legs in plaster.'

'Sometimes you can be very crude Harriet. Give her a break, will you? She just needed a shoulder to cry on.'

'So Mark. You haven't told me yet. Have you got to go down there again? Or not?'

'There was some mention of calling back the troops next spring. It depends on the progress they make down there.'

'Well it doesn't have to be you. Does it Mark?'

'Not if I can help it Harriet. Not if I can help it.'

The surge of tension rendered the warmth of the bed defunct. It was more than sufficient to propel Mark into the day.

'It's bloody well pissing down out there.'

'You can be very crude when you like Mark.'

'What time is it anyway? At this rate those guys'll be there before me.'

He stretched across to look at his watch. 'Good grief Harriet I've got just about fifteen minutes to get down there.'

'What about your breakfast, Mark?'

He jumped out of bed. 'I'll grab something to eat when Iris opens up. I won't starve. What time did you say you were going out tonight?'

'I'm picking Tricia up at six.'

'I'll be back well before then. Let's hope your mood's improved Harriet.' A superficial kiss landed on her cheek.

She lay in bed to the scramble of Mark getting dressed. She parted the curtains to peer through the running lines of rain drenching the window as the front door slammed shut. She waved briefly and returned to the warmth of her bed.

'Just a few more minutes,' she said to herself.

She wrapped the duvet around her ears. This was certainly the best place to be on a cold, wet December day. She heard Mark drive off. She wondered about him. About Melissa Scott.

'No Melissa's far too steeped in being green to get diverted like that.' She tried to convince herself.

'No Mark's not the type, either. Well he chats up Tricia a bit, especially when she goes over the top flattering him, but there's never been any question of anything like that.'

Then she remembered the call he'd made to Starboard Marine North West. He'd said Tricia had put him straight through to enquiries. But Tricia knew too much. It didn't quite tally. There was something else too that momentarily alerted her. She was trying desperately hard to remember just what it was. Harriet had now completely diverted herself.

'But he did carve me in ice. He's right. He has asked me to marry him. Not an easy one for Mark. Especially after all he'd had to put up with at Clarissa's wedding.'

She turned over and buried her head in the duvet.

'It's a wonder he's prepared to take on Mummy, though. Legally.' She mellowed. 'Anyhow I might just be pregnant. Wow that was certainly a bit different on the rug. Oh, I hope he didn't get that from her. Melissa Scott. No Melissa Rogers. She's married now. No, I can't imagine from what Mark's said about Geoffrey he'd ever come up with that one. Still waters, Harriet? No. No. He wouldn't carve my statue in ice if he'd been doing that with her. Oops. Maybe that's what inspired him. I bet that's made me pregnant.'

Her thoughts receded as the certainty of being pregnant rapidly lifted her mood. The warmth of the soft quilt recharged the atmosphere, fuelling her contentment. 'How serious was he about carving my statue in ice? Now that *is* romantic. Very romantic. Was it then he decided he wanted to marry me?' Her thoughts, in total, were pleasing. Very pleasing. She wondered when their wedding would be. At last after all this time she would finally be married. She kept her thoughts very close to Mark as she drifted in and out of consciousness. She suddenly disturbed to the sound of him returning. She could hear the car engine running and a quick sharp tap on the doorbell.

'Trust Mark, he's going to get soaked. What's he forgotten now?' she said to herself as she went down the stairs in her nightdress.

She hid behind the front door and opened it sufficiently to let him in.

She jumped.

'Oh Mr. Sanderson. I thought it was Mark. Back.'

'May I come in for a moment Miss Glover? I was hoping to catch him actually before he left. Just a tick, let me switch the engine off.'

Harriet watched him through the hall window while she clung on to the front door. She was still half-asleep. He strode back brushing the raindrops from his jacket. He closed the door behind him.

'Still in your nightdress Miss Glover? I do apologise for disturbing you. This won't take a tick.'

Harriet crossed her arms and clasped her shoulders. She felt exposed. She felt like Mark's ice statue. She felt herself melting.

'You've gone a very pretty shade of pink Miss Glover. Come now we've been here before. Admittedly you're undoubtedly stone cold sober this time so this can't be easy for you. He took her hands from her shoulders uncrossing her arms, only letting go once they'd reached her sides

She could feel every word against her body as he moved his eyes back and forth slowly down to her bare feet. This man with his blonde tousled damp hair. Taking her breath away. Again.

'Be good enough to tell Mark I've had a word with GRP Repairs, will you? There won't be any charge. It'll save him the bother of an insurance claim. None of us need to go there if we can help it.'

He coughed slightly. She knew he meant that cone. *His* car.

'Oh thank you Mr. Sanderson. That's very good of you. I'm sure he'll be delighted.'

She didn't know how she got the words out. She didn't want Mr. Sanderson to start being nice to Mark, either.

'Now, briefly to more important matters. The barn dance this evening. I've asked Mrs. Harrington to give out the flyers. Perhaps you could give her a hand? As Mark and Mr. Harrington have been so instrumental in getting this sailing thing off the ground I thought between them they might like to give a brief speech to the parents. A bit short notice I'm afraid but sometimes these things are better for being impromptu. Would you be good enough to pass the message on?'

Harriet nodded her head. He was looking at her. He was seriously looking at her. Oh how much she wanted him to stay, wanted him to go.

'Oh, just before I go Miss Glover.'

His face was serious. Just a hint of a smile breaking. She watched the curl of blonde hair move slightly down his collar towards his shoulder as he took a deep breath, raised his eyebrows and tilted his head.

'How could he possibly get any more gorgeous?' Harriet was nursing the urgent need for him, now spreading uncontrollably through her body. It was gathering into a mounting, overwhelming throbbing sensation settling low between her hips. She was desperately drawing him in with every look he gave her.

'I trust you've acknowledged acceptance of the honour? It's merely a formality of course, but it keeps the record straight.'

Harriet took a deep breath.

'I can't accept it Mr. Sanderson. I just can't.'

'I'm afraid you don't have any choice Miss Glover, although you were perfectly at liberty to reject the ring, of course.'

She felt his eyes resting on her breasts.

'Although looking at you. I don't know why you did? Your response to me is as natural as a boat drifting on the tide. Come to think of it, isn't that exactly what you're doing Miss Glover? At some point you're going to have to take hold of the sheets and steer the tiller.'

She heard him close the front door. She couldn't move. She was melting in her frozen state. Just like Mark's statue. She looked down at the white diaphanous organza hardly covering her. This man had just turned her world upside down again.

She closed the kitchen door on the cat. She needed space to think this through. Her trembling legs could barely carry her up the stairs. She pushed the bedroom door open and caught her reflection in the full length mirror of the wardrobe. She stood in front of it and tried to retain the stance she'd just held. In front of *him*. She swallowed hard on the mirror. She crossed her arms and placed her hands on her shoulders. Then she dropped them to her sides as he had done. She forced herself to look slowly down. Slowly down all the way to her bare feet. Between the diaphanous organza folds there was very little he wouldn't have seen.

She lay on the bed. She was floundering. Her mind was somewhere else.

'This is worse than the cruise. *I'm trying to put that man out of my life.*'

She stretched her body taught and rolled to one side with her arms over her head. Then she lay face down to feel her body hard against the edge of the mattress. Steeling herself against the saturating flood of desire. Against the urge to be taken. By *him*.

Oh how she wished she'd been wearing her red silk nightdress. At least it wasn't see- through.

Chapter 11

It was a good hour before Harriet had calmed down sufficiently to phone Mark with the message. She felt bad. Sat on the edge of the bed. In that nightdress. With the phone in her hand.

'He didn't exactly have to come to the house to say that Harriet.'

'But he called in hoping to catch you Mark. He wanted to sound you out about you and Bob giving a talk to the parents tonight.'

'About what?' snapped Mark.

'Sailing Mark. I told you he's trying to generate interest in the area. There's nothing wrong with that. Anyway I think you're being horrible. It was really nice of him to settle that repair work without you having to make a claim.'

'No it wasn't Harriet. That lump of lard doesn't do nice.'

'Well are you going or not? I've got to give Tricia a ring now.'

'Most definitely not Harriet. This isn't a five minute job you know. The thing was cracked right along the hull. I'm staying here until the job's done.'

'So you won't be back before I go then?'

'I shouldn't think so Harriet. You mind how you go in that car and *don't* be giving lard ball my apologies. I'll see you when you get back.'

Harriet replaced the receiver. It was barely out of her hand when it rang again.

'Ooh 'ello 'arriet. It's only me. Only guess who's been round 'ere this mornin'? I was expectin' a call from you 'arriet seein' as 'e said 'e'd asked you to ring me. But 'e changed 'is mind and called in 'imself seein' as 'e wanted to 'ave a word with Bob. I told 'im Bob 'ad made an early start at the gym on account of 'im tryin' to reduce all that podge round 'is waistline. 'e laughed 'arriet. Ooh that man 'arriet. I don't think I can go on like this any more.'

Harriet took a very deep breath. She'd just been there. Oh how she'd just been there.

'I'm terribly sorry Tricia. I've been trying to get to phone you but I've been all at sixes and sevens this morning.'

'It's not because 'e's been round to your 'ouse is it 'arriet?'

Harriet paused.

'Oh it's Mark. He's been getting all wound up about the boat being repaired. Anyway he's staying down there until the job's finished so he won't be going to school tonight.'

'Oh what a pity 'arriet. I got Bob on 'is moby and 'e said 'e'll pop down later on seein' as your Mark would be goin'. So I'll still have that lift 'arriet if that's all right with you. I'd far rather go in with you, if you don't mind. I may as well come 'ome with Bob though. Save you goin' out of your way droppin' me off.'

'No, that's fine Tricia. I'll pick you up at six.'

'Ooh 'arriet just before you go. 'e said my boat idea for the draw prize was first class. 'e said e's looked into it and doesn't see a problem. 'e also said I could announce it seein' as it was my idea 'arriet. I've a good mind to tell them all there could just be somethin` special in store for the ten lucky runner-ups as well. What do you think `arriet?'

'Has he agreed it Tricia?'

'Well not exactly `arriet, but I don't think `e'll take much persuadin`. I might be able to catch `im before I make my announcement.'

'Rather you than me Tricia. See you later.'

Harriet put the phone down and went straight into the shower. The running beads of hot water ran off her face and on to her breasts. For a fleeting few seconds she went back to him before forcing herself away.

'He hasn't actually committed himself. Actually. What's stopping him? It could all be spin as far as he's concerned. I don't know what he's up to, do I? But what about the ring? He didn't have to do that.' Harriet's thoughts were going round in circles.

'Anyway things are different now. Mark actually *wants* to marry me and as he's the father of my, our children, that's precisely where it's going. Marry Mark. Anyway *he* might just be another commitophobe. Suppose that's why he finished with Belinda Oxfordshire because he couldn't bring himself to do it? I don't know. I can't go there again. No I'm definitely not going there!'

Her circling thoughts absorbed themselves in the soft warm towel as she concentrated on getting herself dry. She knew she didn't have the steel for it, anyway, even if he'd meant what he'd said. A huge blackness crossed her mind. 'I just don't know what to do about the honour. I've got myself into a right mess over that.' She tugged the corner of towel away from the cat.

'Down Pepper. Just leave it. I'm trying to get dry.'

It leaped onto the bed.

'What should I do Pepper?'

The cat stood up, turned a full circle and a half before making itself comfortable again, leaving Harriet talking to its tail end.

'No use. You're just a load of trouble you are. I don't want Mark finding out about you, either.'

Harriet rushed her breakfast. She needed to call in at the shops. There was the lottery to do. She wondered if Mrs. Bustard had done anything about booking their holiday. Whether she'd turn up with Mr. Bustard at the barn dance after all.

She backed the car off the drive hardly able to see behind her for the pelting rain on the windows.

'Little windscreen wipers for side mirrors. I wonder why someone hasn't thought of that? No doubt *his* top of the range Mercedes is equipped with something automatic to solve the problem.'

She drove up the road desperately trying to change the default setting her mind wouldn't let go of. 'I'm just *not* going to go there any more. Not. Not. Not.'

She was glad she didn't have to go as far as the traffic lights this morning. She didn't want to look across at Starboard Marine North West. Whellread's stopped a little short of it on the left. She was lucky to find a parking spot on the corner, right outside.

She turned the engine off, grabbed her bag and slammed the car door shut. She screwed her face up in frustration with the rain and pushed hard on the door of the newsagents. Hardly anyone in there. Harriet was grateful for that. She pushed the lottery ticket at Mr. Whellread. He didn't usually do this.

'I believe you had a bit of good luck a couple of months back Harriet. I also believe you were a bit off your head and gave it all away, did you.'

Harriet gasped. She watched his portly face crease into a huge smile.

'It was one of those mothers from your school told me. She comes in here regularly does she, to do the lottery. You gave it all to her so she could take that lad of hers on holiday. You might have been a bit off your head love but it was bloody kind. I reckon that should have gone in The Stetmead News. It wouldn't have done me any harm to get a mention either.'

'Oh no Mr. Whellread. No need for that!' Harriet grabbed the lottery ticket and ran to the door. She heaved it open and landed in the wine shop.

In a complete state of shock she wandered around the shelves. 'Oh no, I don't want Mark to find out about that, either.'

She grabbed a couple of bottles of red and plonked them on the counter.

'£45.98, please.'

Harriet gasped. She fumbled for her debit card. She didn't have the nerve to put them back. She wondered who else Mrs. Bustard had told.

She placed the wet bottles on the seat next to her and then slammed the car door shut. She meant to reverse into the short road behind her but indicated right and pulled out to go straight ahead. She stopped as the lights changed to red. Then she realised what she'd done. She couldn't sit on the compunction to look across at Starboard Marine North West.

'Oh no. There's his *car*.' Harriet told the dashboard. 'There's *his* car.'

She suddenly felt peculiar. Faint. She decided to drive on. She needed to see her mother about Christmas, anyway.

'You've brought the rain with you Harriet. Still it's very nice to see you. Shush dear, Daddy and I have just managed to get Susannah to sleep. Susan was here at the crack of dawn. At her wits end with her crying all the time. Paul's had to go into work today. The children are off out lunching with their friends and Susan's desperate to get some Christmas shopping done. The time's moving on Harriet. Just over a fortnight to go.'

'Too right Mummy. That's why I needed to see you.'

'Oh yes, Harriet. Daddy and I have decided what we'd like. We'd like a spring planter Harriet. They've got them at the garden centre. The biggest terracotta pots I've ever seen. Just filled with spring bulbs. So they say. Anyway you know how much Daddy loves his garden and I really do want to brighten up our front a bit. You know sometimes I think that bit by the porch looks very dowdy, especially when I'm chatting to the neighbours over the fence out there. Would that be alright Harriet?'

'Of course Mummy. That's another one, I mean two, solved.'

'Where's Daddy?'

'Here, Harriet.' He tiptoed over to give her a peck on the cheek.

'She's just gone down. What a bawler! We're getting a bit past this game Harriet.'

'Well I'm always available, weekends and holidays anyway if Susan needs a hand.'

'That's nice of you to offer Harriet, but we'll manage Daddy and I. She's used to us you know.'

'How's Mark doing, Harriet? Things settled down between you two?'

'Yes thanks Daddy,' Harriet replied. 'You never know we might have some good news for you.'

'You're not pregnant again I hope Harriet. Well you weren't were you, but you know what I mean? Sometimes I really worry about you Harriet. I hope you're not still under the influence of that common girl.'

'Steady on love, she said she had good news for us. Take no notice of your mother Harriet. You know what she's like when she starts worrying.'

'Thank you Daddy. It will be good news I promise.' She turned to her mother. 'That's all behind us Mummy.'

'Sorry Harriet. I'm still a bit sensitive since the wedding. I'm not sure I like surprises anymore.'

'Oh don't give up on surprises Mummy. Was that supposed to be one, Geraldine booking us all in to the Tideside Hotel?'

'No I don't think so Harriet. I don't remember her saying not to tell anyone.'

'Well in that case Clare and Rachael are coming up with one big surprise for us all on Christmas Day.'

'Both of them?' queried her mother.

'Seems like it. We'll all just have to wait for Christmas Day to find out.'

'Oh I can't wait Harriet. What on earth can be going on with the two of them?'

Harriet caught the wink from her father.

'Glad you haven't completely given up on surprises, Mummy. After all you've decided that's what we're all getting for Christmas.'

Harriet's mother laughed.

'Alright Harriet, you win. You don't change. You were just the same with James and Paul when you were all little.'

Chapter 12

The day had gone quickly. There had been a message from Mark when she got home.

'Just to let you know Hat it's been one pig of a job. The boat rolled off the trestle when we were trying to turn it and the crack's gone from the bow to the stern. We're still not finished. I'll see you later on Hat. And don't leave braking until the last minute when you're out in that thing tonight. It's wet out there.'

She wasn't looking forward to tonight. She rummaged in the drawer for her black tights. She gave a tug, pulling them out. The gold ring hidden somewhere between them jumped out, dropping to the floor. A nervous pang shot through her. She quickly put it back. She was trying not to go there. She changed into her long blue denim skirt and covered her white pin-tucked blouse with an almost matching denim waistcoat. She pulled the zips on her boots. Said goodbye to the cat and went on her way to pick up Tricia.

'Oh `ello `arriet. Am I glad to see you. Do you know `arriet Bob's been in a right mood with `imself ever since `e came `ome from the gym. `e did say `e'd go tonight didn't `e `arriet? I told you on the phone, didn't I?'

Harried nodded.

'Well ever since lunch time `e said `e only said `e might go and it depended on your Mark goin` too. When I told `im Mark might not be able to go `arriet because of `im bein` down at the club mendin` `is boat, `e `it the roof `arriet. `e said "I'm not doin` that for that pillock on my own." That wasn't a nice thing to call Joris was it `arriet? A pillock. I could feel myself gettin` very annoyed with `im. So I said well `e's expectin` you now and you'll make it very difficult for me at my work if you start goin` funny on `im. Anyway `arriet `e said `e's not goin` and `e doesn't give a sod about `im. Well that's not very nice either, is it `arriet?'

Harriet smiled.

'So I will `ave that lift `ome `arriet. If that's still alright with you, of course?'

'Of course it is Tricia.'

'Ah, thanks `arriet, you're a real chum. Oh just a tick `arriet. I won't keep you a moment. I nearly forgot my brown envelopes then.'

'I'll wait in the car Tricia.'

Tricia came out loaded down with six carrier bags full of brown envelopes.

'Just a minute `arriet. I'll go and get the rest.'

Harriet got out of the car to open the rear door for her.

'There `arriet. That's the lot. `e could see me strugglin` in there but `e wouldn't budge from that television. I `aven't got a clue what I'm goin` to say to Mr. Sanderson.'

'I wouldn't bother Tricia,' said Harriet as they drove off. 'Just pretend you thought he was coming. How would you know why he hadn't turned up?'

'You're right `arriet. I won't mention a thing. Anyway I've got more important things to think about. I can't wait to tell them all about the big prize, and maybe the ten little prizes too. You never know what I might end up sayin` to everybody.'

Harriet laughed. She pulled up at the lights at the crossroads by Starboard Marine North West.

'Ooh look `arriet. That's funny. The light's on over there. They should `ave closed by now. I can't see any cars though. Oh maybe just one. I wonder what's goin` on in there?'

'Strange,' agreed Harriet, 'perhaps the cleaners are still there?'

'Oh of course `arriet. That's what it will be. What time is it now?' She looked at her watch. 'They don't go `ome until six.'

Harriet moved slowly through as the lights changed. She was glad to be nearly there. She hated driving in the rain. In the dark. The noisy windscreen wipers adding to the cacophony of screeching brakes, only to scratch the rain away to the dazzle of wet, magnified light. Jumping off headlights. Bouncing off cars. Sheeting off shop windows. Blazing the pavements. Scattering off street lights to shine on the soaked. 'At least we're dry,' Harriet thought.

Chapter 13

The school playground was already filling with cars.

'Ooh 'arriet. There's 'is car. I go all nervous when I see 'is car. There's a space right next to 'im arriet. Go on 'arriet. It will be easier for you to get out when we're goin' 'ome.'

Against her better judgement, Harriet went for it. She was just about to get out when she spotted *him* coming out of the main entrance door.

'Ooh 'arriet. Look. There 'e is. Ooh 'e's smilin' at us 'arriet. Isn't 'e nice?'

Harriet felt the waft of wet night air as he swung back Tricia's door. She felt exposed, as if she was still wearing that flimsy diaphanous nightdress.

'Come, come Mrs. Harrington. You must have noticed it's sheeting down. 'Ooh Mr. Sanderson. Forgive me. I thought you said somethin' else then.' She giggled. 'Thank you ever so much,' and then stepped out of the car.

Harriet struggled out and then struggled into the back.

'Here. Let me give you a hand with these Miss Glover.'

His hand briefly touched hers as she passed the carrier bags over. She wondered if he'd even noticed.

''ere you are 'arriet. Pass some over to me. It wouldn't be fair if I didn't take some in. As well.'

Harriet grabbed her bag and locked the car trying to keep the mass of dripping polythene bags upright between her knees.

She followed Tricia to the open door. Being heavily leant on.

Harriet could hardly bear to look up. At *him*. Leaning against the door like that.

'Into my office ladies. Dump them in here. Mrs Harrington if you don't mind drying them off. You might have to sit those few on the radiator.'

He pointed across as he took his jacket off.

'Oh no. He's wearing that Aran sweater. That deep sea-green shirt. Those black cords.' Harriet had only ever seen him in a suit at work. Only ever seen him in these once. Once when he lay with her in the field of flowers. She didn't know how she would ever negotiate her way through the evening. Without fixing her eyes on *him*.

Mr. Sanderson strode out. Leaving them to it.

'Oh 'arriet. Didn't 'e look just gorgeous? I've never seen 'im in a sweater before and did you notice those black cord trousers, 'arriet? Do you think I might get a chance to do a barn dance with 'im? In the barn 'arriet? In the hay. Ooh 'arriet I wouldn't mind where we did it. Ooh I can feel myself goin' funny all over.'

Harriet emptied the last carrier bag. 'Shush Tricia I can hear him coming back.'

'Splendid ladies. Jolly well done. I think we'll distribute these during the interval Mrs. Harrington. And if you could inform them the draw prize will be a brand new sailing dinghy. We won't go into the class at this juncture. Not necessary at this point.'

'Oh I'm very relieved about that Mr. Sanderson. I don't think I know my way round your school yet. I 'aven't been 'ere long enough. 'ave I 'arriet?'

Harriet was just about to answer when Mr. Sanderson whipped the words away from her.

'Miss Glover. Go and find Mr. Brown will you? We'll need a table centre forward on the stage so all the parents can see Mrs. Harrington.'

He smiled across at her. Harriet could see her eyes widening. Her eyelashes fluttering. She absolutely forced herself to smile at them both and then went off to find Mr. Brown.

She didn't want to find him. She didn't want to see him. Since she'd sent him flying with the lunch box trolley. Since he was hell bent on setting that union leader on her.

She went straight to the hall. It was glowing with bright red cheeks. Moving up and down. In and out. Driven by chattering mouths. Noisy mouths. Laughing. Screeching. Excited. Damp coats and jackets, hats and scarves sat abandoned over the straight wooden chair backs, lining the perimeters. Squashed against climbing bars. The hall was noisy, damp and full.

Harriet stood on tiptoe in the doorway trying to spot Mr. Brown. She could sense a crowd gathering behind her. She knew she was blocking the way. She craned her neck. No luck. Then she stretched her legs as far as they would go. Too far. Her toes couldn't take the strain. She rocked back. The high but substantial heels spiked the pair of feet that had been forcefully shuffled into her parking spot.

'Ouch!'

Harriet turned round. Mr. Brown was nursing his feet.

'Oh Mr. Brown. I'm most terribly sorr...'

'Bugger off.' With his elbows and fists Mr. Brown forced a path through the crowd of babbling parents now choking the corridor to the hall. He stopped short of Mr. Sanderson's office door. He bent down and started taking his shoes off. Swearing. Rubbing at the tops of his toes.

Mr. Sanderson came out of his office.

'Ah Mr. Brown. I sent Miss Glover to find you. Hmm. Do you have a problem down there, Mr. Brown?'

'That bloody woman again. She's just driven 'er 'igh 'eeled boots into my feet.'

Harriet turned the corner only to see them both. She backtracked. The hall would be a safer place.

'Look. Did you not see that? She's just buggered off again.'

Harriet retraced her steps in haste. 'Serves him right.' It brought back memories. 'It was Mark that copped it last time I did that. At university. Standing in that queue. The first time I'd ever met him. Jerk I said.'

'Miss Glover. A word please, if you don't mind.' Her thoughts suddenly became submerged in panic. She looked round. She could see Mr. Sanderson standing at the turn in the corridor. Beckoning. Then he disappeared.

She arrived in a panting heap to the sight of Mr. Brown hobbling off.

'Miss Glover! He's now gone home. That's the second time you've sent him scuttling away this week. See me on Monday morning will you. Be here for eight. Prompt!'

He strode back into his office ushering Tricia out at the same time. They both heard the door bang shut.

'Ooh `arriet. What `ave you gone and done? `e didn't look too pleased to me `arriet.'

'He wasn't Tricia. I was supposed to be finding Mr. Brown, that's the caretaker by the way, to ask him to put a table on the stage for you. The doorway was packed and the stupid man somehow got himself stuck behind me, right under my feet. I didn't know I was going to stab him with my heels.'

'Ooh `arriet. That's so funny `arriet.'

Tricia got the giggles.

'Can't you see the funny side `arriet,' she asked, digging Harriet in the ribs with her elbow.

'Ooh `arriet , `ow can I do…' She started shaking. She took a deep breath.

'Ooh `arriet, `ow can…' Her arm clasped her waist as she bent over. Shrieking.

'Ooh `arriet `ow…' The tears started streaming down her red, flushed cheeks, catching the brittle blonde wisps of hair falling forward as she creased herself in two.

Harriet took one look. In less than a split second they were both trying to prop themselves up against the red tiled window sill much to the amusement of the parents filing in.

'What in the name of fortune is going on with you two?'

They both turned round. Mr. Sanderson looked absolutely furious.

'The pair of you. Get that table on the stage will you? NOW!'

Harriet looked at Tricia.

'Ooh `arriet now we're both in trouble.' Suddenly she found herself running behind Harriet down the corridor.

'Do you think `e might cane us `arriet?' she panted from behind.

'Only I wouldn't mind `im takin` down my knickers and `im givin` me a couple of whacks on my bum `arriet. Would you?'

Harriet didn't turn round to answer. From behind Tricia could just see her shoulders starting to shake again.

'Ooh `arriet so this is your classroom. Ooh they did make a mess of your walls, didn't they? `ave they found the `amster yet `arriet? Maybe we should find it and let it loose on that Belinda Oxfordshire. I've `ad enough of `er comin` in to our place deliberately tryin` to find Joris. I might just come back in `ere `arriet and `ave a good look round for it.'

'There you go Tricia. Can you take that end please?' Harriet was trying desperately hard not to set herself off again. She raised one end of the science table laid bare by the intruders. Tricia took the other.

'ave I got to go backwards all the way 'arriet? Only I 'aven't a clue where I'm supposed to be goin'. Watch that drawer 'arriet. If you start wobblin' it like that it's going to start slidin' open again. You never know there might be somethin' like a clue in it as to who did your classroom in, arriet.'

Between them they just about managed to tilt it through the doorway before Harriet started shaking again. She couldn't avoid the look on Tricia's face as she shunted her backwards along the corridor.

'ow much more 'ave we got of this 'arriet? I don't think I can carry it much further. My arms are droppin' off.'

'Actually there's a side door to the stage from outside. It's just the other side of those fire-exit doors. We'll have to cross the playground Tricia but it'll save us trying to get it past all those parents.'

'Oh aren't we goin' to get just a teeny bit wet out there 'arriet. It's still pourin' down.'

'We'll have to get a move on Tricia. We would anyway. The barn dance'll be over before we get there at this rate.'

Harriet downed the rods and leant against the double doors to open them.

'ere 'arriet. Let me 'elp you.'

'OK Tricia if you can hold this one back I'll pull it through. We should be able to manage.'

With a final tug Harriet pulled the table out and Tricia jumped clear of the two doors to let them bang shut.

'Ooh eh 'arriet. Can you see what I can see? Look who's stumblin' and wobblin' 'er way in. Over there. Look.'

'Good grief Tricia, it's Belinda Oxfordshire. She can hardly stand up. Let alone walk.'

'Yes 'arriet I would say 'er feet are killin' 'er. Wouldn't you 'arriet? I would also say that she doesn't look very glamorous now. In fact I would say that she looks very like a drowned rat.' Tricia slowed down to reach across to the sliding drawer. 'Or even a drowned 'amster 'arriet.'

'Shh Tricia, she's almost behind us.'

'I am absolutely drenched. I've walked my feet off for that man and they're absolutely killing me. I've done every road imaginable from the showrooms to the garden centre and back again to here. Still I'll get a wad of appreciation from Joris.'

'Oh and what exactly 'ave you been doin' then?' Tricia suddenly piped up.

'Well you of all people should know. As you gave me them.'

'Oh, you mean those leaflets don't you? You've been deliverin' those leaflets everywhere 'aven't you? Wouldn't you 'ave been better goin' 'ome to dry out rather than comin' back 'ere?'

The three of them and the table staggered towards the side entrance of the hall.

'Quite. One would have been only too pleased to have done so except I left my car at Starboard Marine North West. I started walking. Further away from it of course. I was near the garden centre when I realised I'd come too far to go back.'

'Oh what a pity,' chirped Tricia.

'I've no doubt Joris will be only too pleased to give me a lift home. After all I've done for him.'

'She had that one weighed up,' Harriet thought as she stopped at the side entrance door to the stage.

'This is it Tricia. In we go.'

'Oh I may as well come in this way then,' Belinda Oxfordshire decided.

'Oh I'm very sorry but you are definitely not allowed to come in this way on account of my surprises. Mr. Sanderson said I am to do what I 'ave to do from this table on the stage. And no one is to be lookin' over my shoulder, as it were. That's right 'arriet. Isn't it? I'm afraid you'll just 'ave to go the long way round. Sorry about that.'

Between them they got the table through the doorway. Tricia slammed the door closed on a hobbling Belinda Oxfordshire forced to retrace her steps.

'There 'arriet. That's got 'er out of the way for the moment. Watch that drawer 'arriet. Remember what I said? There might just be somethin' useful in there.'

They right-turned the table up three wooden steps and Harriet pushed the stage door open with her back. Immediately a deafening six beats to the bar came bouncing out of the gap.

'They've already started,' mouthed Harriet, stating the obvious.

'That's splittin' my ear drums that is 'arriet. That'll do my 'ead in before the night's finished. Look, there's the speakers 'arriet and that box with those wires comin' out the back. The knob's on there 'arriet. I'm goin' to turn it down *now*. You see if they don't even notice. I can't stand that noise.'

She plonked her side of the table down and scooted over to the other side of the stage terminating 'The Dashing White Sergeant' in full flow. Suddenly the skipping pairs halted abruptly. Too abruptly. There was a crash to the floor. Harriet saw Mrs. Bustard land on top of her Bert and Mrs. Atkins.

Mr. Sanderson glared at Harriet and Tricia as he took the platform.

'We seem to have encountered some difficulty with the music. I apologise for that.' He looked down below him at the fallen, struggling to their feet.

'No harm done, I trust.'

'No 'arm Mr. Sanderson,' came Mrs. Bustard's shaky voice.

'Jolly good.' He looked at his watch. 'In that case we're almost half-time. Ready for a break. We'll call it now. Refreshments in the canteen as usual.'

The hall cleared whilst Mrs. Bustard headed for Harriet. 'You got your friend to do that for me didn't you? I've always wanted to flatten that Mrs. Atkins. You're a good'n you.'

She rushed off before Harriet could speak.

Mr. Sanderson pointed to the packs of brown envelopes now falling in a heap behind the stage curtain.

'Get them distributed Mrs. Harrington. Catch them at the door as they filter back. And dry that table top before you put anything on it.'

He turned to Harriet.

'It would seem you've managed to jinx the evening Miss Glover.'

'Oh no Mr. Sanderson, that wasn't 'arriet that was me. I'm ever so sorry I was only tryin' to turn it down a bit. It was doin' my 'ead in and I wanted to 'ave a very clear 'ead for when I 'ave to make my speech.'

'Quite Mrs. Harrington. Now where's your husband. And Mr. Glover?' He turned back to Harriet.

'Oh sorry, I meant to tell you he does send his apologies though. I'm afraid the job went a bit wrong.' Harriet looked at her watch. 'He's most probably still down there. He expected it to take all evening, anyway.'

'And Mr. Harrington? Surely he's going to turn up?'

'I'm terribly sorry Mr. Sanderson. I'm afraid 'e broke 'is leg at the gym this mornin'. 'e got a bit over enthusiastic I'm afraid and off 'e went. Fallin' off that runnin' machine. Oh 'e did come an awful cropper. All covered in plaster it is.'

Harriet watched the look of concern cut through those distressingly handsome features.

'Oh I'm frightfully sorry to hear that Mrs. Harrington. Give him my best will you?'

'I most certainly will Mr. Sanderson. Thank you very much.'

They watched him descending the stairs from the platform. He didn't get to the bottom. Tricia jumped. She thought she could hear Bob.

'Who left the bloody lights on at that flaming place of yours? I've had the security patrol on the phone. Ours was the only number they could reach.'

Tricia jumped off the stage covering her mouth with her hands.

'Oh it's you Bob. I'm so pleased your leg's alright now. I thought it would take longer than that.'

Mr. Sanderson glowered.

'Mr. Harrington. I'm most grateful to you. Were you able to get them switched off?'

Bob fished in his pocket.

'It's all sorted now.' He sensed Mr. Sanderson was about to call on him. 'I wouldn't be here if I hadn't had to let him in with Tricia's keys.' He dangled them in the air. 'I wasn't exactly planning to go out on a night like this.'

'No, quite, quite, Mr. Harrington. Though I was rather hoping for your input this evening. Maybe now you're here? I'm sure you'll agree, to say the least, it's in all our interests to keep a healthy membership at the club.'

Mr. Sanderson smiled. Harriet watched him smile that most charming of smiles. Oh how she wanted that man.

They moved away from the steps, down to the parquet floor and into the doorway. He snapped his fingers at Tricia.

'Door Mrs. Harrington. Miss Glover start bringing the envelopes down will you?'

Harriet struggled to pick them up. She watched his broad shoulders from behind, moving slightly as he put one hand in the side pocket of his black cord trousers and lifted the other to stroke his chin.

'Now who would have been foolish enough to leave Starboard Marine North West ablaze with light?'

'I'm afraid that was me Joris,' came a highly cultured voice.

From nowhere Belinda Oxfordshire suddenly appeared. She plonked her soggy designer shopping bag down on the floor. 'I called back there for more leaflets. I soon delivered those you'd allocated me.'

Mr. Sanderson looked puzzled. He scratched his head and looked as though he was about to speak. Belinda Oxfordshire got there first.

'Well, there were a few loitering school boys on the corner, only too happy to give me a hand. So I let them. I'm most terribly sorry. I was only trying to help you.'

'Most kind. I hadn't anticipated your involvement Belinda.'

She turned and glared at Harriet. Harriet could feel the colour rushing to her cheeks.

She seethed as she watched him move closer. Watched him tighten his arm around her.

'Those soaking wet clothes. You must get them off immediately. Such frightful weather. You look like you can hardly stand. Come, come to my office.'

Belinda looked back to give Tricia a filthy look. Tricia drew a very deep breath and turned to look at Harriet. She grabbed the designer bag left on the floor and banged it down on the table in the middle of the stage. Harriet, raging with jealousy, stomped off to get some more brown envelopes.

'Shove over Bob and stop gazin' at Belinda Oxfordshire like some stricken youth will you please? She'll only be takin' 'er coat off. Nothing else. I can assure you.'

'What the bloody 'ell were you going on about Tricia? I haven't done anything to my leg. Though I wouldn't mind breaking a leg for that one. I wouldn't mind drying her down either.'

'Are you lookin' for a row or somethin' Bob? You've been in an 'orrible mood all day. You might have noticed she's not the only one round 'ere soakin' wet. Just look at me and 'arriet.'

'What am I supposed to say to this bloody lot, anyway?'

'Oh say what you bleedin` well like Bob. Why didn't you just go back `ome?'

'No. I'm *not* doing his fucking publicity for him Tricia. That's for sure.'

'Well don't do it then. Nobody asked you to come back `ere.'

'Someone's let the tyres down on that car parked at the centre. I got sucked into sorting that one as well...'

Tricia turned her back on him and stomped off to join Harriet at the door giving out packs of brown envelopes to the returning parents.

'`e's still talkin` to `imself `arriet,' she said, 'oh `ere they come. Oh I don`t believe it `arriet she's wearin` `*is* raincoat.'

Harriet chose not to look. She kept her head down until the last of the parents had filed in. Then no choice. Mr. Sanderson. Belinda Oxfordshire. Right alongside. Bob walked over to join the four of them.

Mr. Sanderson took command.

'If you three could possibly hold the fort whilst I run Belinda back to the centre to pick up her car? Yes?'

'Oh it's *your* car then is it, Belinda?' Bob smiled as he spoke. 'I'm afraid your tyres have had it.'

Belinda covered her face with her hands. Turned to Mr. Sanderson. 'I'll run you home then Belinda. We'll get that sorted in the morning.'

Harriet was absolutely gutted. With envy.

Bob suddenly chipped in.

'I'm on my way back anyway. I'll drop you home and we'll check out the car on the way. That security guy was a bit concerned. It might be as well to suss out the damage.'

'That's jolly decent of you Mr. Harrington. Er Bob...,' said Mr. Sanderson. Harriet and Tricia caught his frown. 'I'm far better employed here.'

Tricia's fury emerged in trembling threads, somehow distorting her voice.

'Just before you go Miss Oxfordshire. Oh excuse me I think I've got a frog in my throat. Your bag's on the table. You left it behind and I put it up there, out of `arm's way. Open the drawer while you're up there I think you might just find a nice little present inside it for you.'

'A present for me? For all my hard work and you pretended not to know.' She turned to Mr. Sanderson. 'Oh thank you Joris. You can be such a sweetie when you like.'

Mr. Sanderson blanked completely. She was up on the stage before he could speak.

'Nothing, I can't see anything in here.' She banged the drawer closed.

'`ave a look in your bag then. I might `ave popped it in there. I can't remember now.'

Suddenly there was a loud squeal. She rushed down the steps of the platform carrying the soggy designer bag at arm's length.

'It's dead. In there. The fattest dead mouse I've ever seen.' The colour drained completely from her cheeks. 'Oh I think I'm going to faint.'

'A chair Mrs. Harrington. Bring that chair over will you? Now!'

Tricia rushed to get the chair. Belinda Oxfordshire dropped the bag and sat down.

'A glass of water Miss Glover. Move!'

Harriet flew to the cloakroom and picked up a dirty white plastic cup rolling on the floor. Quickly she filled it and ran back to the hall.

Belinda Oxfordshire snatched it from her hand.

She raised it to her lips just as the thing leapt out of the bag, ran up her legs, up Mr. Sanderson's raincoat and down over her shoulder. She squealed. Jumped. Then dropped the beaker of water all over herself.

Instant panic. It darted across the hall floor ensuring a guaranteed right of way as everyone jumped back squealing. Tricia was not to be distracted.

'Ooh, I could 'ave swore I saw a present in that table drawer with your name written all over it. Did you not pull it open and 'ave a really good look like I thought you were goin' to? I did tell you to 'ave a good look in there. I do 'ope nobody 'as pinched it.'

Belinda Oxfordshire stood up. 'It's not the first time I've had this kind of encounter in your company Harriet Glover. Are you sure you didn't cook it up between the pair of you?'

'No we didn't,' returned Harriet, her anger mounting. She turned to Mr. Sanderson. 'I'm sure you will confirm it Mr. Sanderson. That's the classroom hamster. Missing since we were broken into. It's obviously been scurrying round the hall since then.'

Mr. Sanderson brushed them all aside. Instantly he was standing on the stage explaining just that to all the parents.

'Please. Do take me home if you don't mind Mr. Harrington.' Then she managed a smile, glancing at Tricia. 'I mean Bob. Please. If you will?'

'Now if you would all like to resume your seats,' Mr. Sanderson demanded, 'Mrs. Harrington will explain a little more about delivering the leaflets. Oh, and the surprise draw. Miss Glover will first of all explain the benefits of family sailing. Carry on Miss Glover!'

Tricia clambered up the platform steps in a fluster, absolutely raging with Bob. She'd watched him guide Belinda Oxfordshire through the doorway without him hardly waving goodbye.

Harriet felt sick. She hated sailing. Hadn't a clue what to say. 'How could he spring that one on me just like that?' Jellied with fear she followed Tricia on to the stage.

Mr. Sanderson sat himself on the piano stool. His expression defaulted to furious.

Harriet coughed a little to clear her throat. She walked over to the table to pick one off the pile of brown envelopes still to be distributed. She needed to hold on to something. It was shaking in her hand.

'Good evening to you all.' She clasped the trembling envelope behind her back. 'First of all I would like to welcome you.'

''e's already done that,' came a shrill shout from a chair near the front. Mr. Sanderson was being pointed at.

'Of course. Sorry!' Harriet knew her face could well be mistaken for one big strawberry. 'In that case perhaps you will allow me to thank you all for coming out in such large numbers on this dreadful evening. As you can see I'm soaked to the skin and so is my colleague Mrs. Harrington.'

'Stick to the point Miss Glover.'

She looked across at Mr. Sanderson. Was that man putting her through the wringer? She began to feel annoyed. Cross. Angry.

'That's exactly the point Mr. Sanderson. We're soaked because we didn't exactly have any choice.' She turned to Tricia. 'Did we Mrs. Harrington?'

'Oh no we most certainly did not. As a matter of fact I'm gettin' used to it. Gettin' soaked that is. You 'ave to watch screamin' fast cars in this weather. Especially if you're walkin' on the edge of the pavement. Only a few days ago I got my suede jacket completely ruined by a silver one. I think it was a Mercedes. Went like a bat out of 'ell it did. Soaked me. I was nearly drowned by the time I rang your doorbell wasn't I 'arriet?'

Harriet could hear Mr. Sanderson clearing his throat. She wanted to die. There and then. She was drawing on all those silent gestures that might just have shut her up. Tricia finally got the message. Tittering round the hall broke into screams of laughter. The place was rocking.

'And we 'ad to carry that 'eavy table over 'ere in the rain. Only the 'amster in the drawer kept dry. I'm afraid.'

Hands slapped against legs as the laughter translated into clapping and cheers.

Harriet froze. Completely mortified. 'Good grief. What on earth was Tricia thinking of?' Her mind was whizzing. She couldn't believe she'd presented Tricia with the opportunity.

She tried to pull herself together. To pick up the threads.

'You good people didn't have to come out at all. But you chose to.'

The clapping and cheers translated into loud wolf whistles.

'So thank you very much indeed for that. Now...' Harriet opened the envelope and produced the leaflet.

'If you turn your envelope over you'll see the roads listed. The delivery route you've been given.'

The hall hushed to the sound of rustling brown envelopes.

'Now, are there any of you here unable to do that?'

The hall fell silent.

'Good, is anyone without one of these?' She waved the brown envelope in the air and watched a few hands go up.

'If you would like to help out please leave your hand raised or if you feel you could do extra please also put your hand up. Thank you. Mr. Sanderson will give them out now.'

Mr. Sanderson jumped off the piano stool and marched straight over to Tricia. Then he sat down again. Tricia stumbled down the stage steps with two arms full of brown envelopes.

Harriet gulped. 'What made me ask *him*?' She cringed at what she'd just done. Then found her voice.

'Thank you all so very much indeed. Your response has been tremendous. Now let's get to the point of all this.'

Harriet cleared her throat again. It tightened. She sensed his fury. Oh how she wished she had Belinda Oxfordshire's dirty white plastic beaker of water.

'We have all seen how much the children have benefited from their sailing lessons this year. Haven't we?'

A huge cheer chorused 'Yes!'

'Well, let's face it. It's been all about the children for some time now. As it should be of course. But don't you think you deserve something for yourselves, too?'

A laugh went up. Then all went quiet. The atmosphere immediately charged with a negative impossibility.

'Now, be honest with me. Who thinks sailing clubs are only for toffs? And kids, of course?'

Harriet looked around.

'Too many waving hands. If the sailing club's good enough for your children, why can't it be good enough for you?'

'She's right.' His voice was so deep as to be funny. Harriet's anxiety suddenly transmuted to a silent giggle. She over-smiled at him. 'I'll get in your boat any time Miss.' His words. Deep. Slow. Deliberate. Against the claps and whistles. Harriet turned. Mr. Sanderson tapped her shoulder.

'Speed it up Miss Glover. Get on with it. Just remember I'm asking for a *professional* take on this.' He returned to the piano stool. She was glad she couldn't see his face.

'We won't all make sailors, of course. I can't tell you how many times I've landed in the drink.'

Everyone laughed.

'And there's plenty down there that are much too snooty for me.'

'Miss Glover. *Get on with it.*'

Another huge roar of laughter and clapping. 'She's a good'n she is!' Mrs. Bustard was leading the way. The singing started. "For she's a jolly good fellow." Harriet had to call a halt. She knew he would all but wipe the floor with her. With them both. Just as soon as he got the chance.

He was looking furiously agitated. He marched over again. Determined. 'Wind it up. *Now*, Miss Glover. Will you?'

'Anyway for those of us who prefer to stay dry there's plenty of activities going on down there. We want you to give it a try, at least.' She half-turned to Mr. Sanderson and then back again to the listening parents.

'Mr. Sanderson would like Starboard Marine North West to take an active role in supporting the sailing club. For that reason he's opening a new coffee shop at the centre. This will be a place where you can congregate. Learn about sailing. He'll be giving talks and showing sailing videos. Running courses. Selling books. Organising flotilla holidays. This will be a real opportunity for each and every one of you, not only to offer informed help and support to your children as you gain in understanding. But a chance for you all to open up new avenues. Come on let's break down some of those barriers between the haves and have-nots.'

Harriet thought the clapping would never stop. They all stood up cheering, waving their envelopes. She looked over to Mr. Sanderson still seated on the piano stool. His head was down. He was looking up at her from under his eyebrows. His legs astride. His hands on his knees. She knew only too well what he was thinking.

'I hope all your appreciation was going that way.' She nodded at Mr. Sanderson.

A laugh went up and the clapping started again. Mr. Sanderson stood up and contolled the volume of noise to a halt with his hands.

'Thank you Miss Glover. I'll now pass you over to Mrs. Harrington.'

Tricia clicked her high heels all the way to the front of the stage, ignoring Mr. Sanderson.

'Well I'm not sure I've got very much to add to that actually. Miss Glover's said it all.'

Then she suddenly took fright. Complete silence. She turned to Mr. Sanderson.

'Prize draw. Mrs. Harrington. Prize draw.'

'Oh yes. Sorry. Where was I now? Oh yes. If you look on the leaflets you will notice a number at the bottom right `and side. Right `and side.' She turned to Mr. Sanderson. 'That is the right `and side, isn't it?'

He nodded. Impatiently.

'Very sorry about that. You'll `ave to forgive me as I'm just a little bit furious. I mean nervous. Gettin` my words all mixed up now. Anyway that number is for you to check to see if you `ave won the prize draw. Which will be drawn at the sailin` club dance on New Year's eve. So you'll all `ave to be there to see if you `ave won. Anyway it's all there on the leaflet. Just make sure you keep one back for yourselves.'

Tricia suddenly got a cheer. 'What's the prize then love? A kiss off you?' She looked across to see a large chap with combed back greasy black hair, almost out of his chair.

'I wish Mr. Bustard would keep quiet,' thought Harriet.

'Oh I nearly forgot to tell you, didn't I?' Tricia glanced nervously back at Mr. Sanderson. 'It's a brand new sailin` dinghy. I can't tell you which class. Er which classroom it will be in as Mr. Sanderson doesn't know yet, but I'm sure `e'll tell you when he finds out.'

'No, no Mrs. Harrington.' He stood up. 'Class as in type. It will be a fourteen foot Wanderer. A family dinghy. Ready for the start of the season next year.'

Suddenly all hands were being driven by a rush of enthusiasm.

'Oh I `aven't quite finished yet.' Tricia looked up at Mr. Sanderson. She was just in the mood for dropping him in it. 'There will also be ten runner-up prizes.'

Mr. Sanderson took a very deep breath and covered his mouth with his hand. His voice was lowered.

'No, no Mrs. Harrington. That's quite enough!'

She looked at him and decided to go for it anyway.

'Mr. Sanderson `as very kindly offered to take the ten lucky runners up for a day sail from `ere to Anglesey and back, of course. On `is very posh yacht.'

She heaved a sigh of relief. She'd said it. There was no way she could stop herself.

'Oooooooooh!' shot from pursed lips around the hall and then disintegrated into much babble and chatter.

Mr. Sanderson moved to centre front stage.

'Guaranteed support?' He stretched his arms wide open and managed to force a smile. Not with his eyes though. Harriet knew they would be devoid of any twinkle. She didn't want to see the expression on his face once he'd turned round.

'Guaranteed support!'

The parental response hit the ceiling and bounced off the walls into loud, excited chatter.

'It's time to go Tricia.' Harriet grabbed her elbow. 'Come on Tricia. It's time to go!'

'We can't just go. Can we `arriet? Aren't we supposed to be `ere?'

'You can stay if you like Tricia. I'm going. Do you want a lift or not?'

'I'm comin` `arriet.'

'Quick, out of the back stage door whilst he's mingling with parents.'

They grabbed their wet coats and bags from the floor at the back of the stage and ran across the playground. Slamming the car doors shut. Harriet panicked, turned the steering wheel to the left too soon and clanked into *his* car.

'Oh bloody hell!' She went into first gear, pulled forward and just about managed a straight rear exit. Now, well clear, she backed up and then forward and out of those gates. As fast as first gear would carry her.

'Ooh `arriet. Do you reckon we've got ourselves into trouble?'

'I would say so. I would most definitely say so Tricia.'

Chapter 14

Harriet woke the next morning in a panic. She had to be in school for eight. She had to see *him*. Then she suddenly remembered it was Sunday. Mark was still asleep. She wondered what time he'd got in last night. She'd had enough. She'd taken her aching head to bed just as soon as she could get in and up the stairs. What an evening!

'I don't think we'll get away with that one,' she worried to herself as she got out of bed to make the tea. She met the cat at the bedroom door. 'Down you come Pepper. Breakfast.' With mounting enthusiasm the soft fur brushed hard against her legs. The cat rapidly became a menace. 'Get down Pepper. No breakfast for anyone if I break my neck on the stairs.' It took no notice. She clung on to the banister, relieved to reach the bottom in one piece.

She shoved a bowl of dry food under the cat's nose. It walked away. 'Oh leave it then. Suit yourself. If you were really hungry you'd eat it.' She knew she'd woken up anxious. Nervous. In more than a bit of a bad mood. She thrust the kettle under the tap. Cursed the white splashing line of noisy running water. She thought she could hear the phone. Noisy. Too noisy for her to be sure. She whammed the tap off and switched the kettle on to boil. It *was* the phone. She rushed to answer it.

'Ooh `arriet, I'm terribly sorry to phone you so early in the mornin` but I `ad to tell you that Bob didn't get in until one o'clock this mornin`. I was absolutely furious `arriet. I just pretended to be asleep. What was `e doin` with `er all that time? Oh don't tell me `arriet. I just don't want to know.'

'Don't jump to any conclusions Tricia,' Harriet whispered. She didn't want to wake Mark. 'I went to bed as soon as I got back so I don't know what time Mark got in either.'

'Oh `arriet. Thanks for that `arriet. Do you think Bob could `ave dropped `er off and then gone back to the sailin` club to see Mark?'

'I bet that's just what he did Tricia. Now stop worrying. She's not really his type. Wouldn't you say?'

'Oh I most definitely would say that `arriet. That she wasn't `is type but you did tell me that `er and Joris weren't together any more. You must be right `arriet. All the world can see she's doin` `er best to get `im back. Now that's what worries me `arriet. If she's been jilted she most probably will go for anythin`. Wouldn't you say? Even my porky Bob would do if she's desperate.'

'Stop flapping Tricia. We've both got plenty more to worry about after last night.'

'Yes, well I did think of that `arriet. Do you think `e'll sack me for lettin` that dead `amster loose on `er? Well it looked dead `arriet when I spotted it in the back of the drawer. When we were carryin` your table. You know, when it slid open. But it must `ave been `ibernatin` `arriet. I didn't for one minute think it was goin` to jump out of `er bag and run all over `er, though. I must `ave disturbed it when I lifted it out. But not enough 'arriet. It still looked dead to me.'

'*He* had a night of it Tricia. What with me stabbing Mr. Brown's feet as well. The hamster would be the least of it. I'd be more concerned about dropping him in it if I were you. He's not going to be exactly thrilled at filling his yacht with half the school's parents. Is he?'

'Not 'alf 'arriet. I did only say ten.'

'You volunteered ten prizes. They'll all be expecting a family day out Tricia. He'll end up having to hire one of the Liverpool ferries.'

'Oooh 'arriet. I never thought of that. No, I shouldn't think 'e's goin' to wake up in a very good mood this mornin'. Anyway 'arriet. What about you? 'e never mentioned 'alf of those things to me that you told all those parents 'e was goin' to do at the centre. I think you just over did it a tiny bit there 'arriet.'

'I know Tricia. I honestly didn't know what else to say. Am I not looking forward to tomorrow morning?'

'Oh yes 'arriet. You've got to go and see 'im aven't you?'

'Too right Tricia.'

Harriet's stomach turned over. She'd been called to his office too many times.

'I think you scraped 'is car, too 'arriet. Ooh I wouldn't like to be in your shoes 'arriet. Oh that's another metathingy. I'm gettin' really good at them now. It might not be one though 'arriet. If we 'ad the same size feet then I really could be in your shoes and that wouldn't count then, would it?'

'Oh Tricia I really can't get my head round working it all out. Anyway I think I can hear Mark moving about. I'll phone you when I get back from school tomorrow. I hope *he* stays away from your place Tricia, or we might both be in for a day of it.'

'You're right 'arriet. Oh 'arriet. Just before I go. Do you think 'e got the message about splashin' me with 'is car like that? I couldn't 'elp myself 'arriet. I was so angry with everythin' I just 'ad to say it 'arriet.'

'Let's hope he didn't Tricia. He had enough to be going on with.'

'Well I don't want to 'ave to say it all again 'arriet. 'e should be made to think twice before 'e drives like that. In the rain. I still want my compensation. 'e's not gettin' away with that. Maybe I'll wait until 'e's in a better mood 'arriet. Anyway after what you've said at least I've stopped worryin' about Bob and 'er. For the moment at least.'

'Keep it like that Tricia. Thanks for phoning.'

Harriet returned to the kitchen, reboiled the water in the kettle and made the tea. She looked down to see the cat's little pink tongue cleaning the last from its plate.

'Good grief Harriet. What have you been doing down there? It's taken you ages to finally bring it up.'

'Make it yourself next time Mark.'

'I usually do Harriet. Better than this, too. I can always tell when you've reboiled the kettle.'

Harriet turned her back on him. Glad to drink her tea.

'How did it go down there last night, anyway? Did you manage to get the job finished?'

'NO.'

'Oh. Is that all? NO?'

'No we bloody didn't. It was too damp out there. The resin wouldn't set. Must have been something up with it. Has it finally stopped pissing down yet?'

'That's very vulgar Mark. I'm not in the least bit impressed.'

'Oh you're not, are you? Look Harriet I didn't spend the evening cavorting with lard ball. Barn dancing.'

'I'd be concerned if you had.'

'Very funny Harriet. You know exactly what I mean. It was bloody cold out there last night. Somebody had to try and get the thing sorted.'

'I thought you had a couple of guys Mr. Sanderson organised. Didn't they turn up?'

'Well they weren't going to spend half the night down there Harriet. They did have homes to go to.'

'So did you Mark. I suppose there wasn't too much you could do on your own. What were you doing out until one o'clock in the morning?' Harriet knew she was on a bit of a gamble. It was a grossly unfair accusation, but well worth a try.

Mark suddenly grinned.

'You win Hat. You wouldn't have wanted me to miss Bob bragging on about taking Belinda Oxfordshire home. Would you?'

'You what Mark? Bragging until one o'clock in the morning?'

'He had a bit to drink Hat. It was a long story. By the time he'd finished she was desperately trying to get him into bed.'

'You're joking, I hope, Mark. That's not very nice for Tricia.'

'Her, not him Harriet. He was doing his best to get away.'

'He didn't actually have to go in with her. Did he?'

'Oh she wanted him to have a look at a dodgy light switch, or something like that. Anyway he sorted it for her. Apparently. She then sat him down with a coffee telling him how choked she was at breaking-up with *him*. Lard ball. She must be off her head. Actually Harriet, Bob said she was blaming you.'

'Bloody cheek,' Harriet fumed.

'Well she was hardly going to trust him after that do with you and him at the wedding Harriet. How would you have felt having that lot tipped all over your head? What was it doing in there anyway? It all seems a bit sick to me.'

'I don't know do I Mark? It wasn't my carrier bag. Remember? I was only asked to carry it.'

'You knew who it belonged to though Harriet.'

'Oh I'm getting up Mark. I've had enough of this. I hope I'm not going to be getting this all day.'

'No. I'm back down there. All day I expect. Just to please you!'

Harriet was glad about that. Very glad about that. She wasn't in the mood for an inquisition. She was glad to see him go. A brief peck. A quick good-bye. She closed the front door and went back to bed. Even though it was now nine o'clock.

She'd hardly had chance to snuggle back under the duvet when the phone rang again.

'Harriet. I hope it's not too early for you dear? But Percy's slipped out for the paper and I thought I must ring Harriet with the news.'

'Oh gosh Molly. It's lovely to hear from you. How are you and Percy doing? Alright?'

'Oh we're fine Harriet. And what about you and Mark. Did he get back alright from the South Pole?'

'He did, thank you Molly. He's just gone off to the sailing club. Flapping for Britain about getting the boat repaired.'

She could hear Molly starting to laugh.

'That's what they do Harriet. And believe you me dear, the older they get the worse they become.'

'Very reassuring, Molly,' Harriet sighed.

'Now dear. What about our handsome friend? Have you seen anything more of him? I was so pleased he took you home after the wedding. But you know you were very welcome to stay.'

'Oh I know that Molly. Thank you. It was far better for me to get back though.'

'Of course it was dear. Now for the surprise. Percy and I have been doing a bit of research on the internet and we've seen some beautiful houses overlooking the Welsh side of the river. That's where you are. Isn't it Harriet?'

'Not quite Molly. Not far away but we haven't aspired to Lower Tideside yet.'

'Oh you're still young Harriet. Plenty of time. Not like Percy and I. We've both had a hankering to live by the sea all our lives. Isn't that strange Harriet? So we decided there's no time like the present. Percy's got his cottage on the market and guess what Harriet? We've sold this.'

'Well done Molly. The housing market's in freefall. How did you manage it?'

'A property developer, Harriet. No doubt he'll knock it down, but there you are.'

'Oh Molly. It's such a beautiful old house.'

'The place has been far to big for me for a long time now, Harriet. We'll enjoy retirement by the sea. Percy's very fond of Wales. We'll be handy for visiting his relatives.'

'Well that's super news Molly. We're supposed to be house-hunting ourselves, actually. Guess what Molly?'

'No. Go on.'

'Well you're the first one to know Molly. Mark's asked me to marry him. We're selling this and going for a fresh start.'

'Congratulations Harriet. I couldn't be more pleased for you. Wait until I tell Percy.'

'Anyway dear I must get on with Percy's breakfast. He'll be back soon. Oh by the way Harriet you left your clothes here and your diamond pendant's still on the dressing table. I'll bring them with me when we meet up.'

'Thanks Molly. Thanks for phoning. Regards to Percy. Talk to you soon.'

Harriet replaced the receiver and curled herself back in the duvet. She was pleased Molly had phoned. Pleased Molly had distracted her from the thought of having to face *him* tomorrow morning.

Chapter 15

Monday morning. Harriet had spent all yesterday dreading it. She didn't see why she should have to be up so early either. Just so *he* could have words with her.

She reversed off the drive. Glad to be marrying Mark. Now she just wanted to move. A fresh start for them both. A Baby.

'We've got to start looking around for another house. With a nursery.' She tried desperately hard to focus her mind.

'It would help if I was actually expecting.'

She still had a week to wait to the start of her next period.

'How could I have possibly saved that one for *him*? A ring on the wrong hand isn't much to go on. Being a dame to a sir absolutely doesn't mean a thing. Unless of course he's trying to up my status. Appropriate to living in Lower Tideside.'

She jumped on the thought. It merely translated itself into fear. Fear of telling Mark. Fear of telling *him*. An uninvited honour. It took hold of her mind for the rest of the journey. She barely recorded seeing Belinda Oxfordshire's car still parked outside Starboard Marine North West.

She approached the school gateway. His car was already there, parked in its usual place to the right of the door. She decided to stop alongside the newly painted railings. She gathered her books and bags, locked the car and scurried past his with her head down. She didn't want to know if she'd damaged it on Saturday night. She wasn't about to look.

She pushed against the old heavy door and marched quickly down the corridor to her classroom. The science table had been returned to the corner.

'Mr. Brown must be back in.' The thought set every nerve ending on edge.

'My room Miss Glover.'

She jumped.

'I'll be with you in a minute.'

Harriet slung her bag over her shoulder, following him briefly before he turned into Amanda Woods's classroom. Their voices faded as she carried on to his office. She didn't know whether to wait outside or go straight in. She hopped from one leg to the other just wishing it was all over and done with.

'In Miss Glover. I told you to go in. Take a seat. Take a seat Mr. Potts.'

Harriet looked at Mr. Potts. For a second she couldn't think what he was doing there and then she suddenly remembered. Mr. Brown!

There was a loud knock on the door.

'Yes,' Mr. Sanderson shouted, impatiently.

'Don't you let `er get away with anythin` Sydney. Look at these feet. I've hardly been able to walk since Saturday night.'

'Alright Mr. Brown. You'll have a chance to state your case shortly. If you don't mind leaving us for a few moments. Er I think Miss Woods would like a word. You should still catch her in her room.'

Very reluctantly Mr. Brown departed. Harriet threw her bag down and shifted on her chair as she watched the strap settle into almost a heart shape on the floor. Mr. Potts stared at her. Then turned to Mr. Sanderson.

'I'm not here to listen to any of that fancy talking of yours Mr. Anderson. If you don't mind. You are failing in your health and safety duties by not keeping this little minx under control.'

Mr. Sanderson coughed. Harriet could see he wasn't looking at all pleased.

'Mr. Potts may I introduce you to Miss Glover. I don't think we'll abandon all sense of common courtesy. Shall we?'

'Now that's something this young woman doesn't seem to know much about.'

Mr. Potts glared at Harriet. Harriet could feel herself going bright red.

'I can see I'm not going to get anywhere with this one.' Mr. Potts raised himself from his chair.

'I'm terribly sorr...'

'No. No it's too late for that, young woman. You've 'ad him again since the last complaint was filed. As union leader I have the right to decide and we'll sort this one out in court.' He scowled at Mr. Sanderson. 'Unless you're prepared to dismiss her. You've more than sufficient grounds.' He stepped sideways. Upright alongside Harriet's chair.

Mr. Sanderson stood up and took a very deep breath.

'I think you've forgotten there's a procedure to follow. "Homo praesumitur bonus donec probetur malus." One is innocent until proven guilty, Mr. Potts.'

'I told you I didn't want any of that fancy talk. Always trying to put the likes of us down. Your kind. With your posh cars. Rollin' in money. Anyway what are you doin' here? This doesn't seem much of a job for the likes of you? Sure you haven't got a nice little sideline going on? Banking? Oh it's all coming to light now. Isn't it just Mr. Anderson? The likes of you have caused this recession. You won't even have noticed we're in one.'

Harriet couldn't believe the look on Mr. Sanderson's face. He was absolutely outraged.

'You're in serious danger of overstepping the mark Mr. Potts. Now would you mind leaving?'

'I don't have a problem with that Mr. Anderson.'

He moved to go at precisely the same time as Harriet reached for her bag. Without looking she pulled at the strap tossing the bag up between Mr. Potts's legs. He landed side-saddle on the floor.

Harriet put her hand over her mouth, trying to stifle the onset of hysterics.

Nose in the air, Mr. Potts hauled himself up and marched towards the door. Harriet watched her bag whipping across the floor, disappearing into the corridor. Following him like an eager dog. Harriet jumped off the chair to try to catch it.

'It's still wrapped round your ankle Mr. Potts.' Mr. Sanderson called out.

Mr. Potts looked down and shuffled his foot out from the strap. 'You'll be hearing from me.'

Mr. Sanderson ushered Harriet back into his room and closed the door on him as he stomped off to find Mr. Brown.

Harriet looked up to see Mr. Sanderson, one foot raised to the bar on his chair. His elbow pressing down hard on the desk. His hand clasping his head. Bent over. Shaking. Laughing.

'Oh go away Miss Glover. Just go away.'

Harriet returned to her room. Her eyes were streaming. She went straight to the box of tissues on her desk. She blew her nose. And then started off again. Suddenly the door swung open. Mr. Brown and Mr. Potts stepped inside.

'See what I mean now, Sydney? She thinks it's funny. See what I'm up against Sydney?'

'She'll be laughin' the other side of 'er face, Eric. Before too long.'

They left. Banging the door closed behind them.

Harriet blew her nose again and looked out of the window to see Mr. Sanderson driving away. She felt a strange mix of disappointment and relief. She hoped the briefly shared moment of humour would soften him. Excuse her. Negate Saturday night and the barn dance. At least.

She spent the day wondering if he'd gone off to see Tricia. She couldn't wait to get home to phone her. The three-thirty bell rang. She opened the classroom door allowing the children to spill out noisily into the corridor. Mrs. Bustard pushed her way past into the unaccustomed silence of the empty room.

'Did you see that Mrs. Atkins floozy woman all over our Bert? Do you know Miss Glover I don't think it's 'im so much as 'er. Anyway I 'ad to thank you again. And your friend if you don't mind passin' the message on. I changed me mind about stayin' 'ome after talkin' to you. Of course 'e didn't need any persuadin'. Anyway I'm fuckin' glad I did. Wouldn't have missed that for the world. Trust our Bert to carry on when everyone else 'ad stopped. But it was well worth goin' down to see 'im squash 'er flat. 'ave you seen 'er fingernails Miss Glover? Each one's painted a different flamin' colour. Then she must of decided to sprinkle them with silver glitter before they'd dried off. She'll come in 'andy, anyway. That Christmas tree your caretaker's put up this mornin', by the front door. We could stand 'er behind it and make 'er poke 'er fingers through. Save you the trouble of decoratin' it Miss Glover. Stop pullin' at my coat Danny. I'm 'avin' a private word with Miss Glover.'

'Ah Miss Glover, Mrs. Bustard...'

Harriet looked up. 'Not excused. No trace of submission on his face.' Her thoughts took over.

'Are we all finished here Mrs. Bustard? If you don't mind.'

'We are. Thank you very much Mr. Sanderson. Ah just look at 'im. Lookin' in the 'amster's cage. Is it still not in there Dannybabes?'

'Oh get going for goodness sake Mrs. Bustard,' Harriet silently panicked.

Mr. Sanderson drummed his fingers on the side of the door. He didn't like being kept waiting. Harriet didn't dare look at him.

Suddenly Danny ran aeroplane arms round all the tables and then took his mum's hand. 'Are you givin' me Dad onions again for 'is dinner tonight Mum? You gave 'im onions on Saturday and 'e's been in a good mood ever since!'

'I'll say goodnight to you both then. Mr. Sanderson. Miss Glover.' She marched Danny down the corridor and out over the playground.

'My office if you will, Miss Glover?'

Harriet trembled her way behind him. Oh how she wished he'd stayed out all day.

He stepped back to allow her in and then closed the door behind her. He swept his hand at the chair facing his desk.

'Take a seat Miss Glover.'

Harriet sat down. She lowered her bag from her shoulder.

'No. Out of the way Miss Glover.' He pointed under the chair. 'We could well have Mr. Brown back. I'm afraid he took his feet home this morning saying if he rested them he might manage the three-thirty shift. We don't actually want a repeat of this morning's performance.'

Harriet could feel her shoulders starting to shake. She knew the momentum was coming from nervous energy. She felt like laughing and crying all at the same time.

'I couldn't fail to admit to a fleeting moment of mirth, Miss Glover. However it's over. Done with. Settle yourself down.'

Harriet smoothed her hair away from her face, repositioned herself on the chair and pushed the last of the strap to the top of her bag, under the seat. She checked the three sides of the floor around her to make sure there was nothing sticking out.

'I've spoken to Mrs. Harrington, Miss Glover. If you recall I gave you a large brown envelope along with those three files destined for Belinda Oxfordshire?'

His eyes were serious, questioning. Harriet's stomach hit the ground. She couldn't speak.

'Well,' he said, standing with his back to the window, looking straight at her.

She still couldn't speak.

'It certainly didn't contain leaflets Miss Glover.'

She looked down. His voice was sharp. Angry. This was and wasn't what she'd been expecting. All day.

'According to Mrs. Harrington she gave Belinda the files and same envelope you'd left for her. Now it certainly *didn't* contain leaflets Miss Glover.'

Harriet could feel herself blushing profusely.

'It's the only one I had Mr. Sanderson. Could it not have possibly got mixed up with all those Mrs. Harrington had stored for Saturday night?'

'We've spent the best part of the day on our hands and knees Miss Glover. On the floor, behind the shelves, combing every square inch of Starboard Marine North West and it certainly isn't there.'

'Well how did I know what you gave me Mr. Sanderson? I just passed it all over.'

'You wouldn't lie to me. Would you? Miss Glover?'

Mercifully the colour of Harriet's face couldn't have intensified any more.

'I suggest you have a good look at home. Oh and in that car of yours. I want it back Miss Glover. If you please.'

Harriet fidgeted on her seat. She was caught in the primeval fear thing. The flight option would suit her admirably just at this moment.

'Now, to other matters Miss Glover. I cannot comprehend how you've more than likely placed us in exactly the same damned situation as we were in earlier this year with that Bastard woman. I don't like to recall how much getting closure on that one cost me. We've hit a recession, if you haven't already noticed Miss Glover. I've no intention of bailing you out "unofficially" again, as it were. Think about it Miss Glover. Will you? Think about it seriously for a moment. You've done a grand job here and that's not in dispute of course. However, you do recognise, I hope, that in the circles I move in, "Manus manum lavat" inevitably creates obligations.'

Harriet looked at him completely blank.

'One hand washes the other Miss Glover. The favour for the favour.'

Harriet stiffened herself. She could feel herself plucking up the courage. He'd presented her with the perfect get-out.

'Well, it was most kind of you Mr. Sanderson, but if it's not all above board I don't want to be involved.'

She thought he was going to hit the roof. He paced back and forth in front of the window. Then he thumped his fist down on the table. She jumped.

'Of course it's above board Miss Glover. You've done the work haven't you? It's just a question of timing. These things normally take far longer than that to get through the system. Concentrate will you? Mr. Whittle already has serious doubts about my decision. We don't need Brown and that Potts fellow stoking the boiler. I'll be receiving my knighthood too, don't forget. I'm not prepared to face the glare of negative publicity you seem intent on surrounding yourself in. Do you think you could make an exceptional effort Miss Glover and try to stay out of trouble at least until the end of June?'

Harriet now knew what going into shock felt like. It wasn't pleasant. She might just as well go for it.

'What about Tarquin Bridgewater, anyway? Mrs. Harrington says he's always down at the centre asking if you've left anything for him.' She could see the anger in his face intensifying. Oh gosh what had she just said? She felt compelled to continue. 'I also believe he's up for an honour too. As well as questioning?' Harriet was immediately mortified. She hadn't meant to drop Tricia in it.

'Er that wasn't Mrs. Harrington. That was on the news. And Mrs. Harrington was always most concerned that you might be forgetting to leave something for him that was very important. Like shackles for his boat,' she tried to explain.

'I doubt if Mrs. Harrington even knows what shackles are Miss Glover. And as for Tarquin Bridgewater. Not part of the old schoolboy network I'm afraid. At least not Eton. What he does is his business Miss Glover and nobody elses.'

Harriet cupped her hands and twisted them in her lap.

'Get that acceptance sorted Miss Glover. I refuse to be made a fool of.'

Harriet looked up. His anger accentuated all of the best of those good looking features. As did his humour. His concern. His passion. She'd just let the last shreds of hope for this man slip through her fingers. She'd finally let go of this most gorgeous of men.

She scrambled under the chair for her bag and stood for a moment watching him take a small key out of his pocket. He bent forward to unlock the drawer. His head was down. Harriet was transfixed by that mop of thick blonde hair. Curling at the neck of his clean white collar.

'Atrocious behaviour Miss Glover. Absolutely atrocious. Had trouble reversing once you and Mrs. Harrington absconded on Saturday night?'

Harriet couldn't answer. She felt absolutely flattened.

'Here. Dispose of these will you. As you see fit.'

She took his washed-up bow tie, still clinging to her dingy grey bra, from his hand and walked the ever lengthening miles of corridors back to her classroom.

She closed the door behind her and pushed them into her bag. She sat on the empty science table just staring out of the window. Trying hard to choke back the tears. 'It's all over now. All over.'

Chapter 16

With tears blurring her vision Harriet arrived home to the phone ringing. She ran upstairs and shoved the bra and bow tie to the back of the top drawer in the dressing table. She ran downstairs. The answer machine clicked in. She picked the phone up quickly at the sound of Tricia's voice.

'Oh `arriet. Is that you `arriet? Oh you are there, aren't you?'

'Yes, sorry Tricia. I've only just got in. How did you get on? I believe you've had *him* there most of the day.'

'Oh `aven't I just `arriet. I don't think I've ever seen `im in such a bad mood. `e gave me a right goin` over about Saturday night `arriet. I can tell you. `e said I `ad no right to overstep the mark offering runner-up prizes on `is yacht `arriet. `e said there was absolutely no way `e could get out of it. `e said `ad I any conception of the safety issues involved? I did `ave to say "No" `arriet. Do you know `arriet I don't think anybody `as ever wiped the floor with me like `e did. And what made it worse `arriet was `er. *She* was sittin` in `is office earwiggin` the `ole of the time. You should `ave seen the smirk on `er face when she came out.'

'Oh poor thing Tricia. I got exactly the same but at least *she* wasn't around.'

'We were only tryin` to `elp `im `arriet. There's no pleasin` some people is there?'

'No Tricia.' Harriet rubbed at her eyes with her sleeve. Tricia had just made her feel a tiny bit better. 'Tricia I've got a confession to make.'

'A confession `arriet. What do you mean?'

'I think I might have dropped you in it a bit, I'm really sorry. I told him you'd mentioned Tarquin Bridgewater always coming in asking if there was anything for him.'

'Oh I wouldn't be worryin` about that `arriet. I forgot to tell you. I said to `im only the other day: "What is it Tarquin Bridgewater's `opin` to collect off you? `e's in `ere by the minute." And do you know what he said `arriet?'

'No. Go on.'

'Cor `arriet did `e smile one of those smiles at me? `e said "Not your concern Mrs. Harrington. Unless, of course, he's making it the excuse to come and see you." Oh `arriet that man `ad me swoonin` for the rest of the day. `e only `as to smile like that. One of these days `e's goin` to `ave to take me to `ospital `arriet. When I collapse at `is feet.'

'Not one of those days today though Tricia?'

'Certainly not `arriet. To tell you the truth `arriet I felt a bit bad about tellin' `im I'd only passed on the files and brown envelope to *her* that you'd given me. I said "`ow did I know what was in it?" '

'Oh Tricia I told him exactly the same myself. No wonder he was raging. He didn't get any sense out of either of us.'

'Too right `arriet. `e won't either. If it was that important `e shouldn't `ave given it to you in the first place. You should `ave seen `im lookin` for it in places it could never `ave been, `arriet. I reckon `e's missin` somethin` very important. Something `e `ad to give to `er `arriet. I wonder what it could `ave been?'

'Best not to go there Tricia. Not our concern. As *he* would say.'

'Ooh `arriet. Did your Mark say Bob `ad been down to the club after `e'd taken that drip `ome? Like you thought `ad `appened.'

'Yes he did Tricia. Mark couldn't bring himself to come home leaving the boat like that. Though what good it did I'll never know.'

'Oh I know `arriet. I know that Bob wasn't tellin` porkies after all. That's what good it did. Anyway `arriet. I'll `ave to go. `e's `ome early tonight so as `e can get to the gym again. `e's becomin` totally obsessed `arriet. I was tellin` your Mark all about it.'

'Could be doing worse things Tricia. Anyway thanks for phoning. Call in any time you see the car.'

'Will do `arriet. Bye.'

Harriet replaced the receiver. She felt a slight concern. But she couldn't put her finger on it. 'Oh yes. That was it. Mark never mentioned Tricia telling him all about Bob.' She pushed the thought to the back of her mind. It was insignificant in relation to the day she'd just had.

'Oh no. That's the phone again Pepper.' She plonked the cat's bowl down and went to answer it.

'Good afternoon, Mrs. Glover? Bryce Rae Roberts here. Mr. Roberts speaking.'

Harriet jumped. This was the chap that sounded far too much like Mr. Sanderson for her liking.

'Yes. Speaking. Good afternoon.' Harriet waited.

'The offer of the full asking price made by a Miss Belinda Oxfordshire, I believe, has now been reinstated. She's requesting access to the property for survey purposes this coming Saturday morning at ten o'clock.'

Harriet couldn't be doing with it. Not now. Not after today.

'It's not a very convenient time Mr. Roberts I'm afraid.'

'Look Mrs. Glover. You've been on our books for some time now. If you don't wish to sell the property do kindly inform us. You are most fortunate Miss Oxfordshire is maintaining the original offer. Are you aware that prices have fallen twenty per cent or more in the last six months? I'll be quite frank with you Mrs. Glover. There's no mortgages to be had out there. She's definitely a cash buyer. Now we'll go with ten o'clock Saturday morning. Shall we Mrs. Glover?'

Reluctantly Harriet agreed. She put the phone down and filled the cat's saucer with milk. 'We're seriously going to have to do some house-hunting Pepper.'

Chapter 17

'See if you can get an appointment to view this one Hat?'

Harriet leant over Mark's shoulder. He'd been online scrolling down houses all evening.

'But I don't want to live in Millington, Mark. It's miles away.'

'It's not miles away. I thought we were looking for a fresh start Hat?'

'Well it might be on the way to *your* work Mark, but it would take me ages to get to school from there.'

'You won't be at school Harriet. I don't want you anywhere near the place once we're married.'

'Well we might just need my salary if you're looking at those kind of prices. Anyway Mr. Roberts said there were no mortgages to be had.'

'Of course there are Harriet. He's trying to put the frighteners on. Isn't he?'

'Well, it said on the news this morning that building societies, what's left of them that is, are looking for deposits of twenty per cent. Where are we supposed to be finding that from if I give up work? Even if we can borrow it, it's still got to be paid back.'

'Look Harriet it's a buyer's market. We've been offered the asking price relevant to six months ago. People are accepting all sorts of low offers to get rid. Give them a call tomorrow.'

Harriet watched him click on all the rooms. It looked nice. She didn't want it to look nice. It had a lovely big garden. There was nothing overlooking it only fields.

'It's got a nursery Hat.' Mark turned so she could see him smiling.

Her mind was elsewhere.

'If we're looking at those kind of prices Mark. How about Lower Tideside?'

'No Harriet. Most definitely not.'

Harriet went downstairs and put the dirty dishes in the sink.

'That kitchen had a dishwasher,' she thought. 'Everything fitted. Everything tidy.'

She let the hot water run over each soapy plate before placing it in the dish rack as she looked out of the window.

'Overlooked. Definitely overlooked. If we move there we'll be nearer to James and Geraldine. Posh like them.'

Something about it appealed to her. Something about it didn't. She shouted up the stairs.

'We'll go and see it Mark as long as we can also see a few more a bit closer to home.'

'OK Hat. I'll leave this on. You can have a surf and see if there's anything else out there. I want to go down to the club. They should have sorted the boat by now.'

Harriet passed Mark on the stairs. She was glad he hadn't twigged the bottle of red wine jogging up the stairs alongside her. She went into the small back bedroom and reached for one of the two glasses they kept in the wall cupboard above the computer. They weren't averse to a drink in bed.

'See you later Hat,' Mark called up.

'Have a look round for that brown envelope while you're there Mark. Someone might just have put it down.'

'Lard ball can find his own brown envelope Harriet.'

The front door banged closed. Harriet went back into worry mode. She opened the bottle of wine. After a quick scroll down she turned the computer off. This was spoiling her drink. Two glasses and still the events of the day refused to go away. Not after the second gulp of the third one though. It was all softening now. She still had a feeling *he* hadn't quite finished with her yet. She had a feeling she wasn't all that bothered. She went into their bedroom and back into the top drawer of the dressing table. She brought the brown envelope out wondering if Mark had actually read the letter inside. Wondering if he knew. She put the glass to her lips. Tried to gulp this unpleasant dose of reality away.

'I daren't accept it. I daren't. We really will be finished if I go there.' She placed her hand across her waist. She moved it downwards. She could almost feel this microscopic embryonic form. Cells rapidly multiplying, gathering, shaping its beating heart. Tiny, nowhere near the size of her little finger nail. Not yet. Anyway.

'Even if I managed to hang on to Mark in the face of an honour, he wouldn't go through with the wedding. I'm going to refuse it.'

She shook the envelope in her hand. Took another gulp of wine. The decision was made.

She went across to the window. And wished she hadn't. Her stomach turned a full 360 degrees. She drew a deep breath as she watched *his* silver Mercedes draw up outside. She downed the remainder of the wine and placed the empty glass on the dressing table.

'He doesn't care! Mark could have been in for all *he* knew.'

She shoved the letter back in the drawer. Twisted the seam in her skirt back to centre and went down to the bottom stair. Waiting. Waiting for the ring on the doorbell.

'May I come in Miss Glover?' He looked around. 'Mark down at the club?'

Harriet nodded her head as she showed him into the lounge.

'Any luck Miss Glover?'

Harriet was flummoxed. She couldn't think what he was talking about. He looked at her. Hard. Straight in her eyes.

'I asked if you'd had any luck Miss Glover.'

'Well, as a matter of fact I think I have Mr. Sanderson.' She watched just a hint of a smile crossing his face.'

'Well. Go on Miss Glover. No on second thoughts get that damned brown envelope first. Then explain.'

Harriet went upstairs. Came down and popped it on the hall window sill. She could hear him. Impatient. Hardly waiting for her to get back into the room.

'Where is it then Miss Glover?' He opened out his hand then closed it again, lifting it to stroke his chin.

'It's on the window sill in the hall.'

'OK I'll pick it up on the way out. Now explain if you will. Miss Glover. This should be interesting, indeed. You're not normally prone to good luck. I can't say how relieved I am. Tell me all about it.'

'Not all about it Mr. Sanderson. You don't want to know absolutely everything. Surely?'

She could feel herself going a bit dizzy. The red wine was whooshing its way round her head. Saturating her brain cells. Stripping down her defences.

'Yes Miss Glover. I need to know absolutely everything.'

'Sit down will you Mr. Sanderson?'

Harriet was relieved to see him lean back on the sofa. She watched him lift his right foot up on to his left knee, angling his long leg out towards the door.

She sat down on the sofa opposite.

'Fire away Miss Glover.'

'Well that's exactly what Mark did on the rug the other night. He fired away. He'd never actually done it like that before Mr. Sanderson. It was what he did before that though. Wow. It could have been all that ice and snow. All that cold weather. Trying to warm his thoughts up. Absolutely nothing to do with Melissa Scott. I can assure you. Anyway he most certainly managed it Mr. Sanderson. It was a second honeymoon really. Well we didn't really have a first. Well you can't if you don't actually get married. Can you? And yes to get back to the point. No I never do have any luck. But this time I have. I absolutely know I'm pregnant Mr. Sanderson. Well I've just got to wait until tomorrow now to see if I start my period. It won't happen though. I'm not even going to bother with one of those testing kits.'

'Miss Glover. Have you been drinking?'

Harriet watched him stand to his full height. Somehow the look on his face reminded her of this morning. Of this afternoon. 'Well he did ask!' She was starting to feel puzzled.

'I'll speak to you in the morning Miss Glover. That's if you're in a fit state to come in. Now where did you say the envelope was?'

He was out of the lounge door before Harriet could answer.

'Not this one Miss Glover. Haven't you done anything about that yet? You've been home well long enough to have posted the reply. Acceptance Miss Glover. Get it done. Now. I'll wait and post it.'

She left him standing in the hall while she took it into the dining room.

'Do hurry Miss Glover. It's not rocket science.'

She met him in the doorway and handed it over.

'Well at least I've seen one glimmer of common sense from you today. Even if I did have to lead you by the hand.'

He marched to the front door and closed it behind him without looking back. Harriet struggled up the stairs to finish the bottle of wine. She wasn't quite sure whether she'd done the right thing or not.

'I think there'sh a problem with that. Shomehow.'

She curled up on the bed and fell fast asleep.

Chapter 18

'Oh. My head's killing me Mark.'

No answer. Harriet was hardly awake. She rolled over to a flake of paper leaping from Mark's pillow. It landed on her nose.

"Impossible to wake you Harriet. Empty wine bottle on the dressing table. Might just be a clue? See you later."

'Oh no. What time is it anyway?' Even the cat hadn't managed to wake her up. 'Alright Pepper. I'm on my way down.'

She crawled out of bed nursing her head. She should have been in school an hour ago. She shook the last of the packet into the cat's bowl. Four and a half whole pieces and a few crumbs.

'Oh sod.'

She baulked at having to open a tin of cat food.

'Off Pepper. Wait will you?'

She just managed to lump it into the bowl before heaving violently. It was sheer determination that propelled her to the bathroom. Just in time.

She crawled back to bed.

'Oh I said I'd never get like this again.'

Filled with remorse she sank into that semi-conscious hell. In and out. Unable to move. Then somewhere from within this mess that was supposed to be her head she finally surfaced to the needling ringing of the phone. She was vaguely aware that someone, intent on disturbing her, had persisted in trying all morning. She looked at the clock. It was nearly lunch time. It was nearly time for the bell to go. The children would be lining up by the door. In her classroom. She should be there. 'Oh no. P.E. this afternoon.' She decided against it. She fumbled for the phone holding it at arms length. She could just hear a man's voice coming through. She dithered. Didn't know whether or not to put it down.

'... Glover?' She didn't quite catch it.

'Yes. Oh yes Mr. Roberts. If you don't mind letting that woman in on Saturday morning. She can get on with the survey.' She scratched her head. She was about to lose the thread.

'No need for him, er Mr. Sanderson to be with her though. He'll only end up crawling round on his hands and knees with the tape measure. For her. Do you know Mr. Roberts he's a very busy man. He's got far better things to do with his time. She'll no doubt insist. But you're under instruction not to let him in here. With her. Now we'd like an appointment to view the one you have for sale in Millington. Around 9.30 tomorrow morning if you can. Please?'

She pressed her hand against her head and waited for the reply. She thought she'd been very coherent, considering...

'Miss Glover. Do you realise you haven't reported absent yet?'

She almost fell off the bed.

'Oh I'm terribly sorry Mr. Sanderson. I haven't been very well.'

'I'm not exactly surprised Miss Glover. What you do in your own time is your own affair. When the effects cut into your working hours, however, it becomes my affair. Now what's been the matter with you? Apart from being hung over, that is?'

'I've been sick Mr. Sanderson.'

'That goes with the territory Miss Glover. Now get yourself back here for 1.30 will you? I don't think the rest of the staff will be too happy carrying the excess of a split class all afternoon as well, Miss Glover.'

Harriet dragged herself off the bed and into the shower. She was trying to remember just what she'd said about Belinda Oxfordshire. Said about *him*. She shuddered cold in the hot water. He had been too angry to even mention it.

Somehow. Eventually. She got herself out. And into school. His car wasn't there. What a relief. She'd just about manage the afternoon. If they spent it making Christmas cards, calendars, tree decorations. Harriet suddenly realised how very far behind she was.

'That door's not usually left open,' she thought as she hurried past the stock room to her classroom. The bell clanged in her ear. Promptly terminated the thought to go back.

'Right. In everybody.'

The children rushed past her to sit on the carpet in the story corner.

'Melanie, pop along to the office will you please and see if you can find the register for me?'

'Why can't I go? I'm supposed to be the register monster, aren't I?'

'Oh, of course, Danny'

'Definitely not quite with it,' she thought.

'Look Danny, you go along with Melanie. You know where the stock room is. Don't you?'

They both nodded their heads.

'The door is open. On the way back just pop in and on the shelf nearest to the floor behind it you'll see some packs of white card. Just bring one back will you?'

A burst of enthusiasm propelled them to the door.

'Oh and while you're there. On the shelf above that you'll see some packs of coloured paper. Do you think you can manage one of those large containers of glue, as well Danny?'

She looked back at the children sitting patiently on the carpet.

'Robert. Pop along with them, please. Give them a hand. Oh and a large tub of silver glitter. It's next to the coloured paper I think.'

'That's that then,' she said to herself and proceeded to do a head count. 'Twenty four and three outside. Twenty seven. All in today. They've done better than me!'

She put her hand across her mouth. She was still feeling sick. But her head was starting to clear.

'Right everybody. Craft. Group leaders to the cupboards now. The rest of you put your aprons on.'

Harriet congratulated herself on the speed of response. All sets of tables were quickly covered in scissors, paper shapes of all colours and sizes, half-empty glue pots, felt tips, cotton wool. And a host of miscellaneous junk.

She was just beginning to wonder where the three others had got to when the door swung open.

Melanie marched straight over proudly offering Harriet the register, discharging her albeit fleeting responsibilities, with much aplomb. All the time glancing sideways at Danny struggling to drag the huge white plastic container along the floor behind him. Danny sniggered through the distortions of dissatisfaction screwing up his face. He shook the big tub of glitter at her.

'Well, I've got this,' came the proud boast.

'Danny. Watch the lid doesn't come off,' Harriet shouted, 'wasn't there a full tub there?'

Danny shrugged his shoulders.

They'd both left Robert trailing, now completely transmogrified into a walking roll of coloured paper, save the white card in his hand. Which he pushed into Harriet's face.

'There Miss.'

'Thank you Robert. Danny. Melanie.' She turned to the class. 'Now this afternoon we're going to make Christmas cards, calendars and tree decorations. A whole afternoon of craft.'

'What about P.E. Miss? I wanna do P.E.'

'Not this afternoon Danny. We'll skip that one today. We want all this finished in time for the Christmas party.'

'Don't we even have to play out Miss Glover?' came a little voice from the back.

'What a good idea,' Harriet decided to herself. 'Well done Charlotte.'

'No. We've got a lot to get through this afternoon. Those of you who want to miss playtime can stay in with me. Whilst you're all getting on I'll be putting the Christmas decorations up.'

A buzz went round the room. A fizzing excitement took over. All faces beaming. Except Danny's.

Danny went out to play. All on his own.

Harriet tied the last balloon to the hook holding the paper streamers. She looked down from the chair she was standing on. The window sill was rapidly filling with Christmas cards. That opened the wrong way. Calendars. With back to front date pads pasted on the bottom. Some at the top. And some so stuck together nobody would ever be able to prise the pages apart, never mind find out what day of the week it was. A whole variety of red faced drunken looking angels stared up at her. Preferable that to the poor things looking at their feet, to the cut out Christmas puddings, not dissimilar to horse droppings, shining with glittery yellow custard. Surrounded by what looked like a host of black monsters.

Not very Christmassy looking items, save they were covered in glitter. As were the children. The tables. The floor.

The three-thirty bell rang.

'Clear up everyone. Now. Quickly. The bell's just gone.'

Harriet stepped off the chair. Danny put his hand up.

'Miss. You made me play out on me own and I'm gonna tell me mum of you for not doin` P.E.'

Harriet looked at his sleeve. She was horrified. It was covered in thick white glue. Glittering away for Britain.

'What on earth have you done to yourself, Danny?'

'I dunno Miss. I must of got it from somewhere?'

'You most certainly did young man.'

Harriet turned round. Mortified. She wondered just how long *he'd* been standing behind her.

'See them out Miss Glover.' He wandered over to the window sill. And back again. Harriet didn't much go with the expression on his face.

She closed the door then felt it push back on her. Mrs. Bustard. Of course. It would be. With Danny's glittering arm pulled up in front of her.

'Oh `ello Mr. Sanderson. Oh. It's not important. I'll catch you again Miss Glover.'

She ushered Danny towards the door, to Harriet's relief.

'Mr. Brown's been taken to accident and emergency Miss Glover.'

Harriet wasn't sure what it had to do with her. She completely blanked.

'By *me*. Have you seen the mess that stock room's in Miss Glover? Apparently not, you'd be looking a little more cognisant. I can only assume you sent Danny and whoever else down there. Since when have children been allowed into the stock room Miss Glover? You know it's for teaching staff only. Other than that it remains locked at all times. He's had the lid off the glue. Must have tipped at least half of it all over the floor and then decided it would look better if it shone. Silver.'

Harriet suddenly remembered the half tub of glitter. She put both hands over her mouth.

'Of course Brown goes straight in and over. It's dark in there Miss Glover. He's hardly going to look down at his feet every time he wants to move. Although I think it wouldn't be an unwise thing to do in the circumstances. He jolted his back. Not helped of course by you shooting this damned thing at him.'

He banged the lunchbox trolley with the palm of his hand.

'Unfortunately it was me that had to shove his glittering backside into the Mercedes to get him there.'

'What about the seat?' Harriet managed.

'Well for want of anything else I had to sit him on top of my Aran jumper Miss Glover. Actually hand-knitted by my mother. Needless to say it wouldn't come off. I had to march him through endless hospital corridors with the sleeves tied round his middle.'

He stopped and glared. He'd even surpassed his fury of yesterday.

Harriet swallowed hard. She knew one day she'd look back and die laughing. Not now though. She knew *he'd* just about had enough of her.

'But the door was already open Mr. Sanderson. That's why I sent them down. Having missed the morning I wanted to make the most of the afternoon.'

'Absolutely no excuse whatsoever Miss Glover. You do not, I repeat, DO NOT send children into the stock room. What with guillotines and the like, the place is a minefield. That's why the door remains locked.'

'I'm terribly sorry Mr. Sanderson.'

'It might have been better if you'd remained at home Miss Glover. My misjudgement. I don't expect for one moment you'd have reported for duty. I can only put all of this down to, to use a euphemism, to the fact that you've been unwell. Or PMT or some other such damned thing you women get before your periods. Has it started Miss Glover?'

Harriet's face went redder than some of the angels' haphazardly caught between the drooping streamers and the curling Christmas puddings.

'No, Mr. Sanderson.'

He rested his chin in his hand, pushing hard against his cheek. Looking straight at the centre seam in her skirt, just below her waist.

'Totally irresponsible Miss Glover.'

Then strode out.

Chapter 19

'What was that all about Harriet?'

Mark was hardly through the door.

'What all about?'

Harriet rushed upstairs. She suddenly remembered the wine glass left on the dressing table.

'It's no good washing it up there Harriet. Did you actually manage to get yourself to school? I bet you didn't.'

'As a matter of fact I did Mark. Anyway I'm getting just a little bit tired of you disappearing every night. Isn't that flipping boat sorted yet?'

'We won't exactly know until we get it in the water. It looks OK. I'll give it a go on Saturday morning. Come down. We'll try it out together.'

'No thank you Mark. I'm not scrambling up the side of the hull soaking wet while you try to heave the blinking thing over.'

'On the water Harriet. Not in it. We float it first and see what happens.'

'Can't go anyway we've got an appointment to see that house in Millington.'

'Oh. Well done Hat. Pleased you were compos mentis enough to sort that one.'

'Not you as well Mark. I've had just about enough of Latin overtures for this week.'

'Been winding lard ball up then?'

'No.'

'Come off it Hat. Has he found his brown envelope yet?'

'No.'

'I'd like to catch the bugger that did the boat in. Have we heard anything from Bridgewater yet?'

'No.'

'You've become very monosyllabic Harriet. What's the matter with you? PMT or something? Have you started yet?'

'No.'

A wide grin spread across Mark's face.

'Not like you Harriet. Not like you at all. Looks like it's got a ready made nursery too, Hat. Let's keep our fingers crossed, shall we?'

Chapter 20

Saturday morning saw Harriet and Mark scurrying round the house trying to make it look at least a bit presentable.

'Come on Harriet. Stop messing about. What time did you say we had to be there? It's going to take us a good half-hour. You know what the traffic's like on a Saturday morning.'

'9.30 it was and I'm *not* messing about. It's *your* mess I'm trying to tidy up if you did but know it.'

'Well, we're going to be late then. Aren't we? Stop fiddling will you? It's bad manners to keep people waiting.'

Harriet wiped the draining board dry one more time and hid the towel in the tumble dryer. She grabbed her coat and bag and followed Mark to the car. Impatient. He backed off the drive and swung the car round hard to gather speed down the road.

'Steady on Mark. It's not exactly going to be the end of the world if we're a few minutes late.'

The lights were on green at the cross roads. She barely had chance to catch a glimpse of Starboard Marine North West.

He looked across. 'Did you bring the brochure?'

'No. We haven't got a brochure. You found it online. Remember?'

'Well how the bloody hell are we supposed to know where we're going, Harriet?'

'I do happen to know exactly where it is Mark. It's on or off that straight road you turn into from James and Geraldine's. Only we don't go left. We go right. You should know anyway. I thought it was on the way to your work.'

'I'll take your word for it Harriet.'

They drove away from the town, past the thinning trails of suburbia into the countryside.

'Carry on straight Mark.' Her head turned. 'We'd go down there if we were going to James and Geraldine's.'

'I do know where I am Harriet.'

'Stop complaining then.'

Mark continued driving. The countryside drab. Grey. Damp. Disinterested trees. Standing. Still. Stencilling bare black branches to a mantle of disinterest. The flat grey sky reluctant. Just occasionally parting to let the pale watery sun through. Endlessly, mile after mile through stark winter countryside. He kept going.

'Mark there was a left turn back there. Maybe we should have gone that way?'

'Thanks Harriet. I thought you were supposed to be navigating.'

He spotted a lay-by. Too late. Now rendered useless in his rear mirror. He screeched to a halt. Reversed.

'You're not allowed to drive backwards on a main road Mark. Mind that digger coming up.'

'You want to bloody drive Harriet?'

Harriet decided to shut up. She knew it was a few miles back.

Then she spotted it.

'There Mark. There. Now. Turn now.'

He swerved right.

'There's not one bloody house to be seen Harriet.'

'Carry on a bit Mark. It *was* surrounded by countryside.'

'Phone the agents Harriet. We're never going to find this sodding place.'

Harriet scrambled in her bag.

'Hang on a minute. There's a board there. Harriet. Yes that's the one, Bryce Rae Roberts.'

'Not on its own though. Is it?'

'No Harriet. But there's plenty of space between them.'

They were looking at three detached houses cornered into a piece of land sitting between a lane to the right and an old stone farmhouse to the left. The clutter of barns and sheds and other low rise buildings geared to service the farm, fell away with the sloping land behind. Mark drove in and parked outside the house on the end. The one edged by the lane.

'We're only quarter of an hour late Harriet.'

'Oh stop going on Mark.'

Harriet saw the curtain twitch in the front window. Then a face appeared from behind.

'Get going Mark. She's about to open the door.'

He locked the car. Harriet got impatient.

'Who's going to pinch it here Mark?'

'Oh don't talk to me about unlocked cars Harriet. Or brown envelopes.'

She kept quiet. They hurried up the long front drive.

'Plenty of parking space here, anyway. Two cars and the boat. No problem.' Mark looked pleased.

Harriet nodded. She felt nervous. This was far removed from the familiar. Undoubtedly up-market. But strange. Miles away. She could hear the children playing in the side garden. The noise stopped as someone called them in.

'I'd have left them outside,' she decided to herself. She didn't fancy being trailed round the house by kids.

'Press the bell Harriet. They won't answer unless you ring.'

'Really?' She gave a short light tap.

'They won't bloody hear that,' Mark suddenly found himself addressing the frown just sitting under the brown fringed bobbed head of hair, swinging round the door.

'Oh good morning,' rushed Harrriet. 'We're so sorry we're late. Got caught in traffic going through the town I'm afraid.'

'Late for what?' She pushed her glasses up her nose.

'The viewing.' Harriet pointed at the board.

'I don't know of any viewing this morning. No one's told me.'

'9.30,' stepped in Mark, 'well it was supposed to 9.30, but as we say...'

'No. Definitely not. Not without an appointment. I'm afraid I've got the children to see to. Anyway it's under offer. I'm surprised they didn't tell you.'

'Not on the website it isn't.' insisted Mark.

'Well they won't have got round to that yet. The offer only went in last week. Anyway we agreed to take it off the market. I don't know what they're playing at down there.

I'll get straight on to them. Flaming estate agents. I ...'

She slammed the front door closed on the unfinished sentence. Harriet and Mark stood looking at each other.

'She's right. Bryce Rae and bloody Roberts. They couldn't organise a piss up in a brewery!'

'That's not very nice Mark. You're not the same since you came back. Obviously been in undesirable company while you've been away. Down there.'

'Phone them up Harriet. Stop babbling and find out what's going on.'

'No. You can do it when we get back. I've had enough for one day.'

They drove back. Neither of them inclined to break the silence. Harriet racked her brains trying to remember the call she'd made. Who she'd spoken to. Mark drove in. Annoyed. His time would have been better spent trying the boat out.

He held the door to let Harriet and the cat through. She turned to him.

'At least it's all nice and tidy. Let's hope she got finished. Oh a message Mark.'

He terminated the green flashing light. His index finger just a bit quicker than hers.

Just enough to seal her bad mood.

'Bryce Rae Roberts here. Mr. Roberts speaking. We were unable to gain access to your property today Mr. and Mrs. Glover due to the fact you failed to leave us a key. Unfortunately Miss Oxfordshire and a Mr. Sanderson, I believe, waited outside for a full half hour for someone to turn up. Needless to say they're not best pleased.'

'Cheeky sod.' Harriet was furious. She curtailed the message to dial their number. Then changed her mind. Played it all back again.

'That voice. It could almost be Mr. Sanderson.' She went into a trance. Completely distracted by the thought.

'Stop messing about with it Harriet. Why didn't you leave them the key?'

Then it occurred to her. It was *him* she'd spoken to. She'd completely forgotten to phone the estate agents after that.

'I forgot Mark. Probably engrossed in my pregnancy. Sorry I just forgot.'

'Do it. Now. Harriet.'

'Stop being so bossy. I won't do it at all if that's the way you're going to be.'

'So where did you get that 9.30 appointment from Harriet?'

'I was *going* to make it for then. Wasn't I Mark?'

'Drinking too much bloody wine Harriet. Completely irresponsible whatever condition you're in.'

'Oh leave off Mark. What time should I say they can come back?'

'Suit yourself Harriet. I'm off to float the boat while it's still dry. I'll be back later. Oh and don't forget to lock the shed. It's a bit of a death trap.'

She winced at the thought of phoning them. The front door banged on her mood. She decided to get on with it..

'Bryce Rae Roberts. Mr. Roberts speaking.'

Harriet jumped. She was expecting to be put through. Expecting a few seconds grace in which to prepare herself.

'Oh, er, Mr. Roberts...'

'Yes I recognise your voice Mrs. Glover. I've had Mrs. Foster on the phone absolutely furious you chose to view the property without an appointment. Not to mention letting Miss Oxfordshire and Mr. Sanderson down like that. Do you know Mrs. Glover our reputation is paramount? We're in difficult times. We can't afford to offend one single client. You'd be surprised how quickly the word gets round. Now I suggest you allow Miss Oxfordshire and her partner back at two o'clock.'

'Right,' Harriet instantly agreed. Only to that though. 'He's not her partner Mr. Roberts. Let's get the facts straight here.'

'Business partner Mrs. Glover.'

'Not business partner either. He employs her.'

'I'm just not prepared to spend the rest of the day arguing the toss with you Mrs. Glover. Getting the house surveyed and the sale underway, that's the issue we're dealing with here. Oh yes. A mailing's been posted to you. I can assure you all the properties on the list, without exception, are fully available to purchase.'

'Thank you Mr. Roberts,' finished Harriet, taking a deep breath and flaring her nostrils as she put the receiver down. Was she not looking forward to dealing with those two on her own!

Chapter 21

'Well that was nice of Mark to leave me to deal with those two all by myself.'

The cat meowed back brushing in between her legs.

'Yes. You most definitely agree with me Pepper. She'll be watching my every move. With him! Next thing is she'll be suing me. As well as Mr. Brown. No Pepper. I'll be back in a tick. I'm just taking the spare keys down to Mr. Roberts. He can sort it out.'

She jumped in the car. Determined. Determined to avoid them at all costs.

'Not in this afternoon, Mrs. Glover? I'm afraid it's rather difficult to accompany clients at such short notice.' Mr. Roberts peered disapprovingly at her over the tops of his black-rimmed spectacles.

'Well you might sound a bit like him, but you certainly don't look like him. Not in the least.' Harriet's thoughts stalled her response.

'I repeat. I'm afraid we can't do it Mrs. Glover.'

'Oh. Just phone them then. Get them to collect these.' She pushed the keys at him. 'They can let themselves in. Just get them to drop them back into here when they've finished.'

'That isn't our policy I'm afraid Mrs. Glover. We can't accept responsibility for unaccompanied viewings.'

'Oh don't then. I accept full responsibility. They're not likely to run off with the silver exactly. Are they?'

Mr. Roberts fished under the counter and slammed a form down in front of her.

'Sign this Mrs. Glover.'

'Not necessary Mr. Roberts. Just dropped in to make sure she hasn't changed her mind.'

Harriet jumped. *Oh how* did she just *know that voice*. Stunned, she turned to see Mr. Sanderson and Belinda Oxfordshire standing behind her.

'I'll take those if you don't mind.'

Mr. Roberts obligingly passed them over.

'Two o'clock it is then.' He pushed the keys into his pocket. Held open the door for Belinda Oxfordshire. Departing with not so much as a backward glance at Harriet.

'Cheek. What cheek!'

'Good day Mrs. Glover. Let's trust all will be well with the survey.'

Harriet stomped out of the office and back to her car round the corner. She fished in her pocket. No keys. Then the other pocket. No keys. Then, in her hurry, realised she'd come out without her bag. No spare keys. 'Bloody hell I've just given *him* my keys.' They were long gone.

'Oh no. I'm not sitting in the estate agent's 'til gone four o'clock. Not with that Mr. Roberts.'

She started walking. Walking all the way home.

Chapter 22

Exactly one hour, twenty three minutes and four seconds later Harriet stumbled round the corner of her road only to see *his* car already parked outside. She looked at her watch again.

'Bloody cheek. There's still thirty three minutes and fifty six seconds to go.'

She'd stopped to give her aching feet a rest while she worked it out. Bought a bit more time.

'The shed. Mark wanted it locked. No, I'll wait in there. They must be nearly finished by now. Then I'll catch them. On their way out.'

Her mind was racing. She was getting nearer to the house.

'Can't do that. No that won't do. I might miss them. Might not hear them if I'm in there.'

She dithered about unable to decide. She looked around, then stooped as she reached the wall. She ran low, down the side and into the back, hiding behind the bin housing. She was tempted. Very tempted to go in the shed.

'No Harriet. No. You might be stuck there all night waiting for Mark to come in.'

The door was slightly open. The lock was hanging open on the catch.

'No. I'm going. I'm NOT facing HER with *him*.'

She crawled alongside the garage. The shed.

'No. Can't do it.'

She looked around. No sign of them. Quickly she stood up. Pushed the door closed. Secured it with the catch. Then slipped the lock through. Clicking it shut. Just as Mark had asked.

With temptation out of the way she flew to the front door. Took a deep breath. And rang the doorbell. She was dreading this.

'Ah Miss Glover. Do come in. We're nearly finished here.'

Mr. Sanderson stepped back to allow Harriet in.

'We gathered you'd be out for the rest of the afternoon and as we weren't given a specific time we thought it better to get it out of the way.'

'Two o'clock Mr. Sanderson.'

'Belinda took the call. Anyhow no grounds for complaint Miss Glover. We seem to have been messing about all day with this one.' He beckoned her through.

'A word Miss Glover. Belinda's outside somewhere. Checking the roof and gutters and other such things.'

The relief was sweeter than being able to take the weight off her feet. She hoped she'd stay there. Outside. And not come back in. She flopped on the sofa.

'Consent has finally come through from the planning department Miss Glover. We'll be getting the placed fitted out as from next week. It's the smaller showroom at the back we'll be converting. It's totally Belinda's project, as you would expect. However we're going to need to sell it. Hard.'

Harriet watched him smile. She pushed her hair away from her eyes. She felt exposed. Like she was still in her diaphanous nightdress. Embarrassment mingled with pleasure as she tried to rid herself of the thought.

'You're the one for that Miss Glover. You draw them like a magnet.'

He cleared his throat and looked down. 'Not a bad speech off the cuff Miss Glover. Flotilla a bit off the mark. Still you got them interested. That's the point. I'm afraid the company's taking a bit of a knock. To be expected in a recession. Stock market diving. Having to put the flotation plans on hold for the time being. Starboard Marine North West not had chance to get properly established. Certainly isn't looking good I'm afraid. Falling behind the rest of it. Still. Diversification. That's what it's all about.'

Harriet didn't speak. She didn't even feel the need to forgive him. He was praising her again. She was enjoying this. It was just so worth the walk to be able to watch him. Like this.

'The property portfolio's hit the wall. This is the last one for the time being.'

He tossed his head and looked round the room. 'Of course it will recover. It always does. Eventually. It's going to be a long time though. This is a global recession. We've all hit the fan at once. Damned bankers. Anyhow. Still. Now you have your answer, Miss Glover.'

'Answer?' Harriet suddenly felt herself floating away from the plot.

'Education? I suspect you've always wondered, like Mr. Potts just why I'm where I am. Oh I've tried my hand at most things Miss Glover, and I'm not finished yet by any means. No no. I'd never be satisfied in one job. I like to spread myself around. Just at this moment however I'm very grateful for it. The school. Call it stability Miss Glover. Oh it's not necessarily the money. No. It's just that one can't loaf one's way through life. One needs some kind of gainful employment.'

Harriet felt quite dazed. All of a sudden. All this revelation?

'Anyhow back to the point. Have you found somewhere to go yourselves?'

'No. We've only just started looking, really.'

'Well it's certainly a buyer's market out there. You shouldn't have too much difficulty.'

He scratched his head, then stroked his chin.

'I'm not sure about the asking price for this you know. Belinda's picked up on a few bits and pieces. Nothing too serious, mind you. Still I do think the offer should now reflect current market conditions. She's too interested in keeping you on board, I suspect. Though I'm not sure the company can stand this kind of investment without it affecting the overall cash flow considerably. Phil Newton's looking into it all at the moment. I'm trying to bring it home to her. Sometimes these things sink in better for the reading. The written word. Might do the trick. Brown envelope Miss Glover. Confidential. Damned confidential now, I suspect. Anyhow, as I said, it was important information. I wanted her to see it. More valuable to me than running her backside off posting leaflets, I might add.'

He paused and took a deep breath. Harriet fidgeted on the sofa. Feeling uncomfortable. Again. He continued.

'I'm trying to go a bit easy on her. She's taken a bit of a bashing of late. Broken engagements take their toll. For both of us. Especially when friends of the family are involved.'

He pulled himself forward to rest his hands either side of his legs on the cushions under him. Then he pressed his right hand hard down as he lifted the other to his face. He covered his chin and allowed his index finger to cross his mouth to touch the tip of his nose.

'Still. It had to be done. She's a beautiful woman Miss Glover. Very attentive. Vulnerable in some respects. I'm not made of steel. Family approval. Family pressure. All that kind of thing, you know.'

Harriet's diaphanous nightdress suddenly turned green. With jealousy. Her mind flooded with it. She was angry, too.

'Beautiful indeed?' she hissed to herself. 'She's only *blackmailing* me.'

She wanted to tell him. Then drew the words back into her mouth. She couldn't. She couldn't risk it.

'So. Where was I? Yes. I've been that route before. No shortage of prospective brides, shall we say? That's without my mother lining them up at the back door. So to speak. Off-putting to say the least.'

He shook his head. Harriet watched the layers of thick blonde hair shift against the curl at his collar.

'Wrong move Miss Glover. Getting engaged. One should never mix business with pleasure.'

Harriet could feel the finality emerging from his words.

'I asked you to wait.' He looked hard into her eyes.

She lowered her head. Nothing more to say.

'We got engaged. A bit on the rebound I suppose. I thought you were pregnant. It looks like you've now wrong-footed me in both directions Miss Glover.'

Harriet was unable to speak.

'Has your period started yet?'

Somehow he'd just stripped her worse than naked.

'No need to blush Miss Glover. Charles wasn't that far from the mark actually.'

Harriet pricked her ears.

'That night on the ship when he let me into your cabin…'

'Yes, Mr. Sanderson.'

'I qualified as a GP, you know?'

She could scarcely conceal the shock.

'I thought you were a classics scholar. I thought you read classics at university?'

'Just for a year Miss Glover. Got in on A-level Latin. The rest of them were sciences. I changed over.'

'But why didn't you continue as a doctor?'

'Damned hard work Miss Glover. I reckoned there had to be an alternative route to usefulness. Topped it all off with a PGCE and shot through the ranks. As it were.'

She moved to stand. Could feel her legs starting to sway from under her. Sat down again. She'd known absolutely nothing about him. Until now.

He stood up, looked at his watch. Held her fully in the intensity of those serious blue eyes.

'Period Miss Glover? I asked you had it started?'

'No Mr. Sanderson.'

'Just how regular are you Miss Glover?'

'Very.'

'Hot flushes? Any unusual symptoms?'

'No Mr. Sanderson.'

'Get one of those damned kits will you and let me know the results.'

'No Mr. Sanderson.'

'You're going to have to tell me at some stage Miss Glover. It's a lot easier for me to work things out if I know in advance. Amanda Woods is leaving. I was at some stage going to suggest you apply for the post. On balance I would say your achievements outweigh the rest of it. It should be nothing more than a formality.'

Harriet liked that. He'd already promised her promotion.

'What about Mr. Whittle? I'd never get past him. And there's Mr. Brown. I might end up being prosecuted?'

'Not if I can unwind it Miss Glover. Though no doubt somebody will have told him where the trail of glitter finished up.'

Harriet clutched both hands into her lap. She couldn't look at him.

'You've a tendency to exaggerate the significance of such incidents in the wider scheme of things. Not of course where people get hurt as a result of your carelessness. That's a different matter.'

He stroked his chin again.

'Of course you were off the premises when you signed offensively at Mr. Whittle?'

'Yes. I've never, ever met him Mr. Sanderson. Before then. I'd never have done that.'

'Quite. Indeed not. Still. He doesn't appear to remember you prior to that incident. I think he's almost taken that on board. We'll need to tread carefully with him.'

'What's Mr. Potts going to do about Mr. Brown?' Harriet just managed to get it out.

'We'll have to wait and see Miss Glover. It'll just have to run concurrent with the job application, I'm afraid. Anyway that won't be advertised until next term.'

'Now be sensible will you? Your period? Keep me posted.'

Harriet filled her lungs with resolve. 'I'm not getting one of those kits though. I'll just wait and see what happens next month.'

Suddenly she *didn't* want to be pregnant.

Mr. Sanderson shook his head in disbelief. 'And then the month after that, no doubt. Miss Glover, at your age, the sooner you avail yourself of antenatal care the better.'

Harriet had just been insulted. 'That's it,' she thought. 'That's bloody well it.' Then suddenly she *did*.

She followed his quick march to the door. He turned as he opened it.

'Is he going to marry you?'

'Yes Mr. Sanderson. He *is*.'

She closed the door and ran to the front window to see him get into his car. Suddenly he was on his way back. She ducked and waited for the doorbell.

'Miss Glover. Your keys.'

Harriet took them. She'd hardly managed to close the front door when the bell rang again.

'Belinda Oxfordshire. I almost went without her. Where could she have got to Miss Glover?'

He strode in front of her. Through the hall and into the kitchen. He opened the back door. They both stepped out.

'Where's that damned woman got to?'

His words oozed delight into Harriet's ears. She followed him out. But not as far as the shed window. He marched past and then turned. A loud banging sent the blackbirds fluttering from the lawn. Harriet jumped. He could see Belinda Oxfordshire's face pressed to the glass from the inside. He waved at her. Went straight round to the door. Clutched at the small locked padlock.

'Key Miss Glover. Get the damned key.' His face was red. Absolutely furious.

Harriet panicked, desperately tossing each of the keys in the palm of her hand until she finally managed to find the smallest on the ring.

'Pass it over. Now. Miss Glover.' He rattled away at the lock until it finally dropped open.

'Move back Belinda. You're stopping the door. How the devil did you get locked in there?'

Belinda burst into tears. 'Someone locked it. Why did it take you so long to find me, Joris?'

'Miss Glover. Have you got anything to do with this?'

'Me?' feigned Harriet. 'How can it possibly have anything to do with me?'

'See me on Monday morning Miss Glover. This is getting to be a bit of a habit. Oh. And I want that brown envelope found.'

Chapter 23

Sunday. Harriet was glad it was Sunday. She woke to Mark biking it round the room. Revving his nostrils to the capacity of six cylinders. He'd been at it all night. Throttling away. She decided on making the tea. She banged the kettle under the tap, clattering herself a gap in last night's dishes as they fought for space in the flat grey water brimming the circumference of the washing-up bowl.

She grabbed a new pack of cat food. Pressed her thumb hard into the almost perforated semi-circle invitation at the top saying 'Open here', then shook a hefty portion into the cat's bowl.

She was trying desperately to get her head round the revelations of yesterday afternoon. She was kicking herself for telling him Mark had proposed. She didn't want it to be that final. Not yet. Anyway.

'There would have been a better time to tell him. We haven't even fixed a date yet. But he asked. He went and *asked*.' Her thoughts turned to Mark. She was glad he'd at last got the boat sorted. 'I might finally get to see him.' She poured the thought out with the cat's milk and took the tray upstairs.

'Tea, Mark.' She poked him. Immediately the revs galvanised into one heavy kickstart and the snoring stopped.

'You turned yourself into a motorbike last night, Mark. Well it might just as well have been. You kept waking me up.'

'Funny you should say that Hat.' He yawned and stretched and started rubbing his eyes. 'I dreamed I was biking it across the ice.'

'Who with Mark? Who was on the back?'

'Definitely a sultry beauty.'

Harriet stopped there. 'Melissa Scott er Rogers.' She decided to herself. 'He's been dreaming about her all night.'

'And what happened?' Harriet had to ask.

'The shelf started to split and she flew us over the chasm to safety. Actually to your cup of tea. Thanks Hat.'

'Why wasn't it me on the back Mark?'

'Well I don't know. Do I? How can I decide who's going to be in my dreams?'

'Your subconscious can Mark. Who was it?'

'Come here. Daft bat Hat. It was only a dream.'

Harriet snuggled into his neck. 'I still haven't started Mark. Do you think this time we might have...?'

'Sure thing Hat. Bound to have hit the target after that night on the rug.'

He drew her very close. Quite perversely Melissa Rogers suddenly came to mind. On the back of that motorbike.

'No Mark. We've got to watch the baby now. Don't want it to become dislodged.'

'You're absolutely right Harriet. We've got responsibilities. More's the pity.'

'I thought you wanted one too?'

'Of course I do Hat. We could always stop short of *that*.'

'No. Anyway I'm not in the mood. I can still feel my feet.'

'You won't need your feet Hat. What's wrong with them anyway?'

No answer. Harriet hadn't told him everything.

'Anyway. Just *who* did you dream about?'

'It was you Harriet.'

'Oh no it wasn't, or you'd have told me. Straight away.'

'Let's get up Harriet. It sounds more like you've got PMT to me.'

Harriet shook the last of the cereal into the bowls then struggled to tear the triangle bit away from the rest of the stubborn strip sitting along the top of the orange juice carton.

'Cut it Hat. You'll have that stuff all over the place.'

Too late. She tugged and held the pulsating carton, watching it spout gathering rations of orange juice all over the cat. It shot out.

'Well done Hat. Lack of co-ordination. Definitely PMT.'

'It sounds like you want it to be Mark.' She threw the kitchen roll across. 'Here, you mop it up.' She wasn't sure about him. Wasn't sure where he was coming from.

'*Then* you can bath the cat.' She jumped out of the way to dislodge the soggy wet fur pushing at her legs. 'Oh no. No way you're getting your own back.'

'Push off.' Mark opened the back door and shooed it out. The phone rang. 'Get that Harriet.'

'Hello,'

'Is Mark there?'

'Mark? Who's speaking please?'

'Melissa. So sorry to bother you Harriet.'

'Oh Melissa. No terribly sorry. He's out.' She could feel Mark's chin suddenly perch on her shoulder.

'Outside putting the cat out. Actually. No he's just come in. I'll pass you over.'

'Get that mess off the floor. It'll be back again.' Mark instructed as he took the receiver from her.

'Sorry about that Melissa. I...'

Harriet looked back at him. With great reluctance she left him to it. Mopping up the thick sticky orange. Too low down to be able to hear what was going on. 'Oh come here you.'

She grabbed the cat and held it under the running tap, long enough for the water to clear before it leapt from her hands.

'Where is it?' Mark demanded.

'Out. Get out of the way while I wash the floor.'

'OK Hat keep your hair on.'

'What was that all about?'

'Geoffrey's walked out on her.'

'Bit difficult with both legs in plaster Mark?'

'Well she's walked out on him then. Same difference.'

'No. It's not the same Mark. Why's she telling you, anyway? Bloody cheek when I'm here.'

'That's the point Harriet. You are here. It's a shoulder to cry on. She's feeling vulnerable at the moment. Do you think she'd have phoned here if there'd been anything going on?'

'I've had enough of vulnerable women for this week,' she fumed, 'I'll just have to believe you Mark.'

'Touché Harriet.'

Harriet dried off the last of the rinsing water. She stared at the floor. At the patch of four very clean tiles.

'Meaning?'

'Meaning. At least she's not coming round to the house every five minutes like lard ball. He's not exactly out of our lives yet. Is he Harriet?'

'Well that's where you're wrong Mark. As from yesterday afternoon, he most definitely is.'

'You haven't told me about all that yet. How did it go?'

'Oh I'll tell you all about it on the way to the garden centre.'

'Garden centre. What are we going there for?'

'A Christmas tree Mark. A real one. And I also want to pick up one of those spring planters for Mummy and Daddy. For Christmas.'

* * *

Mark carefully slotted the car between two of the white lines neatly drawn all over the car park. Skinny oblongs. They squeezed themselves out and walked sideways to the pedestrian path.

'Don't look now. But there. Over there. Look over there. Just the other side of those sheds.'

'Well well. Bob's bit of stuff.'

'It's Belinda Oxfordshire Mark. I don't want to see her. I've just told you about locking her in the shed. Mark. It's Belinda Oxfordshire!'

'I know. That's what I said. "Bob's bit of stuff." She's just given that shed a filthy look Harriet. Or was it meant for you?'

Harriet kept her head down. 'It was your fault Mark. You told me to lock the flipping thing.'

'She's spotted us Harriet. She's marching over.'

'Quick Mark. That shed on the end. In.'

Harriet pushed him through the doorway and pulled the door closed on them both. They could hear the click of high heels getting louder as they hid under the window. The door rattled a bit. Then the click, click got fainter.

'She's gone Harriet. Let's get to hell out of here.'

He tried to push the door open. It wouldn't budge.

Harriet went white.

'What's she done?'

Mark kicked hard on the door. It shot open breaking a thick twig in two.

'She tried to lock us in Mark,' Harriet exclaimed.

'It's only what you did to her Harriet.' He grinned and then didn't. Suddenly they were face to face with Guy. Harriet was glued to his name sitting in the flower embroidered on the top pocket of his dark green overall.

'You buyin` this or not?'

'Not,' declared Mark.

The salesman rubbed his hands up and down the nylon. 'What a racket. I came to see what's goin` on. If you see what I mean? Eh look `ere. You've kicked that panel off down there. I'm reportin` this. That's deliberate destruction. That is.'

Harriet looked at Mark.

'He meant "Not," as in not until he gets his wallet out of the car. Left it there by mistake. We're definitely buying it Guy. He was testing it for strength. But never mind. He'll put that bit back on. Won't you Mark? MARK. Go and get your wallet.'

'Won't be a tick Guy.'

'What the bloody hell are you playing at Harriet. We've got a shed. We don't want another one.'

'Just unlock the car Mark. He's watching us.'

'Get round the other side Harriet. Quick.'

'Just pretend to get your wallet out from under the dashboard Mark. Now. Better another shed than a court case.'

'Stuff that. Get in Harriet. NOW! We're going.'

Harriet ran round the back of the car and jumped in. Mark squealed his way out and on to the road.

'They've got security cameras Mark. They'll get us. I'm not marrying you Mark unless you turn back.'

'Sod this Harriet.'

He screeched to a halt.

'I'm not bloody going back in there Harriet. You want two sheds. You have two sheds. I'll wait for you here.'

'Right.' Harriet slammed the car door and half ran, half walked back to the garden centre. By the time she got back there were three of them. All in dark green nylon overalls weighing up the damage.

'There she is. That's `er.'

'Left his wallet at home.' she panted. 'Didn't he? Shot off to get it and I suddenly realised I could pay. Terribly sorry about that. Yes please. Will you deliver it for us?'

Two of them drifted away leaving Guy to complete the sale. 'Funny fella that. You're not married to `im I `ope?'

'No most definitely not.' She flared her ringless fingers at him as he took the credit card. 'This one Miss. This one's got the swipe in it.'

She followed him into the end shed.

'There. There you go Miss. That's your receipt with your card. It'll be delivered on Monday mornin`. Er not like that though. `e'll `ave to assemble it. If `e knows `ow. Funny bugger. I wouldn't be marryin` `im if I were you. If you see what I mean.'

'No. No. Most definitely not. I can assure you of that Guy.'

He winked at her.

She caught a hint of triumph in his smile as she walked away.

'`ope to see you again Miss. If you see what I mean?'

Chapter 24

They'd both gone to bed in the foulest of moods. And awoke steeped in the despondency of aftermath.

'I don't want another bloody shed Harriet. Where the hell are we going to put the sodding thing.'

'Oh drink your tea Mark.'

'£329.99 Harriet. And you're more than likely going to have to give up work.'

'Oh give over Mark. We can always sell it.'

'You can sell it Harriet. I'm not having anything to do with it.'

Mark jumped out of bed. He gulped his tea whamming the empty mug down on the tray.

'And that's another thing Harriet. From what you've told me it sounds like lard ball's gone cold on buying this.'

'No he hasn't. It's just that he's going a bit easy on *her*. Trying to get her to realise the state of the company. That's all. He did say this was going to be the last one, though. He wouldn't be surveying it with her. Wasting his time like that if they weren't going to proceed.'

'We'll see. This wedding isn't going to be cheap either. Not the way you'll want to do it Harriet. I know you. It won't be far short of Clarissa's. Well I'm telling you Harriet I'm banking on the sale of this to recoup some capital to pay for it all.'

'What are we doing looking at houses in Millington for then Mark?'

'Because I want out of here Harriet. I want to start married life away from anywhere lard ball's planted his feet. Understand?'

'Well, even if it was still available I don't see them dropping that much.'

'Look Harriet. You don't know just how much they've gone down already. If it falls through we'd probably get it for peanuts.'

Mark stomped off to the bathroom leaving Harriet to finish her tea. 'We haven't even fixed a date yet,' she thought. 'He hasn't exactly committed himself.'

'I'm off Harriet.' His voice faded behind the closing door. Then returned. 'Harriet where's your bloody car? Was it there last night? Has some bugger pinched that now?'

Harriet braced herself. She could hear him thumping up the stairs.

'First the boat, then a flaming shed. Now this. I'd have been better staying on the ice cap. Did you forget to lock it Harriet?'

Harriet suddenly remembered. She hid her flushing cheeks under the duvet. Only her eyes showing.

'No Mark. I know where it is. It's parked just round the corner from Bryce Rae Roberts.'

'What in the name of fortune is it doing there Harriet?'

'Well if you hadn't gone off in a bad mood desperate to float that stupid boat I might not have forgotten my bag. With the spare keys in.'

'Oh so you handed over the house keys? And walked back. That's why your feet are still killing you. So you'll just have to get the bus to school this morning and pick it up on the way back. That's if it's still there. Good grief even Tricia's got more sense than you these days.'

'It's taken you long enough to notice it missing Mark. Too obsessed with Melissa, or is it Tricia, now?'

Off he went leaving Harriet furious. 'I'm not getting the bus. I'll get a taxi. Right call a taxi.' She picked up the phone and then put it down again. 'Can't. Got that blinking shed coming this morning. Oh no. I'm supposed to be seeing *him* as well.' She heaved. Her thoughts sent her stomach churning. 'I'm pregnant. I've got morning sickness. I'll phone in.'

'Stetmead Primary, Amanda Woods speaking. How may I help?'

'Oh hi Amanda. Harriet here. Feeling dreadfully sick this morning. Must be a bug or something. I'm afraid I won't be in today.'

'Sorry to hear that Harriet. You weren't too good on Friday either. Probably came back too soon. I'll let Joris know. I do hope you'll be feeling better soon.'

Harriet got back into bed and then thought better of it. She opted for getting washed and dressed. She didn't know how soon delivery would be.

'Out Pepper. No paw marks on the tiles please. I've just mopped the floor.' She couldn't stand it any more. Looking at that one clean patch stripped to the glaze of dirt by the orange juice. She followed the cat out and tipped the bucket of water down the grid.

'Phone, Pepper. Get out of the way.'

She hesitated before lifting it.

'Oh it's you Tricia. Oh I'm so glad it's you.'

'Why `arriet. What `ave you been up to now?'

'Oh you wouldn't believe it Tricia.'

'Oh I would `arriet. You've just bought a shed that you didn't really want. `aven't you?'

'How on earth did you know that Tricia?'

'I've `ad your Mark on the phone `arriet. I'm at work of course. `e just wanted me to pass `is thanks on to our friend Mr. Sanderson for organisin` the GRP repair team free of charge. Then `e let rip `arriet. Ooh `e did sound cross. `e told me all about it. Fancy `er lockin` you both in like that and you endin` up `avin` to buy it `arriet. That wasn't very nice. Was it? I'm glad you didn't check your shed, though, `arriet to make sure no one was in before you locked it. Ooh I wish I'd been there to see `er face when she got out.'

'In tears Tricia. She was blubbing at him. They were both there doing the survey. *He* nobbled me and forgot all about her. It was Mark that kept going on about locking the shed so I did. Anyway. Can't you just picture it? "Why did it take you so long Joris?" Anyway it was something like that.'

'Ooh `arriet that's just so funny. She's not `avin` a very good time at the moment what with that hamster and all. `ave you found it yet `arriet? Oh sorry about the bangin` in `ere. Can you `ear them workin` away? `e's told them `e wants it ready for the 23rd `arriet. `e wants to `ave `is first "in-`ouse coffee shop" on Christmas Eve. I told `im `arriet. Nobody will come. They'll all be too busy getting` ready for Christmas Day. `e said, "That's down to Miss Glover. Marketing and promotion. She'd better get her skates on".'

'Cheeky sod.' Harriet could feel her fury surfacing. She went prickly all over. 'Bloody cheek. There's only just over a week to go.'

'Now don't you worry `arriet. I'll `elp you out. I've got a few good ideas of my own for bringin` them all in.'

'Oh thanks Tricia. I honestly don't know where to start.'

'Anyway `arriet I thought I'd better let you know. All day. `e's expectin` us both to be `ere. *All day.*'

'All day,' Harriet fumed, 'I haven't even got the Christmas tree yet. Never mind the presents.'

'Anyway `arriet what I'm really phonin` to tell you. I `ad those lads in `ere first thing. You know they're always `angin` about outside swingin` on those traffic lights.'

'Yes. I know them.' She immediately recalled pointing her two fingers at them. The ones that unfortunately hit Belinda Oxfordshire's line of sight.

'Well `arriet they came in `ere grinnin` all over their faces. The thin, very gangly lookin` one chirped up. `e said "That woman that comes in `ere. That posh woman that speaks like this," Then `e brought a rubber out of `is pocket and stuck it in `is mouth `arriet. "Like this," `e said, tryin` to sound posh. They all started laughin` `arriet. So I said, "`ave you come in `ere to tell me somethin` or not?" So they said she was drivin` up the road `arriet. This mornin`, that is and stopped and called them over. They all opened their `ands `arriet. Each one `ad a pound. She'd given them a pound each `arriet.'

'What on earth for? Why would she do that?' Harriet was puzzled. Then it suddenly dawned on her.

'That's it Tricia. She will have paid them for delivering those leaflets.'

'Oh you're right `arriet. Of course that's what it would be. I've been tryin` to work that one out since they all went leapin` out of the shop. Wouldn't `ave said it was all that funny though `arriet, myself. They were jumpin` around like mad things. I `ad to tell them to go `arriet. Anyway `arriet. I should `ave told you this first really. I've just `ad *im* in. Oh I'm really sorry `arriet I forgot to ask you `ow you are feelin`. Are you feelin` any better now `arriet?'

'Oh, yes thank you Tricia.'

'That's good `arriet. Now where was I? Oh yes. First of all `e said Belinda, I mean that long streak of misery, needed to go back to the estate agents so wouldn't be in `til later. As if I'm interested `arriet. Then `e asked me for the activity schedule I `ad to make out for `im the other day. `e said `e wanted to speak to you this mornin` but you'd reported sick. Oh `arriet. `e scratched `is `ead. `e looked gorgeous. `e always does, but when `e's lookin` as serious as that `arriet. Oh I can't tell you what `e does to me. When it warms up `arriet I swear

I'm goin' to take my knickers off and throw them at 'im. Do you think 'e might just get the message then, 'arriet?'

'Most definitely Tricia. What else did he say?'

'Well 'e waved my typin' around. Four sheets that was 'arriet. 'e asn't 'alf got plans for this coffee shop. Sorry 'arriet I'm diversifying myself.'

'Diverting yourself Tricia.'

'Oh yes that's the word 'arriet. I'm gettin' all mixed up with 'im. "Diversifying," that's 'is favourite word at the moment. Anyway 'e said "Miss Glover will need to see this." 'e 'ad a quick look round at them all workin' and then off 'e went 'arriet.'

'He's not coming here is he Tricia?'

'I don't really know 'arriet. 'e might be. That's why I phoned you. Just in case.'

'Thanks Tricia. You're a real pal. Look I'll give you a ring later when you get in from work.'

'Ooh just before you go. 'e's left a small brown envelope for Tarquin Bridgewater 'arriet. Now I wonder what's in that?'

'I wonder?'

'We'll just 'ave to find out 'arriet. Speak to you later.'

Harriet put the phone down in a flap. Intrigued as she was, Tarquin Bridgewater's small brown envelope wasn't exactly a priority at this moment in time.

'I'm supposed to be ill. Feeling sick.' She thought about hiding. 'No. I can't. My car's not there. He'll think I'm out. I've got this stupid shed coming. He'll think I've taken the day off for that.'

She looked in the mirror. She looked a bit pale. Not pale enough. She pulled her powder puff from her compact and ran to the bathroom. She sprinkled it with talcum powder then dabbed it at her face. Just in time. The doorbell went. She didn't know whether it was *him* or the shed. She didn't dare go to the window.

It rang again. Her legs were taking her somewhere she didn't want to be. The front door.

'Good morning Miss Glover. May I come in? I promise this won't take long.'

She stood behind the door, pulling it towards her to allow him through. 'Lounge Miss Glover? Come through.'

'He's right,' she thought. It felt like anything but *her* house. Just at this moment.

'Take a seat Miss Glover.'

He seated himself in his usual spot, by the door, on the sofa opposite the fireplace.

Harriet was facing the window. She sat on her hands and stared out. Thinking hard. 'That flipping delivery wagon is not, *not* to arrive now.'

'Are you alright Miss Glover? You're looking exceptionally pale.'

'Oh a bit better thank you. She crossed her arm over her waist.'

'Sick Miss Glover. Amanda said you've been sick?'

'Oh yes Mr. Sanderson. Going off a bit now. Thank you.'

'Just how overdue are you Miss Glover?'

She could feel herself blushing. She wasn't sure how it would look peppered with talcum powder. She counted.

'Five days.'

'Loosely termed morning sickness. It doesn't normally kick in this early Miss Glover. Not to be confused with hyper emesis gravidarum I hope.'

'No Mr. Sanderson.' Harriet didn't know what he was talking about.

'I do wish you'd go to your GP and get this diagnosed Miss Glover. You're not exactly in the first flush of youth. Are you?'

'No Mr. Sanderson.' She sat tight. She didn't know how she'd managed to ignore that one.

'These Miss Glover. Take a look at these will you? Just a few ideas. A springboard for this marketing exercise.'

'Oh. Right.'

'They're cracking on down there. I'm planning for the opening of the coffee shop on Christmas Eve. I'd like you to be there.'

Harriet nodded.

'I appreciate it will be a day out of your Christmas holidays. We'll split your class Miss Glover. Take a day off will you before we break up? Avoid this Thursday and Friday. Let's get the parties and the carol concert out of the way. We're looking at tomorrow or Wednesday, basically. Or Monday, Tuesday of next week. Possibly. Though I'd prefer you kept that clear if you can.'

Harriet hardly replied. Her worst nightmare was bumping along the top of the hedge and then ground to a halt. She could hear the door slam.

'Expecting a delivery Miss Glover?'

'Er, no. Er yes. Er I'm not really sure.'

'Whatever do you mean Miss Glover? You either are or you aren't.'

The doorbell suffered the onslaught of continued persistent pressure.

'I should answer it Miss Glover, or would you prefer me to go?'

She went to the door.

'No not expecting that. I don't think. Unless Mark hasn't told me about it.'

She could feel Mr. Sanderson standing behind her.

'No mention of a Mark, Miss Glover. Definitely your name 'ere. Look. Oh that's a laugh. Just look what 'e's written 'ere. "You're the girl of my dreams. You're as sweet as sugar. Remember your promise. Don't marry *that* funny bugger. If you see what I mean? Yours sincerely Guy. P.S. Come and see me any time." There you are then Miss. And it's not even Valentine's day. Where do you want it love?'

'Oh round the back please. Just leave it all against the side wall of the garage.'

'Right Miss. Just sign 'ere. Then we won't need to bother you again.'

Mr. Sanderson swept up the delivery note as the lad released it from the clipboard. 'Thank you young man,' he said.

He closed the front door on them. Harriet, in utter embarrassment went straight to the lounge window to see them unloading the large sides of the shed. He stood behind her. She turned. Her hair almost touched his jacket. He stepped back.

'Now Miss Glover. So you've had a delivery. Without a doubt it was intended for you.'

He looked down at the note in his hand.

'The metre's not right. I can't say I totally disagree with the sentiment, however.'

Harriet put that one away. To the back of her mind. For the moment. He'd just stood far too close to her. Far too close.

'Did you arrange for that thing to be delivered here this morning Miss Glover?'

Harriet didn't answer.

'Where's your car, anyway? It would have been rather difficult for you to get in without that.'

Harriet didn't answer.

'Can we pick it up from anywhere? Is it being serviced Miss Glover?'

'No, actually. Unfortunately not. It's parked just round the corner from Bryce Rae Roberts.'

'What on earth is it doing there Miss Glover?'

'It's been there since Saturday. Forgot my bag. You took the only keys I had.'

'Good heavens Miss Glover why haven't you collected it before now?'

Harriet couldn't answer.

'In the car Miss Glover. We'll bring it back immediately.'

Harriet grabbed her jacket, her bag and the house keys. He held the door open for her. Ran his hand across the seat.

'That should be alright Miss Glover. Can't legislate for the glitter though. Damned stuff. Impossible to shift.'

Harriet got in. He was right. It was sparkling in the darkest of corners. She felt bad. That was her third unintended assault on his car.

'Now Miss Glover. Round the corner from the agents did you say?'

She watched him into first. In a flash he'd turned the steering wheel. Reversed on to her drive. First, second, third, fourth. He was well on his way.

'Oh no this man. This handsome, gorgeous man. Will this feeling ever, ever, go away?'

'We'll go the back way Miss Glover. Save time. I need to get back.'

Harriet sank into a swamp of disappointment.

He turned left, then left again. She could see her car coming into view. He drew up in front of it. Got out and opened her door.

'Thank you Mr. Sanderson. Thank you so very much.'

He bent down placing his hand on the front offside tyre. Then raised his head to speak.

'Mark's not been away this weekend?'

'No. No Mr. Sanderson.'

'In that case it might have been better if you'd picked it up sooner.'

He looked across to the rear wheel and then strode to the pavement side.

'Yes Miss Glover. It looks like some bastard's let them all down.'

He threw his head towards the Mercedes.

'Get in Miss Glover. I'll run you back.'

'It's worth four flat tyres,' Harriet thought, 'just to be back in here.'

She watched his hand on the gear lever. The movement teasing the weak winter sunshine into action. First catching then losing the chance to gleam off his expensive gold cufflink. She felt in awe of Mrs. Harris.

'Just how does she manage to get those cuffs as white as that?'

'There's obviously a spate of this going on. Same thing happened to Belinda's car the other week. I must give Brian Andrews a ring. See what they're doing about it.'

Harriet looked across.

'You've gone very quiet Miss Glover. Day dreaming about Guy?'

'Most certainly not Mr. Sanderson. I can't think why he wrote that.'

'You must have given him some encouragement Miss Glover. As with Mr. Fishwick.'

'No I most certainly did not Mr. Sanderson. Not Mr. Fishwick either.'

She caught just a hint of a smile. Not at her. He was looking straight ahead. Then he cleared his throat.

'Speaking of Mr. Fishwick Miss Glover. Have you heard anything from them?'

'Actually yes, Mr. Sanderson. Molly phoned. They've decided to live by the sea.'

'Indeed.'

'Yes Mr. Sanderson. They're thinking of moving out this way.'

'Interesting. I was going to arrange for the collection of your things Miss Glover. Haven't got round to it yet.'

He pulled back his shirt cuff to look at his watch. His Rolex watch. Harriet knew. She'd carried her mental photograph and checked it out on the internet. She'd never managed to get close enough to read for herself the code of wealth that manifested itself in those five letters, ROLEX. It was definitely the Yacht-Master 11 in yellow gold.

'Saturday morning Miss Glover. I've got to go out that way anyhow. Can you manage Saturday morning? I'll give them a call. We won't need to take up any of their time.'

A rush of delight met his suggestion.

'Oh yes Mr. Sanderson. That's very kind of you.'

'Right. Done. I'll pick you up at 9.00.'

He'd just turned into her road. They could have been anywhere. She had to pull herself together. This man had swept her away. Completely away. Again.

They stopped alongside the hedge. Her stomach buckled from the need for him as she watched him walk round the car to let her out.

'I'll give Oliver Goldsmith's a call. Get them to sort it out. They'll bring it back for you.'

Harriet looked at him. A complete blank.

'The car Miss Glover. Oliver'll get it sorted.'

'Oh thank you so much Mr. Sanderson. That's a load off my mind.'

'Really? After leaving it hanging around all weekend?' He looked hard at her. 'Anyhow it should be with you by the end of the day.'

Harriet turned to go.

'Just one moment Miss Glover. Feeling any better?'

He ran his hand down the side of her face. Then looked at his finger tips.

'You appear to have talcum powder, or some other such stuff, all down the side of your skirt, too, Miss Glover.'

Harriet looked down as her face turned crimson.

'Skip the day off in lieu of Christmas Eve. It looks like you've already taken it Miss Glover. I expect to see you back in school tomorrow morning.'

Chapter 25

'How did you manage to get that thing back Harriet? I was going to run you down there after we'd eaten.'

Harriet glared at him.

'Hello Harriet. How are you? Did you manage alright on the bus? Especially as you're pregnant. It would be nice Mark, if you could come home and be civil for a change. I don't know what's got into you since you came back from that stupid South Pole. I'm doing my best Mark.'

'Best to bankrupt us Harriet. Did that bloody big three-dimensional wooden jigsaw come today?'

'Yes it did Mark. No thanks to you.'

'I wasn't the one who shoved us in, remember? It was you Harriet. We would have still been in it if I hadn't kicked the door down.'

Harriet went quiet. She didn't need this. She'd wrestled all afternoon with the bittersweet words of Mr. Sanderson. He'd given her the most beautiful gift of Saturday morning and tied it with barbed wire. How she wished she'd left the talcum powder alone.

'Look. You were the one who told me to lock it. I hadn't any idea she was in there.'

'You really want to watch yourself with her Harriet. You were very lucky to get away with that at the wedding. It won't take much for her to start considering legal action. You know Harriet. It really is time you made an effort to grow up.'

'Bloody cheek Mark. And you consider yourself to be grown up. If you'd done the grown-up thing and married me. None. Absolutely none of this would have happened.'

'Right!'

Harriet followed him into the kitchen. She stood behind as he lifted the pages to the back of the calendar. To the whole of next year's dates.

'Right Harriet. Saturday 26th June. Should be well back by then. Get it booked. We're getting married.'

'Really Mark?'

'Really Harriet. No messing about. Make it eleven o'clock in the morning Wherever you want it to be.'

'I'll do it Mark. I *will* you know. Are you really sure?'

'As sure as I'll ever be. As sure as you're pregnant.'

'Well back by then you've just said Mark. So you *have* got to go again?'

'Afraid so Harriet. It's work. That's what I'm paid to do. Anyway you'll have plenty to keep you occupied now. Are you sure you'll want to be walking down the aisle at that stage? Six months Harriet. It'll show. We could do it before. Say March?'

'Well no. We can't do it any sooner Mark. I remember Geraldine saying how booked up places get. How long it takes to get everything organised. No that'll be alright. I've still got quite a bit of that blue silk left from Molly's bridesmaid's dress. I'll be able to put a panel in from under the bust.'

'That's not the blue one I meant Harriet. I wanted you to wear what you wore for Clarissa's wedding.'

'No way Mark. There's no way I'm going to fit into that. I wouldn't be able to alter it either. No I'd have to have something made. It would be very expensive.'

She looked out of the window at the garage wall propping up the shed panels. 'Probably cost around three hundred and ninety nine pounds, ninety nine pence. We can't afford it,' she smiled. She wanted it all to be OK. She wanted this to work. As from now.

'Too right we can't afford it Harriet. I've a good mind to paint it blue and make you wear it.'

'What? Wear what?'

'That shed.' He suddenly grinned. 'Anyway, just how did you get that car back?'

'Does it really matter Mark?'

She put herself in his arms. Rested her head below his shoulder and pressed hard into the lapel of his jacket.

'Not just at this moment Hat. Not just at this moment.'

Chapter 26

'Back in today,' Harriet groaned to herself. She never liked going back after being off ill. It was as well those occasions were most infrequent. She was experiencing a strange mix of apprehension and excitement. All she'd ever wanted had almost come together. Just now. Just for this briefest of spells. She wanted to hold it together. Just like this.

She stopped at the traffic lights as red gave way to amber. She looked across to Starboard Marine North West. In spite of the barbed wire, she couldn't wait for Saturday morning. To be with *him*. All that way to Molly's. And back. She was happy. She was pregnant. Or not. She couldn't decide.

'Not actually confirmed, as good as though.'

At this moment there was absolutely no need to get it confirmed. She basked in the choice it gave her.

'The wedding to plan. Mr. Sanderson? Well he's not actually mentioned marriage. Really. Told me to "save that one for him." How could I wait and wait? At my age? I must. I've got to have another baby before it's too late. Anyway it must have crossed his mind "that special ceremony, sometime following the spring." He must have known I'd misinterpret *that*. Not that nice of him really. To do that to me. He's a drifter. Just one of those gorgeous hunks of men. Elusive. Like Mark. No, not like Mark. Now. Saturday 26th June.' She swallowed hard on her thoughts. She preferred them to remain on amber.

She drove off to the discomfort of her deliberations gathering momentum, paralleling the lights as they moved from amber to green. She tried to brush the thoughts away to concentrate on her driving.

She parked as far away from *his* car as she could. She felt sick again. Her stomach started to churn.

'Ah there you are Miss Glover. The Health and Safety Executive have contacted me. There'll be a representative coming in at about 9.30, I believe. Brown and Potts don't appear to want to let go, I'm afraid. It's more than likely he'll want to speak with you Miss Glover. I'd find a more suitable position for the lunch box trolley if I were you. You did do a risk assessment of your room and surrounding areas, I presume?'

'Yes Mr. Sanderson. I submitted it along with everyone else. It was checked and written off by you.'

'Hmm. Quite, Miss Glover. In that case it's fairly obvious you are aware of the pitfalls but for the most part chose to ignore them, perhaps? Leaving the fire-exit doors open. A case in point?'

Harriet looked down.

'Anyhow Miss Glover, fortunately Brown's recovered sufficiently from the accident to enable him to attend to his duties. It's not as if we've suffered a fatality, exactly. It's this paranoia of his that could prove difficult. We'll just have to see how it goes. Mrs. Lacey's got them all in the hall after break rehearsing the carol concert. Amanda will be taking your class before then, until you're cleared of this. It should be finished by the end of the morning. I suggest you wait in the library Miss Glover and try to tidy up some of those angels before you let them loose on our unsuspecting parents.'

'Right. Thank you Mr. Sanderson.'

'Oliver got the car back to you, I presume?'

'Oh yes. Thank you so much Mr. Sanderson. As you said. It arrived late afternoon.'

'Good. Oh and yes Miss Glover. When you've finished sobering up those angels perhaps you'd like to give some thought to your promotion strategy. Coffee shop. Not a great deal of time left to Christmas Eve.'

Harriet met Amanda by her classroom door.

'Terribly sorry about this Amanda. Thanks for taking them.'

'Not to worry Harriet. Between you and me Joris reckons Mr. Brown's a bit of an old fusspot. To tell you the truth I nearly burst out laughing when he told me about it. Shouldn't really, I know. But you've got to see the funny side. Haven't you Harriet?'

Harriet nodded. She liked Amanda. She suddenly felt very sorry she was leaving.

'Just come to shift this trolley Amanda. Then I'll get out of your way.'

Armed with the Christmas cards, calendars and angels, Harriet went to the library wondering just where Mr. Brown's complaint would land her. She looked at the heap she'd just plonked on the table. It was an impossible task.

'They don't bother with them anyway,' she thought. 'Who's going to put one of these on the wall?'

Her mind wandered to her own calendar. To the picture of Switzerland. To the flower-laden meadow. To Saturday morning. Oh how she was looking forward to that.

She gathered the mountain of stumbled creativity into her bag.

'Right. They can make hats. Large conical hats. Large enough to hide this lot in.' She hurried down the corridor and round the corner to the stock room.

'Is this usually left unlocked?'

Harriet walked straight into the face of a dark haired, good looking young man.

Her stomach sank.

'Er no it isn't.'

She pointed to the hook screwed into the corner of the door frame. High. Well out of reach of the children.

'The key's usually hung up there. Anyway, just popped along to collect a few bits. But I don't have to. Actually I can come back.'

'No. No. Here just look at this.'

She followed him into the long narrow store.

'The lid's not been screwed down on this one for a start.' He lifted a large plastic container filled with white glue. She felt sick again. Then remembered.

126

The offending one was still in the classroom. She watched him jotting something down on the paper in his clipboard.

'Whose responsibility is it to make sure this place remains locked? Save me checking.'

'Overall I think it's the caretaker's, but we, the teachers are supposed to lock it after we've finished. He has to keep an eye on it though.'

'Right. Yes that's right. I remember.' He wrote something else down. 'I'm finished in here now. I'll leave you in peace.'

Harriet gathered up all she required and made her way back to the library. She felt a little less apprehensive now she'd met him. 'Of course that door should have been locked,' she thought, 'maybe, maybe not all completely my fault though.'

Break time came and went. With the hat cut-outs stacking high, she was nearly finished. The sound of Christmas tip-toed into the room. She loved to hear the children singing carols.

'Right Miss Glover.'

Harriet jumped.

'My office if you would.' He held the door open for her while she tried to rein in the cascading angels, slipping as she gathered her bag up from the floor. Only one left.

'A soul mate perhaps?' he shot her that glance. 'Just leave it Miss Glover. That one looks incapable of stance, never mind flying.'

Harriet pretended not to hear. She zipped her bag closed on the rest of them as she followed him out.

'Most interesting Miss Glover. One might say, if you'll allow me to draw on my Latin, "Angelus Delapsus". '

Harriet caught that look again. The one that sent her head spinning all the way down to her toes.

'Not inappropriate, wouldn't you say?'

Harriet couldn't say. She kept her head down. Followed him into his room.

'Still no period, Miss Glover?'

Harriet shook her head.

' "One fallen angel" Miss Glover. Most unfortunate.'

Harriet sat down as he opened his hand towards the chair nearest him. She wished he hadn't just said that.

'Ah here they come.' He opened the door. 'Right take a seat one and all if you will.'

Mr. Andrews sat next to Harriet. He nodded briefly. Smiled. She welcomed his flash of recognition. Mr. Brown and Mr. Potts had decided they were only going to look at each other. Until Mr. Sanderson sat down in his chair.

'Why does he keep asking me that?' she thought. He'd side-tracked her. She watched him shift in his seat. Put his hand to his mouth. Actually catch that blonde curl at his collar between his thumb and his forefinger. Then he suddenly banged both hands on the big wooden desk and stood up.

'Now Mr. Andrews, perhaps you'd like to deliver the same verdict to these good people you gave me a few moments ago? Relevant to the complaint, that is.'

Mr. Andrews coughed. Looked down at his clipboard.

'Having completed a thorough investigation of the school, the risk assessment currently operative is satisfactory in every respect. I've been unable to identify anything additional that would compromise the health and safety of all those who use the building.'

Harriet caught Mr. Potts in a scowl. Now reflected in Mr. Brown's face.

'However,' he continued, it falls down only in as much as a certain laxity has crept in. For example. Where's the key to the stock cupboard? It's down here in black and white whose area of responsibility this is.'

'Quite,' agreed Mr. Sanderson, catching Mr. Brown's eye.

Mr. Brown pressed his thumb to the inside of his grey overall pocket before allowing his fingers in to lift the knotted bit of old string from which the key reluctantly dangled.

'Enough said, Mr. Brown. Explain yourself.' Mr. Sanderson was becoming impatient with the charade.

Mr. Brown looked at Mr. Potts and then back to Mr. Sanderson.

'I can't stretch up there to put this back since she dug `er `eels into these.'

They all looked at his feet.

'No defence I'm afraid Mr. Brown. You didn't seem to be having too much difficulty stretching to the top of the tree with all the Christmas lights,' cut in Mr. Sanderson.

'Aye, that was before she got `er `ands on the glue, leaving me to go over on my backside.'

'Nonsense Mr. Brown, you're the only one with a key. The cupboard must have been open for Miss Glover's children to get in there. You were well within stretching capability on that day. If you can reach for the key to unlock it, you can just as easily reach for it to lock it again Mr. Brown. In any case Mrs. Blackthorn's class watched you decorate the tree, if you recall, well before your encounter with the glue.'

Mr. Brown watched Mr. Potts throw his hands open. He shrugged his shoulders and then looked at Harriet.

'Do you have a dislike of Mr. Brown young woman?'

'No. No Mr. Potts, of course I don't,' protested Harriet.

Mr. Andrews rose to his feet.

'Stress can be a vital factor in clumsiness.' He looked across to Harriet. 'It might be worth your while to consider some de-stressing techniques.'

'What a nice smile he's got,' Harriet thought.

'Other than that I can't offer any further advice. This is outside of my domain now.' He looked at Mr. Brown and Mr. Potts. 'As far as I'm concerned there's no case to make. I'll submit a report.' He nodded at Mr. Sanderson. 'You'll get a copy.'

Mr. Sanderson walked him to the door. Harriet watched them shake hands. She couldn't remember feeling so relieved in the whole of her life.

'Now. Mr. Brown. Mr. Potts. Is there anything further you would like to say?' Silence.

'I take it that's a "no". See me at 3.30 Mr. Brown will you?'

He held the door open for them. Harriet watched them stomp out. She stood up to go.

'Take a seat for a few moments Miss Glover.'

'That may well be the end of it. Certainly the initial fault lies with Mr. Brown. You should not, however, have sent those children to the stock room Miss Glover.'

She watched him jotting something down on his note pad.

'I'll call an emergency staff meeting for half an hour after school tomorrow. Get this damned thing sorted once and for all. Give Alice Atkinson the message will you? Get her to send the word with the registers this afternoon.'

Harriet nodded. She was beginning to feel uneasy again.

'Are you not certain that that's the end of it Mr. Sanderson?'

'Well it's a bit like the Bast er the Bustard woman. Broadbent knew she didn't stand a cat in hell's chance of pulling it off. Post traumatic stress and bed wetting? Was it? I seem to recall something of that nature. As I said before, it depends more likely than not on how far Potts decides to wind Brown's paranoia up.'

'Oh,' said Harriet.

He stood up to place his hand on her shoulder.

'I wouldn't worry too much Miss Glover. You witnessed Potts's somewhat slanderous comments the other day, didn't you?'

'Yes,' Harriet agreed. 'He really had no right to speak to you like that.'

'Quite Miss Glover. I'll make damned sure he doesn't get anywhere with this one.'

He walked over to the door holding it open for her as she stood up.

'I don't know how to thank you Mr. Sanderson.'

'I *do* Miss Glover.'

She walked away and as she reached the corridor windows she stood for a moment to watch him get into his car and drive off.

Chapter 27

Still on amber Harriet drove home basking in the increasing luxury of indecision.

'Wow. Oh wow. What exactly did he mean? "I *do* Miss Glover." How *would* he want me to thank him?'

Her thoughts moved along with the lights. 'Could somebody please stop the clock? Leave it all just like this. Forever?' She hadn't felt so deliriously happy since the field of flowers. Or since he'd given her the ring. Though that was short lived. 'Bittersweet that one. Oh why can't that man just marry me?' Then she remembered she was pregnant. 'What am I playing at?'

By the time she'd got home she'd managed to pop every bubbling thought until there was nothing left. But doubt. 'No, not pregnant. Mummy could be right. I've started the menopause. No definitely not pregnant. A kit. I'll get one. No. No I won't. I don't want to know.'

She opened the car door. The cat bounded over.

'At least *you're* pleased to see me Pepper. Maybe I should just stow away. Like you did. Mark doesn't know about that yet, either. You certainly took a chance there. Could have ended up as another Davy Crockett hat for that awful girl.'

She opened the front door to the sound of the phone ringing.

'Out of the way Pepper. I'm trying to answer it.'

'Oh `ello `arriet. It's only me. I thought I'd give you a call seein` as you didn't get chance to phone me last night.'

'Oh sorry Tricia. What with school and everything. Do you know Tricia some cheeky sod let the tyres down on my car?'

'Ooh `arriet that's what `appened to `er ladyship's didn't it? When my Bob `ad to take `er `ome that night. `e's never been the same since `arriet. `e keeps measurin` `is porky middle. `e keeps takin` the tape measure out of my bag of knittin` `arriet, `til I `id it. It's really funny watchin` im struggle with that long steel one. `e keeps pressin` the button by mistake. `e gets it `alf way round `arriet then it twangs back on `im. I said to `im "serves you right for bein` so vain." It's `er `arriet. I `ad to buy `im some aftershave. The designer stuff `arriet. I ask you? I said "I `ope you've made me buy that for my benefit and no one else's." All of a sudden `e can't wait for this coffee shop to open `arriet. `e's bought `imself a new sweatshirt `arriet with 'BANKER'S? MY ARSE' written all over the front. I said "and just when are you plannin` to wear *that* Bob?" and do you know `arriet `e said on Christmas Eve at the coffee shop for a laugh. Festive season and all that. So I told `im that was a really good idea `arriet. I thought that would put `er off `im for good. I shouldn't think she'd want to be seen anywhere near `im in that!'

'Good thinking Tricia. Talking of Christmas Eve. Have you managed to get any publicity going yet?'

'Too right I `ave `arriet. Just wait `til you see the Stetmead News. I just got it in before the "stop". Whatever that is. Well I think for today's paper it would be too late to change anythin`. I think that's what it means `arriet. Not that I want to. The whole place will be crowded `arriet. I wouldn't bother doing anythin` more. That's if you `aven't already done anythin` `arriet?'

'No I haven't had chance yet Tricia. Thanks so much. He doesn't give you much time for these things. Does he?'

'No `e does not `arriet. You should see those poor men slavin` away for `im. Do you know `arriet they've nearly finished. I can't believe it. Toilets as well. They've made two lovely cloakrooms from those stores at the back. We're expectin` the tables and chairs to be delivered tomorrow. `e wants it all signed off on Friday. Actually `arriet I'll be glad when it's all done with. I've really `ad enough of `er waltzin` in and out. Cottoned on to the managin` director of that garden centre too, she `as. I'm sick of `earin` about `ow they've organised their bloody coffee shop `arriet. Sick of `earin` about Guy. That's the managin` director `arriet. Well it would be wouldn't it? She wouldn't stoop to talk to anyone of them down there if they were in a green overall.'

'You're probably right Tricia.' Puzzled, Harriet scratched her head.

'Anyway `arriet I told my Bob. I said "If you're tryin` to lose all that pork round your middle for Belinda Oxfordshire you're wastin` your time. She's got a new boyfriend now. ` is name is Guy and `e's the owner of the garden centre. Chain of garden centres." I said. "She's `ardly goin` to be botherin` with you." '

'Too right Tricia. Men! What would you do with them?'

'Ooh `arriet I know what I'd do with `*im* given `alf a chance. `e's just gorgeous. `e's been `ere all afternoon `arriet. Oh `ave I `ad some smiles off `im. `e seemed to be in a very good mood. Do you know `arriet Bob could bugger off with who `e liked and it wouldn't bother me if I `ad `im. You can never be quite sure what Joris's thinkin` though, can you `arriet? I definitely know `e's very attracted to me. It's probably because of Bob. I bet that's stoppin` `im from makin` a move. Don't you think? Maybe I should `ide that sweatshirt after all `arriet. Come to think of it Belinda Oxfordshire could be quite useful `arriet. If she goes for Bob that would leave me free for Joris. I'm sure Joris would be very pleased not to `ave `er flappin` around `im all the time. We'd be free for each other then, apart from the kids, that is. Me mum would have them. They're always fightin` and squabblin` anyway `arriet. I've `ad enough of them. We wouldn't be wantin` anythin` to disturb us when we're lyin` in our marital bed. Would we `arriet?'

Harriet laughed. 'Of course not Tricia. Anyway what did you put in the paper? Go on tell me. Ours doesn't always come. Never mind on time.'

'No `arriet. I want you to read it for yourself. Just look for the by-line, I think that's what they called it. Anyway `arriet just look for the one by Holly Berry. I gave myself a stage name `arriet as I don't think I could `andle any publicity. I tried to sound festive `arriet. Anyway I don't want that Simon Barnes `avin` anythin` to do with this. Just in case `e found out my name `arriet. Anyway when you've read it `arriet I want you to tell me if it makes you feel as though you can't wait to come on Christmas Eve. It should do 'arriet. Phone me as soon as you've read it 'arriet. Oh I think Joris will be very proud of me.'

'Will do Tricia. Holly Berry did you say? You've taken a load off my mind. Thanks again Tricia.'

Harriet put the phone down. A series of nervous pangs instantly stitched their way through her stomach. She wondered just what Tricia had been up to. She looked out of the lounge window in the hope of getting the paper. In the hope of seeing the old shopping trolley flanked either end by those two rowdy lads. One pushing, the other pulling the load of free local news along the uneven pavements.

'So Guy's got the hots for Belinda Oxfordshire,' she mused as she went to the kitchen to start the evening meal. 'Bit of a lad that. Creative to say the least.' She wondered where the delivery note had gone. The last she remembered Mr. Sanderson had taken it. Poem and all. 'Well he's either wearing his best suit under that overall before whipping it off when he sees her coming, or she's trying to send the signal out to Bob via Tricia there's another man in her life. In which case Bob might have been telling the truth. Now there's a thought,' she decided, as she put the last potato into the pan of water. She returned to the sink. Tried to hold all the peeling against the side of the bowl with one hand as she emptied the muddy residue of water down the drain.

'Oh brilliant. That sounded like the paper, Pepper.'

She almost fell over the cat as she scrambled to the door. The letterbox snapped. She grabbed the headlines. 'Oh no Pepper. This is it. It's made the front page. **"by Holly Berry"**.'

She placed it on the kitchen table. Still folded. And gathered the curling escapees of potato bits from the edges of the sink before drying her hands.

SANTA'S BIG SURPRISE
by Holly Berry

"You are in for a treat if you come to the opening of the brand new coffee shop called 'The Bean-S-Talk' on Christmas Eve at Starboard Marine North West.

Just why are you in for a treat? You don't know? Of course you don't know. Because we are keeping it one big surprise.

Just who will be giving out all those special Christmas gifts to your children? Just who will be sitting in the grotto all day waiting for them to arrive? Still guessing? Well here's a teeny weenie clue.

We've got a very famous celebrity behind that long white beard. Looking out from under that red and white hood. He might be a pop star. He might be a sports personality. He might be an actor. He might be a very famous politician. He might even be a member of the Royal Family. What's more. He might even be the most famous man in the world.

At four o'clock the grotto will close. Then it will be up to you to spot him in the crowd. He has very kindly offered to autograph anything you might buy from Starboard Marine North West.

Don't miss this! This is going to be the highlight of your Christmas holiday.

Our fun will start on Christmas Eve 10.00am - 5.00pm. Drink your coffee then keep coming back with all your friends to see who our very special celebrity is."

Harriet couldn't believe what she'd just read. 'She must have cleared this with Mr. Sanderson first.' Harriet tried to remember exactly what she'd said. 'Whoever are they going to get on Christmas Eve?' The cat meowed at her. 'You don't know either, do you? Well I'm sure I don't. Bloody hell Tricia. What have you gone and done?'

Suddenly she felt as if it was all of her own making. *He'd* asked *her* to come up with some ideas. She couldn't drop Tricia in it. Just like that. 'I bet she hasn't got anyone. Who can we get? Who can we get?' She babbled incessantly at the cat. Went straight to phone Tricia. It rang.

'She's beaten me to it.'

Harriet lifted the receiver just as the doorbell went. She didn't know what to do. Its persistent rings outstripped the phone. She left it dangling unable to answer it.

In less than a second she found herself sandwiched between the front door and Mr. Sanderson. The folded paper almost in her nose.

'Miss Glover. Who the fucking hell is responsible for this?'

He marched into the hall.

'`arriet are you still there `arriet. Only I think this line's gone funny again `arriet.'

He walked straight to it. Held it to his ear. Then passed it over.

'Answer it Miss Glover. Then pass it back.'

Harriet did as she was told.

'Mrs. Harrington. I'm standing next to Miss Glover. Standing here with this damned paper in my hand.'

He turned to Harriet, pinning his eyes to her as he continued.

'I don't want to know which one of you was responsible for this. Possibly both. In fact you Miss Glover, having initiated this very strong link to our extra-curricular school activities, were given the job of marketing as I recall. Now! Would the pair of you mind telling me who this celebrity is? Who exactly has agreed to spend all day Christmas Eve dressed up as Santa? There isn't anyone of them out there would be so fucking stupid. I want the answer. Now. Right now!'

'Well you do know lots of people in `igh places Mr. Sanderson. You did `ave the PM to the very first openin` of it.`as `e's your friend I'm sure `e wouldn't mind doin` you another favour Mr. Sanderson.'

Harriet heard every word. He'd whammed up the volume to make sure she did.

'NO, NO, NO, Mrs. Harrington. Absolutely NOT!'

Harriet picked up the cat. Shoved it in the kitchen, then struggled to close the door on it.

'The pair of you. You'd better start thinking. Fast. With that build up it had better be good. Very good. I want no involvement. Repeat NO INVOLVEMENT. You find your own world famous celebrity. Got it? And if either of you jeopardizes this launch I swear you'll both be out of a job. It wouldn't be hard to topple the cards stacked against you Miss Glover.'

Harriet felt a strange sensation in her throat as he slammed the phone down. Completely ignited he flung the paper to the bottom stair as he swept past her. She swallowed hard then tried to catch her breath as she went to the lounge window to hear only the sound of the engine speeding away.

Harriet picked up the paper. She didn't need two. At this moment she didn't need any. Then she picked up the phone.

'Ooh 'ello 'arriet. 'as 'e gone? 'e wasn't very pleased was 'e 'arriet? I didn't mean to drop you in it 'arriet. I thought I was 'elpin`.'

'Don't worry about it Tricia. You were helping. I haven't had chance to get to it. We'll bloody well make him eat his words Tricia. Let's see who we can find.'

'Ooh 'arriet it isn't goin` to be easy. With 'im knowin` all them people I thought 'e'd only 'ave to ask 'arriet. Shows you 'ow wrong you can be. You know 'arriet we 'ave some very nice people in the Royal Family. I'm sure if I gave the Palace a ring and explained exactly what 'ad 'appened they'd send someone. Of course I'd 'ave to mention 'is name. They're probably not going to be too impressed with 'olly Berry 'arriet. I'd just 'ave to say Joris Sanderson. I'm sure if I did that someone would get the train up.'

'Don't think so Tricia. Look. We're going to have to think of someone. Quick. Give me a ring if you come up with any ideas and I'll do the same. Think local Tricia, then we might stand a chance.'

'Right 'arriet. Don't you worry. We'll come up with somebody. Speak soon.'

Harriet returned to the kitchen. Shaking. Angry. She was scanning every cell in her brain trying to turn up an answer.

She sat down pulling her chair into the kitchen table as she turned the pages of the Stetmead News.

'Entertainment. Right.' She glued her eyes to each and every line. One jumped out.

' "Arena Central. Rapping Hammer and the Ironing Bards. ALL SOLD OUT" '

'That's him. He's the one. Rachael said he was local. He'll do it. We've got to get hold of him. Ask him. He's got to do it. I must phone Tricia.' She turned to the cat. 'Disappeared. Been talking to myself. So what? Stupid cat. Vanishes at the critical moment.'

Her fingers were too excited. Hardly able to press the right numbers.

'Tricia I've got the answer.'

'Well I'm glad you 'ave 'arriet. I 'aven't got a clue myself. I've been rackin' my brains 'ere 'arriet. I still think we've got a better chance with the Royal Family than anyone else.'

'Tricia have you heard of Rapping Hammer and the Ironing Bards?'

''eard of them 'arriet. Our Adam's got them plastered all over 'is bedroom wall. I told 'im I'm not makin' 'is bed until 'e takes them down. Too scary 'arriet. The lot of them look evil 'arriet. Really evil. And that Rappin' 'ammer looks like 'e wants to kill me just for goin' in there. I wouldn't mind 'arriet. I know they're only pictures but they've made 'is room look like 'ell itself with that black ceilin' and walls. 'e's only thirteen 'arriet. I don't know why 'e can't be a boy scout. At least he'd be doin' somethin' useful there.'

'Too right Tricia. Thank goodness we do still have such things. Our girls loved the brownies and guides. I swear it was the making of them.'

'Oh I'm goin' to 'ave another go at our Adam when 'e comes in tonight. Anyway 'arriet are you thinkin' of *them*?'

'Well yes Tricia. They're famous aren't they? That's what we've promised. I'm going online. See if I can find the website, the fan club, the agent. Anyone I can ask.'

'I'll definitely do the same 'arriet. Bob can 'ave beans for 'is tea. 'e can get them 'imself. I've 'ad enough of all these fancy salads 'arriet. Grillin' bits of lean bacon and tossin' them at lettuce. I told 'im I'm not as green as you're lettuce lookin' 'arriet. I said I know who you're doin' all this for. Well you're wastin' your time. It's Guy she fancies. One of these days I'll just go 'arriet. What with 'im and the kids. I'll phone you the minute I get a breakthrough 'arriet.'

'Me too Tricia. Thanks.'

Harriet put the phone down, anxious to progress her enquiries.

'No I don't want to become a member of the flipping fan club. Thank you. For the thousandth time. No I don't want to chat with like minded punks. I'm not a flipping punk. No I don't want to buy tickets for their Boxing Day gig. Thank you. They're sold out. Anyway. Trying to con me now?' Harriet turned off the computer. Completely frustrated. She looked at her watch. Felt under pressure. Came downstairs. She panicked. There wasn't a hint of Christmas anywhere.

'Never mind his blinking coffee shop. I haven't even got the tree yet. Oh, I'm going to get it. Sod *him*!'

She backed the car off the drive and headed for the garden centre, hoping not to see Guy.

'Sheds are not by the Christmas trees. It'll be OK. I'll pick up Mummy's planter too. Good thinking Harriet. Everyone can have one. Let's see.' She started counting to herself.

'Yes. Good idea. They can all have one between them. No. One between the two of them. So that's James and Geraldine, one. Paul and Susan two, ... Right. So I'm going to need seven. Oh and one for Molly and Mr. Fishwick, eight. We can take that over with us on Saturday. *Saturday.* Oh no. Oh golly.With *him* on Saturday. All that way to Molly's. I *can't* go now. Definitely can't go. Need to think of something. Now why can't I go? What am I going to tell him?'

Her thoughts took her right through the entrance and into the car park facing the sheds. She stopped the car and looked over to the gap where hers had been. The one she'd been forced to buy.

'No sign. No sign of him. In fact no sign of anyone in a green overall anywhere. Good.'

She hurried along the other path. Just in case. The double set of glass doors sensed her arrival and obligingly separated to let her in. She was thankful for the extended opening hours in the run-up to Christmas. It was full on. The place sparkled with baubles and tinsel and all manner of Yuletide things on strings, bobbing around to the rocking Christmas music. Plastic mistletoe hanging complacent over cribs, showing no shame. Now so entrenched in the tradition its pagan origin long since rendered insignificant.

Harriet grabbed a trolley. 'Christmas cards. They'll do. And gift wrap. Just a band round the bottom of each planter. Mark's not going to want one of those.' She diverted to the compost bins. 'I'll fill it. That's it.'

She put a garden hose in the trolley. An outside tap. A hand trowel. A fork. A pair of secateurs. Some bean netting. Oh and a pair of wellingtons. She lifted the big cardboard box containing the self assembly compost bin on to the shelf sticking out at the bottom of the trolley. Toyed with the idea of a new lawn mower. 'Better not. No. he'll say we can't afford it.'

She returned to the gift tags. The Christmas crackers. Popped them in the trolley. The serviettes. Then put them back again.

'Thank goodness I'm not doing Christmas dinner.'

She grabbed a couple of packets of green bean seeds, about to tumble from the stand anyway.

'Wires to tie them.'

She threw them in. 'Oh fertilizer. They won't grow without that.'

She moved along to the full-to-bursting bags shaped liked pillows stacked against the wall.

'Too big.'

Then she spotted some packets.

'That's better. Two should do. Yes he'll definitely like this present. All done. Better check these out and come back for the rest.'

Pleased with herself Harriet pushed the trolley to the car. Opened the boot and shoved it all in. She kept her head down.

'No sign of Guy. Good. Jolly good.' Harriet was steaming her way to Christmas now. She decided on the side entrance this time. 'Nearer the trees and the pots. All outside.' She remembered.

'No. No. they've changed it all. Indoor water fountains. Mine. I'll get that one for me. From Mark. And one for Tricia. Clare and Rachael too.' The trolley was stacking. Again.

'I'll go through here and then out that way. Oh crafts. That's new. Didn't know they'd diversified. "Diversify". That word. *Him?* He was furious. How can we get in touch with Rapping Hammer?'

She pushed her way round the revolving baskets of soft toys, then the rolls of fabric, then the baskets of wool. Then face to face with the knitting patterns. A good looking chap with blonde hair smiled down at her from just under the 99p sticker in the top right hand corner.

'That's an Aran sweater. I'll knit him one. That'll do the trick.'

Immediate action overtook her thoughts. She pulled the pattern out. Took it to the counter and instructed the girl who looked as though she wanted to go home, to supply her with all the materials required.

'No need to look at me like that,' Harriet thought. 'I am a paying customer. We are in a recession.'

The girl opened up the pattern and flattened it to the counter with both hands.

'Be choosing your wool. Will you?' She ran her hand down a run of wooden shelving all joined together with uprights to make squares.

'Aran. Aran. Aran.' She punched at the balls as she ran down each box. Then returned to the counter.

'You'll need. Sodding hell. It depends whether you want a huge big ball rolling around the carpet or not? Depends if you've got a cat. If you want 50g balls you'll need. Let me see now? Say twenty. How big is he?'

'Very big actually. Looks a bit like him on the front. Much better looking though. He hasn't got a silly grin like him. And his hair's much thicker. And longer. His eyebrows don't look like that either. They're quite dark for a blonde and so are his eyelashes, in fact. He doesn't really look like that at all. Now I come to think of it. Anyway you would never ever find *him* on the front of a knitting pattern.'

'Madam I'm not that interested in looking for him on the front of a knitting pattern. Would you kindly choose your wool. I'm not on a late tonight. I'm due off just as soon as Paula Sloe gets here.' She threw her eyes up.

'Sloe by name. Slow by nature. Wouldn't you know? Trust me to get paired with a dozy one. I always seem to end up serving them as well.' She placed both hands on her hips. 'You just take your time. She can serve you if you like?'

'Oh no. Sorry. I'm in a hurry myself. I've still got things to get. Sorry about that. Got carried away.'

Harriet loaded the carrier bag full of wool and needles into the trolley as her credit card ran through the swipe.

'You forgot this.'

Harriet watched the knitting pattern land in the trolley. It was time to move away from this very bad tempered girl.

'Outside. At last.' The cold evening air smacked at Harriet's face. She was glad to be out of there. She walked past the planters.

'Eight. Yes it was eight. Tree first.' She walked on. ' "TREES DELIVERED. ASK HERE". Brilliant. Planters as well. I'm sure they'll do that. All sorted.'

A young girl tottered past as Harriet pushed her trolley at the bark chippings forcing a sideways path to the big shed directly ahead.

'See you later Paula love. If you see what I mean?'

Harriet looked up.

'You'll never get that thing through this love.' He kicked at the dark brown flakes.

She turned round. It was Guy.

'Got your shed alright then love?'

His grin was determined to tie itself in a knot somewhere round the back of his head.

'Yes. Thank you. Thank you very much indeed. Very reliable. Very prompt delivery.'

'You signed it off didn't you love?'

'Er yes. Thank you. Yes I did. Christmas trees. I've just come for a Christmas tree. Please. If you don't mind. In a terrible hurry. Got to get back.'

'That funny bugger want feedin' does 'e?'

'Something like that. Anyway this tree'll do. If that's alright. And I'd like eight of those planters please. Those over there. Just against the fence. Could I possibly have them all delivered together please? All at the same time. Oh and all these in the trolley. If you could, please?'

'Anything for you love. It'll be OK. I'll just park this in there. No on second thoughts, bring that bag with you. A bit easy to lift that one. We've 'ad a few light fingers in 'ere lately. If you see what I mean? Talkin' of which.' Suddenly he stopped to take her hand. He eyed her fingers.

'Good. Glad you 'aven't married 'im. If you see what I mean?'

Harriet was relieved to reach the shed. At least he'd have something to do. She took her card from her purse.

'Shed up yet?'

'Er not yet I'm afraid.'

She watched him write on his pad.

'Delivery address same as the card? Yes. I remember now love. Well I wouldn't be forgettin' that one would I?'

Harriet wanted to go. Her feet were running away without her. It was dark outside. She didn't want to be in there. On her own with him. And her bag of wool.

'Don't suppose 'e'd know one end of an 'ammer from another. That funny bugger. I'll put it up for you love. If you like?'

'Most kind of you, Guy. Actually Daddy's offered. More time. Retired you know.'

'Well. If you're sure. Talkin` about `ammers. They're comin` `ere. Doin` a gig on Boxin` Day. Fancy it?'

'Oh that's most kind of you Guy. But it's sold out. Noticed it in the paper just before I came out.'

She put her credit card back in her purse and nervously crumpled the receipt in her pocket.

'Sold out! Don't take any notice of that love. Our Wayne'll get us in. No probs!'

'Your Wayne?' Harriet backed out of the shed.

'`e's me cousin. Isn't `e? Wayne `ammer. You don't think `is mum would `ave called `im Rappin` do you? No `e thought that one up for `imself. Rappin` `ammer and the Ironing Bards. Good eh? `eavy metal. Rock and all that. `is name was already `ammer, so iron. Metal. `eavy metal. Get it? And Bards. Their poets like, aren't they? A bit like me.'

His mouth began to wander off again into a huge grin.

'All a bit of a pun on ironing boards. You'd never guess `ow many of them out there `ad to use their ironing boards to `elp them get on the road. Clever eh? It's worked for them anyway. I'd call myself Rappin` if it meant not working in this friggin` garden centre. `ang on a minute. I'll give `im a buzz.'

Harriet was struck. Dumb. Just for a fraction of a second. Recovery was instantaneous. She could hardly get the words out fast enough.

'Guy. We're looking for a celebrity to open the new coffee shop at Starboard Marine North West.'

'Oh yeah. I get me sailin` gear down there. There's a right funny chick serves me. Nice enough. But does she flap? She `ates bein` disturbed from `er dustin`. Someone should tell `er the wind blows it all off anyway.'

'Got to refocus him,' Harried panicked. Without need.

'Anyway I'm sure `e'll do that for you. You should see `is forty five foot ketch. It's a corker. With `im comin` from the other side and bein` on the road `e `asn't `ad chance to get to the joint yet. *"Joint"* I just said, didn't I? Now that's a good word.' He winked at her. Harriet just wanted him to get on with it. 'Speakin` of which there's another old spud `e talks about. Somethin` to do with `im, Sanderson, the guy that owns it. Oh that's it. `e calls `im Barkin` Ditchwater. If you see what I mean? I've told `im `ow good the place is though. `e's very keen to meet that Sanderson chap. You know `e skippered the team that came second in the Fastnet race a couple of years ago. Yeah, our Wayne's bustin` a gut to meet `im. Been droppin` `ints at Barkin Ditchwater for yonks.'

'Never?' Amazement threatened to stun Harriet's mind. She came to. Could she just see *him* heaving the sails in. She touched the wool in her bag. 'And no. I don't suppose Mark would have told me that, either.' What a thought!

'When did you say it was love?'

'Christmas Eve. All day, nine 'til five o'clock. We'd need him to dress up as Father Christmas. And give the children their presents. Do you think that would be alright Guy? Do you think he'd mind? We'll pay him of course. Just tell him to name his fee.'

'Knowin' our Wayne 'e won't want anythin'. The band'll probably want somethin' though. 'e never goes anywhere without them. Somethin' to do with their contracts. They're all contracted to appear together. At all times. If you see what I mean?'

'Yes. Of course. That's absolutely fine.'

''ang on love.' He pulled his mobile from his overall pocket and hit a button somewhere centre left. Harriet watched him kick the chippings back to the shed. Then watched him come out again.

'All sorted love. 'e's done that sort of thing before. 'e's got a sack load of presents left over from last year. 'e likes to give the kids a momento. Somethin' to do with the band. If you see what I mean? If 'e gets to meet Sanderson 'e's not goin' to charge for anythin'. The band'll be comin' in at around ten grand.'

'That's fine,' gulped Harriet. 'I can't thank you enough.'

'That's alright love. 'e's put our name on that box in the gods. Usually reserved for royalty. But it's ours for the night.'

Harriet smiled on her sinking heart. She took the receipt from him.

'Delivery?'

'That's OK. I'll be takin' Paula 'ome in the van. I'll drop 'em in on the way.'

'Thanks Guy. Ever so much.'

'It's all my pleasure. If you know what I mean?'

Harried marched her carrier bag full of wool along all the dimly lit side paths back to her car. She couldn't wait to get home.

Chapter 28

'Late tonight Hat? Or have you been in and gone out again?'

Mark was looking at her school bags sitting at the bottom of the stairs.

'I'm very pleased with myself. Actually. Done all the Christmas shopping at the garden centre.'

'Mine as well Hat?'

'Not telling you Mark.'

'It's not that bag of wool is it? Not quite ready for sitting in the shed cross-legged knitting.'

'Of course it isn't Mark. Just fancied having a go. I don't know who it's going to be for yet.'

'Doesn't look like baby wool Hat. Not pink or blue. As long as it's not for lard ball. He's been on the phone by the way.'

'On the phone? What did he say?'

'Not much. I thanked him again for sending the repair team out. Then he said something about Saturday morning. There were no other plans. You should be using the time to get this damned celebrity issue thing sorted out. To pass the message on. Then he said he wouldn't be in school until Monday. Then he went Harriet. Which is just the way I like it.'

She didn't know whether to be relieved or disappointed. Whichever, she tried to keep it from Mark.

'No other plans Harriet? What's he talking about?'

'Oh. Well. No. It's just that I offered to help get the place sorted. You know? The coffee shop. There's a lot to do before it opens on Christmas Eve. Right. He wants me to work on it on Saturday morning, instead. Is that all he said, then? Oh well, that's fine with me. More than fine. As it's sorted.' She tried to hide her disappointment.

'Just as well it is Harriet. He doesn't own you, you know. I've had enough of you being at his beck and call without you volunteering our weekends. We're going to see that house again on Saturday at ten. I've been checking it out. They can't get a mortgage. It's back on the market.'

'Oh, isn't it getting a bit too near Christmas for viewings Mark?'

He pointed to the post. To the top letter sitting on the hall window sill.

'We need to find somewhere. There's a load of bumph in there from the solicitor. It's under way. They're buying it.'

'Well that's very nice. Nobody told us.'

'It was a foregone conclusion Harriet. That's why she surveyed it.'

'The takeaway Mark. Do you mind going? Get a couple of bottles of red on the way past.'

'I'm not sure you should be drinking Harriet in that condition. It's high time you shifted yourself to find out what's what you know.'

'Oh sod off will you Mark? I'm having a bot... er glass of wine. It won't do any harm.'

'I hope you're right Harriet.'

Harriet needed to phone Tricia. She lifted the receiver just as soon as he'd slammed the front door closed.

'Tricia. It's me Harriet.'

'Oh `ello `arriet. It's bad news I'm afraid. I couldn't bring myself to enquire about that evil `ammer boy so I took the bull by the `orns `arriet. So to speak. I don't think that's a proper metathingy `arriet. Is it? Anyway I tried to email the Palace `arriet and the bloody thing kept comin` back at me just like a boomerang. Now that is a metathingy I think. Is that right `arriet?'

'Sorry Tricia. I think that one's a similie.'

'Oh bloody `ell `arriet `ow many more of these are there? Anyway. No luck I'm afraid. I do `ope you're phonin` me with good news.'

'Well Tricia, it's good and bad.'

'What do you mean `arriet. `ow can it be both?'

'We've got Rapping Hammer. He'll do it Tricia.'

'Oh `arriet. `ow on earth did you manage that?'

'That lad Guy. Belinda Oxfordshire's latest from the garden centre.'

'No `arriet. `e's not a lad. `e's the managing director. `e's the one who fancies `er, Belinda Oxfordshire. Ooh what's `e like `arriet? Is `e nice? If I can't swing it with our friend Joris, maybe I could `ave `im `arriet? That's if she ends up with my Bob.'

'No Tricia. She's been trying to impress you I'm afraid. He's a real jerk, just one of the assistants down there.'

'Oh *really* `arriet? `as she been `opin` I'd tell Bob about this "managing director" of `ers so as to make `im jealous?'

'Could be Tricia.'

'So if she ends up with my Bob because I've been `elpin` it all along on a lie, who am I goin` to end up with `arriet? I think I'd better try a bit `arder for the true man of my dreams `arriet. I've got to make all this effort worthwhile, I would say. Anyway `arriet where was I before all that? Oh that's it, we don't want `er to be involved in this. Not really. We don't want `er gettin` any praise she doesn't deserve. Do we?'

'No. It's alright Tricia. She isn't. It's just that Guy's only turned out to be Rapping Hammer's cousin. Well Wayne actually. His name's Wayne Hammer. Guy phoned him there and then. It seems he's done it before. He's even going to bring the presents. He's got a load left over from last year.'

'Oh `arriet. That is just marvellous. Oh thank goodness for that `arriet. Why would `e want to `elp us though `arriet? Just like that?'

'Always wanted to meet Joris Sanderson, Tricia. He sails, too. He probably wants to discuss the pros and cons of Fastnet with him. Seems Mr. Sanderson and his crew came in a close second a few years ago.'

'Well I didn't know that `arriet. Bob never mentioned that. You know `arriet I've come to the conclusion Bob is really jealous of `im. I'm gettin` really fed up with `is sarcastic comments. Anyway `arriet, well done you. `e'll go down really well round 'ere. It's funny that I said it could be a pop star right at the start of my list. When I was doing my 'olly Berry that is 'arriet.'

'Yes. Well there you go Tricia. Psychically inspired. He's not claiming a fee either just as long he gets to meet Mr. Sanderson.'

'Well there you 'ave it 'arriet. It couldn't 'ave gone better. Surely you 'aven't got any bad news after all that?'

'Bad news Tricia. He's not coming on his own. He's bringing the Ironing Bards with him. The rest of the group. They're contracted never to split, whatever the appearance.'

'Well that's alright 'arriet. We'll soon find somethin' for them to do. We'll be there all day don't forget.'

'I think we'll have to be finding them plenty to do Tricia. They'll want *their* fee, or so they told Guy.'

'Ooh 'arriet. 'ow much will they be lookin' for? We can't 'ave 'im fizzin' again. We can 'ardly go back to 'im again. 'e was off the planet 'arriet when 'e 'ad to part with that £3,000 for All about Buffet's. Remember?'

'Only too well Tricia. Except these rockers are looking at £10,000.'

'Ooh no 'arriet. And what did you say to that?'

'I told Guy that would be absolutely fine. Well I couldn't risk them all backing off, Tricia. We haven't got time to mess about. It's not so much losing our jobs as not being able to produce a decent reference from *him*. You're always asked about your last place of employment. *He* knows everyone Tricia. We can't afford to make a fool of him.'

'Oh I know 'arriet. I don't want to lose my job. I love workin' there. It's the best job I've 'ad in my life 'arriet and I need somethin' now Adam and Michelle are growin' up. Ooh wait 'til I tell our Adam about Rappin' 'ammer. All the kids from 'is school will be there. That was a real brainwave 'arriet. 'ow are we goin' to get 'im to pay for the Ironing Bards though? That's a very silly name. Don't you think 'arriet? I would say that boards would 'ave been far more appropriate. Booring boards. Apart from when I go into 'is bedroom. That is. Really scary 'arriet.'

'There's got to be a way of putting it across Tricia. Have a think. Between us we've got to come up with something. You never know? He might just consider it worth paying for all the publicity.'

'Too right 'arriet. Oh I can 'ear Bob comin' back from the gym. I'd bettter go 'arriet. I'll give you a call.'

'Perfect timing,' Harriet thought as the door bell rang. 'Mark's got his keys. No. Of course, he's got the takeaways. And the wine. Hands full. Hopefully. With the wine.'

Harriet pulled the door back wide. She could just see Guy's face smiling through the branches of a large Christmas tree.

'Shall I leave this one just 'ere then love?'

'Oh yes please. That's fine. Yes. If you just pass those over to me I'll pop them down there.'

Harriet stacked the boxes in the corner under the hall window.

'That's it then love. I've lined them pots up alongside the door, there. `ope that's OK? Would you mind signin` `ere?'

He shuffled from one foot to the other.

'Er I don't like to `ave to `ask you this but Paula. She's in the van. She's moanin` `er `ead off about goin` to see our Wayne. I don't like askin` `im for any more favours. You know what I mean?'

Harriet flooded with the sweet sense of relief. She nodded.

'You know I wanted to go with you. Now I'm gonna `ave to take Paula. I'm sorry love. I couldn't stand to `ave `er naggin` me all over Christmas. I meant what I said in my poem though. You're different. You've got somethin` Paula `asn't.'

'Just a few more years Guy. Now you take her and enjoy it together. My two daughters are going. I'll get them to look out for you. In the gods you'll be? They'll be so impressed to meet Rapping Hammer's cousin.'

'`ow `old are they then?'

'Just a bit younger than you. But not much.'

'Well `ow old are you then love?'

'*Well* old enough to be your mother Guy.'

'Well. Knock me down with a feather. I thought you were probably a bit more than `er in the van. Say about three or four years.'

Harriet had to sit on a very powerful urge to fling her arms round him.

'It don't bother me at all. I'm drawn to older women. Me. If you know what I mean?'

Belinda Oxfordshire suddenly sprang to Harriet's mind.

'Well thank you so much Guy. We'll see you at the coffee shop on Christmas Eve. Maybe?

'Bloody workin`. Aren't I? `ave a good Christmas love. Keep poppin` in.'

Harriet was glad to close the door on him. She flew upstairs to hide Mark's presents. And then down to answer it again. She let him in.

'That cheeky swine from the garden centre. Just pushed this at me.' He nudged the knitting pattern, sitting on top of the hot white paper wrapped cartons, towards her with his chin.

' "Give `er this," he's just said.'

Harriet took the pattern. She could see Mark was furious.

' "You don't deserve `er you funny bugger. If you know what I mean?" The bloody nerve of him Harriet. I told him I didn't know what he bloody meant and I'd kick his arse if he ever came round here again.'

'Well he did watch you hare off like that Mark. You did leave me to sort it.'

'You what Harriet? I don't believe I'm hearing this. And just what do you suggest we do with that monstrosity out there?'

'Oh these are going cold. Come on. Let's get Christmas out of the way. Anyway that house has got an enormous garden. We'll take it with us.'

'Good thinking Hat. Why didn't I think of that?'

Chapter 29

Only half awake, Harriet reluctantly let the morning seep into her consciousness, bringing with it an emerging sense of disappointment.

'Thursday. Oh no. Only Thursday. And I've blown Saturday. I *could* let Mr. Sanderson know it's all sorted. No, he's bound to want to know who we've got. Rapping Hammer might just not be his first choice. Then he'll ask what it's all going to cost. No Harriet. Just leave everything where it is.'

Still thinking, she decided to make the tea.

She struggled past the skirting of prickly branches as she met with the Christmas tree at the bottom of the stairs.

She continued to ponder it as she rattled the carton at the cat's saucer.

'Oh I was really looking forward to that. With *him*! I wanted to take Molly's planter over, too. Oh sod!'

She pulled at the bottom of the kitchen door with her foot as she steered the tray of overfilled mugs into the hall. She noticed the green light flashing on the answer machine.

'Get out from under will you Pepper? If you don't want to be scalded with hot tea. That's funny. We didn't hear that go last night. Surely we didn't drink that much?'

She decided on getting the tea upstairs first. It wasn't going to be easy struggling past all those prickly branches again, especially with tray in hand.

'Did you hear the phone last night Mark?'

'You what Harriet? Give me a chance to wake up.'

'There's a message on it. How much did we drink Mark?'

'Too much probably. You certainly did. You don't care, do you Harriet?'

Harriet couldn't answer. She didn't know how she felt. She wanted to stay on amber.

'I didn't tell you who we got for Christmas Eve, did I?'

'Who you got Harriet? What do you mean?'

'We've got Rapping Hammer for the opening of the coffee shop at Starboard Marine North West, Mark. That should draw the crowds.'

'The wrong kind I would think. Wasn't he the twerp that got done for drugs?'

'I didn't know that Mark. He's going to be Father Christmas. Oh golly I hope he's not high on Christmas Eve.'

'I should think he'd save the hard stuff for when he gets home. He'll probably have a joint or two while he's fishing in the sack. Good grief Harriet. He's not exactly your first choice when it comes to being Father Christmas. What were you thinking of?'

'A joint?' Harriet panicked, suddenly she could hear Guy's words, ' "… 'e 'asn't 'ad chance to get to the *joint* yet. If you see what I mean?" '

'You'll have to watch he doesn't start giving them out to the kids Harriet.'

'Giving what out Mark? Joints? What are they anyway?'

'Marijuana cigarettes. If you want the exact definition. Well slang for.'

'I can't deal with this Mark. Surely he's not going to be doing drugs with children around? I wish you hadn't told me.'

'Face facts Harriet. Ow! What was that?' He delved under the duvet and instantly produced a sharp pointed pine needle.

'Serves you right Mark!'

'Thanks Harriet. I've got to drive today. I don't wish to be stabbed by these things all the way there.'

'All the way where Mark? You didn't say.'

'Only over to Newcastle. She's docked there. I volunteered to pick up some equipment for them.'

'I hope you're referring to a ship Mark and not Melissa Rogers?'

'She's returned to the use of her maiden name Harriet and no as far as I know she's not involved. I'll call you before I leave if I get a chance. In any case I'll be back before nine.'

This was all too much. Harriet felt decidedly nauseous.

Chapter 30

Feeling very sick Harriet closed the front door and waved him off from the hall window. She struggled past the tree, anxious not to attract any more of its sharp green spikes to her nightdress. She hovered on the bottom stair, then decided against playing the message back.

'No not. Not just yet, anyway. It's probably green Melissa. Making me feel ill. And *him*. Making me feel ill. I just need to go back to bed.'

Her legs refused to support her churning stomach any longer. It was beginning to cramp with anxiety. She looked at the clock. Then at the bed. Then remembered the carol concert.

'Better get going or I'll be late.'

No response. Harriet couldn't talk herself into getting ready for school. The bed won. She curled up in the duvet. 'No. No. It's not anxiety. It's morning sickness. Definitely. Most definitely. I'm pregnant. Most definitely pregnant. I'll be leaving anyway. It's all those maternal instincts kicking in. *He's* not in anyway. I'll phone in. Now.' Immediately she translated her thoughts into action.

'Sorry Amanda. I don't think I've got over that bug yet.'

'I'd give yourself the weekend Harriet. I wouldn't think of coming in before Monday.'

'Feel a bit bad Amanda. There's the Christmas party and the carol concert.'

'You can't do it if you're not well Harriet. You need to get over it. You don't want it to spoil your Christmas. Joris isn't in for the next couple of days. He won't mind me getting a supply in.'

'Thanks Amanda. I appreciate that.'

Harriet replaced the receiver. Every nerve ending in her body was telling her she was pregnant. Every thinking, conscious brain cell was telling her she wasn't.

'Why can't I just stay on amber?'

The tension between the two states of mind was starting to take its toll.

'Why can't I just get that man out of my mind? Out of my life? Mark's finally won out over his phobia. For me. Or Melissa Rogers? Perhaps? No Harriet. Silly thought. Don't go there.'

She'd been tossing it all around for twenty minutes, or more. Then jumped from under the duvet as the phone rang. She was grateful for the distraction.

'Not well again Miss Glover? I've just been down there. Amanda was organising a supply.'

'No. Not. Er. Not very well Mr. Sanderson. Terribly sorry. Just feeling so sick.'

'Have you seen the doctor yet Miss Glover?'

'No. No I haven't. Not yet.'

'Let me in will you Miss Glover. I'm sitting outside.'

Harriet could feel her heart pounding. Her knees went weak as she got out of bed. The doorbell rang as she parted the bedroom curtains to see his car.

'He's not supposed to be in school. This isn't school. Oh flip!'

148

She scrambled for her dressing gown and stumbled past the Christmas tree to open the door.

'Right Miss Glover. Let's get this thing sorted once and for all shall we? That's why I'm here.'

He ushered her into the lounge. Sat her down. Then paced to the window and back. He stood. Watching her. Arm across her middle. Clasping her hand to her side. The colour draining from her face.

'I trust you will forgive this intervention Miss Glover, er Harriet.'

Harriet looked up pulling the gaping edges of her dressing gown together.

'Whilst I acknowlege it's not necessarily my place to insist on a diagnosis Miss Glover, it concerns me greatly that you do seem intent on side-stepping the issue completely.'

Harriet swallowed hard.

'Your symptoms could be indicative of other conditions Miss Glover and this is something that should be ruled in or out. As the case may be. Right now!'

'What do you mean Mr. Sanderson?'

She watched him standing tall. Serious. So very serious, as his hand reached to the inside pocket of his jacket.

'Use this will you? If you don't mind I'll wait here. I'm not leaving without a result.'

Harriet stunned looked down at the testing kit now in her hand.

'You know Miss Glover there's a certain flippancy about you which overrides your common sense. You look anything but well. Unlike you I find myself unable to switch off my feelings. My feelings of concern, Miss Glover. Now this shouldn't take a couple of minutes.'

He sat down. Harriet, shaking, went upstairs.

'It's now been ten minutes Miss Glover. Are you alright?'

She came down the stairs, struggling past the Christmas tree. She met him in the lounge doorway. Then sank into the sofa stretching across to hand it back.

'But you haven't used it Miss Glover. Come. Come now. You've got to know sooner or later. It might just as well be now.'

'No Mr. Sanderson. No.'

She bent forward clasping her hand to her stomach.

'Your period's started?'

Harriet nodded.

'Come, Harriet. Let's get you back to bed.'

Harriet lay down, her head deep into the pillow. He was standing over her. She looked at his face. Set. Deeply serious. Deeply concerned. She could feel her eyes filling. She looked away.

'Mark. Can I get hold of him. What's his number Harriet?'

'He's well on his way to Newcastle Mr. Sanderson. There's no need anyway. I'll be alright. It's just a period. Bound to be difficult with it being so late.'

'You're probably right Harriet with the sudden onset, but we can't rule out a miscarriage entirely. Very early stage. I think we can rule out a D&C.'

'What's that,' Harriet panicked, 'no I'm not going to hospital. No I'm not.'

'Dilation and Curettage. Sorry Harriet. Just thinking aloud. No. No I'm sure there won't be any need. Anyhow it might not even be a miscarriage.'

She buried her head in the duvet to soak away her tears. She felt him reach for her hand. He clasped it as he sat on the edge of the mattress.

'Look Harriet. I'm going to phone your GP. Who will it be? Mike Holden? Dr. Holden?'

'Yes Mr. Sanderson, but they don't come out anymore.'

'Oh he won't mind Harriet. I know Mike very well. It's not going to set him back more than half an hour.'

Harriet listened as he spoke. Charming. Compelling. Commanding. She nudged under her pillow and filled her hand with tissues.

'He'll be out just before one. Earlier if he can manage it.'

'Thank you Mr. Sanderson. He won't send me to hospital will he?'

'No Harriet. He'll just check you out. Now there really isn't any need to hide from me. Do come out from under there.'

He pulled the duvet back a little then gently turned her face towards him.

'Oh dear me Harriet. Really no need for tears. Come now.'

He shifted himself down along the edge of the bed. She felt his arm around her shoulders. Her head rested against his suit jacket as he held her sobbing against his chest.

'Now Harriet. There's really no need for all this.'

She looked up along the line of his tie, neatly knotted. The sharp points of his pristine white collar, either side.

'Your shirt's wet. I'm terribly sorry Mr. Sanderson.'

'How's it feeling now?'

'Not so cramped, thank you.' Her words were muffled in soggy tissues.

'Good. Jolly good. I'll get my stuff out of the car. There's things I can be attending to whilst I'm here.'

'While you're here? You're not staying are you Mr. Sanderson?'

'Well I'm certainly not going to leave you like this.'

He allowed her to ease back as he placed his hand on her forehead, brushing away her hair.

'I'm so sorry about all this Mr. Sanderson.' She knew she was blushing.

'There's really no need for embarrassment Harriet. This isn't new to me you know. I'll be in the lounge if you need me.'

She watched him walk out. For a second she lay back on the pillow. Overwhelmed.

'The hassle I give him yet he's still so, so kind.'

The thought was overwhelming. Overwhelming her fear. She lay very still, all she wanted was, yet again, to stay on amber.

* * *

'Still asleep Mike.'

Harriet awoke with a start.

'Good afternoon Miss Glover. Now let's see what we can do for you?'

'Thanks Mike. I'll catch you on your way out.'

Mr. Sanderson disappeared.

'Can't be a hundred percent certain but it's looking like a late period. Could even be the onset of the menopause. Things can start to get a bit erratic at your age, you know. Stay in bed. See how it goes. Give it forty eight hours unless it becomes excessive. In which case call an ambulance.'

Harriet panicked.

'Don't worry. It's not that likely. I shouldn't think so, anyway.'

She felt a tiny bit better.

'You've definitely got a virus Miss Glover. "Nausea and stomach cramps" you say? It's going round. You've a temperature. Just some paracetamol. You won't feel much like coping with a class of children for a few days.' He tore a note from his pad. 'You can self-certify this if you like.'

'Thank you very much indeed Dr. Holden. Thank you for coming out.'

'Don't worry about it. You'll be fine. In any case all thanks to Joris Sanderson, Miss Glover.'

He left. Harriet could just hear the low exchange of conversation as Mr. Sanderson saw him out.

'Now, it wasn't that bad was it Harriet? How are you feeling now?'

'Very relieved thank you Mr. Sanderson. Dr. Holden says I've got a virus. Does that make it less likely to be a miscarriage?'

'Possibly. You know Harriet you really shouldn't be playing around with this pregnancy thing. If you seriously want a baby, then between you, you should both commit to it. I suspect you do and you don't, but there's no going back once you conceive. As I've said, at your age the sooner you partake of antenatal care the better. Your total lack of responsibility towards diagnosis, not to mention anything else suggests you're game playing. It's a very dangerous thing to do Harriet.'

She watched him walk to the window. He put both hands in his trouser pockets and turned to face her.

'It's bad enough game playing with me Harriet. I didn't give you that ring lightly, you know. You're unmarried. Therefore as far as I was concerned available. You would agree?'

She watched him take his right hand from his pocket to stroke his chin. His presence filled the whole room. This gorgeous, gorgeous man. So serious. So very, very serious. Stern in his postulation. Reading her with precision. Penetrating her every thought. Exposing her in naked reality.

'Was it too much to ask you to wait?'

Eternity crossed her mind.

'Belinda Oxfordshire. There's her. Mark. There's him. How can I let him down?'

She remained silent. Kept her thoughts to herself.

'Not pregnant. Might not ever have been.'

She let the full flood of relief surge through her anguished body. She knew she'd wait forever for him. If only she could.

'Just ask me. Ask me now. Ask me to marry you now.'

She blew her nose as she felt her eyes brimming again. 'No. You're not going to. Of course you're not going to.' She swallowed very hard on her thoughts.

'What do these tears and such silence suggest Harriet?'

'Just thinking Mr. Sanderson.'

'Just thinking Harriet? Thinking what?'

'Just thinking. I won't need that testing kit now, but thank you. So much.'

'It's on the coffee table in the lounge Harriet. I suggest you keep it but I sincerely hope you won't be needing to use it. I am asking you *not* to put us through this experience again. For heaven's sake don't go in for unprotected sex unless you're absolutely certain which way you want your life to go. Understand?'

Harriet sank further under the duvet.

'Understand.'

'I hope you do Miss Glover. Now lunch. Got a larder to raid Harriet?'

She nodded.

'Am I likely to find any clear soup?'

'In the fridge next to the milk. Help yourself to anything you like.'

'Thank you Harriet. Can you manage a little?'

She nodded. For for the first time she caught just a hint of a smile overtaking those serious blue eyes.

She lay looking at the ceiling, listening to him going down the stairs. She felt strangely euphoric. She thought of the field of flowers. How he'd taken the fullness of her breast into his hand. His lips gently against her. Kissing her. How so very much she wanted him. Was so ready for him. How easily he could have made her pregnant. If he hadn't held back.

'I'll always love him. I know I'm marrying Mark but I'll always love *him*. I'll never give up work while *he's* there. I've *got* to be able to see him.'

'That damned cat Harriet. It's been shuffling round my legs meowing at me. Where's its food. Do you know?'

Jolted from her thoughts she smiled as he put the tray down. He propped her up against her pillow as he reached for Mark's, then rested the tray on the duvet across her lap.

'Thank you so much Mr. Sanderson. I think you've been so very kind.'

He touched her shoulder and smiled.

'The cat food Harriet?'

'Oh sorry. It's in the packet by the kettle.'

The bowl of soup jumped with Harriet as the phone rang.

'I'll take that.' He lifted the receiver.

'Oh you're there Harriet. Mummy here.' He opened it out in his hand for her to hear.

'Only I tried yesterday Harriet and no answer. I left a message and you haven't returned it. Is anything the matter Harriet? You're not getting yourself into trouble again with that common girl are you?'

'Not just at this moment she isn't Mrs. Glover. I've no doubt whatsoever that will come.'

'Oh. Oh. And which gentleman am I speaking with?'

'Joris Sanderson Mrs. Glover.'

'Oh. Congratulations on your forthcoming knighthood, by the way. Unfortunately I really didn't get the opportunity to speak with you for very long at the wedding. You seemed to be moving around everybody. Each time I attempted to come over you were with somebody else. Anyway it's very nice to have this opportunity now. You must forgive Harriet's behaviour Mr. Sanderson. Of course if that Bohemian boyfriend of hers had married her it would never have happened. Two daughters out of wedlock Mr. Sanderson. Two of *my* granddaughters. Thank goodness he had the same surname. His only redeeming feature and he wasn't even responsible for that. It was the only way I've been able to keep it quiet from my friends at the W.I. for all these years. Until the wedding of course. Now they all know. My word, it soon gets round. They abandon all morals Mr. Sanderson but they don't think of the effect their behaviour has on the rest of us.'

'Quite Mrs. Glover. I can see exactly where you're coming from.'

'You know I said exactly that to Harriet's daddy. I said I'm sure Mr. Sanderson can't approve of those kind of morals. It must be quite difficult for you at school. Children need example. Good example. Anyway we're hoping Daddy and I that having been away for so long he might just do the decent thing and marry her.'

'Quite Mrs. Glover. Now would you like me to pass you over to Harriet?'

He watched her slip herself away from her soup to disappear from the bedroom.

'Yes please if you would be so kind.'

'Oh I'm afraid she's not anywhere to be seen just now. Gone to the bathroom I expect. Look Mrs. Glover I'm afraid Harriet isn't too well. She needed someone to be with her this morning. That's why I'm here.'

'How very kind Mr. Sanderson. Do you know what's the matter with her?'

'Not entirely. She's certainly got a virus. I organized Dr. Holden to visit her. Anyhow she'll explain everything, I'm sure. She's not going to be too long.'

'I feel there's more to it than that. The fact that you are there. I'm on my way Mr. Sanderson. I'll get her daddy to drop me off as soon as he comes in. It'll be within the hour. Can you wait with her that long? You are so kind.'

'Not a problem Mrs. Glover. It's a pleasure to be of help.'

'Well I can assure you it's very much appreciated. I can't think what that good-for-nothing hippie's playing at. Has she tried to phone him?'

'Unfortunately he's in Newcastle today, Mrs. Glover.'

'Typical. Good afternoon Mr. Sanderson. I'll see you shortly.'

Harriet crept round the door as Mr. Sanderson put the phone down. She could see he was laughing.

'She's coming round. Isn't she?'

'Get in and get this before it goes cold.'

'Isn't she?'

'She is. By the kettle did you say?'

Harriet heard him go down.

'NO. NO. NO. Mummy. I don't *want* you round. Things were perfect just the way they were.'

She lay for fifteen minutes in a complete pelt with her mother. Then she heard his footsteps coming up the stairs.

'Right Harriet. Fought off the Christmas tree. Fed the cat. Washed the dog. Let the budgie out. Washed up last night's dishes.'

'Oh you didn't Mr. Sanderson?' Harriet was mortified.

'You're too right I didn't Harriet. I'm sure your mother will enjoy doing those. As well as tidying up, washing the floor, doing the ironing.' He was laughing. 'Wise woman your mother, Harriet. I think she's quite taken to me.'

He looked at his watch.

'Is it easing up at all?'

'Yes thank you Mr. Sanderson.'

'I think you'll be alright Harriet. Stay there for the rest of the day. We finish on Tuesday, don't we? So that's you finished until we go back in January.'

His back was against the window. The afternoon sun had finally eased its way round to outline his tall, solid frame. The curl resting on his collar shone defiantly at the rest of his straight layers of thick blonde hair. She watched the sunlight bounce off his gold cufflink as he lifted his hand to his mouth before putting both hands back in his pockets. Harriet's eyes were drawn to her tear stains on his otherwise faultless white shirt.

'Hopefully we'll see you on Christmas Eve at Starboard Marine North West?' He looked at his watch again. 'Yes. That'll be a week tomorrow.' He frowned momentarily. Then looked up and across at her from under his eyebrows. 'Another unknown quantity. If you're feeling better tomorrow you might see your way to getting this celebrity thing sorted out. Hmm?'

'I've sorted it Mr. Sanderson. I've already sorted it. It's all fixed.'

'Oh yes. And who have we got?'

'Rapping Hammer and the Ironing Bards,' Mr. Sanderson.

'Oh no! Crikey! That's all I damned well need.'

'I think that was the doorbell Mr. Sanderson.'

'Right I'll let her in on the way out.'

Suddenly he was gone. Then he was back again. He passed her the testing kit.

'Keep it under your pillow Harriet. In case you need a reminder.'
She tucked it away as the doorbell rang again.
'Right I'm off. Better still. Just lay off sex for a while. Will you?'

* * *

'Harriet how are you dear? I only wanted one spring planter for Christmas, you know. Not eight!'

Chapter 31

'It's Saturday Hat. Are you sure you're feeling up to the viewing this morning?'

'Well. If you wouldn't mind Mark. Would you mind going on your own and then if you like it we can make an appointment for a second one after Christmas? Together.'

'Sounds OK to me Hat. You've got a bit more colour but it's probably a better idea to rest. I can't get over your timing Hat. Trust you to wait until I'm on the road. Just as well your mother was able to get round. Was that her who left the message by the way? I forgot to ask.'

'It was. She did go on about me not phoning back.'

'Well I've got no complaints in the food line Hat. She's a better cook than you.'

'Oh thanks Mark. Don't let your stomach get the better of you. You might just end up liking her.'

'Awesome mother-in-law, though Harriet. Not auctionable online. Apparently Geoffrey reckoned he'd get well past the reserve for his.'

'Oh so she's been trying to sell you her mother has she?'

'Together with her horses and camels Hat.'

'Well that wouldn't surprise me either. Greener than a frog with those little bulging eyes, chubby jowls and big flat feet. I don't know what you see in her Mark?'

'Chameleon Hat. She's a sexy chameleon with a lovely mummy.'

'You'd better be joking Mark.'

'Daft bat Hat. Now your mother. That's a different matter. I'm definitely not looking forward to that legal entanglement on the 26th June.'

'Are you looking forward to the rest of it then?'

'Of course I am Harriet. I wouldn't have asked you if I hadn't meant it.'

He stretched over to give her a kiss.

'I really thought we'd scored the bull's-eye this time Harriet. Still, once you're over this, plenty more evenings to come. On the rug?'

'Not, Mark, most definitely not.' Harriet was feeling distinctly annoyed.

'What do you mean Hat? Not?'

'Exactly that Mark. We'll save it for once we're married. We'll keep it something really special to look forward to.'

'Harriet. It's six months away. You've got to be joking!'

'Not joking Mark. I haven't particularly enjoyed these last few days.'

'Well that's understandable Hat, but don't let it send you over the top.'

'It's not over the top Mark. It's just about the right time to do it. Once we're married. To try for a baby, I mean. It's something we should think about, together. Take joint responsibility for. Plan it properly.'

'I wasn't wrong. It's your mother again. Isn't it Harriet? She's been putting her oar in.'

'No. That's unfair Mark. She hasn't said anything. I just want to act more responsibly for a change.'

'Well act responsibly and go on the pill until then Harriet. I don't know why you suddenly want to deprive me of my birthright. You can be such a misery when you like.'

'Birthright Mark? After all these years not being married? I don't believe I'm hearing it.'

Mark grinned.

'Soon to be addressed Hat. If you don't want to risk getting pregnant six months on the pill won't do you any harm.'

'I'll think about it. And I want that Christmas tree up when you come back. Decorated.'

'Bloody hell Harriet. You're going more like your mother every day. What does a chap have to do to melt his ice maiden?'

'Which one are you talking about Mark. The one that hopped out of the frog mould?'

'Right Harriet. I'm going. Should be back before eleven.'

Harriet sat on the sofa with her carrier bag of wool at her feet. The cat sniffed into the neatly wound balls.

'Now guess who's not going to get this one, Pepper?'

Chapter 32

The next few days saw Harriet feeling so very much better. She'd got Mark to post all the Christmas cards on his way to work.

'Everyone'll understand if I don't wrap the planters,' she thought after she'd finished wrapping everything else.

She liked the feeling of being in control. She looked at the packet Mark had collected from the pharmacy. She'd asked Dr. Holden for 'the pill' after all. As Mark had made her go back for a check-up anyway. She didn't see the harm really.

'It's going to be a bit hard on him this abstinence thing. No. Definitely not fair on Mark. No phone calls. *He* hasn't rung. *He* might be a qualified GP but it doesn't give him the right to dictate what we do. When we're together. On our own. I bet *he's* not abstaining. He really can be very bossy.'

She suddenly recalled Mrs. Harris trawling through so many girl's names in an attempt to identify Belinda Oxfordshire. 'I bet he's done it with *her*. I just bet he has. And the rest.' The thought suddenly filled her with unrelenting jealousy.

'Right that sweater's going to be for Mark.'

She went into the lounge and started knitting as furiously as her thinking.

'That was a very embarrassing experience. With him. Too, too personal. Too intimate. What's he waiting for anyway? How could he be so involved, like that, and it never crossed his mind to ask me to marry him? I could have said "No Mr. Sanderson. Belinda Oxfordshire's threatened to take me to court if I say yes." And he could have said "What nonsense Harriet," and then he could have persuaded me to marry him. What about all those very important posh people that come with him though? No, no Harriet. That's exactly why he won't commit. Definitely wouldn't fit in. That's why I haven't heard from him since. Could have phoned to see how I was.'

Her needles slowed as the questions barely formed, negated in the face of the answers.

'Knit one. Purl one. Knit one. Drop one. Oh sod I've gone wrong. It's turning into moss stitch. He won't notice. Mark won't notice. It was never going to be for *him* anyway. That house sounds really nice. Look forward to seeing it after Christmas. Might not need the nursery though. Well not just yet. I wonder if I *was* pregnant? Amber please. I don't want to know. Far too young for the menopause. That's a fact. I do wish people would stop saying that. I did feel sick. Virus Harriet, virus. We'll try again. On the rug. On our rug. I'll never lie on *his*. Must have a baby before it's too late. Now where was I? K1, P1, K1. Ooh why is knitting so boring?'

She flung it down as the phone rang. Never so pleased to escape from the task in hand.

'Oh hello Amanda. It's nice to hear from you.'

'Feeling any better Harriet?'

'Oh yes much better, thank you.'

'That's good Harriet. Joris asked me to phone to see how you are? Should have done it yesterday actually but it's been manic here. End of term and everything.'

'I know what you mean Amanda. Don't worry about it. My class get on alright with the carols and the Christmas party?'

'Yes no problems at all Harriet. I managed to get hold of Lucinda Lawton again. Remember? She was in the other week covering for Enid.'

'Oh yes, I remember her.'

'Well you couldn't forget her easily Harriet. Could you? She's so pretty with legs to die for. I wish I looked like that Harriet. Between you and me I've seen old Joris giving her the eye once or twice.'

'Really? That's very sweet Amanda. Anyway thank you so much for phoning. I'll see you when we start back. Have a lovely Christmas with your family.'

'Thanks Harriet. Same to you. Oh by the way my job's come up on the bulletin. I'll pop an application form in the post. Joris said for you to just sign it and send it back. It's just a formality.' Harriet thanked her. Put the phone down.

'Not interested! I'm in recovery and I've got to cope with that. Bloody Lucinda Lawton now. That's why he hasn't phoned. Well he needn't bloody well bother. Ever. Boy did I make the right decision to marry Mark. I am not. Repeat NOT going to be dangled any more. Decision made.'

She picked up the phone. She needed to get those wedding arrangements sorted.

Chapter 33

It was Christmas Eve.

'Thanks for putting the tree up Mark. The place looks really nice. We'll enjoy Christmas together, especially after you having been away for so long.'

'Not if you're going to deprive me of my marital rights Harriet. I did pick up that prescription.'

'Yes Mark but I haven't decided yet. Anyway we're not quite there yet. Not marital rights just yet. June the 26th I believe.'

'Oh well done Hat. When did you get that booked?'

'Oh yesterday morning just after Amanda Woods phoned. I was too tired to tell you last night.'

'Reception as well? Did you manage to get anywhere decent?'

'I did. We're going to The Gerald Roper Hotel.'

'Wow Harriet. A bit pricey?'

'We're worth it Mark. I've waited a long time for this and I want it to be right.'

'Harriet you'll be in for a bitter disappointment if I've got to wait until June. Don't forget I'll be away for a month before then anyway. I'll have lost it Harriet. I'll have forgotten how to do it. Or I'll remember and won't be able to do it. No baby then Harriet?'

'I'm thinking about it Mark. It depends what you get me for Christmas.'

'The bigger the better you mean Hat?' Mark was grinning.

'I'll be a bit late tonight Hat. Need to get to the shops. Just a bit of extra shopping Hat. If I can get parked.'

'Well I'm down at Starboard Marine North West all day anyway. *Him* and his flipping coffee shop. What a day to decide to have the opening.'

'No brain. All lard.'

'I couldn't agree more.'

'Now that makes a nice change Hat. Make sure you don't overdo it down there. See you later.'

He kissed her cheek then bent down to pick up the post. Passed her a long white envelope.

'Ah, Amanda said she'd post this. Hang on a minute Mark, just let me get a pen. Thanks Mark. No need for a stamp. Pop it in the box will you please?'

'What is it?'

'Just a formality. Deputy job. We'll need the money if we're going for that house.'

'Not too sure about that Hat.'

A hand reappeared round the open door. It was the post man back again. Harriet grabbed her purse.

'Oh, thank you very much,' declared Mark. 'Hang on a sec. She's just coming.'

'For you. Have a lovely Christmas,' she smiled.

The postman waved the tenner at her as he went down the path.

'Even more cards Hat. You'll get mine tonight. Thought I'd forgotten?'

'Hoped you'd forgotten Mark. Anyway I'm in denial.'

'Daft Bat Hat. Happy Birthday!'

Harriet sighed. The kiss she blew him from the hall window barely left her hand as the phone rang.

'Mum. We're on our way. We're all coming up in Tristan's car. Can't wait to see you and Dad. Wow fancy us staying in the Tideside Hotel. You didn't mind did you? It will save you and Dad a lot of work.'

'No of course not Clare. It's worked out really well. Look. You have a good journey and phone us early this evening. Your Dad's at work and I'm tied up with the opening of the coffee shop at Starboard Marine North West. I didn't tell you did I? We've managed to get Rapping Hammer and his gang to open it.'

'Never? You never have? Well done you! Wait until I tell Rachael. The boys wanted to come via Bristol for some reason, so we'll be late. There's something on there. See if we can talk them out of it. Might get to see them. Not every day you get the chance to get so close to Rapping Hammer. Hope to see you down there Mum.'

'I hope so Clare. Anyway love to Rachael and the boys. Safe journey.'

'Will do. Bye Mum.'

She'd barely replaced the receiver when it rang again.

'Oh `ello `arriet. I `aven't phoned because Joris said you `aven't been well `arriet and I didn't want to disturb you. `e seemed very concerned `arriet. Anyway are you feelin` better now?'

'Yes thank you Tricia. I'm fine. Just a virus really.'

'Oh I am pleased to `ear that `arriet. Good, so you'll still be comin` I `ope?'

'Almost ready to go Tricia.'

'I thought I'd just tell you `arriet. `as you did all the work gettin` Rappin` `ammer and all that I felt as though I `adn't `ardly done anythin` so I got this kids' Christmas party together `arriet. Not much. Just a few sandwiches and crisps, cake and jellies. That sort of thing `arriet. Oh and some lemonade. I was wonderin` if you `ad any paper plates `arriet. I thought you might `ave got some for your party at school?'

'Oh yes Tricia. I've got a stack here. I'll bring them with me.'

'Thanks `arriet. That's lovely. I've got the plastic beakers and spoons for the jelly. Ooh `ave you got any serviettes `arriet? I forgot about those.'

'No sorry Tricia. No I haven't.'

'Never mind `arriet I'll bring some rolls of kitchen paper I got from Bargains `ome. That'll do `arriet. Oh `arriet `ave you `ad any thought on `ow we're goin` to tell `im about `im `avin` to pay all that money to the band?'

'No Tricia. I think we probably don't. We'll let them ask for it. He can hardly blow a fuse at them. Can he?'

'Ooh I don't know 'arriet. 'e's been a bit snappy round 'ere over the last few days. To be 'onest 'arriet I wish 'e wasn't comin`.'

'Oh don't say that Tricia. If Wayne Hammer doesn't get to see him he'll have to pay his fee as well. We'll have cleaned *him* out of about thirteen or fourteen thousand.'

'Oooh 'arriet. I think we're best keeping` our 'eads down if we can. Do you reckon we might be able to do a runner like we did from the grand openin` `arriet?'

'Don't go there Tricia, I'm struggling with going as it is.'

'We'll stick together 'arriet. 'e's very lucky to 'ave us. I bet that Rappin` 'ammer'll make 'im a fortune. 'e's more than lucky 'arriet. 'e's bloody lucky.'

'You're absolutely right Tricia. I'll see you down there in about quarter of an hour.'

'Why don't I pick you up 'arriet? You can give me an 'and with the jellies. I'll be right with you.'

'Oh, thanks Tricia. I'll look out for you. Don't bother getting out of the car.'

Chapter 34

'`ave you closed that door properly `arriet. I don't want you fallin` out?'

'No. Yes. Yes that's all right now, thanks Tricia.'

'We're stickin` together `arriet. I don't know why we're so scared of `im. Well I `ave tried to work it out. I think it's because `e's so important `arriet. `e mixes with people of power. If you see what I'm gettin` at. Take the likes of the Prime Minister `arriet. Fancy `avin` `im round for dinner? `e's `ob-nobbin` with them that `ave to make all those world decisions `arriet. I mean the Prime Minister `arriet. Well `e as to go to America and important places like that, doesn't `e? Then `e `as to meet their leaders. Imagine meetin` the President, `arriet. There's no one more important than `im in the world. Or better lookin` `arriet. I'm always lookin` out for `im on the news. Wouldn't you say so `arriet?'

'You know Tricia, you could just be right. He's got a lot more than good looks though. Can you imagine anyone having the steel for that job?'

'Oh no `arriet. I can't. We might be scared of `im `arriet but I don't think our friend Joris Sanderson could do it. I wonder if the President would ever turn up for dinner at `is `ouse, though? Do you think our PM might just take `im along? I wouldn't mind offerin` my `ostessin` services on that night `arriet. I could give them all `aggis. I'm used to doin` that.'

Harriet smiled.

'I'd love to know what our friend Joris's `ouse is like, though `arriet. It would `ave to be very posh, I would say, for all that entertainin`. I wouldn't mind seein` that. I bet that's not your average semi on the main road.'

'It certainly isn't Tricia.'

'Ooh what `ave you slowed down for you stupid man? I very nearly went up your bum then. Sorry `arriet. What were you sayin`?'

'Mr. Sanderson's house Tricia. That time I had to give him a lift. It's really something else. Now that would frighten you being in there. That really made me realise just how high up the social ladder he is.'

'Umm. `e talks posh too. Doesn't `e `arriet? Just like the Royal Family really. Like anyone of them I tried to get for this bloody openin`.'

'I know Tricia. Same as Belinda Oxfordshire. Makes you scared to open your mouth.'

'You can say that again `arriet. I've tried copyin` `er but it didn't work `arriet. She sort of sneered a smile at me so I went back to droppin` my aitches.'

'I wouldn't have bothered Tricia.'

'No. You're right `arriet. And another thing `arriet, `ow come `e's so rich? You've got to `ave plenty of money to live in a big `ouse like you say `e does. And that car of `is. Bob's really jealous. `e says it must `ave cost `im the thick end of a `undred thousand pounds `arriet. And `ave you seen `is watch? They don't come cheap either. Unless `e's been sold a fake. We must `ave been right `arriet. `e's gettin` all that money from somewhere. And what about `is stacks of cash? I bet that suitcase was full of it `arriet. I never did find out what I'd been carryin` over for `im. "Little star" `arriet. I was supposed to be `is little star. If you ask me `arriet `e's more than likely got millions of them twinklin` away just waitin` for `im to call `arriet. I'm nothin` more than a tiny grain of sand in `is life. Oh `arriet do you think those lights'll stay on green if I `urry up? I've been talkin` so much I didn't realise we were `ere. Anyway `arriet, to use my metathingy again. You've got to admit `arriet I could win a prize for my metathingies now, I'm gettin` really good at them. Where was I? Oh yes. Even if it costs `im fourteen thousand `arriet, to `im it will be like fourteen grains of sand from a mile long beach. `e'd never miss it.'

'Brilliant Tricia. That really puts it into perspective. No we're definitely not scared of *him*.'

Chapter 35

'Oh look `arriet. `is car's already there. I'll just go the other end I think. Right. If you don't mind openin` the back door `arriet and gettin` the jellies out, I'll go round the other side for the carrier bags.'

'Ah. Good morning ladies. All fit and well are we?'

'Yes thank you Mr. Sanderson,' they chorused.

Harriet looked down, determined not to catch his eye.

'Oh Miss Glover. There's a carrier bag down there. Your things from Molly. She sends her best. Over today as a matter of fact. House hunting. I invited them along. Said they'd call by to say hello.'

'Oh thank you Mr. Sanderson. I'll look forward to that. Must keep an eye open for them.'

She looked up, sensing he'd moved along. She could hear Belinda Oxfordshire by the door, over-greeting him.

'Did you see `er `arriet? She's just clacked `er way in on those `igh `eels. I think they're glued to `er feet `arriet. She looks just like an upside down cactus in those tight jeans, I would say. She's certainly got the prickles `arriet. She `asn't even given us a glance. I've pushed those tables together for the party food. I don't think we've got room to sit all the children down `arriet so we'll let them `elp themselves. It'll be alright if we keep an eye on it.'

'Right Tricia. So we start putting this lot out?'

'Yes please `arriet. Look `arriet do you like the grotto? If you look out of that back window you can just see it behind that bit of old wall.'

'Oh. A tent. What a good idea Tricia.'

'Well I thought if I covered it in a white sheet and stapled rolls of cotton wool round the doorway the kids would think it was Lapland. The balloons are blowin` a bit but they'll be alright. Plenty left in `ere if they blow away, anyway.'

Harriet looked round the room.

'Gosh Tricia. It must have taken you hours blowing that lot up. With all this red and green the place looks really festive.'

'Ah thanks `arriet. Talkin` about red and green, you `aven't seen anythin` yet.'

She dived under the table to surface with a jangling bag, spilling out elf costumes. Just waiting their opportunity.

'I `ad such a good idea `arriet. We `ave to make them work for their money those Ironing Bards. Don't we? And we don't exactly want them under our feet all day do we? So they can be Santa's elves. Or they don't get paid `arriet. That's what we'll tell them anyway. So `arriet it's all going to look even more Christmassy. Which reminds me.'

Harriet laughed as Tricia rooted in her bag. A twig of holly appeared.

'I wonder if this'll stay put in my `air with this clip?'

Harriet followed her out to stand behind the one-way mirror. Tricia peered into the tiny square bit stuck to the bottom, now reflecting her ever widening lips.

'I stuck this on 'ere 'arriet. Well you 'ave to do your lipstick when you 'ear the door go 'arriet. Don't you? There that'll do. Red lipstick to match. 'olly Berry. I've got to 'ave my five minutes of fame. I'm entitled 'arriet.'

'Oh look! They've arrived Tricia.'

The reception area of Starboard Marine North West went into shadow as the huge pantechnicon rolled up.

'Bloody 'ell 'arriet. Will that be them? They didn't 'ave to come in that bloody big thing. Did they? They're only goin' to be outside in the grotto. Not exactly doin' a gig. Surely not 'arriet?'

'Surely not Mrs. Harrington?'

Mr. Sanderson walked on and out to greet them.

'I think we'd better follow him Tricia. We don't want him sending them away.'

'Right there Gov?'

A thin tall wiry chap painted in black leather leapt down from the driving seat. He thrust a tattooed hand at Mr. Sanderson while Harriet counted the gold rings pierced in along each of his eyebrows. Curtain rings came to mind. His bright orange and purple nylon sheath sat criss-crossed on his chest while the tail ends flapped in the wind.

'No those eyebrows would not, could not have taken any more.'

The rest were stacked knuckle high on each finger. She watched the wind catching at his hair. First lifting the thin, long greasy streaks into tramlines above his head, then blowing round to catch his mouth as he spoke.

'You? You actually that Sanderson dude? Fastnet and all that? Cool guy. Fill me in Gov.'

'I beg your pardon?'

Harriet and Tricia looked at each other. Breathing in hard to try to stifle the giggles.

'Rock man rock.' He started prancing about. Then disappeared behind the van to let the other five out.'

'Miss Glover. Mrs. Harrington. This is *not* the kind of publicity I had in mind.'

'Rapping Hammer.' His hand stretched out again.

'Er quite. Joris Sanderson. Pleased to meet you.' He weighed the others up. 'All of you. In fact.'

'They just look as though they've struggled their way out of some thick primeval sludge,' Harriet decided to herself.

Up went their flattened hands against the breeze before waving them swiftly from left to right. Rox suddenly positioned Mr. Sanderson's hand for a high five slap. 1.2.3.4.5! He'd barely time to pull away. The five of them rubbed at their hands, grinning.

'That's cool man. Cool. You've loaded that one now. Try it on `er.'

Harriet was suddenly being pointed at.

'Hmm. I rather think not. Now I'll pass you over to Miss Glover. With Mrs. Harrington's assistance they'll be completely responsible for directing your time here.'

'Directing our time here?'

They all looked at each other.

'Rock man rock. We don't do anything unless we swing. Get the matchbox unloaded guys. Yah. Yah. Yah. It's Christmas Eve. Rock to the rhythm. Rock to the beat. Rock. Rock. Rock. Get rockin` them feet.'

'Hmm. Right I'll leave you to it.'

Harriet and Tricia watched Mr. Sanderson march back in.

'That guy sucks Rapping. He never did that Fastnet trip? You scooped the wrong babe man!'

'He did. I can assure you he did,' cut in Harriet. 'I know he'll be more than happy to speak to you later.'

'Cool dig Mama.'

Harriet stiffened. 'Bloody cheek,' she thought. 'So I now look like a menopausal mama.' She was beginning to regret getting involved with Guy Hammer at the garden centre the other evening.

'Cool chick Rix?'

'Cool chick Rax?'

'Cool chick Rox. Rex, Rux?'

'Cooool chick.'

'Oh well they're not so bad really,' thought Harriet.

'Cool chick. Taking roots. Growing like a tree. From the bottom of her boots. Sprouting Holly leaves. For all to see. One. Two. Three. Well fuck me.'

To Harriet's fury they all started dancing to their impromptu song as they gave Tricia the thumbs up.

'Burn them matches Rix. Unload the baby.'

Suddenly they all shot round the back of the van. Leaving Rapping Hammer hopping about on his own.

'Suss the joint for the big bangers. NOW!'

Harriet and Tricia jumped as he clapped his hands together hard behind their backs.

'Lead the way Mummy-Mamma. Dig the path Chick-Lips.'

Harriet glanced at Tricia. She'd raised the back of her hand to her mouth.

'Kiss me on my hand. Kiss me on my toe. Kiss me on my arse. Go. Go. Go.'

Before they knew it he was mooning in front of them.

Harriet was mortified. Speechless. She could feel herself blushing to the core.

'Squeeze that back into your leathers will you? `arriet and I are not very interested in seein` it. Are we `arriet? I'd say it was just a bit porky to let loose on the innocent. I don't think you can 'ave very much round the front if that leather's got to work so 'ard to get all the way round the back.'

'Mutton dressed as lamb. Wham. Wham. Wham. You're no chick. Just a bit of cold ham.'

If it made Harriet feel a bit better. It certainly didn't do very much for Tricia. She could see the back seam gaping at the waist as he struggled to pull up the front zip. In went the holly from her hair just as he forced it closed.

'Ouch. My fucking arse.'

He was dancing around struggling to get the zip back down.

'Fuck you.'

'No thank you Rappin`. You're most definitely not my type.'

She reached at her hair.

'Now where's my 'olly gone 'arriet?' She turned to Rapping Hammer.

'It couldn't 'ave fallen down the middle of your bum. Could it? Maybe that's what's makin` you just a teeny weenie bit uncomfortable?'

'Fuckin` uncomfortable? It's diggin` 'oles in my arse. This bleedin` zip's gone now.'

'Well you'll just 'ave to wrap those orange and purple tails blowin` from round your back to the front. If you tie them in a nice fluffy bow I'm sure it'll 'ide what little you've got very nicely. Don't you think 'arriet?'

All Harriet could do was try to keep from laughing.

'`olly is a bit on the spiky side. It might 'ave been better if you'd kept it all to yourself in the first place.'

Harriet was on her way in. The tears were streaming. She was shaking. About to explode. Laughing. Inside. As quietly as was almost impossible. She sat herself at Tricia's desk and buried her head in her hands. She didn't see Tricia running in. Running out.

Suddenly she felt a hand on her shoulder. He kept it there. She didn't dare look up.

'Try not to get upset Miss Glover. I expect it will take a little time for your hormones to settle down.'

She cupped her hands round her eyes and tried to nod her head in the right direction. She could see Tricia wrestling with flying arms and legs. Struggling away in their black leather. Gradually transforming him into the red and white chrysalis from which he would eventually emerge as Father Christmas.

'My word, he's jolly anxious to get started Miss Glover.'

He lifted his hand to stroke his chin, then went out to join them.

'Good morning Harriet.'

A different voice. Refocused. She looked up.

'Oh good morning Mr. Bridgewater.'

'See you managed to pull young Wayne, then?'

Harriet went bright red. She wasn't quite sure of his terminology.

'Well, he very kindly agreed to provide us with the celebrity opening we were looking for.'

'Ah. Good choice. That's if you want the place packed out. There's hoards of them on their way. Amazing how the word gets round.'

'Hoards of what?' Harriet was starting to feel a bit alarmed.

'Well what would you call them these days? No. I'll be polite. Unfair to generalise.'

'Oh. You mean heavy rock fans? All on their way?'

'They're heaving like ants all along the pavements. You should see the traffic out there. All hanging out of the windows. Razzing those noisy things from their mouths. I doubt if you'll get them all in?'

Harriet tried to ignore the series of nervous pangs that suddenly laced themselves in and out of her stomach.

'Mark been trying to get hold of me then?'

'Yes. Someone pranged the boat. I think he was having a real struggle getting at it. Wondered if you could do something about those people that bang themselves up against everyone else?'

'Aye. It's a shambles down there. Wants a good sort out. His boat got damaged, did you say? Was that around the time of the the break-ins? There were a number of cars got done as well. Some damaged. Mindless.'

'Yes Mr. Bridgewater. To be fair Mark was too flapped about the boat and he didn't bother to lock it but we had something taken from the back seat.'

'Hmm. That's interesting is that Harriet. I don't know if they've caught the buggers yet, but one or two stolen items have been recovered.'

'Recovered? Where?' Harriet was impatient to find out. Tarquin Bridgewater turned away.

'Morning Joris. Tricia. Ah Father Christmas! Is that you Wayne in there? And the lads. Be with you in a tick.'

He turned back to Harriet.

'You were saying some things had been found. I'd love to know where Mr. Bridgewater?'

'Don't know where exactly but I do know Phil King got his stereo back. That's it. Yes. I think all the stuff had been dumped somewhere. Not far away as I recall.'

'Oh could you please find out for me Mr. Bridgewater?'

'What went missing Harriet?'

'Oh,' she stalled. She didn't know whether or not to go on. 'Just some notes. Some of Mark's notes from work in a brown envelope. Something to do with the South Pole project I think. Anyway he wants them back.'

'I'll do my best for you Harriet.'

His arm appeared round her waist. She felt the squeeze.

'A little bird tells me you'll be off to the Palace too?'

'Oh yes. I think so anyway.' Harriet looked down. Horrendous thought. Didn't need that one just now.

'Congratulations my dear. By all accounts you've earned it. Me? You could call it charity work of sorts. Levelling the playing field to keep our good old democracy in good shape.'

He gave her a huge wink as he walked away.

'`arriet could you give me an `and gettin` all these Ironing Bards into their elf costumes please? I've told them dressin` the part `as been agreed and that's the only way they'll get paid.'

'Of course Tricia. I just had to come in. It was so funny. How did you keep a straight face?'

'Well I wanted my `olly back `arriet. Not that I fancied puttin` it back in my `air after it `ad been down `is bum but it's the only piece I've got. There was no way I was laughin` `arriet, I can tell you. Every time `e tried to grab it `e yelped for Britain so in the end I `ad to fish it out myself. It wasn't very nice rummagin` round `is porky pink bum. I can tell you'

The giggles found their way back. Harriet struggled to control them.

'Stop it `arriet. You'll start me off. Do you know `arriet I thought we were never comin` in. I thought we'll never get started `ere. At least `e won't want payin`. They've been talkin` about boats bloody boats and nothin` else all that time. Father Chrysalis out there, well `e's got a catamaran. And our friend Joris. Well `e couldn't just `ave one. Could `e? No `e's got... Now what did `e call them now?'

She looked at her feet.

'Two Tenatoes `arriet. That's right because I thought two feet. Ten toes. I tried to remember it `arriet because I knew you'd know more about them than me.'

'Beneteaus Tricia. That'll be it. Two? Golly he must be absolutely loaded.'

'Ooh I `aven't finished yet `arriet. One's thirty five feet.'

'That'll be the biggest Tricia. Wow.'

'Oh no it isn't `arriet. Wait `til you `ear this. The other one's fifty two feet. `e brought it back to Falmouth from the south of France `arriet in the summer.'

'And how long is Father Chrysalis's Tricia?'

'Oh not very long `arriet. I couldn't `elp but see tryin` to squeeze `im into that costume. No underpants `arriet. I should think `is bum is well used to uncomfortable experiences by now.'

Harriet could feel her shoulders starting to shake again. She caught the tears just as they threatened to roll down her cheeks.

'That's funny Tricia. Great minds! We both thought of chrysalis at the same time.'

'Oh we did `arriet. It was a nightmare tryin` to shove `im into that lot. Of course you can`t tell `ow big `e is from our Adam's posters on the wall `arriet. Anyway I got my tape measure, the one I `id from Bob and measured `is bum and doubled it. That was the smallest one though `arriet.

The ones that start at the ceilin` and finish on the floor would probably `ave been better but I couldn't bring myself to measure `im from the front with those evil eyes starin` at me. They were the biggest pictures though. More `is size really. Anyway I've squashed `im in now. Not really my idea of Santa Claus `arriet I thought `e'd look better `angin` from a tree. All set to emerge like a creepy black moth.'

Harriet couldn't contain herself. She collapsed in a heap trying to hang on to Tricia's shoulders for support. Until she saw 'INTERNEWS TV' slowly drive past. It backed up behind the pantechnicon.

Panic won out.

'Tricia. Tricia just look.'

'Oh no `arriet. You know who that is `arriet, don't you? Bloody Simon Barnes.'

She answered herself as Harriet frantically searched her mind.

'He's got nothing on us Tricia. There's absolutely nothing he can say.'

'Oh I wouldn't be so sure of that `arriet. Just don't look at `im. `e'll be too interested in Rappin` `ammer to be bothered about us. Quick `arriet to the grotto. Let's get these elves sorted out. `e won't see us in there.'

The place was filling up. Harriet looked at her watch. It wasn't ten o'clock yet. The leaders of the ant pack had already straggled their way through. Suddenly the drums rolled. Harriet and Tricia picked there way round the tangle of black wire trailing the ground that led to the tent.

They went in.

'You can stop that racket for a start. Who said you could fill my grotto with this lot?'

'We `ad to plant it somewhere Chick-Lips. Or we're off!'

'Can you just STOP twangin` that guitar string? You Rox. Just put this on. And you get off those drums this minute. `ere.'

She threw the costumes at them.

'No. That pointed bit with the bell on the end goes on your `ead. Take it away from there NOW. I've never seen anythin` so disgustin` in the `ole of my life. `ave you `arriet? Apart from `is bum that is.'

Harriet had little control over her returning mirth.

'`elp me do their zips up `arriet. They `aven't got a clue.'

'Ow! Stop it will yer Chick-Lips. She's got me splinter in `er tweezers.'

'I can't think what you're talkin` about?'

'Get your fuckin` nutcrackers off me nuts will you?'

'I `aven't got any nutcrackers. Only at `ome. My Bob cracks away all Christmas Day.'

'You've got me friggin` poker stuck in your vice. Will you bloody undo it? Before I `ave a bleedin` sex change?'

Tricia stopped tugging and moved along.

'Oh no Ham Fists. Don't come near me. I'll do it my friggin` self.'

'Ah five green pixies.' Mr. Sanderson managed a smile.

'Was this your fuckin` idea or what?'

'I beg your pardon young man?'

'She's nearly snipped away me bonker.'

He pointed two fingers at Tricia. as he turned to Tarquin Bridgewater. 'Mushroom the soup man. I'm fuckin` *desperate*.'

Harriet was near collapse as she tried to hide herself in loose balloons by the door of the tent.

'That's very coarse, young man. I suggest you conduct yourself in a manner more appropriate to your costume.'

'Miss Glover. Are you feeling ill again? What *are* you doing down there? The place is filling up. Give Iris a hand with the coffees will you? Mrs. Harrington. To the till. There are people queuing out there. Oh, and get Belinda to give you a pack of white labels. They can come back here for the signatures.'

Harriet barely managed to pick herself up. Doubled she was hardly able to see her way through the gathering crowds. She arrived alongside Iris to see Tricia straight ahead. Her elbows paddling in and out while her hands covered her screeching mouth, shaking as she went.

From an uncertain spout the coffee sploshed at the tray full of cups as Harriet wrestled to hold the huge pot steady. Tears flooded down her cheeks dripping into the brew. Finally she gave up. She plonked it down.

'I've been watching you Miss Glover. I'm disappointed you see fit to find the trash in that tent amusing.'

She ducked under the counter.

'Come up immediately Miss Glover. Stop that ridiculous noise. Not the time for hysterics.'

He turned to catch Belinda Oxfordshire's eye.

'Belinda. Take over here will you? Start again with this lot.'

He swept his hand at the half filled cups sitting in the slops. Then turned to Harriet.

'Escort those wanting a signature to the tent will you? This place is getting completely out of control. You could not have failed to hear that racket outside. We've had children crying out there. Too frightened to go into the damned tent. Look. Just look at that Miss Glover. They're the ones that braved it. He's given them all bloody hammers. They're going round bashing everything in sight.'

'Not real hammers Mr. Sanderson? Plastic?'

'I've just told you to look over there. Do they look like plastic hammers to you?'

He pointed. Then shouted. Harriet jumped.

'You boy. Get down from there. Stop banging at those balloons this minute.'

For a second the room went silent. Then it all started again.

Harriet scooted to the counter. The shelves were practically empty. The till was ringing in delight as if satisfying an uncontrollable compulsion.

'Pass those labels over please Tricia.'

'Oh `ave you come to `elp arriet?'

Suddenly her elbows were away again. Harriet had to go.

'Follow me for signings if you don't mind?'

She looked behind her. The Pied Piper came to mind.

'Bridgewater Miss Glover? If you see him send him to me.'

The fevered crowd pushed and shoved their way behind her to the grotto outside.

'Well it's Mummy-Mamma. Wouldn't you know? Hit them drums. Go man go.'

The drum roll was deafening. A shove sent her toppling towards him. Trapped, she thrust the pen and labels at Rapping Hammer.

'Would you mind? Please? Just sign them. Peel them off and stick them wherever.'

'Go man go. Nice and slow. Stick 'em where they fits. Stick 'em on 'er tits.'

Harriet suddenly felt the simultaneous pressure against her jumper as he forced a white sticky label against each breast. Blushing, she whipped them off. Quick.

'Got that. Thanks lads. That'll get the ratings going. Cut!' it was Simon Barnes.

The laughter drowned out the drumming.

She immediately felt a hand on her shoulder.

'Roll again lads.' She could see herself looking into the camera. Stuck in the crowd.

'Turn that flaming thing off.' It was *him*.

She turned her head. Straight into Mr. Sanderson's oatmeal fisherman's knit sweater.

'Out of order. Totally out of order. Virtual assault. Recorded here.' He pointed angrily at the cameras.

'Come off it man. She pushed her tits in my face.'

'Miss Glover?'

'No I did *not*. I was shoved from behind.'

'Tarquin Bridgewater? Anyone seen him? Is he back there?' Mr. Sanderson pointed to the zipped closed inner tent compartment behind them.

'Barkin' Ditchwater? Scrub the joint.' Rux flung his arm around. 'Unless he's still mashin' the mush.'

'Risin' the rizon. Stooped!' Rix scratched his head then fractionally undid the zip. 'Nope. Dope. He's vapourised.'

'I simply don't comprehend this language young man.'

Mr. Sanderson marched forward. Unzipped the inner tent and walked in. And out.

'Get this lot signed off will you! NOW! *IMMEDIATELY!*'

A shock of silence stunned the tent.

'No probs guv.'

'Miss Glover OUT. I insist you DON'T subject yourself to such crudity any longer. They're high. The lot of them are away with the fairies. Judging by the smoke curling into that heap of empty jelly cartons back there. What time is it?'

He looked at his watch. 'Is that all? Anyhow Molly and Percy have turned up. You'll find them in the foyer. See to them will you?'

'Molly, Percy. It's lovely to …..'

'Don't make it obvious Harriet, but look who's just turned up?'

Harriet peered between Molly and Mr. Fishwick to see the whole gang of them. The whole gang of raucous youths from the ship, led from the front by that awful girl. Her tattooed hand pinned to her Davy Crockett hat. Fighting against the wind.

She picked up the threads of nerves weaving out again from the pit of her stomach.

Molly caught her face. 'They won't even think of seeing us here Harriet. We'll be alright if we stay put. Keep our backs to them.'

'Oh they've gone right through. Thanks Molly. You always make me feel better.'

'Look Harriet there's a free table just inside there. We might just be a bit close to the till, here. Come on Percy, Harriet. We'll turn our chairs to the wall.'

'Sitting down Harriet Glover? I must say you've been next to no use all day.'

Harriet turned. She just knew it was Belinda Oxfordshire.

'Joris shouldn't actually have to be serving coffee. Wouldn't you agree?'

Harriet didn't know what to say.

'Ah there's Bob Harrington. Just come in. Maybe he'd be kind enough to relieve Joris.'

'Did our friend get your things back to you Harriet?'

'Oh yes thank you, Molly.'

'Still as handsome as ever.'

Mr. Fishwick side-glanced her. Then turned to Harriet.

'And this young lady's still as beautiful as ever. How are you doing these days my dear?'

Harriet blushed. She tried not to catch his eye.

'Oh fine thank you Mr. Fishwick.'

'Gentleman behind you my dear.' He touched her shoulder.

Harriet turned.

'Oh, Mr. Bridgewater, Mr. Sanderson was looking for you. He's serving the coffee. I think.'

'In a minute Harriet. Now my little darling. This has got to be worth at least a kiss?'

He put his arm around her. She smelt smoke. But different.

'I've got a little something for you. Remember? This morning?'

'Cheer up Percy. Whatever can be the matter?' Molly nudged him with her elbow.

'I've got it,' triumphed Mr. Bridgewater.

Up popped the large brown envelope. Now creased and stained.

'I've also got another surprise for you. Not ready yet mind. Coming on nicely in my greenhouse.'

Harriet hardly heard. Overjoyed she flung her arms round him.

'Where did you get it? Where was it?'

'Had a word with Phil King. Andy Price found the stuff. A while after it disappeared, mind. Didn't know what to do with the bloody thing.' He waved it around.

Mr. Sanderson was on his way over.

'Exactly what are you up to now Miss Glover?'

Mr. Sanderson was more than a little exasperated. Too late. Tarquin Bridgewater refused to let go.

'Put her down Tarquin. She doesn't need one iota of encouragement. Move back. Let these schoolboys in.'

He turned, shouting towards the door.

'Belinda.'

'Yes Joris. We're coming.'

She clacked across the floor, tossing her head backwards, beckoning Bob to follow.

Molly, increasingly excited, kept looking across to Simon Barnes supervising the shifting cameras.

'Oh we're going to be on telly Percy. I think he's coming over. Oh no. Or is he? Cheer up Percy. You won't want to be looking at yourself with a face as long as that if we're on the news tonight.' Molly nudged him.

The schoolboys hovered round the table.

'Traffic lights,' thought Harriet. 'It's those little brats that hang around, outside.'

'It's 'er.' One of them said, pointing at Belinda Oxfordshire.

Harriet suddenly spotted the raucous girl heading straight for them. She looked away. Turned to Mr. Sanderson.

'Look. It's the envelope Mr. Sanderson. This missing brown envelope.'

'Any more tyres you want letting down Miss? Double the price now. The recession and all that.'

Belinda Oxfordshire's porcelain white face instantly turned puce. Mr. Sanderson glared at her. Harriet gasped.

'Don't know what you childish boys are talking about.' She managed to get the words out. Just.

'Look. There's the ole geezer what tried to pinch me 'at.'

The raucous girl snatched it off and waved its tail threateningly at Mr. Fishwick.

The whole gang suddenly encircled the table. Closing it in.

'Locked us in the cupboard onboard that ship. We know it was you. You ole plonker.'

Mr. Fishwick was hardly listening.

Harriet could feel him staring at her. Almost oblivious. But not quite.

'I was very surprised you got that cat of yours back Harriet, my lovely. I had my doubts you know? My, how we searched that ship? High and low.' Mr. Fishwick had become totally transfixed. His face splashed in delight at nudging his way in. Nudging out Tarquin Bridgewater.

'Percy Fishwick will you just shush?' Molly whispered in a panic.

Mr. Sanderson had had just about enough.

'Pass that envelope over to Miss Oxfordshire, Miss Glover. This minute!'

Her long painted nails immediately ripped away at it.

'Not here Miss Oxfordshire. Before the board meeting, but not here.' Mr. Sanderson was blazing.

Too late. She pulled at the scruffy crumpled A4 sheets. Then shook the envelope over the table.

'Oh what's all this?' She drew a line in the brown bitty, fragmented dust as it settled on the table. Then flicked her finger at Harriet.

Harriet coughed. The smell. Unpleasant. Just like Mr. Bridgewater's jacket.

'Blanks. All blanks. Just a load of filthy paper. Is this another of your little jokes Harriet Glover?'

Harriet turned white. Mr. Bridgewater shot off. Smartly followed by Mr. Sanderson.

Simon Barnes swooped like a sparrow-hawk to its prey. Harriet felt herself going into a daze as the camera lens closed in.

'So you were lookin` for your fuckin` cat were you? That's why `e grabbed my `at. Took it with you. On board?'

The raucous girl was stabbing the air with her index finger.

'You can get done for that.'

'Cut. That's all we need.'

Molly watched Simon Barnes and his crew shuffle away.

'I do hope you were smiling Percy. He couldn't have helped but get you. Being so close to Harriet. Do you know? I don't think I got a look in. Oh our *very* handsome friend's coming back.' Her irritation was totally lost on Mr. Fishwick.

'I was just about to find you Joris Sanderson. *You* brought it back *didn't you?* That was the meowing rat-bag we emptied into *her* garden. You *knew* it was *hers* all the time. Didn't you *Joris?*'

'This is neither the time nor the place to behave like a fishwife Miss Oxfordshire. Indeed. Quite outrageous. Just remember your place will you?'

Now fully ignited, Harriet watched her beauty almost evaporate. Her features distorted by trembling rage.

'And what *were* you doing on the ship with *her*, anyway? You told me you flew out from Manchester with that bird-brain on the till.'

'And just who do you think you're calling a bird-brain? Did you `ear that Bob? Just got `ere in time to be insulted. I only came over `ere to be friendly.'

Belinda Oxfordshire, fuming, rolled the sheets of thumbed white paper and whammed them against the back of Harriet's chair. She turned to Mr. Sanderson again.

'I'd hardly got over Ted. Then *you* go and break it off as well. I don't know why we got engaged in the first place?'

'Rebound Miss Oxfordshire.' His eyes narrowed as he glanced at Harriet.

'If you want the truth in public.'

'Who? You or me?' she snapped. Now uncomfortable she moved along.

'And what was supposed to be on these? Written in orange juice I suppose? Well don't expect me to have to iron them all to find out.'

'Childish nonsense Miss Oxfordshire.'

He looked over at Bob, behind her, standing full square. Showing off the scribes across his chest. Beaming. As macho as he could manage.

'Hmm. "**BANKERS? MY ARSE!**" now that wouldn't be a bad place to start,' suggested Mr. Sanderson.

'Come on Robby. She doesn't want any more tyres doin`. Let's `ave a go at `er balloons. I dunno what Rappin` `ammer's thinkin` of comin` `ere. They're weird. They're all weird. The lot of `em. Shall we tell `er we did *`er* tyres in first before we did that one she paid us to do by the estate agents? Or not?'

The lads laughed at Belinda Oxfordshire. We dumped your fuckin` flyers too. You didn't think we were really goin` to trap our `ands in every fuckin` letterbox in Stetmead did you?'

The gang of raucous youths were beginning to look completely out of it.

'They're right. Totally weird. Let's go. Oh look! There's the band out there. They've finished. They've done `ere. Let's catch them loadin`.'

The raucous girl picked up a stray till receipt from the litter on the floor.

'This'll do. We'll get `is autograph on `ere before we go. Come on.'

'`scuse me. If you don't mind. You `ave to buy somethin` first and then `e'll sign a label.' A most indignant Tricia grabbed a bell from the shelf. '`ere. You `aven't bought anythin` yet. This will do. I'll check it out at the till. SHALL I?'

She turned to see Rapping Hammer right behind.

'Chick-Lips flappin`. Ringin` `er bell. Stick it up `er arse. Go to `ell.'

Tricia, seething, pushed the bell at his face, jangling it straight in his ear.

The raucous girl fell about. 'You tell `er Rappin`. You friggin` tell `er.'

She led the way forward as the rest of them mingled with the band, struggling past with drums, wires, yards of white kitchen roll and all else Mr. Sanderson would be so very glad to see the back of.

'That's us finished then gov. Just twelve grand for the lads?'

'On your bike young man. Drugs! I've got enough evidence to put the lot of you behind bars. Think yourselves lucky.' Mr. Sanderson was on the point of explosion. 'I trust you're a damned sight more competent in charge of that catamaran?'

'Chill man chill. Just jokin`. They've pinched the butties. They'll `ave to make do with that.'

'Where `ave you left those costumes? We want them back.' Tricia was furious.

'In the wigwam man. Flappin` like a hen. You never know when. She'll open those pegs. Lay a few eggs.'

'OH! Did you `ear that Bob? `it `im will you?'

She turned round. Neither he nor Belinda Oxfordshire were anywhere to be seen.

'Oh `e would disappear. Gob like a cake frill. Grinnin` at `er.'

Absolutely livid she tugged on the fluffy nylon orange and purple bow holding his leathers together. Sending her backwards into Simon Barnes's arms.

'NOW. Roll again boys.'

'And where did *you* suddenly come from? You weren't `ere a second ago?'

Harriet looked away.

Rapping Hammer covered what was necessary with both hands and shot off. 'Let's get to bleedin` `ell out of `ere. It's a mad `ouse.'

'Almost a compliment Mrs. Harrington,' came Mr. Sanderson's stern voice.

'Get the place cleared will you?' He looked across. 'I'm afraid we're closing young man.'

Harriet spotted Belinda Oxfordshire. Spotted her turn on her heel.

'No it's alright sir. I've only popped in to say hello to our Wayne. And see `er.'

Harriet felt a quick tap on her shoulder.

'Managed to slip out Harriet. Our Wayne's lunch box's all over the place,' he sniggered.

'No. The sandwiches were wrapped in kitchen roll,' insisted Harriet.

Guy Hammer grinned and turned to Mr. Sanderson. 'Isn't she lovely?'

'I got rid of Paula. I got rid of `er. For you Harriet.'

Mr. Fishwick in a rash of jealousy started to rise from his chair. Then caught Molly's glance.

'I can take you now love. We can both go to the Arena Central together. For sure Rapping Hammer'll rock better with you around on Boxing Day. To the gods it is. I'll meet you outside at seven.'

Guy Hammer looked really pleased with himself.

'You most certainly will **not** young man,' Mr. Sanderson fumed. 'Take it from me, Miss Glover will not be going anywhere near the place. Am I correct Miss Glover?'

'Afraid he is Guy. It's really kind of you but I've made other plans now.'

Guy's chin hit the ground.

'I'll `ave to ring `er again now. I don't know if she'll `ave me back.'

He turned to Tricia.

'You wouldn't like to come would you love?'

'You're jokin` me I `ope? Oh there's our Adam `e'll go though. Won't you Adam?'

'Arr, ay! I wanted to take a bird.'

From the cinders of chaos Mr. Whellread suddenly materialised. Almost from nowhere. He turned to Mr. Sanderson, waving at Simon Barnes on his way out to the van.

'Do you know? I've been wanting to get hold of him for ages, have I. Ever since she won three grand or more on that lottery ticket.'

He pointed a steady hand at Harriet.

'Really, indeed.' Mr. Sanderson cleared his throat then briefly scratched his head.

'Aye. Shop's falling back a bit. People stopping their papers. Not buying magazines, comics, sweets, cans. You know? Things like that. Definitely starting to feel the pinch with this recession. Could do with a bit of publicity, could we. He's the man for it, is he. Took down every word I said.'

He glanced back at Harriet.

'You don't come across the likes of her very often. Wouldn't have known she'd won if it weren't for that woman. Now who's that woman with the lad that can't keep still? All over the shop, is he. In her class, she says. Custard? Mustard? No. I've got it, have I? Bustard. Mrs. Bustard. That's it, is that.'

He paused to pat Harriet on the back.

'What does she do with it? Keep it for herself? No. Not our Harriet. Gives it all to Mrs. Bustard does she. So she can take that lad on `oliday.'

Harriet concentrated hard on the small heap of brown strandy dust remaining on the table.

She daren't look up. Mr. Sanderson was glowering at her.

'Got the lottery ticket from us. Didn't you love?' I told that Barnes chap you were the one, did I, when you were behind the counter serving that there coffee. He seemed to know you love. Said there's a lot more to her than meets the eye. I thought that was bit below the belt, was that.'

He nodded at Simon Barnes on his way back. Then on his way out again.

'By gum e'd better mention Whellreads. I'll be looking out for the news tonight, will I.'

Harriet could feel her nerves knotting in the pit of her stomach and decided death would be infinitely preferable.

'So will I Mr. Whellread. So will I,' replied Mr. Sanderson.

Harriet had never seen those handsome features so steeped in severity.

Everyone jumped.

'What on earth was that? What in the name of fortune is going on out there?' Mr. Sanderson marched out, rapidly followed by Mr. Whellread. The crash was deafening.

'Ooh `arriet what was that? I've left our Adam with Guy `ammer. I don't think I can threaten Bob with `*im* any more though arriet. Mind you, I could be wrong. She's probably desperate. Desperate enough to still be gabblin` away to `im. I said "Bob you're looking really bored. `ave you noticed my `olly leaves yet? `olly Berry on the telly." Oh `arriet I've `eard that many rhymes today I'm startin` to do it myself. `e wouldn't budge though `arriet. I think she's frozen `im to the chair. Still. Serves `im right I say. Anyway `arriet what was goin` on out there?'

Harriet put her hand to her mouth and shrugged her shoulders. 'Mr. Sanderson's gone to see.'

'Oh, he's on his way back Harriet,' Molly whispered.

'Crunched!   The whole bloody lot's crunched. The whole caboodle. Cameras and all. The whole shooting match.'

A look of satisfaction shot across Mr. Sanderson's face.

'They'd stacked it all on the ground in favour of chatting to the band. Apparently that Hammer chap freaks. Tries to break it up. Threatens to go, then backs straight into the lot. Barnes not too chuffed.' Mr. Sanderson finished.

'Ooh no `e doesn't look very pleased, does `e?' Tricia declared as he walked across.

'What a shame you've wasted your day. I am sorry to `ear about your crash. So we won't be on the telly then after all?'

Tricia looked at Harriet. Relief generated reciprocal smiles.

Simon Barnes fished in his pocket. Three reels of tape rested in the palm of his hand.

'First rule. Get them out. We don't take any chances. Especially with you two around. There's enough on these to keep that story running and running.'

Harriet could feel the colour drain from her face. Tricia took a very deep breath.

'My Bob's already warned you. `asn't `e? Accusin` me of being pregnant. Bloody cheek. `e said `e'd finish you off next time if you dared to do that again.'

Simon Barnes turned to Harriet.

'I thought I recognised him. That guy over there chatting up that posh bit. She tore your letter up, didn't she? He's hers? Not yours?'

'No `e isn't bloody `ers. `e's supposed to be married to me. But you wouldn't bloody think so,' burst in Tricia.

'Stop talking about my husband like that,' Harriet instantly demanded. 'We might be in the throes of a divorce but we're not there yet. You can fight it out between the two of you, then.'

Complete silence.

'I'm off. I don't know where I fucking am with you two.'

'My sentiments entirely Mr. Barnes.' Mr. Sanderson shook his hand. 'Good day to you.'

Chapter 36

Harriet and Mark stretched out in front of the fire. Warm. Cosy. They sat, drawn to the spread of flames. Tiny. Yellow. Orange. Hissing. Curling cautiously from their hard black beds, spitting wisps of light grey smoke. On their way. Struggling to reach the massive yellow tongues. Busy. Twisting. Turning. Dancing. Licking their way up the chimney.

'More wine Hat?'

He looked at his watch.

'Any minute now.'

The doorbell went.

'Delivered. Get the gobbling rods Harriet.'

'Now that would have been a better name for the Ironing Bards,' she thought. She wondered about Simon Barnes. What he'd draw from the day for the ten o'clock news. The panic returned.

'Bloody Belinda Oxfordshire letting my tyres down,' she fumed to herself.

'And Tarquin Bridgewater. High as the proverbial kite.' She heaved at the smell, vivid again in her mind. 'Even the doziest sleuth could work that one out. For a kiss? Messing about with all that paper just for a kiss? Higher than a kite.' She shuddered at the thought of flinging herself into his arms.

'Another Percy really. Not as nice, but coming from the same place, definitely. Just like Guy Hammer, too.'

She felt a deep sense of relief. She was so grateful for *his* intervention. So grateful to be off the hook.

'Mr. Sanderson certainly put Belinda Oxfordshire in her place. She can hardly sue me now. Not really. Not after that. No Harriet. Don't go there. *He'll* never ask you to marry him.'

'No Hat. Bring them through. We'll have it in here in front of the fire.'

Soon finished, Mark gathered up the empty cartons and returned with the wine bottle.

'Happy Birthday Hat. Cheers.' He passed her a card.

'It couldn't have been that brilliant for your mum having you on Christmas Eve Hat.'

'Actually I've never forgiven her. I've been deprived of that present gap all my life.'

'Ah! The answer at last,' he grinned.

'Oh put some more coal on the fire Mark. It's burning down. Like you.'

'Burning down am I? Not tonight Harriet. Certainly not tonight.'

He threw the scuttle at the hearth then reached in his pocket.

'Happy Birthday Harriet.' He passed her a small square box.

'Mark? What's this? Come here.' She held him very close to her chest. 'Thank you Mark.'

He smothered her words with his mouth to give her a huge kiss.

'Open it Hat. Go on.'

Excited. She tossed the paper on the carpet and lifted the lid. Tears came to her eyes.

'Oh Mark it's beautiful.' The solitaire diamond ring gleamed in the firelight.

'Let me Harriet.'

He lifted it out. 'Will you really marry me Harriet?'

'Of course I will.'

He placed it on her finger.

'Engaged. I've never been engaged before. It's beautiful Mark.'

She curled into his arms and they rolled off the sofa on to the rug. The little flames had suddenly grown up. Crackling their way up the chimney.

'My word you look hot Hat. You'd be better taking this thing off. And that…'

The doorbell went. It was impossible to answer it. Harriet was vaguely aware of something being pushed through the letterbox.

Chapter 37

'Happy Christmas Mark.'

Harriet took the mug of tea round to his side of the bed.

'Thanks Hat. Happy Christmas. Sleep OK?'

'Out like a light Mark. After last night. Engaged! Can't quite believe it. It's a beautiful ring Mark. Can't wait to show it off to Geraldine. They're all going to get such a shock. Wow Harriet and Mark actually engaged! And the wedding booked. Who'd believe it?'

Mark rolled over then pulled up a red Santa sack from somewhere behind the headboard. 'Father Christmas has been Harriet. He comes to good girls.'

'Ooh Mark, you've never done that before. Yours isn't so much in a sack as a garden bag. Father Christmas ran out of those.'

She opened the wardrobe door and dragged the plastic green bag along the carpet.

'There Mark, he's left you lots of surprises.'

'Not as good as the one you gave me last night Harriet. Wow. You're learning fast.'

'Well we are *engaged* Mark.'

'Wow Hat. What's it going to be like when we're married then? Can't wait.'

'You're going to have to Mark.'

She got back into bed.

'Mark, it's a potato peeler. That's not very exciting. Oh a cheese grater. A pair of salad servers. Getting a bit better. A set of pan scrubs. Mark, Father Christmas would never give me these. A new frying pan. A sieve. A pack of dusters. Some spray polish. Where did you go Mark?'

' Bargains Home Hat. You're going to have a fresh start once we're married. Just a few things for the collection.'

She flung her arms around him.

'That's sweet Mark. You're absolutely right.'

Mark heaved his sack on to the duvet.

'A pair of wellies? A watering can? A box of fertilizer? Come off it Harriet. Not my scene.'

'It has got a very big garden Mark. You're going to need them all.'

'Too right Harriet. Very sensible. We've become Mr. and Mrs. Sensible already.'

'Not last night.'

'No. Not last night Hat. Did you take your pill?'

'No I forgot.'

Mark shook his head to the rhythm of the ringing phone.

'Hi Dad, happy Christmas. We called last night. You were both in. The cars were there and we could see the firelight flickering through the closed curtains. I bet you were both fast asleep.'

'That's what we do at our age Clare. We just doze off.'

'We pushed Mum's birthday present through the letterbox. Did she get it?'

'I don't think she's looked yet Clare. Anyway I'll pass you over. Happy Christmas. We'll see you at the hotel. What's it like, anyway?'

'Oooh Dad. It's sumptuous.'

'Happy Christmas Clare. Have a good trip?'

'Yes thanks Mum. Roads weren't too bad once we'd got out of Bristol. Chocked with it being Christmas Eve. How did it go at Starboard Marine North West with Rapping Hammer? There was just a clip on the news. Sorry we didn't make it. Still we'll be seeing him on Boxing Day.'

Harriet breathed a huge sigh of relief. 'Is that all he's going to show? I wonder? Just a clip. Can Simon Barnes be so confused he's now totally given up?' She sank the thought.

'Upper Tideside Hotel nice then, Clare?'

'Oh it's absolutely gorgeous. Posh. Luxurious. Dinner last night was something else. Did you know it's been awarded five stars in the "Same Place?" guide?'

'It doesn't surprise me Clare. We'll look forward to joining you later.'

'Oh Mum your birthday. Did you enjoy it? We pushed your presents through the letterbox. Dad said you'd both dozed off. Gosh I'm not looking forward to being as old as you. When dull becomes the norm.'

'Well it was anything but dull Clare yesterday. Can't wait to tell you. Tricia and I could well have died laughing.'

'Oh don't do that Mum. Dull's cool. It's very *in* at the moment.'

Harriet laughed.

'I'll go and get my presents. Thank you Clare. And your card. That was lovely. Put Rachael on for a minute will you?'

Chapter 38

It was crisp out there. The sun was shining from a transparent sky. Blue all around. It usually did on Christmas Day. Harriet felt a sense of ease. It was finally here. All the preparations over. Almost a promise of spring in the air. The day to enjoy.

Harriet decided on the blue one, to please Mark. It was still a size too big. She'd managed not to put the weight back on, the stone she'd lost while he was away.

She rooted in Molly's carrier bag for her diamond pendant. Perfect match for her ring.

'What was that?' She felt something. 'I didn't take or wear anything else. Did I?'

She pulled out a small square bag. Gold with tiny shimmering handles tightly pressed together.

'What's Molly put in here?' Puzzled. Curious. She cautiously pulled them apart. Inside was a black velvet box. No message. She lifted the lid. Gasped! A wide gold bangle, exquisitely engraved with flowers. Buttercups. All the way round. Her heart leapt. Its inner face engraved, like the ring. Latin.

' "*haec olim meminisse iuvabit*"   "*in somnis veritas*"   *JS*. Oh gosh. Wow! Oh no. It's 22 carat gold.'

She couldn't translate it. Not now. She clasped it close to her chest. Mark was coming upstairs. She pushed it all quickly to the back of her drawer.

'Right Hat. Are you ready? I don't like being late to these places.'

She reached for her coat. Absolutely stunned.

'You've gone all pink Harriet. Are you OK?'

'Fine thanks Mark.'

'Hot flush Harriet? Or are you just warming to the thought of last night?'

'Something like that Mark.'

'Right. Got the presents Hat? Is that all we're taking? Just those two boxes?'

'The rest are lined up outside Mark. Well we'll need to take six with us. Molly's and Tricia's will have to wait now.'

'Harriet, not that lot outside? I thought you'd been collecting them for the new house. How the devil am I supposed to get that lot in the car?'

'Of course you can Mark. You can fold the back seats down. Oh. Hang on a tick. I just need the gift tags for them.'

'I'm not happy Harriet. They're going to wobble off there. No they're going to have to sit on the seats. Bloody hell Harriet. Couldn't you have got everyone a book or something? We're going to be late.'

Chapter 39

'Told you Harriet. They're all here. Girls up in Tristan's car, are they?' He let Harriet out. She glanced over to the foyer. To the massive Christmas tree, twinkling its coloured lights through the long panels of leaded glass. She pulled her coat together as they hurried to the other side. To the main entrance door.

'Oh no! Bloody hell Harriet they haven't invited HIM!?'

'Who Mark? What are you talking about?'

'That's lard ball's car, if I'm not mistaken.'

Harriet could only see a silver roof.

He marched to peer over the thin line of beech hedging separating out the car parks.

'Personalised bloody number plate. I don't know what your Geraldine's playing at Harriet. Probably fancies him. "Oh do join us for dinner Joris..." Can't you just hear her?'

'I'd far rather she hadn't Mark. Not that there's much we can do about it. We'll have sprouted little brown leaves by the time we go in if we stand here much longer.'

'Right. And if you so much as look at him Harriet that ring's going back to the shop.'

'Well that's not very nice Mark.'

'Oh you know what I mean. No Harriet. I don't see why we have to have *him* round our necks on Christmas Day.'

'Not exactly in keeping with the spirit of Christmas Mark.'

'In here Mum. We're all in here. All having a drink before dinner. Happy Christmas!'

Rachael moved from one to the other with Clare hot on her heels.

'Mum! What's that on your left hand? Mum. It's not an engagement ring is it? Clare, look.'

They both flared their left hands at Harriet.

'Snap. Snap. Snap,' bounced Clare. 'That was *our* surprise. The one I told you about Mum, remember?'

'Well, well, congratulations girls.' Mark found his voice first.

'I'm thrilled for the both of you.' Harriet scooped her babies into her arms. She could feel the mix of tears welling. Delight. Regret. The limelight should all have been theirs. 'Identical rings, too. Sapphires and diamonds. They're beautiful. Did you choose them together?'

'We did,' they chorused.

'And you two. Actually getting married?'

'Yes Clare. Your mother will fill you in on all that.'

'You don't have to you know. Not for us. Do they Rachael? We've got kind of used to being born to hippie parents. It's cool. I don't know why Mum spent so much time flapping about it?'

'Oh they'll go their own way Clare,' Rachael piped up. 'They're now doing boring, like dozing off in front of the telly. You've got to be married to do that Clare.'

'Excuse me girls. And what have you both committed yourselves to? If not boring?'

'Oh it's different for us. We're bucking the trend. It's cool to be different. So un-cool to be like your mum and dad.'

'Can't you just break it off?'

'No. 'fraid not Clare. I take it we don't have your blessing then?' Mark grinned.

'Most definitely not,' they almost chimed in unison.

'Not quite reached the age for role reversal, you two.'

Harriet scratched her head. It wasn't quite the reception she'd expected.

Clare looked at Rachael.

'Suppose we'd better congratulate them anyway. We hope you'll both be very happy in your new life together.'

'Well,' said Rachael. 'I thought they were happy anyway?'

'So we're not looking at a triple wedding then?' Mark cut in.

'No most definitely not. Sorry and all that. What a joke. On the 25th June we're all off to the Seychelles. Getting married on the beach. You don't mind do you Mum and Dad? We'll be up for a family celebration though. We might even do a church blessing mightn't we Clare? We'll see how we feel.'

Harriet swallowed hard as the implications from the clout of disappointment sank in. It wasn't even worth telling them their dates had coincided. Not worth the bother of her and Mark changing their arrangements. They wouldn't want to be there anyway. She tried not to let it take the shine off her engagement. She put it down to their upbringing. Having to cope with unmarried parents. She glowered at Mark. 'Why has it taken him so long?' She thought of *him*. She looked at her ring.

She steeled herself. Engaged. The bracelet. The message. How she wished she'd given more time to her Latin homework. How she wished she didn't have to declare her engagement in front of *him*.

'Happy Christmas Harriet, Mark.'

'Happy Christmas Mummy, Daddy. Oh Geraldine. Lovely to see you. It was so kind of you to invite Mark's Mum and Dad as well. I don't think we've ever had so many of the family together at one time. Wow all this? Here as well? Posh. Very posh. Such a special treat. James. Happy Christmas James. Oh Clarissa, Henry. Happy Christmas to you both. Ah Shirley, Harold. Mark's just back there. Happy Christmas anyway.'

Eventually they all sank into the grand settees gracing the elegant old room.

Harriet looked around. She turned to Geraldine.

'Are we all here then?'

Geraldine nodded.

Harriet breathed a huge sigh of relief. Mr. Sanderson was nowhere to be seen.

'Oh. Er. Gin and tonic please.'

'Sweet sherry.'

'Make mine dry.'

'Have they got anything non alcoholic? Oh. Alright. No, no. That'll be fine.'

'Just a lager. A half will be fine. Thank you.'

'Glass of red please.'

'White for me.'

'And me please. That would be lovely.'

'We'll both have a whisky. Er. Yes. Just a drop of ginger ale. Thanks.'

'Cheers! Happy Christmas everyone.'

Clare nudged Rachael. 'We want you all to raise your glasses to Mum and Dad. We don't approve but, both engaged to be married.'

'Well, fancy that. After all this time.' Harriet absorbed the comment from somewhere out of the excitement.

'My dream come true after all these years. Well I don't expect you could do any better than him Harriet.'

'I'll take that the right way Mummy,' Harriet replied.

'Well I never.'

'What do you mean Daddy?'

'Well I never. It's the old bus thing isn't it? You wait forever and three come along at once.'

The chortle went up.

'You never cease to amaze us Mark,' chimed Harold. 'About time too.'

Shirley nodded in agreement. 'Take no notice of your father Mark. Better to take your time. Better to make absolutely sure. Better late than never.'

Harriet looked across. Caught her glance. Almost a hint of disapproval.

'OK Mum. Done it just to please you.' Mark grinned.

'What lovely news Harriet. You can borrow my wedding dress if you like.'

'Oh thank you Clarissa. Already fixed up, though.'

'Well done Sis. What did you threaten him with?'

'Shut up James. We're all different.'

'We'd like to share the limelight with Clare and Sebastian, Rachael and Tristan. If they'll allow,' Mark declared. 'To your double engagement. Every happiness.'

All the glasses lifted. The girls bubbled their way round the group showing off their rings.

'Congratulations lads,' Mark nodded at Harriet. 'We couldn't be more pleased.'

'Absolutely delighted for you all,' said Harriet. 'My, what a surprise that was.'

Chapter 40

'Oh Mark. You can't have that for the main course. Everyone else is having turkey. It's Christmas.'

'I think he can make his own mind up Harriet. Just let him get on with it.'

Mark's mum closed the large maroon folder and handed it back to the waiter.

'All done? Everyone ordered?' James collected the rest.

'Snappy old bat,' Harriet thought. Then dismissed it to wonder about *his* car. Wondered where he was.

'Fingers crossed they've all finished. He'll be gone.'

'Come through now, if you will? Please.'

The waiter directed them towards the dining room. Harriet dawdled behind the rest.

'Well there's Joris with his mum and dad. Looks like the whole family are up.'

Excited, Geraldine announced it to reach Harriet at the back of the queue. She watched Geraldine bustle her way between the tables at the far side of the room.

Harriet watched his broad smile as Geraldine approached. He stood to greet her. Harriet couldn't look anymore. 'Please, please don't have placed us by them.'

Her silent plea fell to the parquet floor as they were led to the adjacent tables, pushed edge to edge alongside theirs. Matching length for length as the hotel had done its best to accommodate each large family.

Hang back or move forward? She didn't know what to for the best. Couldn't face *him*.

'Don't want to be able to see *him*.'

'There Harriet. You and Mark can sit there.'

'No. It's alright Mummy. Someone else can go by the window. We'll go over the other side.'

'Oh I was just about to sit there.' Clarissa nudged Harriet back to where she'd started.

'Harriet stop dancing about and sit somewhere. Will you?' Mark wasn't out to hide his annoyance. The chair staggered back in his hand. Harriet had no choice. She sat. Right opposite *him*.

Head down. She swizzled the diamond round to the inside of her finger. Noticed the sunlight catching at the wine glasses. She didn't want it bouncing off the clear cut facets straight into *his* eyes. She looked around the room. Beautiful gold drapes edging the long elegant windows. Eight ornate columns stretching their way to the high ceiling, gracing the length of the room. Tastefully decorated. Trailing strands of mistletoe, occasionally studded with holly. The Christmas tree. Not like the one in the foyer. Simple. Decorated simply. Nothing on it that wasn't blue or silver.

Chatter. Laughter. Excitement. All the sounds of an affluent Christmas Day filled Harriet's ears. She strained them. Tried to filter it out in order to catch what her mother was saying to the elderly lady behind. Always *his* voice. Lower. Deeper. In the background. Disturbing her.

'Red or white Harriet?' Mark nudged her.

'Oh sorry, white please.' She hadn't noticed the first course on its way. Still listening. Watching. Thinking.

'Go on Daddy. You tell her.' She watched her father turn her mother's shoulder back towards the skewered scallops wrapped in smoky bacon; nestling in a deep green bed of rocket leaves, not quite tipping the elongated apostrophe of wine creamed sauce glowing its way down the white porcelain plate.

'Art,' Harriet decided, 'pure art. Like the rest of the place.'

* * *

'Coffee?' The waiter addressed the table before turning to James.

Harriet stared at the Christmas tree. She could hear Mr. Sanderson saying something to James.

She looked up. Both his arms outstretched. Mr. Sanderson, behind, ushering his party forward towards the door. Relief. She swizzled her diamond back round to the outside of her finger.

'You've made a friend there Mum.' James put his arm around her. 'Mrs. Sanderson insists we all go back to Joris's for coffee.' He turned to the waiter. 'I think that's a no, thank you very much.'

The waiter moved along. James felt for his wallet and headed for reception.

The chairs shuffled and squeaked their way out from under and back again. Pushed well under the tables. White cloths almost cleared, save the odd fork and empty glass. A couple of screwed up serviettes. Half-shells of Christmas crackers strewn around small curling bits of paper printed with time-worn jokes. Just the remnants of affluence, now. They all wound their way to the foyer for their coats.

'Bloody hell Harriet, this is getting worse. So we've got to go ingratiating ourselves to lard ball now? *Where* does he live?'

'Look Mark. I don't want to go. I'd far rather go home.'

'Let's do that. Shall we?'

'We can't Mark. That's stupid. James and Geraldine have paid for that meal. We can't just leave like that. Anyway we haven't given out the presents yet. We won't be long round there. I'm sure. They'll want to have as much of the day on their own all together, I would imagine.'

'It's your bloody mother, Harriet. Can't keep her big trap shut. If she'd turned round and got on with her dinner it wouldn't have happened. She left half of it. So busy gassing. Where *is* the bloody place, anyway?'

'Not far. Probably just up and over the hill.'

'Up the bloody hill Harriet? With the car full of that lot? They'll be all over the place. Soil everywhere by the time we get there.'

'Stop moaning Mark. Hurry up. You won't have anyone to follow if we don't get a move on.'

Harriet got in the car and steeled herself for Mark slamming the door.

'Right,' she thought. 'Engaged? To him? It's off. All off. He's being horrible about Mummy. It's supposed to be Christmas Day. He's done nothing but moan.'

She pulled at her ring and zipped it closed into the back pocket of her bag. In silence they followed Clarissa and Henry out of the entrance and along the road up the hill.

Thud. Harriet jumped.

'What was that Mark?'

'Need you bloody ask? It's gone Harriet. Bloody stupid idea that. Flaming planters for everyone. Now there *will* be compost everywhere. Well you can clean it out Harriet. It's your mess.'

'Absolutely not a problem Mark. The vacuum cleaner isn't exactly an alien object.'

'Don't talk to me in that teacher voice Harriet. I've had enough!'

In sullen silence they watched Clarissa and Henry disappear over the brow of the hill. Harriet looked left. Between the bare branches of trees she noticed the 'For Sale' board. Still there. The last house before *his*.

Almost at the top of the hill. She looked up and out towards the horizon to see the gathering rows of wispy white clouds just holding together. She watched as the spears of sunshine lit their way through. Turning them to all the pastel shades of sugared almonds. A beautiful mackerel sky. Changing. Retreating. The blue back cloth. Now darkening. Receptive. Lifting the mist from the sea. Veiling the merging light. Fusing the palettes of pink, lilac, purple into a deepening, mysterious, evocative, consummate mix. Transfixed, *he* flooded her thoughts. Harriet felt the rush of sweet pain. The desire. The need ached and pulled at every part of her body. She opened out to him. Drew him in. She allowed herself. 'Just one last time.'

'Bloody hell Harriet. Fancy living here? He must be worth a sodding fortune.'

They turned in just as Clarissa and Henry disappeared into the main hall. They parked next to them, near the door.

'I'm sorting these bloody pots out first Harriet. I'm not driving back with that lot rattling around.'

Harriet removed herself from her dream. She followed him. Watched him open the hatch.

'Here take this one for a minute, will you?'

She stretched over.

'Grab it Harriet... Bloody hell. Couldn't you even do that?'

She just managed to catch it. But not before its load of bulbs and compost jumped out. Up. Forward. Then down. All scattered around, in and between the gravel.

Mark weighed up the Cotswold stone chippings.

'He's not going to be too pleased about that.'

'Look Mark. Just try to get the compost up will you? I think I've got all the bulbs.'

Mark kicked his toe at it.

'You're joking Harriet. If you're prepared to spend all night on your hands and knees I'm certainly not.'

From under the raised hatch he rearranged the pots.

'Pass that one over Harriet. It can go by your feet.'

He stretched forward and dropped it on to her seat.

'Come on Mark. Everyone's inside.'

'I don't suppose anyone's missed us Harriet. I'm seriously in two minds whether or not to go in.'

'Well of course they'll miss us Mark. Hurry up before someone closes the door.'

Chapter 41

'Oh there you are Harriet. Just look at this rug.'

'Yes I've already seen it Mummy.' Her next line was silent.

'He's made love to me on it. Actually.'

'Seen it Harriet. Have you been here before?' Her mother was curious.

'Only when I gave Mr. Sanderson a lift home.'

'I thought you were in a hurry to get in,' Mark mumbled.

'We're in the lounge Harriet,' her mother continued. 'We're having coffee in the lounge. Mrs. Harris is serving it.'

The beam on her face said it all.

'She thinks they're bloody royalty now,' Mark whispered at Harriet as they went through.

'Take a seat. Do.' Mr. Sanderson directed them to the small sofa near the fire.

Harriet sank into it. Hardly able to believe she was here. In this beautifully furnished room. Here again. In *his* house. This charming, gracious, exquisite old house. Chattering with people. She watched. Listened. Concentrated on his family. Always picking out the intonation. The long 'A'. The rounded vowels. Cultured. Confident. Natural. A joy to hear. Different. Not irritating like Belinda Oxfordshire. Her mother. Now seated as if she'd never moved. *His* mother. Steeped. Absolutely steeped in conversation. Like they'd known each other for years. Mr. Sanderson. Chatting. Moving around. Coffee cup in hand. Was that his sister? They hadn't been properly introduced.

'Right. Now,' Mr. Sanderson announced, 'if you'd all like to find a seat we'll do the introductions.' He'd read her mind. Geraldine was helping him out.

Too many. So many. Harriet was dazed. Couldn't take it all in. Then their turn came. Her and Mark.

'Now this is Harriet,' she heard him say, 'and Mark,' he cleared his throat. 'Her partner.'

'Oh, a bit more than that now Joris,' her mother called over. 'Her fiancé now. They've just got engaged. I've been telling your mother all about it.'

'Shut up Mummy. Just shut up. Now! Mummy,' Harriet said to herself.

'Show Joris the ring Harriet. Beautiful solitaire diamond. Expensive you know.'

'Well. Crumbs.' He scratched his head and stroked his chin. 'May I offer you both my sincere congratulations? I wish you every possible happiness.' He lifted her hand.

'No ring Harriet?'

'You haven't lost it out there have you? Grovelling around in all that gravel?' Mark piped up.

Mr. Sanderson threw him a look registering confusion.

'No Mark. I haven't. It's here in the back of my bag. Look.'

'What's it doing in there Harriet?' Mark asked suspiciously.

She slid it back on her finger.

Mr. Sanderson took a deep breath, raised his eyebrows and moved swiftly away.

'Joris.' His mother shouted over the noise. 'Mrs. Glover, er Frances,' she gently touched her hand. 'Frances and I would like to watch the Queen's speech. Would you mind turning the television on please?'

Then she changed her mind.

'No don't bother Joris. We'll catch it later. They'll all be staying for tea. Everyone alright with that? Bring me the sherry bottle will you? Oh and a bottle of red. The one Harriet's drinking.'

The chatter lowered to kindle a generally pleasant, agreeable atmosphere. Distinctly over-laced with gratitude from Harriet's mother.

'Well how very kind of you Mrs. Sanderson.'

'Well I'm not about to have Christmas Day spoiled by you leaving early Frances. And you must call me Olivia. Please do. Charles take the men to the billiards room. They might like a change from the small talk.'

She waved the wine bottle at Harriet.

'Come dear. Do come and join us.'

Harriet counted each luxurious step as she crossed the deep pile carpet to the long settee under the window.

'This lady is truly inspired,' she thought, glad to see the back of Mark.

Mrs. Sanderson passed her the wine bottle.

'Do help yourself dear. Now. Do I remember correctly?'

She turned to Harriet's mother.

'This is your daughter Harriet, I believe? What a beautiful young lady she is.'

Harriet blushed. She warmed to her instantly.

'My, what a pretty ring. You know, diamonds are my favourite. You can always wear them.' She lifted her hand to Harriet. 'Even when you get older.'

Harriet smiled. There was something of Molly about her.

'Anyway many congratulations. We wish you and your fiancé every happiness.'

She topped up the sherry glasses.

'Thank you very much. So kind,' Harriet replied, partially distracted. Her mother mouthed something at her. 'Trying to tell me what to say, most probably,' she thought.

'You know Charles and I were most upset when Joris broke off his engagement to Belinda. We've known them for years Suzanna and Robin. Belinda's an only child you know. Her and Joris practically grew up together. She's younger than him, of course, but they seemed to bridge the gap very well.'

Harriet budged back a bit. Tried to get out of her mother's line of sight.

'Of course he's been engaged to be married before. More than once I might add. I was particularly fond of a very pretty little dark haired girl. Both at medical school. We had great hopes for them. Of course he never does tell us very much. Certainly nothing about his failed relationships. You know we thought he'd settle down to making a jolly good GP. Charles and I could never quite understand why he threw it in. For teaching, I ask you?'

She touched Harriet's hand.

'No offence dear. I do know you are the young lady that did so much to turn his school around. Now he *did* tell us that. In fact Charles and I felt he had quite a soft spot for you from the way he spoke.'

Harriet felt herself melting into a cloud of delight. An instantaneous lift from the pleasure of her words. She smiled.

'He wasn't teaching too long before his first headship. We thought he was very settled at Wild Flower Meadow. The primary school. Yes, Wild Flower Meadow Primary School. Beautiful place.'

Harriet pricked up her ears. She'd heard of it. Never forged the connection. With *him*. On both levels.

'Did it ever occur to him?' she wondered, 'as we lay in the field of flowers?'

'Then he just upped and went to your school. Before you started there I think dear. Did he actually appoint you?'

Harriet nodded.

Mrs. Sanderson topped up the sherry glasses. Harriet filled up with wine.

'Just between us three, I don't think he was getting enough free time as a GP. Hard work. Very demanding. Young, good looking doctor. The others were complaining a bit. All the ladies wanted to see him. Wouldn't go to anyone else. Unless they were desperate of course. He never had a free slot. Of course that's all changed now. They do things differently these days.'

She looked at Harriet and then across to her mother.

'Oh dear, I'm talking too much aren't I? I do hope I'm not boring you both.'

Harriet just edged her mother out in reply.

'Certainly not!'

'Good. Now where was I? Yes. That was it. He's always been very clever. Good on the arts. Good on the sciences. It makes life very difficult for people like that. Don't you think? Makes it hard for them to settle. Education gave him the shorter hours. The long holidays, to do other things. Of course that's changed a lot too. He does masses of paperwork well into the early hours most nights, now.'

'Oh. Not so good.' Harriet changed her crossed legs over.

'Exactly my dear. That's just how Charles and I feel. He's involved in so many other things you know. On the board of directors here, there and everywhere. Not to mention the Firstling Bank. Non-executive director there. You know he's frightfully concerned about their goings on. That's another story. Just between us.'

Harriet could suddenly feel her mother shifting in, sending the vibrations along the cushions.

'Between us, he says they've been on the make for years. Now got completely out of control. Lending money to people who can never pay it back. All of them. All the banks selling off debt packages to each other, while all the time house prices are falling. No collateral left in property. No back up. No security. Poor people losing their homes while the big money guys gamble away on the stock markets. Joris can certainly see mass unemployment ahead.'

She hushed her voice as she topped up the sherry for them both.

'Just between us he's tried having a word with the PM. Good friend you know. Eton. Cambridge. They stick together. Things too out of control now for anyone to be able to do anything about it. Of course Joris is very worried about the business. Sailing fanatic I'm afraid. I worry, especially when he's out on the big races. Where was I? Oh yes. They've five now up and down the country. Starboard Marine... Then they tag on the area. South East. South West. You know the sort of thing? I think we're North West up here, aren't we?'

'Yes, that would be it.'

Irritated by her mother's response, Harriet was terrified Mrs. Sanderson would suddenly stop talking.

'Anyhow our bank, Swiss Rollards, mercifully have behaved responsibly, although there will naturally be some effect from the fallout. Joris reckons there's a world crisis looming and there'll be one crash after another. But back to the business. The trouble is property has been part of their investment strategy. They've got a very large portfolio now. Belinda's responsible for that side of it, of course. But do you know? She can't stop herself. She's completely convinced he's got it all wrong. She's forging ahead with the next one. A lovely girl but very headstrong. Joris doesn't like that. I think that's why he broke it off. He's trying not to upset her, I know he feels a bit bad about it all, but Charles and I don't think he should let her carry on buying houses the company can't really afford. He wanted to get the company floated on the stock exchange. Too risky. That's going to have to wait. Anyhow he simply can't keep still. He's now taken over that American franchise coffee company. I think it's called The Bean-S-Talk. He's bought them out. Now a franchisor. Taken on all the franchisees. Running the model in his own outlets then he's going to continue with the franchising.'

Harriet lapped at the information like a cat starved of milk.

'Of course we're a banking family. Historically that is. Merchant bankers. Charles's side goes back to the early eighteenth century. Danish. Started as a small family run business and grew from there. The business was handed down. The next generation moved to London and stayed in the family until Charles's father passed it up. Oh Joris could tell you all about it. He's traced our ancestors back on both sides. Naturally on his father's side they're of Danish origin. Apparently my side originated in Holland. Also bankers I might add. He reckons he can link me right back to Dutch royalty. I ask you!'

'Gosh. That is interesting,' encouraged Harriet. There was an air of regality about her. It wasn't difficult to imagine.

'Well, thank you dear. I don't often get the opportunity to speak to such an attentive audience. Of course with banking in the family Joris is furious about the current situation. I'm sure he feels it's a slight on him.'

Harriet smiled. Wanted her opinion.

'My thoughts dear? Well Charles won't hear of it of course but there's been plenty of stories passed down the family. They've not always been whiter than white you know. Human nature. Doesn't change. Greed and corruption. There'll always be people capable of being tempted. That's why I don't trust them. Any of them. When Charles's father died they tried to squeeze him out of his inheritance. Fortunately he was sharper than them. All that money. It came right in the end. It gave me a thing about it though.'

She paused for the last sip of sherry before reaching for the bottle. She nodded towards Harriet's mother then filled both glasses up.

'Interest, dividends from stocks, shares, things like that. In fact the bulk of my own inheritance. I gradually drew it out. Still do. The chauffeur runs me there. Cash. You can't beat it. Keep it all in a security safe at home. Joris and Charles go mad on account of the interest I'm losing. We don't need it of course. Emily and Rebecca. Joris's sisters, they're just as bad. You met Emily didn't you? Her husband and boys? They're around somewhere.'

Harriet nodded. 'Don't stop now. Please don't stop,' she thought.

'It's safe enough. We're well looked after by our security company. Thousands. There's literally thousands of pounds at home. Joris keeps using it for cash flow. He pays me the interest. I don't want it of course but he sees it as some kind of incentive. Anyhow he deposits it all back into the bank. Just figures. Just numbers. I let him take my cash in exchange for numbers again. We can see what happens to numbers, can't we? All around us. They get wiped off. Cleaned away. Just like that. Millions gone at the touch of a key on a computer keyboard. And they wonder why I want to keep it safe?'

Harriet could just hear her mother articulate her own silent gasp. She desperately hoped that was all it was going to be. Hoped the sherry wouldn't set her talking. It was unlike her to quietly listen for so long.

'The cash. All that cash. That's where he get's it. How could Tricia and I have been so suspicious?' Harriet's thoughts were whirling.

Mrs. Sanderson continued. Continued sipping the sherry, well loosening her tongue.

'He gets a bit too bossy sometimes, you know. Hates me having anything of value around. There's an exquisitely beautiful emerald and diamond set. Collar necklace, bracelet, earrings. Inherited from my mother. You know? Joris insisted on getting it valued. He's never liked it being in the house. Worth over a hundred thousand pounds. Emeralds. Diamonds. Exquisite in cut, clarity and colour. All the c's. I think that's how they classify them. Isn't it? Anyhow, I used to like looking at it. He took it over in the spring. Didn't want family heirlooms in the house. Packed the case up around the last of the gold bullion. Oh just a very few bars left. Very old of course. Then he popped those on top. Now it's hiding away in Switzerland. In some vault or other in the Swiss Rollards Bank. No one can see it. What's the point of that at my age?'

She lifted the sherry bottle and divided the last of it between the two glasses.

Harriet froze. 'Tricia was right,' she thought, 'that case was heavy. It would be even with a few gold bars. The matching set of diamonds and emeralds on top. Gosh! But not for her. Not for Tricia. That *must* have been it. It *was* the spring. He should have taken it himself. That was awful giving it to her.' Then it crossed her mind, 'It was me. He wanted to be with me. He risked giving her all that to take through just to be with me?' She was totally overwhelmed by the thought.

She sipped away at the red in her glass. Thinking hard.

'It's the sherry. It's got to be the sherry. They've had a large bottle between them. She'd never have spilled all that sober.'

Harriet put the wine glass to her lips. 'Oh golly. Gosh,' she thought, 'she's answered so many questions.'

She looked around. Just the three of them and the roaring fire. She didn't realise they'd all drifted off to the billiards room.

She looked up. Mr. Sanderson was in the doorway. Standing tall. Looking at her.

Thick, straight blonde hair. Mop. Just the curl at the neck of his sweater. Serious. Handsome. Rugged. Gorgeous. In the doorway.

'Alcohol not helping this at all Harriet,' she told herself.

He came over to pick up the empty bottle. Held it to the light.

'You two OK? One large bottle between you? I do hope you haven't been giving away the family secrets Mother.'

Harriet went red.

'See what I mean?' said Mrs. Sanderson to them both. 'He's terribly bossy.'

He laughed.

'Mrs. Harris has laid the buffet in the dining room. Some of it's oven heated. She'll get cross if you let it go cold.'

'Suzanna and Robin not arrived yet Joris?'

'No Mother. Not yet. They're not bringing Belinda I hope?'

'Well what else is the poor girl supposed to do Joris. They're not going to leave her behind on Christmas Day.'

Harriet suddenly felt ill. The doorbell chimed. He went to open it. She could hear their voices. Hear Mr. Sanderson. Concerned. In the hall. He returned to the lounge as they rose from the sofa.

'First aid required. Any plasters suitable for gravelled cut knees Mother?'

Mrs. Sanderson stood up.

'Belinda's just gone skidding on this. Poor girl. Can hardly stand.' He held the two halves of Harriet's otherwise large newly split spring bulb in his hand.

Harriet knew it wasn't nice. She was glad.

'Must have a word with Swift.'

Harriet kept quiet.

Chapter 42

Replete, the large gathering returned to the lounge to relax.

'My word. It's not ten already?' Mrs. Sanderson pulled the cuff back from the sleeve of her lilac cardigan to look at her watch.

'Queen's speech Frances. Just in time.' Harriet hadn't ever seen her mother looking so pleasantly out of it.

'Charles. Would you mind turning the television on please? For Frances and I.'

Mr. Sanderson's father winked at Harriet as he brushed past. She turned to Mark.

'Oh Mark. Would you mind taking the men out and giving them their planters? *Please.* They won't be too bothered about missing the Queen's speech, I don't suppose. They'll need to get them in their cars. We'll be going home soon.'

She fished in her bag. 'Here's the gift cards. Thanks Mark.'

They went. The room hushed automatically as the wide flat screen came to life. A different news reader.

'Oh she's drawn the short straw. I haven't seen her face before. She must be standing in. Letting the others enjoy their Christmas. What a kind girl.'

'Mummy, please just shut up,' Harriet said to herself. Her mother was grating at her already raw nerves.

'Now, just before we take you over to the Palace for the Queen's speech, we'll join Simon Barnes for the best of the local news.

Harriet's mouth dropped open. And stayed open.

'A feat of brilliance brought Rapping Hammer and the Ironing Bards to the opening of the new coffee outlet The Bean-S-Talk at Starboard Marine North West yesterday. A sell out. A complete sell out. Laced with narcotics the band turned the grotto into a smoking den. Then it was all Go Man Go. Gambling. Sex and drugs.

Now here's a shot for all you fans.'

The sight of Rapping Hammer's mooning pink bottom sent a gasp round the room.

Harriet kept looking at the door. She didn't know which one of them it would be worst to see first. Mark, Mr. Sanderson or his mother. She glanced back to the television.

Tricia suddenly appeared lifting the holly from her hair only to drop it down the rear end of Rapping Hammer's gaping black leathers.

Harriet could hear her girls giggling as he leaped around in pain, struggling with the zip. Letting go. Rummaging, scrambling to pull it out. The sight of Tricia delving into his backside trying to retrieve it reduced them to tears. Hysterics followed as they watched her forcing him into the Santa Claus costume. At the tug of the orange and purple bow, they were collapsed on the floor. Rapping Hammer shooting his hands across, desperately trying to cover the gap widening at the front of his tight leather pants.

'Now this girl says life's a lottery. Boy does she play while the cat's away? Remember? Concerned to help a deprived pupil for a three thousand pound bet she allowed a little breast play.'

'Oh. Oh no.' Shock charged the room. Harriet covered her bright red face with her hands. She could hear Mr. Sanderson at the doorway sympathising with Belinda Oxfordshire. He stopped. Suddenly she saw her chest filling the screen with Rapping Hammer aiming a white round sticky label at the point of each of her breasts. Mission accomplished. The frame froze. Just like that. Harriet wanted to die. No one could ever have guessed she'd whipped them off so quickly. She felt like she'd just been the centre of some lurid sex orgy.

She heard Mark's mum. Shocked.

'Well Harold I'm quite sure we wouldn't get that kind of behaviour from Melissa Scott.'

'Rogers dear. She got married you know?'

'You've missed the *point* Harold since they're getting divorced. She'll be available soon. I think Mark could do better.'

'I wouldn't miss those *points*, I don't mind telling you.' Harriet could hear him guffaw.

'Harold. That's quite enough!'

Harriet cringed in loud silence to herself.

'I hope the others aren't back yet.'

She didn't dare look round to see who else might be watching.

'Cor Mum. Cool. Maybe you should try that on Dad? Stop you both dozing off in the evenings.' The girls were still choking with laughter. Just about able to speak.

'Clare,' winced Harriet to herself. She stayed silent. Didn't answer her.

Mr. Sanderson returned to the room.

Simon Barnes caught their attention again.

'This innovative approach to dealing with the recession could well catch on. In connection with these events at Starboard Marine North West we've just come into possession of a document. A leaked confidential internal memo originating from the same source in which the founder and managing director of the company Mr Joris Sanderson predicts the collapse of the whole banking system. World-wide.'

Harriet watched Mr. Sanderson turn the sound up.

'He's confident we are as yet only on the edge of a massive, property led, catastrophic collapse. "Desperate times. Desperate measures," he says. And that's exactly where he's gone.'

This is Simon Barnes for Internews TV, Starboard Marine North West, Stetmead.

The kind girl returned.

'Now a quick look at tomorrow's papers before we move on.

"CLOSE FRIEND OF THE PRIME MINISTER TURNS TO ROCK, SEX AND DRUGS TO SAVE HIS FAILING COMPANY" Also a picture there taken at the opening of their new branch earlier this year.

"HAMMER THEM ON" Yes there you can see a picture of Rapping Hammer pressing away at those labels.

"HARD PRESSED" That's a reference there to the state of the company, the Ironing Bards and of course those labels again.

"TEACHER HELPS BOSS KEEP ABREAST OF THE RECESSION." That's another of the same there.

And on a more serious note from the Financial News **"DIRE PREDICTIONS FOR THE STOCK MARKETS."**

There. That's it. Stay tuned for the Queen's Speech. Coming up in just a moment.'

'HARRIET. I warned you about going round with that common girl. Didn't I?'

'Escape Harriet,' she thought, 'away from Mummy. Quick.'

She turned. Stalled. At Mr. Sanderson's feet.

'Harriet. A word.'

She followed him into the drawing room. He closed the door. His eyes were on her, watching her wring her hands.

'What happened to it Harriet?'

'Oh it's beautiful. The gold. The buttercups. Engraved. I put it away in the back of the drawer. To keep it safe. Thank you so very much. I'll always keep it. Always remember you by it. Even after I'm married. I'll always remember you.'

'Hmm. I think I can pretty much say the same of you Harriet. Not for all the right reasons though. I meant the brown envelope. What happened to it?'

Harriet blushed. As red as a letter box. Her mouth as fixed. Oblong. Unable to move.

'So you're not going to tell me?'

Silence.

'Damage done. Some swine's leaked it. All hit the fan at once.' Anger crossed his face.

She watched him stride to the bay window. For a few moments. Staring at the night, painted into Georgian squares. A gallery of starlit skies. Moonlight breathing life into the hard frost on the bare tree branches. Sparkling at the side paths. Forming inquisitively along the glazing bars. Riding its way up the sides of each small frame. Sugar coating every hand blown square of glass. He tapped his knuckle against it.

'You know I'll be under pressure to suspend you. I'll do my best. But I can't guarantee anything.'

She turned to go. Looked up at him.

'Please thank your mother for her kindness.'

'Anyone seen Joris?' Mrs. Sanderson popped her head round the lounge door. Smiled at Harriet's mother.

'Oh there you are. I really think George and I should be making a move Olivia. We've had such a lovely time, thank you. I do hope we can keep in touch.'

'Most certainly Frances. Do you know? I haven't enjoyed a Christmas Day like this for many years.'

Harriet's mother hurried her father into the hall. The drawing room door opened.

'Oh there you are Harriet. Daddy and I are just going. I'll give you a call tomorrow.'

'Joris, I was looking for you.'

He joined his mother as she led him down the hall towards the kitchen.

Harriet hurried into her coat. With barely a wave she was off the entrance steps, crunching into the gravel.

'Mark what are you doing sitting out here? I wondered where you'd got to. I expected you to come back in, at least to say goodbye.'

'Get in Harriet. That's one Christmas Day completely ruined. They're way beyond us Harriet. Beyond James and Geraldine too. I couldn't stand hearing her making such an arse of herself. Fawning all over them. I think it was really winding James up. My parents have never been so uncomfortable. It was written all over their faces. The only one who looked at home was your mother. No surprise there! How the devil did we all end up with them? We were invited back to your brother's. That was the plan. We had every right to sodding well go home. Anyway Harriet, lard ball in a bloody big nutshell. If you've any sense it'll have put you off him for good.'

Harriet closed the door as Mark started the engine. She looked behind her to see the car completely cleared of spring planters. She heaved a sigh of relief. If it hadn't been for those, for sure Mark would have seen the ten o'clock news.

Chapter 43

The roar of a helicopter coming and going round the bedroom all night ensured Harriet little or no sleep. Mark had been snoring all night. Again. Two nights on the run. No sleep. Not like him. He hadn't seen the ten o'clock news on Christmas night. That would have kept him awake. It was as vivid in Harriet's mind as last night. As the night before. She'd been battling for sleep anyway. Simon Barnes permeating every tortuous thought. Tossing. Turning. To the snoring.

'Mark's subconscious determination to get me back,' she decided.

She lay still. Staring at the ceiling. Wanting it all to go away.

'Getting there,' she thought, 'Boxing Day over. Am most definitely NOT going to the sailing club on New Year's Eve. NOT seeing *him*. Not seeing anyone. Hiding. I'm going into hiding. That's fine. Absolutely fine. I'll get suspended. Go into hiding until Mark goes. Until he gets back. Get married quietly. Go into hiding right now. Pretend I've got swine flu. It's actually an ordinary day today. What a relief. Glad that's over. Out of the way. All over and done with for a whole year. Be married by then. That's if...'

Then Mark's mother's words struck home like a thunderbolt.

' "I think Mark could do better." Melissa bloody Rogers Scott. What's he been telling them about her? They must have met her. Must know her, to be talking like that? Surely they won't go out of their way to put him off me? Tell him about the news? Thank goodness the girls didn't mention it yesterday. Boxing Day. When they came for lunch. Neither did the boys. Polite. Nice boys. Not a hint of it. Didn't stay late. Off to see Rapping Hammer at the Arena. We both got to bed early for a change. Not that it made any difference with that racket thundering from Mark's nostrils all night. In bed when the phone rang. Mummy's message? Do I really want to hear it? OK Pepper, I'm coming.'

She decided she better had. It might have been important. The cat wound its way round her legs to the bottom stair. She was surprised to see the green light flashing up two messages.

She pressed 'play'.

'Ooh `arriet. It's only me. I `ope you've `ad a better time than me `arriet. Bob's not at all `appy. And to top it all. Didn't our Adam just go and chicken out last night on seein` that bloody Rappin` `ammer? I `ad to go and meet that gormless cousin of `is to tell `im didn't I `arriet? Ended up on a date with `im. Made such a fuss about bein` let down. I couldn't believe it `arriet. Me `avin` to go in there and watch that lot again. I tell you `arriet I've seen more than enough of that Rappin` `ammer to last me a lifetime and it wasn't very pleasant either. Got into an `ell of a row with Bob when I got `ome. All because our Adam didn't want to give the wrong impression. Didn't want to be seen out with an older man. I ask you `arriet `e's only thirteen. I thought I was doin` `im a favour. Well the only bit of Christmas I `ave enjoyed is takin` all them soddin` posters down off `is bedroom wall. And rippin` them up of course. See you `arriet.'

Harriet smiled and pressed the button again.

'It's Mummy Harriet. There was only a handful of spring bulbs at the bottom of that planter and absolutely no compost whatsoever.'

Chapter 44

Finished, Harriet pushed her cereal bowl away and stared at the new calendar on the wall wondering when Mark was likely to surface.

'New Year's Day. Again?'

The phone rang.

'You did this at exactly the same time last year. Remember? I didn't want a new kitchen then and I don't bloody want one now!'

'I've only just left school. This is my first job. First day. Oh they didn't tell me an old bag like you would answer the phone when I was trainin`. Don't `ave one then. I'm not fuckin` bothered.'

Furious, Harriet returned to her chair. Glared at the calendar.

'South flipping Pole. I've got to look at that all bloody year. If you've seen one lump of ice melting you've flipping well seen them all. Haven't you Pepper?'

Now extremely irritated. Not least with herself. Of course she couldn't go last night to the New Year's Eve bash at the sailing club. But Mark didn't have to go without her.

'No he bloody didn't.'

She didn't want to go last year but he'd managed to stay at home then.

'Oh. It's you. You're up. Happy New Year Mark. How did it go last night?'

'As well as it went for Bob, Harriet. For some reason Tricia decided against it too.'

'Was it packed?'

'Crowded. Full of loud people waving flyers around.'

'Oh. Yes. That would be the draw, Mark. Did you get to see who won the boat?'

'I saw lard ball prancing about. Every female in sight swooning round him. Do you know Harriet, Bob and I are up to bloody here with him.'

'Who won it then?'

'How do I flaming know Harriet? I heard him volunteering himself for sailing lessons anyway. He wouldn't have thrown that in if she'd been wearing an old tweed coat and a headscarf.'

'Lessons were part of the prize Mark. Anyway, what *was* she wearing then?'

'Not enough to cover her long legs. Weren't bad actually. It was better seeing her pink knickers though when she flung herself at him with her legs in the air.'

'What? Did he catch her?'

'He had to catch her. They'd have both gone over.'

Raging with jealousy Harriet could do little more than shuffle on her seat.

'Oh and Tarquin Bridgewater sends his best. Hoped *I* wasn't too disappointed about the brown envelope.'

Jealousy immediately tinged with fear and confusion. Brown envelopes large or small were definitely not her thing at the moment. She thought of the honour. 'Just how much does Mark know?' She wondered as she tried hastily to formulate a reply.

'*You* were disappointed Mark? Why would he say that to you? He was definitely high. Now he's completely bewildered. It's solved now, anyway. Thank goodness. Did I tell you they had a few break-ins at the club when that went missing. He gave it me at the coffee shop opening, on Christmas Eve. I just got told to pass it over to Belinda Oxfordshire. Nothing to do with me now.'

She watched the expression on his face. He'd been holding out ever since he came downstairs. 'I'd stop digging if I were you Harriet.'

She looked away.

'I hear you and Tricia managed to make right arses of yourselves again Harriet.'

'What do you mean?'

'You know exactly what I mean Harriet. Shoving me outside when the news came on.'

Harriet could feel the rush of colour to her cheeks.

'No Mark. They were Christmas presents. They had to be given out.'

'What is it with you two Harriet? The pair of you behave just like a couple of giggling school girls. It's lard ball isn't it? What you two wouldn't do for him? Bob saw the whole thing. Wouldn't let Tricia turn it off. He was absolutely livid with her. Carrying on like that. And from the sound of it you weren't much better. Allowing him to play around with you like that.'

'You what? I beg your pardon? I got shoved forward. He'd stuck those labels on in a flash. I pulled them off quickly. Straight away. Of course Simon Barnes wouldn't have shown that.'

'Well that's precisely the point Harriet. You know exactly what he's like. You'd think after the last do down there you'd have learned a lesson. But no. Oh no. You walk straight into it again.'

Harriet didn't answer.

'This leaked internal report of his. Lard ball's. This bloody brown envelope. If it was that confidential he had no right passing it over to you Harriet. No right at all. You should have refused to take it. "Yes Mr. Sanderson. Three bags full Mr. Sanderson." Where exactly does your common sense go to Harriet?'

'Well I didn't know what was in it. Did I? And what about *your* common sense? Where does yours go Mark? You were the one that forgot to lock the car.'

'In reasonable circumstances Harriet. Anyway that's his look out. More to the point. How many more times is this sodding three grand going to crop up? First of all it's a three grand tip for some bloody steward on that flaming cruise and now you see fit to throw another packet at some kid in your class. Where's it all coming from Harriet? Come on I want to know.'

'Won it on the lottery months ago. I just did an extra line and won three thousand pounds.'

'You what Harriet and you didn't tell me?'

'You were in a very bad mood at the time Mark. I thought I'd keep it. Just in case one day we might need it to pay for our wedding. Then you left didn't you?

You went to the Antarctic in an even worse mood. So I gave it away. On the rebound. I thought at least it would make someone happy. I didn't think we'd ever get back together again at the time.'

Mark scratched his head, stood up, then banged his hand down on the table.

'The decision's made Harriet. Probably not the wisest of decisions. But I'm warning you Harriet if there's any more goings-on with *him* then the whole thing's off. I'm out!'

'There won't be Mark. I promise. You know I've only ever wanted us to get married.'

She blinked at the tears just cornering her eyes. She pushed the chair from under to go straight into his arms. Familiar. Safe. Secure. Things too precious to let go of.

'OK Hat. Let's put it all behind us shall we? Make an appointment to see that house before *they* change their minds about selling it.'

Chapter 45

Ten minutes had passed since Harriet waved Mark off. He was back to work. She still had a few days to go. She tried to put it all from her mind. *Him?* Not an easy ten minutes. She'd been opening and closing the top drawer of her dressing table to the sound of her mother babbling at the answer machine. Something about not even having chance to give out her surprise Christmas presents.

'Well you wanted to stay Mummy,' Harriet thought. 'You were the one who jumped at the chance of staying for tea.'

The distraction was fleeting. The bracelet. She wanted to know. Didn't. Did. Didn't.

'No Pepper. I'm not doing that to Mark. It's staying right there. Just where it is.'

She left the bedroom. Braved the stairs to her mother's message. Skipped the first bit. She'd just heard that.

'Anyway, you haven't phoned me back yet Harriet. Mind you I'm not very surprised after all that scandal on Christmas night. Daddy and I are most disappointed Harriet. I don't know how I'm ever going to look my friends in the face again. Mark's parents hardly looked at us on the way out. You finally bring him on board. On the brink of marrying him and what do you do? Give him every reason not to bother. And who leaked Mr. Sanderson's confidential business information Harriet? You see, you're obviously involved in that as well. Poor man. Quite honestly Harriet it very much looks as if this is all of your own making. Oh and that common girl, as well. That goes without saying. Absolutely disgusting she should be trying to pull the pants off that poor boy. Thank our lucky stars Olivia was out of the room seeing to that poor girl, Belinda. It wouldn't have happened to be one of the bulbs from my pot she skidded on by any chance? There you go again Harriet. Now their poor gardener Mr. Swift will get it in the neck, no doubt because of you. That poor man. You know he's well known locally for his prize tomatoes? Olivia was telling me all about him before you came over. She gave me a small brown envelope. Just a few precious seeds inside. They're very rare. He's cultivated the species himself you know. Everyone's trying to get their hands on them. Anyway I've emptied those bits of bulbs you gave me out of that pot now. Daddy's put it in the greenhouse. Filled it with compost. He's going to get the heating going. See if he can bring a few on early. Not quite the same as showing off a nice display of spring bulbs by the front door Harriet. I was banking on Mrs. Jones next door seeing those. Mark could have at least given that pot to *his* mother. No manners. No *evidence* of good breeding. Bohemian. I don't know where I went wrong with you Harriet? You two are very well matched.'

'Well thank you Mummy for that.' She went into the kitchen and started the nature nurture debate with herself.

Interrupted. The phone again. The line was crackling. 'Mummy's fault, Pepper.'

'Ah, M… Glover.'

'Oh I was going to phone you. We'd both like to see that house together. Saturday morning at ten. Would they be able to do that? Do you think? Please. Just a minute this line's crackling. That's better now. Ten on Saturday. If they can? Please.'

'I'm not your estate agent Miss Glover though I might just as well be for all the antics I have to put up with. Miss Glover I'm afraid to say the balance has gone against you. What with Brown and that union fellow having already filed a complaint I'm afraid there was little I could do to talk Mr. Whittle out of it. You're suspended from duty for one month pending investigation. You'll receive a formal notice of suspension in the post. Of course you'll receive full pay during this period. Damned inconvenient. I could well do without such formality. It was fortunate I witnessed that Hammer lad's lewd behaviour and if it hadn't been for Brown and Potts I don't think this would have happened. However I'm fully confident you'll be allowed to return to your duties shortly. I'll keep you posted Miss Glover. In the meantime I suggest you continue to focus on ways to motivate the parents into lifestyle changes. I noted both your's and Mrs. Harrington's absence from the sailing club on New Year's Eve. Didn't look very good I must say after your involvement at the barn dance. Still probably as well in view of all this. I'm banking on most parents not having turned their televisions on for the news on Christmas night. Can't legislate for the papers though. My phone hasn't stopped. Let's hope you haven't accelerated it. Haven't sent the whole world into a financial black hole Miss Glover. Anyhow, the coffee shop. To return to the minutiae, there was a lot of interest. Very well attended. We need to capitalise on that. Also if you could see your way to giving Mrs. Harrington a hand during this period of suspension? She'll need some assistance shelf stacking as we restock.'

He replaced the receiver. Just like that.

'Not even a "Good day to you Miss Glover." Flipping cheek. Has it not even occurred to him just why he's got to restock? There wasn't a single thing left on a single shelf anywhere. He must have made a fortune. Like he needs it? He's flipping well loaded.'

She rang the estate agents. Made the appointment.

'The sooner we get sold and out the better!'

She'd hardly turned as the phone rang again.

'YES.' She didn't care who it was.

'Oh `arriet. It *is* you. It didn't sound like you then. Are you in a bad mood `arriet?'

'I am Tricia. But not with you.'

'Oh I am glad to `ear that `arriet. You `ad me worried then. Anyway `arriet I `ave to congratulate you on your engagement. I'm really pleased for you `arriet. I must say I felt just a little bit jealous. You must `ave noticed I've always `ad a bit of a soft spot for your Mark. Anyway `arriet I'll give in graciously, especially as

I've never been more off Bob. I've got to tell you about 'im yet. Anyway I didn't think I could wait any longer for our friend Joris. I can't be doin' with 'im messin' me about anymore. So after Bob tellin' me that your Mark was absolutely furious with you, I didn't think you'd go. We both didn't go did we 'arriet? I was so mad at Bob goin' anyway. Without me 'arriet? Supposed to be New Year's bloody Eve 'arriet? Anyway where was I? Oh yes. With your Mark bein' so furious and you two not being married I thought 'e might just become available 'arriet, to be 'onest. I was plannin' on comfortin' 'im after you'd left 'im 'arriet. With my red knickers on. Well off. Of course. I was thinkin' of wavin' them at 'im like a flag 'arriet. You know? To let 'im know I'd surrendered to 'im. If you understand 'arriet? I think 'e quite took to them last Burn's night.'

'Oh I think it's the white flag for surrender Tricia.'

'Oh white then. I've got some new white lacy ones 'arriet. Completely wasted on 'im. Bob. 'e's so busy goin' off to the gym 'e can't see what's under 'is nose 'arriet. Well I've 'ad enough of 'im. Just tell me when you've 'ad enough of your Mark. I'm sure 'e's got a very soft spot for me 'arriet. I know you won't mind me sayin' that. Anyway if you're ever thinkin' of dumpin' 'im send 'im this way. I don't mind second 'and goods 'arriet.'

Harriet laughed. 'I'll bear it in mind.'

'No, I'm not jokin' 'arriet as soon as someone better comes along I'm givin' Bob the big shove. Not worth doin' it for Guy 'ammer though. 'im? 'e'd never own that garden centre in a month of Sundays 'arriet. 'er. That Belinda Oxfordshire tryin' to make 'im out to be somethin' 'e's not. Tryin' to put me off the scent 'arriet in case I think she's after my Bob. She can 'ave 'im 'arriet. Me mum can 'ave the kids. I've 'ad enough of them as well.'

'Not fussed on ours either at the moment,' Harriet replied. 'Cheeky pair. The two of them. Not a bit impressed with us getting engaged. Never mind married.'

'Oh, it'll be the shock 'arriet. They'll get used to it I'm sure.'

'They're both engaged themselves. Just. Coincidence or what? Nice lads and we're really pleased for them but they're off to the Seychelles the four of them. A double wedding on the beach. Same time as ours, so they certainly won't be coming.'

'Never mind 'arriet. I will. It might not be with Bob though. Anyway 'e said Mark told 'im you were all at our friend's 'ouse for tea on Christmas night? Your Mark didn't enjoy it very much, did 'e 'arriet?'

'An understatement Tricia. Of course it was Geraldine trying to go another rung up the social ladder. Mark was absolutely furious.'

''e should have knocked 'er off 'arriet. Er I think that's got to be another one of them metathingies 'arriet. 'e didn't see the news 'imself did 'e 'arriet? Of course Bob couldn't wait to switch it on as it wasn't 'ardly shown on Christmas Eve. I tried to turn it off 'arriet but 'e wouldn't let me. Of course 'e didn't see us outside with Rappin' 'ammer. 'e didn't know what went on 'til 'e saw it on the telly that is. It 'ad all 'appened by the time 'e arrived. Showin' off in that stupid sweatshirt. `e `it the roof `arriet. Do you know `arriet `e called me a little tart. I've `ardly spoken to `im since.'

'I don't blame you Tricia. Mark wasn't much better. I've got to tell you this though.'

'Ooh `arriet. What `ave you got to tell me now?'

'Mr. Sanderson's mother didn't hold anything back. They've come from a long line of merchant bankers. Absolutely loaded. Gosh Tricia you wouldn't have believed it. We've been completely on the wrong track. Nothing so exciting as money laundering. His mother's got a thing about banks. Keeps all her money at home. Mr. Sanderson's busy trying to collect it all up to bank it again. No wonder he's got such easy access to cash.'

'Oh `arriet. I don't believe that. I think you've `ad the metathingy wool pulled over your eyes. Anyway what about that `eavy case `e dumped on me? What was in that?'

'His mother's jewellery.'

'It was `eavier than that `arriet.'

'On top of the rest of the gold bars. She said there were just a few left. Family heirlooms Tricia. Very old. Very heavy'

'Bloody `ell `arriet. You're jokin` me. You've got to be jokin` me.'

'No Tricia. I'm honestly not. They're absolutely rolling in it.'

'Well there is somethin` goin` on with Tarquin Bridgewater and `im `arriet. `e was well away. `e'd been smokin` pot or somethin` in the back end of that grotto with them Ironing Boards. If `e's not comin` in to our place lookin` for money from our friend I reckon it's something like tobacco. Ready to roll broken up drug leaves. I would say. Or marijuana plant seeds so `e can grow `is own.'

'Now there's a thought Tricia. He might be getting that sort of thing from Rapping Hammer and the band, Tricia. They do know him. Call him Barking Ditchwater.'

Tricia giggled.

'As far as Mr. Sanderson goes he's more likely to be passing along seeds from tomato plants.'

'Oh `arriet. Now you are jokin` me. I never `eard the like.'

'His mother gave mine a brown envelope with just a few in. Seeds from a prize species. Everyone wants them apparently.'

'`arriet. It's a cover up. One big cover up. The `ole family's doin` one big cover up. I thought you were cleverer than that `arriet?'

'No brains me Tricia. My heads so full of it all I don't know what to believe any more.'

'Stay vigilant `arriet. That's the motto. That's if `e'd let me in the bloody place. Do you know `arriet `e's suspended me. Just for today `arriet. That's why I've been able to phone you. `e said "I'm not very impressed with your behaviour Mrs. Harrington. Take this as the first warning. You'll receive a copy in writing. Today I'm considering my position with regard to your future employment and I'm instructing you not to return to work until tomorrow." So I said "Oh thank you very much Mr. Sanderson. I could do with an extra day's `oliday." Then `e said in that very posh voice of `is, "It's not a day off Mrs. Harrington. You're to use it to defend your position. I want it written down. All of it in order to be able to make an informed judgement." I ask you `arriet?'

'Done the same to me. Mine's a month though. Mine's going to have to go through the governors right up to that mean faced Mr. Whittle. Area officer for education Tricia.'

'Do you know `arriet `e doesn't deserve either of us. Does `e? Did `e thank either of us for clearing `is shelves? No! We shouldn't `ave bothered `arriet. It just means I've got to fill them all bloody well up again now.'

'Oh he's asked me to give you a hand. Reminded me I've been suspended on full pay. Trying to maximise Tricia. Not that I mind. I'd rather be with you down there than in that school with *him* any day.'

'Too right `arriet. You can `elp me cope with Loppy Lampost.'

Harriet went cold. She'd forgotten all about Belinda Oxfordshire being around.

Chapter 46

In the event Harriet needn't have worried. Belinda Oxfordshire suffering a sprained ankle never appeared. Of course Harriet had filled Tricia in as to the cause.

'Serves `er right `arriet,' she'd said.

The new stock arrived in fits and starts over the next few days.

Harriet spent most of her time down there, helping Tricia. Sorry when her work was done.

'I really miss you `arriet,' Tricia had said. 'We aren't `alf building up the customers in the coffee shop though. I expect that's why `e's decided to keep me on, after `e warned me "not to ever repeat such behaviour" that is. I could do with you back again `arriet.'

Harriet was pleased Tricia still had her job. She was surprised about the continued momentum, as her plans to draw the parents in were barely under way. She was pleased though. She hoped it would continue. She'd ensured plenty ahead to interest them. To expand their thinking. She'd given some thought to Mr. Sanderson's request. Searched out the leaders of groups, clubs, local organisations. Come back with people willing to help, offering painting, drawing, needlework, knitting, weaving. All manner of arts and crafts. Creative writing, books, reading, discussions. The response had been tremendous. People with day time available. All willing to give a hand. For free. She was never far from the computer. Constantly emailing Amanda. Working it all out. Working it all in to suit the offers. Timetabling it all into a fortnightly schedule. Instructing Amanda to get the details out to the parents. One lot after another. She felt Amanda would be getting tired of her.

She'd decided not to tell Mark about her activities. Her suspension.

'No point,' she'd thought. She wasn't about to stack anymore against herself. She only had one aim in view. To marry him. Then try for a baby again. At first she'd got well into the routine of taking the pill. Just one in the morning. All over and done with. Then she did and she didn't as the need for her baby weighed in against *his* advice.

'Not let *him* influence me. Not any more. Over. Done with. "Save that one for me."

How long have I got? No, mummy was right. It's high time I settled down. Definitely keep the suspension to myself. Not going to give Mark one more reason not to go ahead. Not to marry me.'

They'd seen the house. Oh and a few more but that was the one they both really liked. Besides it offered Harriet a fresh start.

'Far better to move away. Out of the area. No one would know. Wouldn't form any association with her and the television news on Christmas night. Better to make a clean break. With Mark.'

He'd been right. Absolutely right. The vendors were so fearful of losing another buyer they'd reduced the price by a whole seventy-five thousand pounds. Of course in order to buy it they needed to retain a small mortgage. Lucky. They were very lucky to get one. Thanks to Belinda Oxfordshire the deposit was no problem. By buying theirs she'd effectively turned her and Mark into cash buyers. That was the pull. That was Mark's strongest negotiating tool.

She'd heard nothing from Mr. Sanderson, as yet. She hadn't wanted to. Her suspension had provided the perfect opportunity to try to put him from her mind. She hadn't even reached for the Latin/English dictionary. The bracelet was still in the drawer. She'd been thinking.

'It's just a reminder, really. Just a seal on the folly of the last few years.'

Since she'd met him. Since she'd been offered the job.

She'd been steeped in thought.

'You hear about men like that. Read about them. They play the field. Not that I want to believe *he's* really like that, but there's something in them. Larger than life. Magnetic. Enough to attract everyone in sight. Wherever. Charming. Alone. Deceptively available. A penetrating immediate presence, alerting the affective in us. Draining the emotions. Drawing admiration, inaccessibility, comparison, competition, jealousy, desire, hopelessness. Yes hopelessness. You fall. You crash the wall down. Crumble the cement of common sense that holds the steady bricks of life in place. Make a complete and utter fool of yourself in pursuit of a dream. No I've been there for too long now. I've fallen too far behind in the race. Let the other poor souls keep running. No one will ever catch him. Not Belinda Oxfordshire. Not Tricia. Not the rest of them. Certainly not me. How could I ever have thought I was in with a chance? Mark's right. The whole family are completely out of our league.'

She'd rationalised herself distance. And the more distance she achieved the harder she cringed. It was so easy now to see where Mark and her mother had been coming from.

Two weeks had passed. It was getting harder to cover up her absence from work. Each time she'd manage to distract Mark's allusion to it by telling him about the wedding preparations. They were all in place. Everything planned down to the tiniest detail. Harriet had waited a long time. This was going to be special. Of course her mother had insisted on paying for it.

'You're our only daughter Harriet. Naturally we didn't get the opportunity to do it for James and Paul. You're are not going to deprive Daddy and I of fulfilling our responsibility, I hope?'

Harriet had had to give in.

'Oh let them,' Mark had said, 'what's the odds? I don't want you working at that school any longer than we have to. It won't even take twelve months to get the new mortgage paid off Harriet if we tighten our belts. Then, pregnant or not. You're out.'

She could see Mark's point. The trouble was he hadn't realised it would put her in charge of the guest list. Harriet had no choice but to go along with it.

'I'm not arguing any more about it Harriet. James and Geraldine insist we invite Mr. Sanderson, besides Olivia and I have become quite good friends. On the telephone that is. Given you work for him Harriet she'll be expecting us to invite him and Belinda of course. You couldn't expect him to come on his own. Anyway we're not leaving that poor girl out. As far as I can make out quite disgraceful the way you and that common girl have treated her.'

'Well I'm definitely asking Tricia and Bob. Otherwise I'm not getting married.'

'Oh have it your own way Harriet. But I'm warning you, I shall seat her as far away from the top table as possible. We don't want that common chit of a girl ruining the day.'

Harriet, her task complete, was getting bored with being at home. Knitting. She hoped her new life would not degenerate into two knitting needles and a permanent ball of wool. The pattern wasn't going at all well. She couldn't count the number of times she'd forgotten to cross cable. The two lines of stocking stitch together and most of the moss stitch had gone its own way. Turned into lumpy, irregular patches of rib. She was confident Mark wouldn't notice. He never seemed to look too closely at anything.

'I'm off Pepper. Had enough of this.'

The cat had leapt at the ball of wool as she threw it down.

'Going to Whellreads to do the lottery.'

* * *

'That Simon Barnes is thick. Is he. I told `im exactly all about you winning that three thousand pounds. Did I. And the bugger twists it. Didn't mention the lottery. Didn't mention you'd bought the ticket `ere. I've been badly let down, have I Harriet. The shop's not doing so well with this recession. Could `ave done with the publicity.

There you go love. That will be just one pound please.'

Harriet had wanted to get out. In a rush she'd taken the lottery ticket and bumped straight into Mrs. Bustard at the door.

'When are you comin' back Miss? I'm gettin` fed-up `avin` `im round me feet all day.' She'd turned to Danny. 'Get yer derty `ands out them penny chews. Stupid place to put the fuckin` things. You won't be goin` to Butlins if you can't be`ave yourself. `ere. Give us them `ere. I'll `ave to buy them now.' She'd turned back to Harriet. 'See what I `ave to put up with? But I'm keepin` `im `ome all the same. We all are. Apart from `er, that Mrs. Atkins. You should `ave seen `er all over `im when she won that boat. Fancy `im givin` `er sailin` lessons as well.'

Indignant, Harriet had suddenly empathised with Mrs. Bustard. Her Bert was most definitely more her type than Mr. Sanderson. If she wanted to indulge in that kind of thing. That Mrs. Atkins.

'She's the only one turnin` up with `er Sara outside your classroom these days. It's spreadin` too. `e's gonna `ave a right fight on `is `ands if `e doesn't get you back in there fuckin` quick. We all saw you and your friend on the telly

Christmas night. No 'arm in any of it. Wish we'd all been there to see it 'appenin' but who 'ad the time to go there drinkin' coffee on Christmas Eve? 'is stupid idea that. It wouldn't 'ert 'im to crack 'is face once in a while, either. 'e only smiles when 'e wants somethin'. You 'ave to be a bit of a miserable sod not to 'ave seen the funny side of all that. We knew that's why we didn't all see you both down the club on New Year's Eve. Anyway Miss. We've all joined up for those free sailin' lessons in the spring. Not for 'im mind. For you. And we'll all be hauntin' is coffee shop 'til 'e gets you back in school. We were down there this mornin'. I reckon 'alf the school 'asn't turned in today. Oh and 'e's watered that runner-up prize down a bit, too. Your friend said ten, didn't she? Well 'e's knocked the Anglesey trip on the 'ead. Blamed it on 'ealth and safety rules your friend didn't know about. 'e did the draw again. 'e only wanted five out of the ten of us. So it's me and our Bert. We 'ad two leaflets stuck together and our Danny of course but 'e doesn't count. That floozie Mrs. Atkins. We said that wasn't fair seein' as she'd won the boat. 'e wouldn't 'ear of it of course. Said it was the way the tickets were drawn. Whatever that means? Of course 'e can do what 'e likes seein' as it was all free. We didn't 'ave to pay to go in the fuckin' 'at. Then there was Fag Bag, Mrs. Bagley and let me think who the other one was? Oh that's it. Nellie the Jelly. I don't know 'ow steady 'is boat is but she's terrified already. I don't know why she put 'ers in the 'at in the first place. Oh and I told 'im if 'e didn't let you and your friend go as well after gettin' us all interested 'e'd be in trouble. I think 'e'd 'ad enough by then. 'e just said that wasn't a problem. Anyway don't bother bringin' a flask. 'e's only takin' us from Tideside down the river, round the island and back again. 'ardly worth the bother.'

Harriet had been both surprised and flattered by the gathering support. She'd arrived home to a message on the answer machine.

'Ring me back will you Miss Glover?'

That's all it was. She'd guessed it would be *him*. No, not Mr. Roberts from the estate agent's this time. Hopefully that was all going through. No problems there.

She'd had to wait a while for Amanda to find him. Her stomach had starting churning. She'd been free of all that for a while. Free of the constant highs and lows. She'd even managed to put Mrs. Atkins to the back of her mind.

'Just another one in the race I've dropped out of. She won't get anywhere,' she'd decided.

'Ah, Miss Glover. Caught you out I'm afraid.'

She'd felt sick at his words.

'But I haven't done anything wrong Mr. Sanderson. You can't pin anything on me. You must have seen Amanda getting all those notices out to the parents?'

'Indeed I have Miss Glover. Simply stating you weren't in when I phoned.'

'Oh, I see. Sorry Mr. Sanderson. No. Not in. Well you can't expect me to spend every sodding day in here. Knitting.'

'I beg your pardon Miss Glover? I would advise you to watch your language, particularly in view of your current situation. I phoned and you weren't in. As simple as that.'

'Oh, I'm sorry Mr. Sanderson. It just slipped out. Been home too long. Most probably.'

'Anyhow Miss Glover, that's precisely why I've phoned. I'm pleased to inform you, your period of suspension has now been lifted. Early of course, due to my intervention on your behalf. I was able to convince them the press had been completely misled by Simon Barnes, as we all were. Mr. Whittle and the governors accept that you were trying to act in the best interests of the school with regard to working towards the promotion of parental support. Indeed they have been most impressed with the contributions you've made during this period of absence.

This business with Brown and Potts didn't hold any weight either since the health and safety directive was followed immediately and they all agreed it would be very difficult for them to prove a case against you in court. However they did express a concern over your penchant for getting yourself into trouble Miss Glover. Unfortunately Mr. Whittle is still smarting from you having raised two fingers at him and whilst I've pointed out to him it didn't happen on school premises and you didn't know who he was at the time, nevertheless, he feels that it is most unbecoming for a professional such as yourself to behave like that anywhere. He's very uncomfortable with the unprecedented amount of support being shown to you by the parents at the present time and feels you've availed yourself of some of their kind of behaviour in order to achieve your goals. I didn't necessarily go along with that. I must add. Anyhow, I'm afraid he's unwilling or unable to come to terms with it all Miss Glover and I'm concerned he may try to block your career path. In spite of it all you're still a very talented teacher I can ill-afford to lose. However, there is no influence he can exert over your forthcoming award Miss Glover. That will always stand you in good stead whatever path you choose to pursue in education.   Still. We'll wait and see. Right Miss Glover. We'll see you back in on Monday morning then. Amanda's posted the formal notifiction out to you.'

Harriet had replaced the receiver dumbfounded. She wouldn't let Mr. Whittle get the better of her. She'd fight her corner. She'd earned promotion. She hadn't quite realised how much getting that deputy post had meant to her.

She'd returned to school. Kept her head down. Got on with the job. Kept bringing the parents on side. Encouraging. Demanding. Convincing them all into taking up the new opportunities she'd created for them down at the coffee shop. It was thriving. Tricia was enjoying the involvement too.

'Much better than dustin` all those ropes every day `arriet. I don't even think about `im standin` behind me anymore. I've really gone off `im this time. After `im suspendin` me like that. I ask you? I don't think `e'd even read my letter of defence `arriet before `e `ad me back!'

Harriet had recognised winter had been on her side. The coffee shop, warm, homely, comforting. Batting away the cold frosty days. One after the other. As fast as that. The evenings were well lengthening. Molly's planter was still there, spilling over with spring colour by the front door where Guy Hammer had left it. She must get it to her. She'd had many a compliment passed on how well they'd all come on. Apart from mummy's of course. It was all about those tomato plants running away with themselves.

"Far too big for the greenhouse."

Harriet loved the spring. The trees reaching for the white fluffs of cloud, scattered endlessly across the sky. Stretching their branches from sleep. Tipping their freshly sprung leaves against the high crystal clear blue. Daisies and buttercups shy, cautiously peeping through the blades of grass. Timidly pushing their way out. Speckling their colour into the suburban blankets of green. Uninvited. Standing proud. Holding their place against the wealth of planted spring colour surrounding them. The blossoms. Lifted high. Pink. White. Lilac. Dabbling colour at the houses, lamposts, telegraph poles. Painting the ordinary. Lifting the dreams. Fulfilling the hope of spring after those dark winter months.

The sailing was under way. Well under way. Harriet couldn't deceive herself. She was definitely relieved when she inadvertently heard Mr. Sanderson had finished giving Mrs. Atkins and her partner their six sailing lessons. Of course if she'd had the wit to realise there was always going to have to be two of them with *him*. Mrs. Atkins could never have learned to sail the boat single handed.

The sailing club was buzzing. She liked going down there, now. It was much friendlier. The parents had given her something back. Their enthusiasm had rubbed off on her, much to Mark's delight. The weather had been good. They'd made the most of it. She'd improved dramatically. Enthusiastic. She could hop in and out of the boat as neatly as the birds around their nests. She was flying too. The breeze in her hair. The jib sheet in her hands. Ducking. Diving. In. Out. From under the boom. Heaving. Letting go. Watching the wind fill the sails only to spill it all out again as they turned about. Tacking their way through the waves. Laughing as the spray caught her cheeks.

She didn't know how often Mr. Sanderson stood back. Watching.

Chapter 48

It was nearly the end of May. Mark would be going away soon. It was supposed to be just for a month. Of course they were sympathetic to the fact he was getting married. They were willing to allow him an early return.

They'd signed the contracts on the sale and purchase of both houses. Having conceded so much on the sale price the vendors were keen to see it tucked away. They'd all had to agree to a long completion date, though. Harriet hadn't much liked that. Especially with Mark away right up to the last. It was bad enough running it all so close to their wedding day without the thought of having to move house all on her own.

The wedding arrangements had been finalised long since. There'd been nothing like Harriet's mother on a mission.

She'd been starting to get nervous anyway. She'd had the date a while for her trip to the Palace. It was getting nearer. She'd managed to keep it from Mark. She was grateful he'd be away. There'd never ever be any need to tell him. She wondered if Mr. Sanderson would offer to take her down. It would be easier. She felt sure she could handle her feelings now.

'Just sit next to him in the car and go. And come back. Simple as that. Virtually last in the race, anyway. Before you pulled out. Remember that Harriet. You've pulled out of the race. Along with Tricia. And no doubt Mrs. Atkins by now.'

Besides she was still licking her wounds. Not getting that job. The deputy's job. On the positive side it just made it easier to keep *him* out of her thoughts. Once she'd got over it, that is. Oh she'd felt very angry. At first. *He'd* all but promised it her. It just piled it on when she knew who she was up against. Who was offered it.

'Bloody Lucinda Lawton.' It still threatened to spark a row in Harriet's mind.

'Of course she's deputised before. Had plenty of experience,' Harriet had thought.

"We were under orders with this one Miss Glover," he'd said. "I'm afraid. For some reason best known to themselves they had to reinstate her. I did my best for you, but as you are well aware, from Mr. Whittle's point of view you've done very little to help yourself. I suggest you keep your head down Miss Glover and see what comes up."

'I don't want to see what comes up!' Harriet had fumed to herself. She'd just wanted to hand her notice in. There and then. Of course she couldn't.

'If only we'd gone for a cheaper house.'

Too late for that, now. Nothing for it.

'Just face facts, Harriet. Let Lucinda Lawton join the race. See how far *she* gets? Anyway he's most definitely getting his ring back before I get married.' She'd decided.

The perfect opportunity arose. She thought it might. She was dreading this trip down the river. Tricia wasn't fussy either. Fully kitted in her inflatable life jacket Mrs. Bustard had arrived with Danny. She'd glowered at Mrs. Atkins from the minute they'd hauled her over the side.

'Our Bert ain't comin` on account of `er.'

Mrs. Atkins had immediately placed her hands on her hips.

'What you goin` on about now Beattie Bustard?'

'`e's ill,' Mrs. Bustard had snapped.

Fortunately Harriet had seen the need to pull them apart before it became dangerous.

'You've upset our Dannybabes you `ave. Flirtin` like that with `is dad. `im bein` late `ome all the time. Out with you. Our Danny thinks you're stealin` `im from us. Tries to keep `im at home with us. Fried onions. That's the trouble. `e can't get enough of them. I'm sick of that fuckin` fryin` pan.'

'That's got nothing to do with me. Anyway…' she'd smiled knowingly, 'far posher fish to fry than your Bert.'

'Oh yes it `as. And we all know who you mean as well. That was disgustin` be`aviour that. Anyway it's my Bert we're talkin` about. If you'd `ave kept `is `ands off `im our Dannybabes wouldn't `ave put those spring bulbs in with me onions. Tryin` to make sure we `ad enough to keep `im at `ome. Poor lamb. Well I didn't know. Fried them all up together and `e's been locked in the bathroom all night. I thought `e was goin` to die. You'd `ave been up for it if `e `ad. Anyway, `e's feelin` a lot better now. Very pale and weak though. Not fit to come on this trip today.'

'You shouldn't be lettin` `im `ave friggin` bulbs in the first place. Where did `e get them from?' Mrs. Atkins had announced.

Danny had pointed at Harriet.

'`er. They were on Miss's lunch trolley. You left them there. Didn't you Miss?'

'She probably didn't Danny.'

Harriet hadn't realised Mr. Sanderson had been standing behind her.

'Yes she did Mr. Sandcastles. I watched `er. She put them on our lunch box trolley.' Danny had said.

'No harm done Mrs. Bustard. I'm sure Mr. Bustard will be fine by the time you get back. A word Miss Glover.'

Harriet had followed him down to the cabin.

'Spring bulbs your thing at the moment Miss Glover? I overheard the chatter. I'm afraid you left a trail of them from the steps right down to where your car was parked on Christmas night. I'd already had words with Mr. Swift on the phone. Had to apologise. Embarrasing. Totally embarrassing Miss Glover.'

'Sorry about that Mr. Sanderson,' Harriet had said as she reached into the back pocket of her jeans.

'I've caused you no end of trouble. Out of the race. Me. Please. I want to give this back. It's not right to keep it now I'm getting married.'

He'd taken the ring with hardly a thank you.

'Head count Miss Glover. Get back on deck. Let's motor our way down. Get this damned trip over with,' he'd said.

Both Harriet and Tricia had been glad it was over. Especially as Danny had escaped from his mother and somehow managed to get hold of a distress flare.

'What you pullin' at now Danny? Stop playin' with that. Get up 'ere this minute.' Mrs. Bustard had ordered.

Too late. He'd managed to set if off. Next thing the lifeboat crew were all offering to rescue them.

'Get them all on board,' Mr. Sanderson had ordered. Safety issue here. Take them back will you to Tideside sailing club. I'll see you there.'

They'd all got off. Tricia was last. Harriet was about to go.

'Stop. Not you Miss Glover. Give me a hand to sail this damned thing back. Will you?'

Harriet had done as she was told.

Chapter 49

Harriet had tossed and turned her way through the night. All night with *him*. She'd just turned her back on this most gorgeous man. Her ring? Not now. *His* now. Back. Back to him. Forever. She'd felt the physical stabs as the pain of finality seared through her body. Sucked away her mind. Just pictures now. Of *him*. His thick blonde hair blowing against his face. His eyes. Sharp. Narrowing. Then twinkling. The blue of the sea, with all its mystery. There, in them. In that look. As he spoke to her. As he watched her. She'd seen the strength in his arms. The determination in his face. How naturally he sat with the boat. Like lovers. Fusing energy. What had she done? She woke the next morning. Drained. Aching for him. Clinging to her dream. Delirious. Restless. *He'd* taken her sailing. Just the two of them. The sea mist had thickened into deep fog. Boat adrift. The black night, then a flashing beacon. He'd rowed the boat towards it, hitting the rocks. He'd scrambled out. Tried to pull her in but she was back drifting on the tide. Then he was suddenly holding her hand. Pulling. Pulling her in. Dark. Drenched, they both sat under the lighthouse. Her clothes had floated away. He'd made love to her. Then she was standing in the 'blue one' the long bridesmaid's dress she'd worn for Molly's wedding. They were getting married. It wasn't Mark. It was *him*.

The dream was powerful. Harriet wanted to stay there. Knew she couldn't. Half awake. Battling the surge of passion still rushing through her body. Trying to focus. Desperately trying to lose the pain. To get back to reality. Mark was going this morning. They'd be getting married in three weeks time.

'No. No. It was only a dream. Mark's not going away leaving me with my head full of this.'

She tried desperately hard to erase it all from her mind.

She jumped out of bed and met Pepper at the bottom of the stairs.

'It's just you and me Pepper. But only for a couple of weeks. Mark'll be back. We're getting married Pepper. At last. I did tell you I'd completely dropped out of the race. Didn't I? Men like *him* don't do marriage Pepper. Men like Mark don't do marriage either. That's why this is so special Pepper. He's doing it for me after all this time. I'm not letting anything stand in the way.'

The cat leapt and bounced and sprang at her legs.

'OK Pepper. As you'll be going to have to put up with my chatter exclusively, I'll feed you first.'

She looked back at Mark's cases stacked under the window in the hall.

'Not as many as last time.' The thought pleased her. 'Just a short trip. It'll give me chance to get on with the packing. We've only got a few weeks. Just after the wedding we'll be moving. Can't wait.'

'Up early Hat?'

Mark's face appeared round the kitchen door.

'Oh it's unsettling when you're about to go off Mark. I wish you didn't have to.'

'Work Hat. Still it's not for long. You've got plenty to be getting on with. What with the wedding and moving house.'

'Did you say Melissa Scott was going Mark. I can't remember?' The question had lay heavy at the back of Harriet's mind.

'She may or may not have been. I can't remember either, it's ages ago this lot was organised. Anyway she's definitely not going now Hat. She got out of it on grounds of needing to be around to finalise the divorce. They're doing a quickie. Don't know what she saw in him in the first place.'

'Well from what little I've seen of her I'd be inclined to put that the other way round.'

'Ah but you haven't seen Geoffrey, Harriet, have you? Great pompous planet obsessed twit.'

'Anyway Hat I don't see that any of it matters.' He switched his line of defence. 'Your mother's not invited lard ball to the wedding I hope?'

Harriet went very red. She hadn't dared to mention it.

'She has. That's it. She has, hasn't she? Why can't the interfering old bat just lay off. For once?'

'It was Geraldine and James, Mark. She didn't want to offend them.'

'It's got sod all to do with them!'

'I know. I really wished she hadn't. Just the last thing I wanted.'

'You're going to have to stand up to her Hat once we're married. I've got no intention of getting drawn into any of her social networking.'

'Don't worry Mark. We won't. Anyway you know how I feel about *him*. Know how I feel about not getting the deputy's job after putting in all that work last time you were away. I'll stay at that school just as long as it takes to get the new mortgage paid. Then I'll be out of it. Won't need to see him. Won't need to have anything more to do with him.' She knew she was trying just a little bit too hard.

'Well we're not letting him stop us from going to the club Harriet. Not now you've finally caught the sailing bug. Of course he has to be in both of them, doesn't he? Why couldn't he just have bloody well stuck with Lower Tideside? His boat's moored there most of the time anyway.'

Harriet shrugged her shoulders. 'Here Mark, we may as well have our tea at the table.'

'Anyway Hat. How did you and Tricia get on yesterday? You were asleep when I got back.'

'Too right I was Mark. It was a complete fiasco. Danny Bustard got hold of a flare from somewhere. I'm surprised it was left lying around, but then that boy's in and out of everything, getting himself into trouble. He managed to set it off and they launched the lifeboat didn't they? He sent them all back to Tideside on it. Except me. Told me to stay back to give him a hand sailing the boat back. He'd motored out but didn't want to motor it back for some reason.'

'Oh yes?'

'Well I couldn't say no. His mother said he's really bossy and she's absolutely right. I didn't know what I was doing. Running from one winch to another turning the handles. I was glad to get back. Tricia was waving us in. Laughing.'

'She seems to have cooled off too, according to Bob.'

'Cooled off Mark? What do you mean?'

'Lard ball Harriet. Bob's not getting him in the face every two minutes anymore. She must have learned some sense. At last.'

'We've both done that Mark. He's a type. A kind. One of those sorts of men that sets the tops off and keeps them all spinning. All at different speeds just to suit himself.'

'So you and Tricia have been tops then? The wooden kind. Brains as thick as planks.'

'Don't push it Mark. None of us are perfect. He's definitely hit us both a bit too hard this time and we're just spinning ourselves out of his life.'

'Tricia going to pack it in then?'

'Probably. I don't know. Haven't had much chance to chat lately.'

'She's alright Tricia. Acts a bit daft but she's actually a very bright intelligent girl. Not bad legs either.'

'Mark. What's with you? Stop it! You needn't talk about me. Go and get ready. You'll have the taxi blasting its horn at the whole street before you know it.'

Chapter 50

Mark had gone. Kissed her a quick goodbye as if he'd just been going off to work. Just as if it had been an ordinary day.

'Don't make a song and dance of it Harriet. I'll be back in a couple of weeks. Just make sure you go through that check-list with the removal people and don't forget to give them the house plan. I've done some labels but you need to get on with the rest of them. Oh and make sure your bloody mother doesn't invite any more of *his* sodding family.'

In the end Harriet had been glad to close the front door. Glad of the peace. Pleased though.

'At least Melissa Scott won't be out there. With him.'

She showered. Got dressed. Pottered about. Decided to spend the rest of Sunday just lounging around. Unwinding. Thinking. Back on track now. It was all back on track. The dream had well receded. Almost as if it had never happened. She must phone Molly. Get them to pick up the planter next time they were over house-hunting. All the bits and pieces needed to be out of the way before the house move. She looked around. Now almost pleased Belinda Oxfordshire had got her way. On both counts. The house and *him*. Then the fear returned. She remembered her words. Her threat. Her deadline for having her engagement to Mr. Sanderson reinstated. She looked out of the window. Wanted the thought to go away. Concentrated hard on the board now upright. Proudly sporting 'SOLD' and then 'subject to contract' in tiny little letters.

'Not relevant. Our contract's signed. Just waiting on the completion date.'

She went to the calendar.

'Monday 28th June.' It was ringed. Her eyes fell back.

'Oh gosh. It's not next Friday is it? Oh Pepper that's really crept up. Don't, don't, don't want to go to that. Get out of it Pepper? How can I get out of that?'

She racked her brains which way and every way to try to conjure up an excuse not to go to the Palace.

'Being forced into it so he doesn't let the old boys down. I didn't ask him to pull the strings in the first place. More publicity? No he won't want me to have any more publicity. Not now, not after that Rapping Hammer affair. This might just be the get out.'

The phone rang. He could almost have been reading her mind.

'Ah you're there are you? Mark gone? Your mother got the word out. Anyhow just to thank you for bringing the boat back yesterday. What a fiasco that was!'

'Exactly my words to Mark.'

Harriet heard him clear his throat.

'Quite Miss Glover. That Bast… er Bustard woman and the other one. One who won the boat. Er… Name?'

'Mrs. Atkins, Mr. Sanderson.'

'Right. Yes. Glad to get that woman out of my hair. It's been a fucking nightmare giving her sailing lessons. Pardon the language Miss Glover. I'll have you know the woman all but propositioned me. Anyhow, can I come round? There are one or two bits outstanding on this seller's property information form, I believe. Just a quick chat.'

'Er yes Mr. Sanderson, that's alright.'

'Give me ten minutes Miss Glover.'

'You can't do much in ten minutes Pepper. Get out of the way. The place is a tip. Oh shove off will you? Now that's the milk all over the floor. Why can't you just flipping well drink it? You make enough fuss about getting it!'

She ran up the stairs with the cloth and bottle of cream cleaner. Squirting everything. Trying to stop that dream from pouring back.

She'd just managed to squeeze the cloth out for the last time when the doorbell went.

'Won't take a tick Miss Glover. I'm sure you're busy.'

He followed her into the kitchen watching her shaking the cloth at the bottle.

'I'd put it away if I were you Miss Glover, the deal's done. Lounge shall we?'

She followed him in. Sat down. Tried to tidy her hair.

He brought an envelope out from the inner pocket of his sports jacket. The solicitor's form.

'All here Miss Glover. Just check those boxes. According to Belinda they should have been ticked.'

He passed his pen over and waited.

'Right. All done Miss Glover. When's he back?'

'It's very close to the wedding actually. Even then they've allowed him to cut the trip a bit short.'

'I see. Hmm.'

'Both sure of what you're doing?'

'Most definitely Mr. Sanderson.' She looked into his serious, deep blue eyes. That blonde curl still sitting in disobedience, touching his collar. She could feel her strong intentions collapsing, her resolve weakening.

'Not letting that dream take over. NOT. NOT. NOT.' Her silent resolution took her to Mrs. Atkins. 'Another one out of the race. Knocked out just like that. She won't realise it. I didn't. She'll wise up. Eventually. Like me.'

'*Absolutely* sure Miss Glover?'

'Never been more certain of anything Mr. Sanderson.'

She could feel herself blushing. She looked down. At the carpet. At her feet. At the legs of the coffee table. Anywhere but at him.

'Oh just before I go Miss Glover. Next Friday. I've arranged to take Belinda down to London. Tarquin Bridgewater will be giving you a lift. We'll all meet down there.'

'Oh. Fine, thank you, Mr. Sanderson. That's fine. Very good of him.'

'Right then Miss Glover, I'll see myself out.'

She heard the front door close. Then his car door bang. Then the engine start. He was away.

'Harriet you had to say it. You had to do it. He's no one's. Never will be. Just get that through your very thick head will you?'

She went to find the cat.

'Tarquin bloody Ditchwater? *He* could have given me a lift. Just one last time. With *him*. Before I get married. What would have been wrong with that? Bloody Belinda Oxfordshire. A damehood for her? Giving them away like sweets. Taking *her* down? After the way she tore him off on Christmas Eve. He didn't even want her to go round on Christmas Day. What changed? What's she said to him? What's she been up to, to be able to swing that? Bloody hell. I most certainly don't want to go now. Not now. Not at all. No I'm definitely not going.'

She fumed for a full fifteen minutes. She'd phone him. Just get out of it once and for all. She picked up the receiver. Replaced it. Would he be back? No. Yes. She picked it up again. Put it down. Her courage failed her. Completely. Utterly. Totally.

She found her knitting and started clacking away at the needles. Furiously.

Chapter 51

It was Thursday afternoon. She'd come back to the answer machine flashing away.

Harriet hadn't enjoyed her week in school. Avoiding *him*. Of course she'd been pleased to hear of Mr. Bustard's complete recovery. She couldn't be doing with *that* on her conscience.

'I told 'im. I told our Bert Miss Glover that she'd set 'er sights on 'igher things, Mrs. Atkins 'ad. You should 'ave seen 'im go down. Just like a balloon. All empty, baggy and wrinkly. Of course 'is jippy tummy 'asn't 'elped 'is looks. 'e said "What are you talkin' about Beattie Bustard. 'igher things?" So I 'ad to come clean. "Only *im*. She's only seen 'er way to 'avin' an affair with *'im*." "Who Beattie? Who are you talkin' about now?" " *'im*," I said. "Do I 'ave to spell it out for you? The *'ead* of the school. *Mr. Sanderson* of course. It all started with 'er winnin' that boat and then the sailin' lessons. You should 'ave seen them together on 'is posh boat sailin' down the river. I bet they ended up down them steps. In the bottom somewhere. If it 'adn't been for our Danny settin' off that rocket, who knows how the pair of them would have ended up?" Do you know Miss Glover 'e suddenly decided 'e'd never been interested in 'er in the first place. As if! Anyway Miss Glover we'll be off to Butlins in the summer 'olidays, thanks to you. I've bought myself a bikini. Now I've got 'im back. I'll soon find out 'ow far 'e got with 'er if 'e manages to do it with me. It's 'ardly been workin' properly for years. You never know those spring bulbs might of just sprung a bit of life back into 'im. You're a good'n you. I mightn't 'ave got my Bert back if it 'adn't been for you gettin' us all to go to the sailin' club on New Year's Eve.'

She'd winked and nudged her elbow into Harriet's side. Harriet had laughed. Glad Danny and her could relax again. Never in her wildest thoughts had she ever imagined being able to empathise with Mrs. Bustard in such a way. That flighty Mrs. Atkins, moving along, leaving Mr. Bustard behind for better things, getting in both of their ways. 'Not anymore though, not that it matters. Mrs. Sensible. That's me now,' Harriet had thought, 'a very wide berth for *him* from now on.'

Not a title Mr. Brown would have sanctioned, however. The other (self-elevated) head, also to be avoided. She'd noticed the door to the stockroom always shut. He was determined to comply with the large notice under the key. Now always there since Mr. Sanderson's health and safety meeting. When they'd occasionally glimpsed one another, Harriet couldn't fail to notice the look of panic cross his face before breaking into a gallop in the other direction. That was fine. That suited her. It could only have been for fear of his safety. She knew him and Mr. Potts were well satisfied she'd been suspended from duties. They knew they weren't going to get any more than that out of it, themselves.

She turned to the answer machine. The cat jumped down.

'Day off tomorrow. Rather not Pepper. Tarquin Bridgewater picking me up at seven in the morning. Ugh! To go down there. The Palace Pepper. I ask you? Me? Stupid idea. Off the planet Pepper. Just got to breathe in and get it over with. All over and done with. Shush Pepper. Our very last secret. Promise. Don't tell Mark.'

She pressed the play button.

'Hi Hat. Hope everything's OK. We had a good trip down. About to turn in for some sleep. Wow Hat! The shelf's completely gone since we were last here. Completely broken away. Afraid it's taken your statue with it. I hope it's not a bad omen Harriet. Just make sure you're completely thawed out for the wedding. I'm not interested in playing second fiddle to your knitting needles either, once we're married. I don't want you turning into your mother. Another thing Harriet, I hope you're not playing up to lard ball while I'm down here. Better not be Harriet. I've had plenty of time to think while I've been sitting on the plane. On both planes. We're supposed to be getting married Harriet Remember that! I'll phone again as soon as I can.'

'Hmm. He sounds like he's in a really bad mood. What exactly did he mean by that? He *knows* I'm just not interested in Mr. Sanderson anymore. Funny thing to say. Definitely not the way to get a new jumper, either. He's supposed to be missing me. Not moaning. Unless. Unless he's getting cold feet.'

She tried to push the thought away as she pressed the button for the next message.

'It's Tricia `arriet. Only me. I know you're off to the Palace tomorrow `arriet and I just wanted to wish you all the very best. And don't worry `arriet, I won't tell anyone. It's our little secret `arriet. Well, not exactly ours because the Queen and everyone else who's there will know `arriet, but you know what I mean. There's no need for anyone to find out before they `ave to `arriet. Especially your Mark.

I've got your keys `andy. `ere they are `arriet. In my `and now. I'll feed the cat tomorrow afternoon and call round again on Sunday mornin` just in case you're delayed for any reason. `ave a good trip `arriet. Keep your eyes and ears open. You never know what you might `ear `arriet. Especially from Barkin` Ditchwater. Oh I do love that name `arriet! Ring me as soon as you get back `arriet. Bye.'

Chapter 52

Friday morning. The sky. Hot. Clear blue. Harriet had set the alarm for six. What she couldn't do in an hour she wasn't going to. She scrambled round. Glad it was just to be a day trip.

'Not much to take really Pepper. Now you be good for Tricia. Don't get under her feet and don't disappear because it's not me. I'll be back tonight.'

She ran through the protocol again before putting it all back in the envelope and then into her bag.

She lifted the large polythene cover from the newly cleaned outfit. Dress and jacket. The blue one again. The one she'd worn on Christmas Day. Still swivelling a bit on her. No one would notice under the jacket. Besides she was getting married. No point in having to buy another set of accessories. Every penny saved meant leaving work a bit sooner.

She checked her handbag. Cards, money, keys. Everything there. Then slipped on her shoes. She heard a car horn beep. She grabbed her coat. Closed the front door behind her to greet Tarquin Bridgewater at the gate.

'It's most kind Mr. Bridgewater to take me down like this. It would have been the train otherwise.'

'Not at all Harriet. My pleasure dear. And do call me Tarquin. Can't be having Mr. Bridgewater all the way down to the smoke.'

'Oh not anymore Mr. Bridgewater. London was the first city to be cleaned up, I think. We don't want to offend anyone. At the Palace. Don't want to end up in the Tower.'

Tarquin Bridgewater snorted. Guffawed.

'Come on dear. Let's be on our way. We can't have Joris and Belinda getting there first. Can we?'

He closed the door on her. Harriet didn't like the smell. It reminded her of the fallen bits from that brown envelope at Starboard Marine North West on Christmas Eve.

'Motorways all the way down Harriet. This won't take long. The paper's on the back seat there if you want to read it.'

'Oh, thanks Mr. Bridg…, er Tarquin. That's kind.'

'I hope you don't mind me saying how nice you look Harriet. Not bad turning up to the investiture with a beautiful young lady on one's arm. A double honour for me, don't you think Harriet?'

'Oh thank you Mr. Bridgewater. You look very smart yourself.'

Harriet was hardly listening. She could just see the curling edges of the newspaper jutting out from under the back of her seat. She twisted round then stretched her arm back and down to the floor. Something else? Just managed to grasp it all to her lap. She sat for a moment. Transfixed. The folded paper angled against the brown paper corners peering out from under. She sat staring at the four points forming an impromptu star with the paper. Wondering. Curious. She nudged it to one side. The sealed end only half pressed down. Already been opened. Peeled it back. Slid her hand in. Had to pull hard at the single A4 sheet. Glanced sideways at Tarquin Bridgewater. Managed to hold it against the inside of the newspaper. Scanned it. Gasped. Silently. Her thoughts well focussed.

'Oh wow! This one got left behind. It's just as well. Talk about dubious friends in high places! No wonder he's predicting a world banking collapse! It was *his* handwriting. Notes. Names. He must have been speaking to someone at the top. He's picked it up along with the rest. By mistake. All in the envelope together. He'd never have passed it over to me, or *her*, with that inside. No wonder he was angry.'

Her hand was shaking as she loosely folded it back into the envelope. The thought of Christmas night at *his* house. And *that* coming on the news. She felt sick. But so profoundly grateful that whoever took it and leaked it had at least left that bit behind.

The newspaper shook in Harriet's hands as Tarquin Bridgewater jerked his way down the road and into the traffic. She watched him from the corner of her eye, raking impatiently at the gear lever. Roaring away and then slowing down. By the time he'd joined the motorway he'd already stalled it twice.

It was still early. Far too early for Harriet. Too early to begin to absorb all she'd just read. She was already shaken and jolted to capacity. The journey had hardly started.

'We'll be meeting up with Joris and Belinda around ten. At the services on the M6 Harriet. I think I know the one he's talking about. A right pair those two Harriet. First it's on, then it's all off. Wouldn't surprise me if it wasn't back on again by the time they get back.'

Harriet held on to the envelope. Mind aghast. She rattled the paper and nodded.

'Just concentrate. Get us down in one piece,' she thought. She hadn't read a word. All the time racking her shocked brains trying to think of an excuse to get the train home.

'Mark wouldn't be too pleased with the envelope Harriet. Just my little joke. I did have the bloody thing in here but could I find it? Couldn't let you down Harriet after promising. Especially with the thought of a kiss.'

'You were well stoned,' she thought. Then coughed politely.

'Don't worry Mr. Bridgewater. I've just brought it up from under my seat with the paper.'

'Little bugger slid under the seat? Pass it over to Mark dear. A bit late for his trip, I'm afraid. Stick it in the post. He's gone now hasn't he? A little bird told me about the engagement Harriet. By the way dear. Congratulations! Myself I don't know why he didn't snap you up long ago. Any particular reason Harriet?'

Harriet peered from behind the page. A bit shocked.

'A bit nosey that,' she thought.

He didn't wait for an answer.

'When's the big day then Harriet? After all this time it will be a short engagement?'

'June 26th actually. Two weeks tomorrow.'

'Oh. As soon as that? And have you got everything in order?'

'All done Mr. Bridgewater, I'm very pleased to say. Actually Mummy took a load off me. You'd have thought it was her big day the way she's been going on about it.'

'Well Harriet. It very much is you know. Our generation want to see our children get married. Get settled down. In the legal sense if you understand?'

They were well on to the motorway. Harriet folded the brown envelope and zipped it into the inside pocket of her bag. She didn't dare look. The inside lane. The far one. Middle. Inside. Then shooting straight over to the far one again trying to overtake two wagons. Getting in their way. In between them. In front. Behind. Spoiling their game. Now neck and neck. Pulling hard. Both at once. The blast from their horns sent waves of fear through her. They'd forced him back.

'Oh bloody hell. What's he doing now? He's having another go!'

Down went his foot. Harriet watched the speedometer hit 90 mph. It didn't fall away until he was miles ahead on the inside lane. She could feel the newspaper turning to papier mache in her hands. She hoped he hadn't been rolling a few before he'd left home.

'Look for the signs now Harriet. They should be coming up. We'll be taking a left turn into the services in a bit. Two or three miles down the road.'

'Anything to get out of here,' she thought. Her mind was racing. It was so bad she was more than prepared to sit in the back of *his* Mercedes behind Belinda Oxfordshire.

'What can I say? What excuse? Rude. No it would be so rude. Can't do it?' Trapped. Her desperate thoughts despaired into temporary oblivion.

'This is it Harriet. In we go.'

Harriet had forgotten to look. She was amazed he'd been able to find it, driving at that speed. She saw Mr. Sanderson's car parked just in front of them to the left. Along side one of those shiny brick edged diamonds, devoid of soil, housing a skinny tree. Tarquin Bridgewater parked the other side. Unparalleled joy when she finally heard the engine silence to the turn of the key.

She grabbed her bag and reached for her coat. She hadn't realised it had landed in a rolled up ball on top of Tarquin Bridgewater's hat. Now dented. She wasn't sure if he'd notice. If it was going to stay like that. The Queen would notice. She began to feel wobbly. Finery? It always made her nervous. She felt like she was off to a wedding. She could scarcely believe she was on her way to the Palace. It felt strange: just about to sit in some services, trying to find a clean bit on the bare red melamine table top for her cup and saucer, dressed like that. All of them dressed like that.

'They're right by the window. Over there. Look.'

Harriet looked. They'd already turned. Mr. Sanderson got up from his seat.

'Wow,' Harriet thought, 'he looks absolutely fantastic.'

He was smiling. In full morning suit. Hat in hand.

'He looks pleased with himself,' Tarquin Bridgewater mimed the words as he approached. 'I told you they'd be back together before the day's out. Look, he's trying to win her over with his hat.'

Harriet didn't wish to hear that. Not just at this moment.

'He needs his hat to keep that mop of blonde hair in place, Mr. Bridgewater.'

'A likely story. He's just showing off Harriet. Trying to impress her. Like I said.'

She remained silent, except in her mind.

'Oh rubbish Mr. Bridgewater.' She was getting impatient. She didn't need this, right now.

'Harriet, Tarquin. Both looking resplendent as ever. What slowed you down then Tarquin?' Mr. Sanderson laughed.

Harriet watched. Looking up at him. At his face. Changing. The distance between his jawline and cheekbone classically perfect. The muscles lifting his cheeks, drawing back that generous, expressive mouth to show those beautiful, strong, white almost even teeth. The laughter lines forming. Long. Short. Almost dimpled. And all the time his eyes, blue, twinkling, laughing as he flicked his mop of blonde hair to the side.

'No no no Harriet. Absolutely NO. You're getting married. Remember?' She stamped as hard as she could on the flurry of weakness. Swirling around. Fogging her mind. Tearing away at her insides. Nil effect.

'Oh I just don't know how to stay out of the bloody race.' She was getting cross with herself. 'I can't. I just can *not*. HE IS GORGEOUS!'

Chapter 53

They were back on the road. Harriet had had to pretend she'd had such a good journey. She wondered how the refreshment would take him. The break. They were nearer now. She hoped against hope it would slow him down.

Not to be. He'd decided not under any circumstances to let Mr. Sanderson's car out of his sight. With total disregard for all else he screeched and hammered the car all the way to the Palace.

They all got out.

'I suggest you knock the dent out of that hat before we go any further.'

Harriet could vaguely hear Mr. Sanderson advising Tarquin Bridgewater. She was shaking. The four of them walked along together. This was the worst moment of her life.

* * *

The Investiture

* * *

Suddenly over. In a flash. Just like that. Well that's how it felt now. Not at the time. Harriet had dreaded having one of her disasters in the middle of it all. Especially having to walk backwards. Fate had smiled kindly. All had gone well.

She was just grateful to Mr. Sanderson. She hadn't realised he'd insisted on no publicity. Of course that was the last thing Tarquin Bridgewater wanted, anyway. But Belinda Oxfordshire? Harriet wondered why she hadn't gone for it. Now she knew. Just a CBE for her. For services rendered to the community. Some kind of charity work.

'Must have tagged along with *him*.' Harriet had decided. She'd noticed her face had grown longer by the minute. Heard her declare her lack of interest in having the record of their investiture on film, to keep. Mr. Sanderson had side glanced Harriet a couple of times, especially over lunch. He looked like he was getting just a bit tired of her.

The four of them walked back to the cars. Harriet was dreading another journey with Tarquin Bridgewater.

'Would you mind?' Mr. Sanderson ushered Belinda Oxfordshire towards Tarquin Bridgewater's car. 'The boat's down at Falmouth. I want to turn her around. If Harriet doesn't mind giving me a hand?'

Harriet was speechless. She opened her coat.

'Oh there's plenty of old jeans, jumpers. All that sort of thing on board. We'll soon get you kitted out.'

Belinda Oxfordshire sniffed loudly. Glowered at him.

'Come on dear. We'll rattle our way back in no time at all.' Tarquin Bridgewater was anxious to get away.

He opened the door for her. Harriet watched her sit. Watched her twitching those fine porcelain nostrils. Screwing her face up against the unpleasant odour intensified from the heat of the sun on the windows.

'Thanks Tarquin.'

Mr. Sanderson nodded and smiled as he unlocked his car to reach into the glove compartment.

'Just a few more from Swift. The very latest propagation I understand.'

Tarquin Bridgewater thanked him, then smiled as he turned to Harriet. 'Oh don't forget these dear.'

He opened the rear door and pulled out a carrier bag, nodding towards Mr. Sanderson.

'There Harriet. Now you know what he's talking about.'

He pulled out a tomato. Heart shaped. 'Not bad eh? Some gardener that man Swift.'

He tossed it in his hand. Winked at Harriet.

'A little beauty. Not unlike you dear.'

Chapter 54

Harriet blushed. Bright red. Just like the thing in his hand. In a daze, she clung on to the carrier bag, sat against her legs. Lumpy with heart shaped tomatoes. They both waved them off. For sure she was relieved not to be going home in Tarquin Bridgewater's car. But this? Going down to Falmouth with *him*? Absolutely gorgeous *him*. How on earth did she get to this?

'Stay out of the race Harriet,' she warned herself.

'I'll pop those in the boot Miss Glover. Do get in.'

He smiled as she handed the bag over.

She sat in the front seat. Again. In the front seat. Next to *him*. Barely able to believe it. He closed the door on her. She watched him stride past the front window and then in. Next to her. Clasping his seatbelt. His brilliant white cuff just moving back to show the face curve of that expensive watch. Lifted his hand to the gear lever. A turn of the key. Foot down. Gliding away from the parking space. Reverse. Steering wheel hard over. Letting it ride to catch it in both hands as they went forward. The smell of leather. Nostalgic. She thought of the field of flowers. She looked at his profile and the smile breaking on that gorgeous, handsome face.

'You OK Miss Glover? Just a hand. Good of you. Won't take us long. Don't mind driving back through the night?'

Harriet smiled. Nodded her head.

'Could motor it of course. We had no problems bringing her back from the Med. Just some routine maintenance. Phil and I needed to get back. Haven't had chance to get down again. Just want to turn her round. Check a couple of things out.'

'No that's fine Mr. Sanderson. Mark's away anyway. There's no panic for me to get back early. I might nod off on the way home though.'

She watched the smile break fully across his face. They'd moved away from the city and were heading towards the motorway.

'Back to the Antarctic then?'

She watched him move effortlessly into the slip road and across the lanes of the motorway to the outside. Still smiling. Set against his window. The sun catching his hair. Blonde against blue. Almost midsummer now. Not a hint of a cloud. Just the vapour trails crossing. Running their kisses against the hot blue summer sky.

'Antarctic is it then?' he asked her again. 'Or has he managed to escape before the big day?'

She heard him laugh.

'How long is it Harriet?'

'Two weeks tomorrow. Actually. Mummy will have invited you and Belinda.'

'Indeed. We're looking forward to it Harriet.'

'No don't say that,' she thought, 'you're not supposed to be looking forward to it. With her. Or anyone else for that matter. It would be much more appropriate for you to be jealous. Madly jealous. You gave me that bracelet. You must still like me? Stay out of the race Harriet.'

For a split second she tried desperately hard to pull her thoughts back. The bracelet wouldn't let go.

'The Latin/English dictionary?'

How she wished she'd opened it.

She watched him, in and out of lanes. As before. Effortless.

'This gorgeous hunk of a man. I just don't see how I'm ever, ever going to be able to forget him.'

The countryside swallowed her thoughts. He'd almost given up trying to speak to her. She was not to be distracted from the aching turmoil of her mind.

'Music Harriet? Might help with those wedding day nerves? It's understandable you've got a lot on your mind at the moment.'

She nodded. She wished she hadn't. Same music. She was on her way back from the field of flowers. Wasn't. She'd caught her dream. Tried to stamp it out. It surfaced. Fluttered. Tried again. Locked it away. Unable to fly. Dying. Fighting for survival. Struggling for life. She wanted him. Desperately wanted him.

'Just once Harriet. Just once. Before I get married.' The thought wouldn't go away.

'We're just about to join the M5 Harriet. There are some services along here. Fancy a stop?'

'Only if you do. Thank you Mr. Sanderson.'

'We'll press on then Harriet. Try closing your eyes.'

He reached for her hand. She allowed her head to rest back. Set alight by his presence. His overwhelming proximity. He'd just turned the key on her mind. Unlocked it. Lifted the supression she'd stuggled so hard to hold on to. Just a touch from his hand. On hers. She closed her eyes, shutting out the reality of her existence. Finally allowing the full flood of freedom to surge her thoughts. Her body. Her soul. For the moment he was hers.

He looked across. Her eyes were closed.

Off the M5 and along the A38. Heading rapidly towards Falmouth. Over the Tamar Bridge. It wouldn't be long now.

He pulled up alongside the jetty.

'Falmouth Harriet.' He smiled as he gently disturbed her from her sleep.

'Already?'

'Already Harriet. Feeling better?'

'Oh yes thank you Mr. Sanderson. Oh that's not yours is it? It's beautiful.'

She sat up to get a clearer view of the Oxford blue hull. The off-white deck. The mast standing tall, proud. The shrouds still, waiting on the wind, anxious to trill. To whistle their warnings around the busy old harbour.

He opened the door. The sun, still high enough, though at the horizon, just brushing the deep blue sky with the soft pink of early evening light.

He led her over the jetty to the sidewalk. He jumped aboard then reached for her hand. Then down below. She was actually on his boat.

'A drink Harriet. Then we'll freshen up and dine at the Quayside Tavern, just over there.' He bent over. Looking out of the wide, narrow window. Nodding his head towards the far side of the harbour. 'Just a short evening stroll Harriet. Stretch our legs.'

It was busy. The long summer evening drawing them all in. They were lucky. Just one table for two by the window.

Harriet watched him walk to the bar. He'd ditched the superfluous. White shirt, open at the neck. Sleeves rolled up. She sat there, holding on to her arms. Looking down at the tiny pearl buttons edging the pale blue lace from the neckline all the way down to the hem of her dress. She watched him walk back. Steady. Holding on to the drinks. He caught her eye. Smiled. She instantly went back to the buttons. He mustn't see the way she was feeling.

'Cheers Harriet. Cheers to we titled people. Not asked for I might add. Mine. Charity work. One of them wired the PM. Still it's unwise to be churlish about these things.'

She suddenly felt bad. She'd almost forgotten. At the Palace this morning? It felt like a dream.

'Cheers Mr. Sanderson and thank you. I don't want anyone to know though. I only told Tricia. Mark doesn't know. I don't want him to ever find out.'

'Not exactly the best start to married life Harriet. It's inevitably going to come out sooner or later.'

She looked down. Didn't want to go there.

'Anyhow only what you deserve Harriet. You know almost all of them boycotted the place? Broke the law. Kept their kids off. Because of you.'

She looked down again. She could feel herself blush.

'Fact Harriet. You've managed to do the impossible down there. Brought almost every last one of them onside. Whittle had to admit it. You've been honoured with his approval.'

'Really?'

'Really Harriet. Not easy for him to eat his words. You see it's one thing raising the standards in school. It's another actually getting the parents to change their lifestyles. The poverty only serves to bring inertia to this insidious class thing. Well rubbed in now of course. Parliament. Not all of them by any means. We hear little of the decent ones. But this ridiculous expenses scandal. They vote them in. Then have to deal with all this? What of life's experiences would have equipped them for this? I doubt if most of them have the cognitive flexibility to facilitate the perceptual change needed to even begin to understand.'

His words were falling away. Harriet was watching him. Serious. Intent.

'Oh this man,' she thought, 'every way he looks, everything he says, every way he is. This gorgeous, gorgeous man.'

'Well OK. It's often very long hours. They should be allowed some of the aesthetics of life to ensure a decent performance. They can hardly cart it all around with them. Can they?'

Harriet nodded in agreement.

'And would any of the complainants actually want to do their job? On the other hand.' He scratched his head. 'On the other hand how is it humanly possible to forget one's mortgage has been paid off? I think not. There's always been plenty of slack at the top, Harriet. In my view far more than at the bottom. "Homini plurima ex homine sunt mala." '

She smiled. 'Translation please.'

' "Man is the root of almost all man's problems." Pliny the younger, I believe. Of course wealth and power increases the correlation dramatically.'

'Ah you've shifted your position, ever so slightly Mr. Sanderson? Empathising?'

He smiled.

'You were right. Of course you were right Harriet. Value judgements? One just can't do it. Criteria for success? Happiness? At whatever level? I depart from you somewhat on that though. What you've done is raised the bar. Offered them choice. Got to make life richer? More fulfilled?'

The brown envelope folded in her bag. It suddenly crossed her mind. A good opportunity to pass it over.

'Confession time Mr. Sanderson.'

'Meaning?'

She took a very deep breath as she pulled it out.

'I'm just so sorry about this. That night, when you gave me it. Mark took the car. He left it open and someone stole it. It happened at the sailing club when Mark was trying to find out what had caused the damage to the boat. Mr. Bridgewater said a few cars had been done. I asked him. Most of it was dumped. I'm afraid this was all there was left. Found it under the seat in his car this morning.'

He took it.

'I thought it must have been something like that Harriet when Belinda found the blanks. He was certainly well out of it old Tarquin on Christmas Eve.'

'Ah the notes.'

'That wasn't folded Mr. Sanderson. It was really stuck hard to the inside of the back of the envelope.'

'Yes. It was all on the desk. Picked the lot up together. Very foolish mistake. I'd guessed I'd done that. At least there's a few in high places spared the indignity of having their names bandied around by the media. As it happened, and deservedly so, it was just you and me Harriet. We took the pasting. Anyhow let's hope the negative publicity keeps the momentum going. I've taken a bit of a flyer with this franchise business. Still. Diversification. That's the name of the game, especially in a recession.'

He shoved it into his pocket.

'Chapter closed Harriet. We'll say no more about it.'

He passed the menus to the waiter. Harriet had gone with his suggestions. Easier that way. Couldn't concentrate. Wasn't hungry anyway. All that had been just too scary.

Unsettled. She fidgeted on her chair. He sensed it.

'All done. All finished with Harriet. Forget it now.'

He leaned forward to catch the silver charms resting on the chain around her neck.

'Molly's bridesmaid's gift? Of course.'

She felt better. He was close. So very close. Resting the back of his hand against her chest.

'A church wedding Harriet? Is that important to you? Do you believe?'

'Yes. Yes I believe. I believe in love. It's simply that. It doesn't matter how it's wrapped.'

'An interesting concept Harriet. Now I think that idea sits very comfortably with the concept of panentheism. Love as the pervading force within the universe yet also transcending it. It leaves room for evolution, too. I like that Harriet. It's a harmonising world view, outstrips all the paradigm shifts that have brought us to this.'

'To this Mr. Sanderson?'

'Yes, to this Harriet. Broadly speaking scientific development has taken us to where we are. The world as we know it. Science. It's virtually become synonymous with truth. We've got to be far more than the product of evolution Harriet.'

He smiled as he separated the tiny charms. Just as he did in the car, before he'd given her the ring. The anchor. The cross. The heart.

'Faith, hope and love. Difficult to quantify. They don't readily lend themselves to the rigour of scientific analysis, but they exist. 'Love' and 'hope' are commonplace. It's 'faith'. That's the tricky one. Squandered to today's methodology. It frightens the scientists Harriet. Yet, in my opinion, it's the most inspired of hypotheses that have created the major breakthroughs. Where does inspiration come from do you suppose if not from somewhere outside of ourselves? Take great works of art and music for example.'

Harriet smiled. It was going completely over the top of her head All she wanted was simply to watch and listen.

'It's just a question of time. They'll get there in the end. Unlike us Harriet. I asked you to remember those three words. I asked you to wait.'

She looked into his eyes. Deep blue. Serious. Deeply serious. One slightly raised eyebrow leaving the other to frown. Questioning.

'Still. He's the father of your daughters. Understandable. Perfectly understandable.'

She could feel it desperate to come out. She had to go for it. Tell him.

'It's not only that. There's something else as well.'

'Something else Harriet? Tell me.'

She pulled back.

'Come now Harriet. Do explain.'

'You mustn't ever, ever say anything. Promise?'

'I'm not promising Harriet. Not for something I don't know.'

'Well if you were to say anything it would most definitely land me in court.'

'In court Harriet? Come now. How many more holes have you been digging yourself into? Who's been threatening you?'

Harriet took a deep breath. Fingered the base of her wine glass.

'Belinda Oxfordshire. She's threatened to sue me for tipping that carrier bag on to her head.'

She could see the smile breaking across his face.

'No. No there's more Mr. Sanderson. She's already discussed it with her lawyer. He told her the case was proven. And if she didn't get back with you that's just what she's going to do. She's threatened to sue me if I don't stay away from you.'

His smile vanished as he sat for a few seconds in silence.

'Hmm. I see. Blackmail. Not a pleasant exercise. With regard to you Harriet, the outcome would probably be little more than an apology. She hasn't suffered any sense of devaluation in the eyes of others, I'm quite sure. We were all at the top end. Most guests, regardless of the fact they don't even know her, wouldn't have caught it anyhow. She hasn't lost by it. She continues to be on the company's payroll. In fact I've gone out of my way to go along with her wishes. Buying your house is a case in point. No Harriet I don't think you should be losing any sleep on that score.'

'Are you sure Mr. Sanderson? I've been worrying about that for ages.'

'Quite sure Harriet. She obviously kept the rest of it from her solicitor. Having implicated me in her threat proves she's using the incident to satisfy her own ends. No. None of it would wash Harriet. Besides there's one big flaw to it all.'

Harriet sat on her hands. Took a very deep breath.

'What would that be Mr. Sanderson?'

'I don't actually want her Harriet, regardless of what you do or don't do.'

Harriet had to suppress the overwhelming urge to throw her arms around him. Kiss him.

'Thank you so much for that. Oh I feel *so* much better now.'

Harriet flopped back in her chair. Mr. Sanderson shook his head. Brushed his hair back to the side.

'Besides, she was responsible for your flat tyres. She'd obviously seen the opportunity. Capitalised on the fact those lads were on the make. Ironic they did her tyres first. I'm sure there's some legal term for paying others to do your dirty work. No Harriet. I wouldn't give it a second thought.'

She smiled. So glad she'd mentioned it.

'Not too sure about palming her off with a brown envelope full of leaflets though. I'll refrain from asking which of the two of you cooked that one up!'

Bright red. She knew he was looking at her bright red cheeks.

He laughed. 'What did she expect? They were never going to shove that lot through every letterbox in Stetmead.'

Meal finished. He caught her hand as they followed the old stone wall rail along the quayside back to the boat.

'We won't be doing anything with this tonight Harriet.'

He helped her aboard. She sank into thought as she sat down on the U-shaped settee.

'Now you know everything. Please just ask me. Ask me. Ask me.' The silent plea wouldn't leave her mind. She knew he wouldn't. She changed it.

'Take me. Take me. Take me. Just once. Just now. I'm single. It's OK. Just once before I get married.' She watched him pour the wine. Her whole being became saturated in desperate, uncontrollable longing.

He sat opposite her. Chatting. Bad place. Harriet kept looking away. It was almost too much being so close to *him*. To this gorgeous, intelligent hunk of a man.

'There couldn't be a better place,' she thought, 'on our own together. Here. Just him and me. What *is* the matter with him?'

She toyed with the idea of just going over to him. Sitting by him. Thanking him again for making her feel so very much better. It would be a start. She looked around.

'This boat is fabulous Mr. Sanderson. What's her name?'

'Mare Libertas, Harriet.' He smiled. 'Translation?'

She nodded.

' "Mare Libertas" that's "From the sea, freedom." '

'Oh that's beautiful Mr. Sanderson. Really lovely. Gosh you're really into Latin.'

'It's pure Harriet. Goes right back to the roots of our language. Lends itself admirably to the profound. Now.' He stood.

'I haven't shown you around.'

She followed him forward. Gasped as he opened the door on a cabin housing a double bed all made. Ready to sleep in.

'You OK in here then Harriet? En suite. Everything there.'

'Oh gosh. Yes thank you.'

He looked at his watch. 'It's late, been a busy day. And another one tomorrow. I suggest we turn in.'

Harriet's heart jumped. Had she just heard that?

He went in. Pulled a T-shirt out of a drawer.

'Should be long enough for you Harriet. Sleep well'

Oh! A wave of disappointment drowned her hopes.

Not even a goodnight kiss. She watched him walk back. His cabin the other end. This was a heavy price to pay for marrying Mark in two weeks time.

Chapter 55

'Good morning Harriet. Sleep well? I'm afraid it's that powdered stuff. Still we'll breakfast on the quay.'

She peered from under the duvet.

'Yes thank you Mr. Sanderson. And you?'

'Flat out. Now your tea's there Harriet. Powdered milk I'm afraid.'

'Oh thank you. Thank you very much. Unexpected. That's very nice. Very nice indeed.'

'Everything all right in here? Everything working?' He walked in to check the shower compartment. Walked out. 'Sorry Harriet. Walked straight into them. You'll be needing these?'

Harriet looked. Blushed. He'd popped her pale blue lace pants on the end of the bed.

'Oh yes. Sorry. Washed them through last night. Left them to dry. Didn't think you'd be going in there. Sorry about that. Didn't bring any spares. Thought I was back home last night. Just out for the day.'

He laughed. 'Absolutely no need whatsoever to apologise. Could hardly have you wandering round the boat minus these. You're getting married two weeks today.'

She looked at him. Felt herself bristle inside. Thought. 'I don't wish to hear that. Thank you.'

He wasn't letting go. Picked them up again. Felt the double lined bit at the bottom.

'Dry? Yes they feel OK Harriet.'

Harriet slid down under the duvet. She couldn't deal with it.

'Right. I'll leave you to it. When you're ready.'

The tea tasted funny. She was glad to drink it though. Sitting on the edge of the bed listening to the water lapping the boat. She was tempted to stay put, just where she was. Just heaven. Couldn't keep him waiting. There were things he wanted to do. She washed and dressed as quickly as she could. He'd been ready for ages.

It was stifling hot. From little rest the morning sun had been working hard away burning off the early mist. Warming the paving flags and old stone walls. Lifting the many white-washed buildings, single, double, triple storey. Packed, rising with the land. Cottages, houses, shops all fighting for prominence in the bustling, busy harbour. Their roof tops stacking across walls and windows until the grand patchwork finally set itself hard against the clear blue sky. Crying, the gulls circled low. Landed. Chattered. Lifted. The old harbour wall a sanctuary. A resting place. Then lifting in flight and returning to balance in long white lines. Looking out from the rails running along the edge, delineating the land from the sea.

They breakfasted. Bought a few bits for lunch.

'It's too hot to do much Harriet. I'll just check the sails then we'll motor out and drop anchor. Just a couple of coves away.' He looked at her dress. 'Best stay like that Harriet. No point sweltering in somebody else's jeans.'

She agreed. Then forced herself to sit on the need to know whose they'd been. She wasn't going to let anything spoil the joys of this hot summer's day. Her very last day with him. Alone with him. Like this.

He helped her into the boat. The feeling changed. Serious. She went down to the galley. Fridge, freezer, cooker, microwave, twin sink, dishwasher. She could scarcely believe it. She put away the bits and pieces they'd bought for lunch. The white wine in the cooler. She went back up. Stood on the teak deck watching as the huge flapping sails made their way to the top of the mast. White, full blown against the clarity of the perfect summer sky. Genoa. Main sail. Watched each furl in their turn as he tested the automatic reefing. He was satisfied. Lowered them. He stood weighing it all up. Called her over. Briefed her thoroughly. Order of slip lines.

'Got that Harriet? Release them as I push the bow off. Make sure they come clear of the water.'

She was nervous. Pleased. She'd managed it. They were motoring out, away from the berth. This was heaven. Cutting their way through the calm turquoise water. Sailing away. Gliding along the silvery ripples. The sun never tiring of painting each tiny wave into one beautiful shimmering sea.

She joined him at the wheel. Along side. Just watching. He'd taken her into a completely different world. A world as natural and appropriate to him as ever there could be.

'I'll cruise her out a bit Harriet. Sailing due west. Then we'll come back. Drop anchor at The Bangles. That's the row of sheltered coves: runs from out there, right the way round to the other side. We'll see how it goes. The last one in is just minutes from here. Go and unwind. Make the most of it Harriet. Relax.'

He'd placed the sun loungers side by side on the deck. She lay down. Stretched to the full length of the sumptuous cushioning under her. The sun was hot. She closed her eyes and let the gentle breeze cool her mind to sleep.

His hand on her shoulder. She woke. Just a gentle sway. Anchored. Not far distant. The clear green water paling away to a duck-egg blue lapping against the golden sand.

He'd gone out and turned back. It felt as if she was on the other side of the world.

'Is this really just round the corner from the marina?'

'It is Harriet. We haven't got the time to do much more than this, now.'

They laughed. Chattered as they wined and dined. Together, stretching lunch well into the evening. She knew this was the best, the very best day of her life. Her living dream. With him. Just him. Come true.

'Harriet. It's not far away.' He pointed across to the shelving sand. 'Fancy a trip to the shore? We can lower the tender. Not a couple of minutes from here.'

Suddenly she felt her stomach knot. Nervous. What had she just agreed to? It was late. The evening sky. Glowing pink. The dipping sun nudging the dark shadows away from the rocks. Stretching along the sand. Beautiful. Compelling. Drawing her in.

In bare feet they paddled, pulling the tender well up on to the bank of sand.

They stood looking out to sea. The sand warm under their feet.

'It's absolutely stunning.'

'Like you Harriet.'

She felt his arms closing her to his chest. His lips against hers. Every inch of her body aching to be his. He lay her down. Pulled back.

'No Harriet. In two weeks time you'll be married.'

'At this minute I'm not, though. I'm absolutely single Mr. Sanderson.'

'Joris, Harriet. Hardly the time for formality.'

He kissed her again. Passionate. Full. Intimate.

She could feel his hand slipping the tiny pearl buttons away from their loops. One by one down the front of her dress, almost to her waist. Slipping the hooks away. Feeling the freedom to her breasts as he lifted them from her white lace bra.

This need for him. This utter and total need. 'It's got to be. It's just this once. Once before I get married. Got to get this man out of my system once and for all.' Silent thoughts weaving from her mind, wiring their way to the touch of his finger tips, gently brushing against her.

'This man. Oh this most beautiful, gorgeous man.' Every thought drawing him in. As vital to her existence as the salt air she was breathing.

He lowered himself to kiss her. Each breast to his lips.

'Harriet I'm so much in love with you.'

'Oh Mr. Sanderson,' she could barely speak, 'I don't really think you can say that. I'm getting married.' She pulled the edges of her dress together.

'That was where I began Harriet. Do you really need to be reminding me of that? Right at this moment. Now?'

'No,' she murmured. 'No. At this point in time. As the sun is setting. I'm no one's.'

'At this moment in time. As the sun is setting. You're mine. All mine Harriet. You've driven me to moral decline Harriet. It's totally unethical.'

'Well, I'd have thought you could at least have said that in Latin?' she whispered.

He laughed. Pulled her very close. Parted the unbuttoned edges of her dress. Looked at her.

He touched at the waist of his jeans.

'Contraception Harriet? Did you take my advice?'

'Yes. It will be alright Mr. Sanderson. I got the pill.'

'You're still taking it, I presume? Maintaining the cycle in the face of your other half's absence?'

She nodded. She didn't care. She closed her eyes. The next kiss penetrating. Intoxicating, washing away his words. Her whole body drawn like a magnet twisting against his. The slip of his hand. From the corner of her eye, just a small patch of blue lace on the sand. The water. Gently lapping. The sound, in and out of her consciousness to the fullness of him deep inside her. Exquisite. Beautiful. Fulfilled.

***

He held her very close. She thought those clear blue eyes of his had misted slightly. She could feel the tears brimming her own.

'Never mention it?' she asked.

'Never mention it. I promise you that my beautiful Harriet.'

He hugged her hard. Touched the tip of her nose. Smiled her that smile.

'We must get back Harriet. The light's fading.'

Hardly undressed, they sorted themselves out. She turned away until it was safe to look back. Then she looked down. Writing in the sand.

'*DO NOT FORGET*'

Her breath caught, pushing her ribs forward. She held it, then let go, helpless to stop the tears. She rubbed them away. Her hand salty against her lips. At one with the sea. At one with *him*.

They stood arm in arm. Still locked together. Watching the tide as the water swept its way into each of the letters he'd channelled; filling them full to overflowing and then drawing back to saturate them again, washing over his words.

Chapter 56

It was ten o'clock. Still light in the sky. Between them they'd brought the boat back to its mooring. Then one last check before they started the long journey home.

He closed the door on her. She watched him walk round the front to his side of the car. He got in. Closed the door. Fastened his seat belt. Turned the key in the engine. They were away.

'I should try to sleep, if I were you Harriet. It's been quite a day.'

His voice was gentle, caring, understanding. He took her hand as he drove out of the harbour.

'Beautiful Harriet. No words. I can't find words to describe this perfect day. What ever you do in life Harriet. Remember this. I love you. I will always love you.'

She squeezed his hand. 'You've always known my feelings. It's just the way life pans out really. Neither of us married. It was just something so right, so very right for us both.'

'Exactly Harriet.'

He accelerated hard. She watched his hands flicking the steering wheel. Safe hands. Sure hands. She looked down to his legs. Strong. Powerful. The strength of his body still in her. The longing still in her. The need for him intensified to a degree she could never have thought possible. His strong handsome profile down to the outline of his lips. Caught, through his window, against the fast fading light. Against the deepening pink and purple hue of the night sky. This perfect day. This perfect man. She knew she would always carry that deep, residual ache. She knew she must now try so very hard to forget him.

Chapter 57

There had been no messages from Mark when she'd got home. She was relieved about that. Just one from Tricia.

'Ooh 'arriet. I 'ope you 'aven't disappeared for good 'arriet. I've fed the cat and watered the plants. Give me a ring as soon as you get back 'arriet. I'm dyin` to know all about it.'

Harriet had phoned her. Thanked her. Tried to match her excitement about the wedding. It was getting easier. She'd hardly seen Mr. Sanderson at school. Huge relief! Apart from the time he'd popped into her classroom. She'd gone as red as a beetroot. 'Well he didn't actually take my dress off. Didn't see anything. Not like being completely naked on the rug with Mark. Don't know how I ever did that!' She'd begun to feel uncomfortable. Exposed. She'd gabbled her thoughts furiously at herself as he'd crossed the room to her table.

'Yours Miss Glover?' He'd handed her that bag of heart shaped tomatoes. The one she'd left in his car. He'd almost sung it. His voice was a fraction too high. Monotone. Detached. Like he wanted to get away.

Helped her to focus. Definitely helped her to focus.

'Always knew it,' she'd thought. 'He's simply a dream. Just got too much of everything to be true. A gorgeous chunk of masculinity. A hunk of dashing good looks. Charmingly, totally unavailable. To the likes of me.'

Chapter 58

Just a couple of days to go to the wedding. Between Harriet and her mother, everything was in place. Except Mark. He'd phoned to say he would be delayed by another couple of days.

'Not to worry Harriet. Just get all my gear round to Mum's. I'll go straight there. Go to the church from there.'

'So I won't get to see you before we get married Mark? That's a bit off.'

Mark hadn't thought so. It was work. She couldn't expect precision from that distance.

Both Clare and Rachael had phoned. Same kind of message.

'Thank you for the cheque Mum. Dad not back yet? You've only got a couple of days to go. Hope he makes it in time. We're all flying out early Friday morning. Can't wait. Actually getting married on Saturday. All of us together. Anyway Mum don't worry too much if he doesn't make it. He might have taken on board what we said at Christmas. Might have decided not to be like us after all. You never know he might just stick with staying cool. There's nothing wrong with living together you know?'

Harriet hadn't wanted to hear that. She'd had enough of being caught between two men. Saturday was her big day. He'd be back.

Chapter 59

Friday evening. Harriet had delivered all of Mark's things to his mother. She'd received her very politely. A bit too polite for Harriet.

'Still frosty from Christmas night,' she thought.

Still no Mark. She was cross. Felt she had PMT. Really bad timing. It hadn't occurred to her to work that side of it out. Her stomach was churning. She lay the long blue bridesmaid's dress on the bed.

'Get off Pepper. I don't want to get married covered in cat hairs!'

The phone rang. She grabbed it.

'Oh Mark. You're back. Oh thank goodness for that. You've no idea how relieved I am. Where are you phoning from? Oh, the airport. Right. Just waiting for the flight back to Manchester. Yes your mother's got everything. And don't be late at the church will you? I don't think I could handle any more delays.'

He'd had to cut the call short. She sat on the bed. Tomorrow she would be married. After all these years. She couldn't believe it. She looked around her. Most of the stuff was packed. All in place. They'd be moved into their new house by the middle of next week.

'Hmm. Mrs. Glover, Pepper. You'll very soon belong to a legal set-up. We're out of this house of ill-repute. Your mistress will be married. Yes Mrs. Glover.' She tried to make it sound good. After all she'd earned it. It was the only title she'd been interested in all along. Hardly given any thought to her damehood since she'd got back. 'Hmm. Mrs. Glover.' It wasn't working. Too many people had got it confused. She'd already been called that too many times.

'Now, Sanderson, Pepper? Would that sound any better? Mrs. Sanderson. Oh! Shouldn't have gone there. No Pepper. That's most definitely one you didn't hear.'

She'd planted the seed. Looked at the top drawer of her dressing table. Felt compelled to open it. To go right to the very back. She felt for the box. The bracelet. Pushed that testing kit he'd given her out of the way to bring it out. Opened it. Held the beautiful solid heavy gold band in her hand. Traced the engravings with her finger. Every single buttercup. The cat bounced its way behind her as she hurried down the stairs to find the dictionary.

'Packed. Haven't I just gone and packed it.' Irritated. Started thinking. Fast. Ended up on the computer. The search engine. Typed it in. Read it out to the cat at her feet.

' "haec olim meminisse iuvabit". One day this will be pleasing to remember.'

' "in somnis veritas". In dreams there is truth.'

She allowed herself to go back on the sand. With him. For the very last time.

Back to the drawer to put it away. A sock. She found a sock to put the box in. Didn't want Mark to see that. Couldn't do it. Left the box in the sock at the back of the drawer and the bracelet on the dressing table.

'For just one more look.'

Went to the back of the drawer again. Brought the testing kit out.

'What to do with this?' She opened the box. It didn't seem that long ago since he'd given it her. Pressing her to find out once and for all what that very late period was all about.

'Late period?' Her stomach dropped to her feet. She should have started yesterday.

'No Harriet. Don't go there. Just don't go there. That very last scare was all about this. And that was alright.'

She looked more closely at the slim glass strip in her hand.

'You know very well Harriet,' she told herself. 'On the pill? You've only ever taken one since Mark went. The first day he went. Wasn't a lie though. Taken one. He only said the pill. Not the pills every day for three weeks in every month. No Harriet. Don't be so stupid. You are absolutely not pregnant.'

It was almost two weeks since they'd been together. Like that. On the beach.

'Due on yesterday?' It suddenly struck her. Absolutely knocked her on to the bed.

'Middle of the month. Two weeks ago. Optimum fertility. The right time to try for a baby. But it never works. Why should it have worked this time? It never works with Mark. Why should it be any different with *him*? She was back on the sand again. He was totally, utterly, completely inside of her. Deep as deep as he could be. No different from Mark. Technically anyway. Otherwise very different from Mark. But absolutely no different from Mark. Technically. Why should it be different? It never, ever works. That blip was due to the menopause. Sometimes Mummy does know best.'

She worked herself up into a complete and utter frenzy. She paced the whole house. Up and down the stairs. Holding the thing in her hand. She couldn't spend the rest of the night like this. She had to know. Just had to know. She sat on the edge of the bed. Read the instructions. Went off to the bathroom. Everything in her hand.

Chapter 60

Early Saturday morning. Feeling very sick, she opened the door to her mother and father. So, so nervous. She wondered just why she'd pushed so hard for all of this. She'd never experienced anxiety like it.

'Come in, Mummy, Daddy. You both look super.'

'Big day Harriet.' It was her father. 'We'll be more than pleased to see you both settle down at last.'

'Did Mark get to his mother's alright Harriet?'

'Oh yes Mummy. It was very late when he got in though. He went straight to bed. His mother just phoned to pass the message on.'

'Well that's not very good the night before your wedding day Harriet. At least he could have seen his way to picking the phone up. Spoken to you himself.'

'She's just told you he was tired Frances. It's not a five minute trip back from the South Pole you know? He hasn't got a magic sleigh and a set of reindeer, you know?'

'That's the North Pole Charles. Father Christmas comes from the North Pole.'

There wasn't a lot of time. Her mother had chattered most of it away. The wedding car arrived. In her long blue dress and carrying a simple bouquet of white roses and freesias she followed them out to the car.

She sat in the back. Next to her father. Nervous. Complete hell. Didn't know if she'd even make it. She felt nervous to the point of collapse. It was well on the cards that her mother would cause them to crash anyway. Gabbing for Britain.

'Shut up Mummy. If you don't want us all to get killed. Stupid man. Stop turning sideways. Just look where you're going!' That was all to herself. It didn't matter of course. Even if she'd chosen to speak it aloud she'd have been ignored by her mother completely. She hated interruption.

She felt a nudge from her father.

'It'll be alright love. We've all had to go through this, you know.'

She managed a smile.

'When is it ever alright for me?' she thought. 'It's all going to go horribly wrong. That's just the way I am. That's just the way it is. For me.'

It wasn't far away. She watched the church coming into view. Thought of Clarissa and Henry. Their wedding. That hat. Belinda Oxfordshire. Thoughts were coming thick and fast.

'Oh just let me hurry ahead Harriet. I must be in my seat before Daddy gets you up the aisle.' Her mother insisted.

Holding on to her hat Harriet and her father watched her scurry ahead. Stalling to shake the vicar's hand before disappearing into the church. He wandered in behind her.

Suddenly she was back. Still clutching at her hat. Running towards them.

'Harriet. He's not there. He's not standing up there at the front. Not at the top of the aisle. There's no sign of him.'

'Oh go back in Mummy, he's waiting for me. He'll be sat down there with Bob waiting for us.'

Her mind was dazed. There was something she needed to do. She felt as though her consciousness was slipping away. She looked helplessly at her father.

'Bob, Harriet? Who's that? What does he look like? Who am I supposed to be looking for?'

'Oh. Sorry Mummy, Bob's Tricia's husband. Big solid sort of chap. Dark hair. Smiley sort of face. It's alright. He'll be there sitting with Mark at the front. Go on in Mummy.'

'That won't be the poor unfortunate husband of that common girl will it? She's called Tricia. Isn't she? Yes it will be. Surely Mark hasn't asked *him* to be best man?'

'Sorry Mummy, his choice.'

'Oh that means we've got that chit of a girl right up front by us all on the top table. Now how did that come about Harriet? How could I have missed that one?'

This was excruciating. Her mother had just sharpened every nerve ending she had.

However hard Harriet tried to wrench her stomach against its deep churning the anxiety just deepened and deepened. She could feel it running its way, sapping every last ounce of strength from her body. She wanted to be sick. She wanted to die. Just die. There was no place for her. No steady equilibrium she could reach. Her mind was everywhere. All that was in her. All that was around her. Quaked. Resonating with her fast-fading consciousness. Too, too much. She could sense it coming and going. Almost fainting.

She could just hear the chords of Handel's Water Music. The organist was firming it up.

'Frances in you go. You're going to be tripping us up at this rate!'

Her mother glared at her father and shot off.

For some reason Harriet glanced behind. She went sick to the pit of her stomach.

'Go on in Daddy. This won't take a minute.'

Her legs went from under her. She tried her best to get down to Mark coming up the path. Coming up the path in his jeans and jumper.

'What's the matter Mark?'

His face was ashen.

'Sorry Harriet. It's Melissa. She's having a terrible time. Just for the moment she needs me. She needs me in a way that you don't. In any case I can't do it Harriet. I just can't do it.'

She could feel the blood draining away. She could barely stand.

'Maybe neither of us can do it Mark. Maybe this has never been the right thing for us both.'

She took the diamond ring from her finger.

'No Harriet. No I want you to keep it.'

He passed her a note.

'Please read it Harriet. Please read it. Consider very carefully all I've written. Promise Harriet. Just promise me that. *Please.*'

'I owe you that Mark. I promise I will.'

She pushed it with her ring into the side pocket of her dress.

He hugged her to his chest. She was helpless to stop her tears from streaming their way down her cheeks.

'Friends Mark. Stay friends?'

'Stay friends Harriet. Stay friends. Read the note Harriet.'

She watched him walk away. Choking. Just stared at her tears dropping, glistening at the petal edges of the pure white roses. Settling like dew drops on the soft green ferns laced at the edges of her bouquet.

She lifted her eyes. Watched him go. The gate. She took a deep, deep breath. Lifted her hands to her face. Melissa Scott. Just ahead of his parents. The four of them turned. Walked away.

She struggled to retain consciousness as her world blackened. She was sinking rapidly into a deep, deep hole. The hole she knew only too well she'd dug far too deeply now for herself.

'Come and sit in my car for a few moments Harriet.'

She jumped.

It was *him*. Mr. Sanderson. She turned. Just saw the vicar raise his hand to him as he walked off.

He passed her his handkerchief. The pristine white corners blew into her hair as she held it to her face. He walked her in silence to his car.

He sat her in the back. Drew her into his arms. Stroking her hair as she sobbed her heart out couched inside the lapels of his smart black jacket.

'Some things are just not meant to be Harriet. You'll get over it. Things have been coming to a head for some time now. It doesn't mean you won't ever see him again. Of course you will. It's painful. It hurts. I know.'

She looked up. Just the blonde curl resting on his collar. He continued.

'What were we saying on the boat about raising the bar? You've done it for our parents at school Harriet. Now do it for *me*.'

She sniffed furiously at the tears. Trying to bring them back up her nose. She looked at him. Looked into those caring, sparkling, intelligent, clear blue eyes.

'I want you to marry me Harriet.'

She couldn't move. She felt suspended in time. Those words? From *him*? He reached into his pocket. Opened his hand. The gold ring he'd once given her resting on his palm. He slipped it on her finger. The wedding ring finger of her left hand.

'This hand now Harriet. You will?'

'I will.'

She smiled. The tears returning. Filling her eyes again. Rolling down her cheeks.

'Now Harriet. No more tears. This is just the beginning. The start of our lives together. And I'll do my utmost to give you the happiness you deserve.'

He kissed her. She was back on the sand. This gorgeous, gorgeous man. She'd just completed the spectrum. A whole rainbow had formed from her tears. A rainbow of beautiful coloured light. Pulling her out of that deep, deep hole. Lighting her world, permeating her senses.

'I've got something for you, too.'

'Really Harriet?'

'Yes. Just a minute. I couldn't cancel it. All arranged. I've been sick with worry. I'd planned on taking Mark by the side door straight to the vestry. To tell him. We never would have got married, unless he'd been prepared to take a chance on it being wrong. No he wouldn't. He wouldn't have understood I needed you that much. Just that one single time before I got married. No he wouldn't have gone for that.' A waterfall of clear pain just flowed from her eyes, streamed down her cheeks. She was sobbing hard again into his chest.

Mr. Sanderson stroked his chin. Looked at her. 'Now Harriet. Calm down. It's probably one of the most traumatic things anyone could ever go through, but you're here, with me. It's over. Finished. Now stop it. I anticipated it Harriet. I could read it like an open book. Why do you think I carried the ring in my pocket?'

She closed her eyes tightly into his chest. His pristine shirt soaked. She was trying desperately to catch her every sob. Her body was shaking. Her chest lifting, her breath catching in regular spasms just as it did as a child. She put her hand in the side pocket of her dress. She passed him the small glass tube.

She tried to smile. 'I'm afraid they don't write it in Latin, Mr. Sanderson.'

He looked at it. Held it up. His face serious. So very serious. Then breaking, breaking into that most gorgeous of smiles.

'PREGNANT Harriet. It reads 'PREGNANT.' He placed it in the inside pocket of his jacket.

He tightened his arms around her. Hugged and hugged her as close as he possibly could. Hard into his chest.

'Harriet my darling, you saved that one for me.'

She watched the tears gather at the corners of his eyes.

'It's the testing kit you told me to keep Mr. Sanderson.' She tried to stop her words from staggering sideways as her ribcage lifted and fell. Forcing her short drawn breaths into a predictable, regular rhythm. 'Just as well I did,' she managed to finish.

'No pill then Harriet?'

'Sorry Mr. Sanderson. No pill.'

He smiled. Placed his hand on her stomach.

'All the wealth in the world could never throw up this joy Harriet. You were so right. I believe in love, too. Oh so very, very much. Our love creating a new life. Our baby. Harriet do you think you could face them all? Could you manage to go in? It would be so much better you know.'

'Red eyes Mr. Sanderson. I must look awful.'

'Awful? Awe fully beautiful Harriet. You will?'

She nodded.

'Come on then. No one will expect you to look any other way. They'll understand. We'll give them this moment. Honest. True. As it is. We'll fill every cubic centimetre of space in there with our love. I've got to thank someone Harriet. *He's* in there.'

He pointed to the church.

They got out of the car. It must have been a full ten minutes. Everybody waiting.

'I've already had a word with the vicar Harriet. He'll be reading the first set of banns tomorrow morning. Then two more Sundays. We'll be married the Saturday following.'

Harriet's mouth dropped wide open. She put her hand in the pocket of her dress. Felt her engagement ring. The unread note. Her mind in a daze.

'I just don't know what to say. Only with all my heart. Thank you.'

He strengthened his arm around her.

'Just think of this as a dress rehearsal. We'll go in now and walk up the aisle together. The vicar's going to announce it. Then we're turning that wedding reception into a celebration of our engagement. For all the guests. Very fortuitous your mother should have invited my parents along.'

He'd planned it all. In a couple of minutes. Harriet couldn't believe her ears. Molly and Percy would be there. What would they think? What would her parents say? What would the girls say? They'd have to work their way through that one. They hadn't ever wanted them to get married. Her and Mark. But this? Oh gosh. Getting married. Getting married to *him*. Carrying his baby.

'Please make Mark happy with Melissa. Make him marry her. Make him just do it. For him. For me. *Please.*'

Her prayer went ahead of her as they approached the church door. She looked up at him.

'Let the pangs happen Harriet. You'll get them. It will all eventually settle down.'

She caught a sob, then smiled briefly. He knew just where she was.

The chattering cut. Stopped. Complete silence.

They walked, hand in hand up the aisle. The vicar smiling. Waiting for them both.

Spoke to them all. Impressive in his long robes. The conviction in his voice hitting the rafters. His presence filling the every last corner of the church.

He'd managed to make a short sermon out of it. Just about forgiveness, love. Pure love. God's love for all of his people.

Mr. Sanderson had glanced across and smiled at her.

The vicar finished, stepped back to let him speak. Mr. Sanderson cleared his throat.

'First let me apologise for keeping you all waiting. Obviously an extremely traumatic time for Harriet and Mark. Both now gone their separate ways but not parted. They've been more than just good friends for many years with two beautiful daughters to show for it. *They'll* ensure the family love that's held them all together for so many years will remain.'

He turned to the vicar and then back to his eager audience.

'As you've heard. Love has many facets. We are fortunate if they remain constant in our lives and we are able to work our way through life from the stability of one secure relationship. However, in one way or another we are all the victims of time. Its ability to change. Throw sorrow and joy in our paths. We have to learn to negotiate our way. Steer as steady a course as we can through the bad times. Learn to make the most of the good.

The announcement of our engagement today will come as a great surprise to you all. Harriet and I have come together in love. Destined at this particular time to give our lives to each other. In the spirit of love we simply ask you to accept our decision. A decision made by us both, but in many ways out of our control.

Harriet was once given the gift of a pendant. A bridesmaid's gift from our dear friend Molly. Here today with her husband, Percy. Like many, they've both loved and lost. A little more than twelve months ago for Percy. Lost his dear wife. Yet this wonderful thing love, this most joyous of gifts that runs through our veins and as vital to us as the blood in them. This wonderful thing allows us to retain all we've held dear yet at the same time, offers friends of faith and hope to enable it to blossom again. Just three tiny silver charms. Speaking volumes. A cross, an anchor, and a heart. Faith, hope and love.'

He turned to the vicar again.

'I think I'm right in saying of these three things love is the greatest.'

The vicar, nodded and smiled. Mr. Sanderson continued.

'You know, like you all, I've loved all my life. Loved my parents. Loved my friends. And yes loved one or two women in my life. Even loved some of those little bast..., er troublemakers we try to teach.'

An instant peal of laughter filled the church.

'Yes we all love. It's the hub of our existence. So? You might think? Of course we all love. That goes without saying. But think on this. Just today. For the first time in my whole life it's come together. I wanted to gather every shred of love I've ever felt. I wanted to move it to one place. I wanted to thank someone, something out there for this most precious of gifts. I wanted to come in here and thank *Him*. He's here, in each and every one of us. He *is* that feeling we all know so well. Simply love, manifesting its many facets in all the aspects of our lives. And so.'

He turned to Harriet then back to the guests.

'I thank Harriet for this insight. For her persistent, unswerving love, revealed more often than not in unconventional ways. But nonetheless there, for all of that. Yes I thank her for all she's given me. And I thank you all for coming here in love of Harriet and Mark. And I hope you'll now turn to a new facet.

Different yet essentially the same. We now ask you to bless *us* with your love and understanding.'

The applause was deafening.

'Thank you,' he continued, 'we'll expect to see you all here, four weeks today for the wedding service. We'll now proceed to the Gerald Roper Hotel for our engagement reception.'

He shook hands with the vicar and guided Harriet down the aisle.

'That was beautiful Mr. Sanderson.' The tears streamed down her face.

He squeezed her hand.

'You're going to have to get used to calling me Joris, you know?'

She just spotted Belinda Oxfordshire sitting behind James and Geraldine, near the pew end. Her face fixed. Like a statue. Looking straight ahead.

Tricia caught Harriet at the church door.

'Ooh `arriet. Stop cryin` `arriet. I wouldn't be cryin` if I was in your shoes. I can't believe all this `as `appened. If I'm `onest `arriet I knew `e always liked *you*. What `appened to your Mark then? Did you decide you'd `ad enough of `im after all? I `eard `e was outside. If I'd `ad known about all of this I'd `ave gone out and surrendered `arriet. I'd `ave waved my white lacy knickers at `im!'

'Too late Tricia. It would seem Melissa Scott got there first.'

'Ooh `arriet. Does that mean I've got to put up with Bob? Do you know `arriet `e was fizzin`. `e said "Surely Mark's not goin` to stand back and just let all this `appen?" `e didn't stay sat up there waitin` for Mark. `e came back to me. We were sat together `arriet by the door. I told `im to keep `is nose out. I told `im `is behaviour wasn't much better. `e said `e wasn't listenin` to that pillock any more, preachin` at everyone. Then `e walked out `arriet, said `e was goin` to try to get `old of Mark. I've been watchin` `im. `e's been followin` that Belinda Oxfordshire around ever since we came. I might as well `ave not been `ere `arriet. I'm not jokin`. If I'd `ave known your Mark was becomin` available that Melissa woman wouldn't `ave stood a chance. That's me `arriet. I'm not even quick enough to catch a second `and one!

In there though `arriet. `im. Joris. Well I think Bob was just a bit jealous of `im. It was beautiful `arriet. `e nearly `ad me in tears. `e should `ave been a vicar `arriet. You never know you might just end up bein` a vicar's wife. I'll come and `elp you `arriet pour out the teas. You're `opeless at it!'

Harriet smiled. She hugged her. Her eyes filled again. 'It's as much as a surprise to me Tricia. I think Bob'll find Mark and I were both bringing our own set of problems to this marriage.'

'Ooh don't get upset again `arriet. You don't still love `im do you? I'm sure you could `ave `im back again if you tried. Problems `arriet? I `ope you're not goin` to keep me guessin` too long?'

Harriet sniffed. Pulled her tears back.

'No Tricia. I promise to keep in touch.'

She knew Tricia was one friend she'd always keep.

'Anyway 'arriet, talkin' of which, you'll be able to while away the mornings down there with me. At the coffee shop 'arriet. Tell me all about it. Ooh you'll certainly get to know what 'e's up to now!'

Harriet smiled. Could feel her mother pushing in.

'Well Harriet. I never did. Your daddy and I Harriet. We never did. My word. It's the first time you've ever done anything really sensible in your whole life. My goodness me Harriet. However did you get to this? Apart from working with him you only really saw him out of school, or met his family, on Christmas Day. I don't understand Harriet. Was it love at first sight? Where is he? Let me congratulate him. My new son-in-law Harriet. Well I never did. Up for a knighthood. Oh a sir in the family. My friends at the WI are certainly going to hear about this Harriet.'

'You've already got a dame in the family, Mummy,' Harriet thought. 'Daren't tell her now. She'd probably spin herself into such a froth of delight she'd explode!'

'I feel for you Harriet, dear.' It was Molly clasping her arm. 'You know Harriet things have a way of working themselves through. He's the one Harriet. Without a doubt he's the one for you.' She smiled. 'If I'd only been twenty years younger. Who knows? I'd like to think it could even have been me in your place. Next best thing Harriet. We're going to be neighbours you know.'

'Molly? Really! How?'

'Percy and I signed the contracts on the house down the lane. The one with the board up on the corner, just before you get to our friend's.' She smiled. 'Oh I mean both of you now, don't I? Your house Harriet. Oh yes, we'll all be in Lower Tideside together.'

Harriet flung her arms around her. She couldn't have heard anything nicer.

The hubbub around the church door grew and grew. Mr. Sanderson stretched his arm through it and took her back to the car.

He held her in his arms and kissed her gently on her lips.

'In Harriet.'

He closed the door on her. She watched him, smiling, handsome, gorgeous walking round the front. He opened his door. Sat alongside her. She thought about Molly. Comforting Molly. Tried to work out how long it would be before she would move in.

'Mr. Sanderson. Your house? Beautiful. Posh. Big. Scary?'

'Your house too now Harriet, together with 4 The Willows, I might add. Still yours. You choose.'

'The cat Mr. Sanderson? You don't like cats?'

'Yours will be different Harriet. I'll make a supreme effort.'

'The Prime Minister? Will he be coming to the wedding?'

'He's terrified of you Harriet. Or at least of that bag of yours.' He laughed. 'Seriously. It's entirely up to you. Nice chap though. Doesn't bite.'

She smiled. Went back to the pocket in her dress.

'Something else in there Harriet?'

She felt her breath catch.

'A note from Mark. His engagement ring. Wants me to keep it.'

'And that's exactly what you should do Harriet. It'll take longer than half-an-hour or so to adjust to all the emotional upheaval you've gone through. You'll learn how to manage. How to let the past sit comfortably with the present. With the future.'

He reached over. Pulled her close. Rested his head on hers.

'This is what I was looking for,' she said, pulling the bangle from her pocket. She raised its inner face to the light to read the words inscribed in the gold.

' "haec olim meminisse iuvabit". '

'Not a bad attempt Harriet. Now what does it say?'

'One day this will be pleasing to remember.'

'Excellent Harriet. Now the next one?'

' "In somnis veritas". '

'And how might you translate that Harriet?' He smiled her that most gorgeous of smiles.

'In dreams there is truth.'

'And "Ne Obliviscaris"? ' His face now serious.

'Do not forget.'

'Once more Harriet.'

'Do not forget.'

He turned the key in the engine. She looked down to the beautiful gold bangle, shining comfortably at her wrist. He reversed. Spun the steering wheel through his hands. Foot down. Into first. Second. Third. Turned left at the church entrance. Clasped his hand tightly to hers. They were away.